The Princesses' Quest

The Princesses' Quest

K.H.Weyerman

ISBN: 979-8-9991648-0-3 (paperback)
979-8-9991648-1-0 (ebook)

Library of Congress Control Number: 2025912106

Cover art and interior art by Abigail Wincentsen
Cover design and interior layout by KaTrina Jackson
Map by Avery Morgan
Author photo by Jason Corder

First edition

To ZTS for being the first person outside my family to read my words and believe in me.

And to my beloved daddy, DSW (1970–2022), whose faith in me still encourages me to move mountains. I miss you.

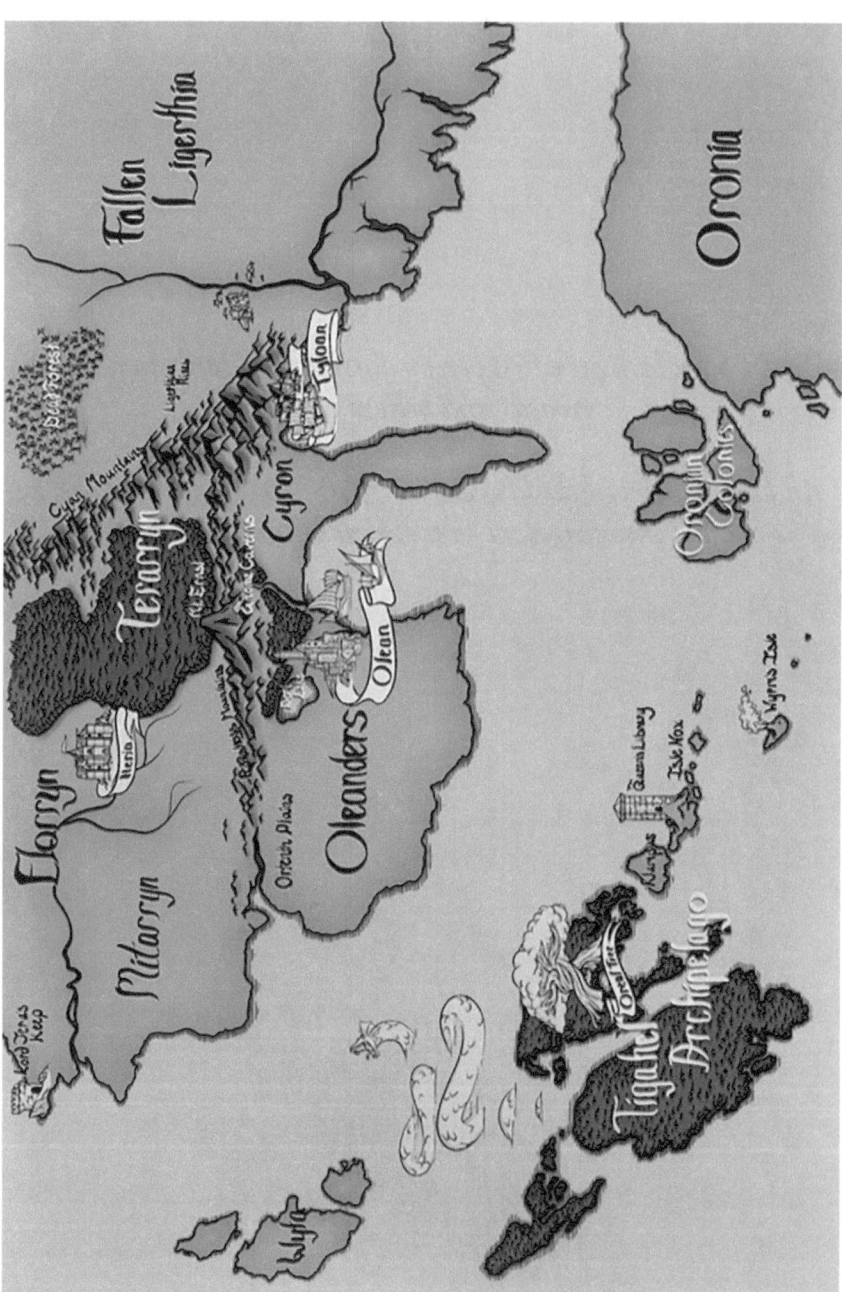

Prologue

It was much the same as it had been for the last six weeks: stand outside the nursery all night long. Barholow didn't mind. He liked knowing that the little princesses were safe. But something still felt odd about his queen's commands. The queen of Ligerthia had placed him undercover as a guard in Florryn a little over six months ago, and in all that time, the only thing that had happened was that the queen of Florryn had given birth to two healthy baby girls.

It was the middle of his shift, but he was wide awake. Alertness was second nature to him. If he drifted off for even a second, his charges would be in danger. And if there was one thing he knew how to do, it was watch.

Which was why it took him completely by surprise when his queen, who he hadn't seen in months, appeared beside him. She was a regal woman with long black hair, draped in white robes with a purple sash. How she had gotten there without him knowing was a mystery.

"Your Majesty!" he exclaimed, bowing low.

She raised a hand. "Quiet, Barholow. You'll wake the whole castle."

He nodded and saluted, but his heart was pounding furiously.

What was she doing here? And in the middle of the night, no less? Surely she had more important things to do than sneak into the Florrynian royal manor?

"Your Majesty, why are you here?" Had he disappointed her somehow? Had she come to replace him? But why? He'd done all she'd asked.

She eyed him coldly. "I am here for my own reasons, Barholow. All I need from you is to guard the door."

He bowed his head, swallowing his questions. "As you wish, Your Majesty."

She smiled at him. "Good man. Stay here. Don't let anyone else into this room."

He nodded and saluted her again. She opened the door and disappeared into the dim nursery. He could hear her footsteps as she approached the two bassinets. His mind was still churning with questions. What did she want with the princesses? Surely she could have come to their christening ceremony a month earlier to visit them? Surely there was no reason why she need come in the middle of the night, all the way from Tigahel?

But she had ordered him to stand guard. And he knew his one role as a Ligerthian Knight was to serve. So he stayed.

His mind buzzed. Everything about this situation was off. Why was the queen of Ligerthia here?

Goddess, please. What should I do?

A sudden scream from the nursery pierced the night. He rushed in and saw, to his great horror, that the queen was gone. The night nurse was sobbing on the floor.

He reached out a hand to help the woman up. "What happened? Where is she?" he demanded.

"The babe! The princess!" She wailed louder, which woke the other child, who started wailing with her.

Barholow walked over to the bassinets, his heart pounding. He could see the dark-haired babe, flailing her tiny fists as she raged in sleepy protest. But the other bassinet—

His heart dropped down to his boots. *No.* It couldn't be.

"Intruder!" he yelled. "Intruder!" He raced out the corridor and ran into three other guards. Sir Wilen, a middle-aged man with graying hair, spoke first.

"Barholow. What is it?"

"Intruder. In the castle. She took the baby."

They didn't hesitate. They started the search.

He cursed under his breath. He should have stopped her. He should have trusted his gut. And now . . .

How could the queen have done this? His blood thundered in his ears. He had to find her. And the babe. He didn't know what she planned to do with the child, but it couldn't be good. Not if it involved stealing her from her rightful home.

Moments later, he ran into King Wendol himself, a bright young man with dark hair and the start of a full beard on his cheeks. His blue eyes, which normally twinkled with merriment, looked worried. "Barholow? Someone said that there is an intruder in the castle."

Barholow bowed. "Yes, my liege. One of the princesses is missing."

"Goddess help us," the king said, his eyes growing wide. Then they sparked with command. "Search the castle!"

The king joined in the search, but as the hours wore on, it proved useless. The queen of Tigahel had vanished, and the child with her.

It wasn't until dawn that Barholow discovered the body. It was abandoned under the larnel bushes, but it was clearly the body of a blond-haired babe. She was still wrapped in the royal

3

blue and silver blanket she had been sleeping with. She was dead. The sight of her still form sent shock waves through Barholow.

"Why would she do this?" Barholow moaned, cradling the little princess. He had failed. He had obeyed his queen, but he had disobeyed his heart. Now the princess was dead, and it was all his fault.

Chapter One

Kailyn

Seventeen Years Later

Princess Kailyn of Oleanders was sitting in her tower, listening to her lesson with only half an ear. Her mind was on the open window, the sunshine beckoning her outside. She could see the sparkle of the Goddess's Library from where she sat. She smoothed her dress, feeling the crinkle of the parchment she had discovered three months ago in the back of that old tome. A thrill of excitement raced through her.

The words were in Old Alarian, a tongue not spoken by anyone in hundreds of years. All that remained of the language were bits preserved like gemstones in the boring rock of the everyday Almarrynian everyone spoke. All Kailyn had been able to make out was the word *Ligerthia*, which she knew was the fallen kingdom of Ligerthia, and *Alaria*, the old name for Almarryn.

It had been enough to get her and her maids excited. No one knew exactly how Ligerthia had fallen fifty years ago, but maybe this parchment held some answers. And if anywhere held answers, it would be the Goddess's Library—the crown jewel of Olean. Kailyn had always wanted to see it, even though, according to her maids, no one had been able to get in for decades. No matter. She had to try.

At the very least, she had to see the library. Anything beat being trapped inside yet again.

She tried not to tap her foot anxiously, but the effort to restrain herself was unbearable.

Lord Don, her portly tutor, was droning on about a peace treaty written twenty years ago between her nation, Oleanders, and their neighbor, Florryn. She'd heard the treaty before, and usually found it thrilling as it ended the One Hundred Year War, but with his high wheezy voice, Lord Don made it sound as dull as the life cycle of a pulong.

"Florryn had, of course, wronged us in their pillaging and looting," he said before coughing daintily. "Which is why your grandfather took matters into his own hands to rally the people to peace . . ."

Kailyn glanced back out the window, trying, with difficulty, to show she wasn't impatient. Lord Don should be asleep by now. What was taking so long? Had Myira's potion not worked like she'd said? Would Kailyn have to stay, enduring yet another lecture about the history of her nation, when all she wanted, more than anything, was to get out and see her people?

"Peace was achieved, but at a steep price—no communication between the two nations, and to this day, each remains on their side of the mountains," Lord Don said, wrapping up the treaty yet again. He let out a yawn and took off his glasses as he settled into his napping posture.

"Now, Princess, if you would read from your book the chapter on the dawn of your father's reign, I think I'll close my eyes for a bit." Lord Don closed his eyes, and his head slowly drifted down. Within a few moments, he was out cold.

Finally.

A knock sounded at her door. Kailyn got to her feet, her

heart hammering wildly. This was it. It was time to implement their plan.

She opened the door and her two maids, Myira and Ilia, slipped inside. Ilia was holding a rumpled pile of clothing, but she was trembling like a leaf. Kailyn felt bad, but they all agreed that with her fair hair and bright blue eyes, Ilia was the one who looked closest to the princess. She had to take her place.

Ilia squealed slightly when she saw Lord Don. "Are you sure he'll stay asleep?"

"I'm sure," Myira said, her voice deep and melodic. "I used a recipe my maman taught me. He'll be sleeping for hours. But we must hurry, Highness. Nea's on lookout, but your father could send someone to check on you any moment."

Myira motioned for Kailyn to stand. They moved to Kailyn's rooms adjacent to her study so her maids could help her switch clothes. Kailyn slipped her hand into her pocket and pulled out the crinkled parchment. Myira set it on the vanity table before she quickly loosed the ties and helped Kailyn slip the gown off.

"Should we be doing this?" Ilia squeaked as Kailyn slipped into the worn but much more comfortable servant dress. It was shorter than her gown, but the humble brown skirt and white apron should be enough of a disguise to ensure someone didn't give her another look. Myira undid some of Kailyn's fair hair so that it looked more frazzled and pronounced her ready. Kailyn looked at herself in the glass of the vanity and nodded once. It would do. She grabbed the parchment from the table and carefully slid it into her new pocket.

"*Ichla huffa*," Myira scolded Ilia in Cyronian, her native tongue. "Just do your part, Ilia. We've been over the plan for weeks. It'll work. Don't you want to know what the parchment says?"

Ilia glanced at Kailyn's hand which was still smoothing the skirt where the parchment resided. "But she might not even get in . . ." Ilia's voice trembled as Myira's well-practiced hands redid the stays of Kailyn's fine gown on the smaller girl. She stiffened as the laces were tugged. "And if we're caught . . . what then?"

"We have to try, don't we?" Kailyn said, echoing the sentiment Myira had told her a dozen times as they'd talked about finding out what the parchment said. The library was their best bet. If they could figure out a way to get inside. Perhaps Kailyn would succeed where her handmaids had failed. Being royal had to count for something, didn't it?

"And if we're caught, then I'll take the blame." Kailyn rested her hand on the younger girl's arm, which was hidden in the deep folds of the pink silk gown the maid now wore. The gown suited Ilia, even if it was a little too large for the girl. "Please, Ilia. I need you to be brave for me."

The girl sniffed and then nodded. Myira quickly braided the girl's hair and pinned it up in a similar style to the one Kailyn had worn.

"Good girl. Now stay here until we return." Kailyn guided Ilia to the chair she had so recently vacated back in the study. "Just act like you're studying. If my father sends someone to check on me, smile and wave, like so." She demonstrated a demure look with a graceful wave. "But you shouldn't worry. He hardly checks on me."

Ilia nodded, her pointy chin quivering. "Please be quick, Princess."

Uneasy about leaving Ilia alone for long, Kailyn followed Myira down the hallway. They passed Nea, who nodded at them before scurrying off in the direction they had come from.

At the end of the hallway was a servant's staircase that led directly to the kitchen. Whatever was cooking was sharp and tangy, but the smells made Kailyn's stomach flutter with nerves.

Was this a good idea? Ilia was right. They didn't even know if she could get into the library. And she hated to think what Lord Shielen would do if he caught their ruse . . . the man was a snake. She shuddered. He'd dismiss her maids. Or worse.

"Are you alright, Your Highness?" Myira asked in a gentle whisper as they waited for some servants to pass before going down the stairs.

Kailyn took a deep breath, easing calm into her tense muscles. She rubbed the side of her dress, feeling the parchment crinkle once more. The motion settled her nerves. *Ligerthia . . . Alaria . . .*

She had to do this. She couldn't back out now. She had to know.

"I'm fine, Myira." She smiled. "Lead the way."

Myira nodded and led her down the stairs to the kitchen.

The kitchen was bustling with activity when they got there, though it was hotter than midday summer. Scullery maids and lower cooks were bustling about in the heat of two giant fire-places, cleaning pots and pans, starching linens, and preparing the evening meal.

Myira waved at one of the scullery maids, who looked similar to her, with her dark skin and black hair pinned up. The younger girl smiled shyly and waved back before getting slapped with a spoon.

Kailyn stiffened. She wanted to scold the woman who had

smacked the girl. That sort of behavior should not be present in the royal house of Oleanders. She was the princess. She could stop this—

She felt a tug on her arm. Myira pulled her to the side door, where the welcoming breeze cooled down her warm skin and helped bring clarity back to her mind. She couldn't blow her cover. Not until she discovered the secret of the parchment.

Myira shoved a basket in Kailyn's arms. "You're going to pick flowers for the princess, Ilia." She said it loudly, likely in case anyone around them was listening. "Don't be gone too long. She needs you back to get ready for the evening meal."

Kailyn nodded, well aware that this was the plan. But she was still troubled by what she had seen in the kitchen. What if Lord Shielen caught her maids? He'd be far less forgiving than the woman with the spoon.

Seeing her concern, Myira dropped her voice to a whisper. "Don't worry about us. We servant girls can handle it, you know. Now go. Hurry." She pointed toward the courtyard where even more people bustled about. Kailyn nodded, but before she could even get a thank you out, Myira had disappeared back into the kitchen.

Squaring her shoulders, Kailyn turned to face the courtyard. Smells accosted her, from rich earthy fragrances of the farmer's crop to the salty tang of the fresh fish from the sea. Most of the men didn't give her a second look as she hurried through the courtyard. She came to the far side, where two guards stood by an arched doorway. Kailyn had only ever seen the arched gateway a few times, and never this close. She could see the carvings of Old Alarian that decorated its surface and wanted to read them, but she had an important mission at hand.

The two guards looked at her, eying her lazily. "State your business, handmaid."

Kailyn swallowed hard but kept her composure. "I'm picking flowers for the princess." The guard nodded and waved her through.

Kailyn knew she should feel elated, but the ease of her escape frightened her. If that's how easy it was to leave the royal castle, how easy would it be for someone unfriendly to enter?

She glanced up at the sun, which was already past mid-afternoon. She had an hour at most before she needed to return to the castle.

Myira and Nea had told her that the library was within easy walking distance from the castle, on the same tier even. She had seen its glowing white steeples from her window, but now that she was on the ground, she wasn't sure which direction that was.

The streets were filled with her people, many dressed in the brilliant yellows, oranges, and blues that Oleanderian dye was known for. Some of the common folk, like Kailyn, were dressed in more humble browns, but here and there she saw some bright colors adorning their simple attire. Those dressed in browns were headed toward the right, which she guessed was where the lower tier was. Those dressed in brighter colors were headed toward the left, which was still part of the noble tier. The library would be in the noble tier, so she headed left, blending in with the crowd. Hardly anyone paid her any attention, which was a relief as her heart was still hammering. She knew her clothing was a little out of place, but she hoped no one would pay her too much attention. She was dressed like a handmaid.

She worried about Ilia, alone in that stuffy classroom with a snoring Lord Don. Myira had said the potion she used would keep him out for at least an hour, possibly two, but Kailyn had to hurry. She couldn't risk Lord Don waking up and finding out his pupil had been replaced by a servant. Despite the fact that she had taught Ilia and all her maids how to read and write, not one of them could compare to the intelligence she had cultivated for years. It was the one thing her father allowed her, and she prided herself on it. But if they were discovered, it would be because of her knowledge. Lord Don would find out the moment he asked Ilia a question. She couldn't let that happen.

Turning a corner, the library loomed in front of her, larger than any other building nearby. It was made out of shining white rock, with five spires that reached up toward the heavens. Graceful, rounded archways made the building look even loftier and taller than it was. She smiled at the beauty of the building. It was unlike anything she'd ever seen before.

"Hey you!" a voice cried out. Kailyn didn't have time to react before she was yanked off her feet, toward a courtyard that opened by the library. A moment later, an out-of-control cart rattled right past where Kailyn had been standing, its driver nowhere to be seen.

Panicked screams filled the air as the cart clattered on before she heard a distant crash. She glanced behind her to see who her rescuer was and saw a dark-haired young man, who was maybe a few years older than her, wearing a simple gray woolen tunic.

He was looking at her with concern.

"Are you alright?" he asked, his voice deep and rough. There was something pleasing about his cadence.

Then she blinked. She was in the arms of a perfect stranger who had yanked her out of the road unceremoniously.

"Yes, thank you," she said, pulling away and straightening herself with what dignity she could muster. "Though I don't appreciate being hauled off my feet like that."

"Hauled off your feet?" the man repeated incredulously. "Look, dilera, I don't know who you are or what you were doing in the middle of the road, but that cart would have run you over had I not pulled you out of the way!"

Kailyn stiffened at the insult. She wasn't naive or foolish. "I appreciate your kindness, good sir. Now, if you'll excuse me, I need to enter the library."

She turned to head back to the road, but the man laughed.

"Enter the library? That's a joke if I've ever heard one."

Kailyn felt her face redden. Who was he to laugh at her? She had a mission—and the library was right there!

She pulled herself up to her full height, though she was still almost a head shorter than this man, and put on her most authoritative voice. "I'll have you know that I'm here on behest of the princess."

Instantly, his eyebrows went up and his face softened. He actually bowed to her. "I'm so sorry, Your Highness, but you won't be able to get in."

Kailyn heart sank as she stared at the strange man. She'd hoped her handmaids had been wrong. "Not get in? Are you sure?"

The man nodded solemnly. "It's locked. Has been for the last fifty years. But you're welcome to try. Perhaps it will open for you."

She blinked. Locked for fifty years? Her handmaids hadn't told her it was locked. All they'd said was that no one had been able to enter. Did that apply to princesses too?

She looked at the man, who was still staring at her curiously.

"Wait . . . how did you know I was the princess?"

The man chuckled, a deep low sound that tickled her to her toes. She bit her lip. Why was it so pleasant to be around him?

"You don't sound like a commoner, Your Highness."

He gestured with his arm to the grand building. "What brings you to the Goddess's Library?"

Kailyn hesitated, wondering if she should tell him. He was pleasant enough, yes. And she found him extremely pleasing to look at.

But telling him what she was up to was dangerous. If her parchment held the secrets to Ligerthia's fall, it would be disastrous if it fell into the wrong hands.

Besides, she hadn't even tried the doors. Maybe he was wrong, and they weren't locked. Or maybe they'd open for her. She had to try, didn't she? She'd come all this way.

"If you please, good sir, I must be on my way."

"As you wish, Your Highness."

The young man gave another bow and walked toward a massive forge Kailyn hadn't noticed when he'd first pulled her into the courtyard. The furnace was blazing, and as she watched, the young man scooped what looked like coal and shoved it into the fire. He then grabbed a bellows and pumped out air to fuel the flames. Fascinated, she approached him again. "What are you doing?"

The young man didn't even look up from his work.

"Smithing, Your Highness."

She watched as he placed a square piece of metal into the blaze.

He looked up at her again, his brown eyes filled with confusion.

"I thought you were going to try the library doors?"

Kailyn's eyes went wide, and she felt her cheeks heat from embarrassment.

"R-right. A thousand apologies, Sir . . ."

The young man grimaced. "It's Benje, but I'm not a knight."

Benje. She toyed with the syllables on her tongue. His name had a pleasing lilt to it.

She mentally shook herself again. She shouldn't be thinking about his name. What was she doing? She was here on a mission, and she was getting distracted by a young, handsome blacksmith.

Handsome?

She blinked, trying to focus. "Yes. Well, thank you, Benje." She looked around the courtyard, trying to see where the doors to the great library might be. The whole building was shining white rock, making it difficult to make out the seam to a door.

But across from the forge was a beautiful white arched doorway covered in curly script. That must be the entrance to the library.

She smiled and walked across the courtyard, admiring the detailed relief sculptures that adorned the building. They depicted the mighty Goddess, fighting the Chaos of the universe. She'd never seen the like before. The Goddess was depicted in her fighting form, with six arms, each holding a different weapon, riding a strange winged creature that also had six limbs.

Kailyn walked up a small flight of stairs but came to a blank wall. There wasn't a door anywhere. She traced the stone lightly with her fingers, but she couldn't find even a hint of a seam. The door was just . . . gone.

She headed back to the forge where Benje was still working. He looked up at her approach.

"Any luck, Your Highness?" he asked.

Kailyn shook her head. "No . . . it's like the door doesn't even exist."

It didn't make sense. All her books said that the Goddess's Libraries were open to all. Her handmaids had told her no one had been able to get in for years, but they'd all agreed that if anyone could, it would be Kailyn. Now it looked like this entire endeavor had been for nothing. The door wasn't even there.

Benje nodded. "They say the Goddess herself locked all of her Libraries after The Fall. That no one can open them until Ligerthia is redeemed. Whatever that means."

He sighed and ran his fingers through his dark hair.

"I'm sorry you came all this way though, Your Highness. What is it that you wanted to find out?"

Kailyn eyed him warily. Should she trust him? He'd picked her up, laughed at her, and then let her futilely try to open a locked building.

Then again, he was also trying to be helpful.

She took the parchment from her pocket and smoothed it out again, not daring to look at the infuriating blacksmith. "I found this in one of my father's tomes. It's old and clearly written in Old Alarian. I can only make out that it says *Ligerthia* and *Alaria*."

She caught a glimpse at Benje, who was staring at her, his eyes wide.

"You escaped from the castle just to find knowledge?"

He sounded impressed.

She nodded once. "Knowledge is power—and the only power allotted to me." She glanced at the parchment again, but the lines of Old Alarian still made no sense to her. She sighed. This whole thing had been pointless. She had to hurry back before Ilia got in trouble. "But it appears that I cannot obtain it, so I must bid you good day." She stuffed the parchment in her pocket and turned to leave. Benje caught her hand with his larger one.

"I might be able to help you," he said quietly, his warm brown eyes staring at her intensely. Kailyn couldn't help but notice how deep his eyes were—they were like pools of the deepest ocean.

She mentally shook herself. She needed to get back and rescue her handmaid, not dwell on this strange blacksmith. She took a step back from him. "I-I should get back to the castle." She felt her cheeks redden again. She needed to get away before she embarrassed herself further.

"But what about the parchment you need translated?" He

asked in a low voice. "I thought knowledge was important to you."

"It is." She nodded. "But as I am at a loss on how to obtain it . . ."

"Let me see it," he asked, his voice soft but insistent.

Reluctantly, she slipped her hand into her pocket and pulled out the parchment. "I want to think it's important, but it might simply be an old piece of parchment someone was using as a bookmark."

Benje tilted the paper closer toward the light from the fire and squinted at it. "Huh. That's odd."

"What?" Kailyn's heart quickened. "Does it talk about how Ligerthia was destroyed?" Might she have found an answer after all?

"No, listen to this. 'Achea lin porluckun Ligerthia, Alaria fespetalta dyoin.'"

She blinked. "You can read it?" Her heart beat hopefully as she repeated the syllables to herself, but she couldn't make out what it meant. "Do you know what it says?"

"It means 'the account of the greatest secret of Ligerthia, and Alaria's only hope.' It then references a prophecy that was given by the Goddess, but it doesn't give an account of that prophecy."

He handed her back the parchment. "I wish it contained more, Your Highness, but that's all it says."

Kailyn glanced at the mysterious blacksmith before tracing the faded letters that made up the word *Alaria*. Her heart felt heavy. She hoped it would have revealed more about how Ligerthia was destroyed, and possibly how to prevent it from happening to Oleanders. Knowledge was all she had to give, and this was her one chance to find something of value to protect her kingdom. But information about a prophecy was useless unless it gave the actual words of that prophecy.

But that still didn't answer how Benje knew what the parchment said. Maybe he was making it up.

"How do you know what it says?" Kailyn asked, suspicion lacing her voice. "No one can read Old Alarian anymore. Are you sure that's what it says?"

The man worked his jaw. "I'm sure." He didn't elaborate, but from his tone, she knew he was certain. She found herself trusting what he said.

Kailyn frowned. He was a man of many secrets, that much was clear. But while she was here, she might as well ask him what else he knew, since he was being so obliging. "What do you think the prophecy is about?"

"I'm not sure, Your Highness. But I don't think it's wise for you to look into this further."

Annoyance shot through her like she'd jabbed herself with sewing pins. "Why?"

"Won't they miss you at the castle?"

Kailyn sighed. "All I ever do is study. I've read all my father's books. This . . . this is something new. And I want to explore everything about this. Especially if it can protect my kingdom." An idea popped into her mind. She looked at him eagerly. "Could you teach me Old Alarian?"

To her surprise, his eyes filled with concern.

"Princess." Benje's voice grew softer. "Please." He licked his lips nervously before he continued. "There is danger here in Olean. You need to go back."

There was something about the way he said it that made her trust him again.

"Alright," she said, pocketing the parchment. "I'll head back."

"I'll guide you," he said.

"That won't be necessary—" she started to protest as he

smiled at her, a charming warm smile that made her lose her train of thought. She swallowed nervously.

"Nonsense, dilera. You need protection."

"I don't need protection!" she said, bristling again at the insult. This was the second time he'd called her a foolish and naive girl.

Though maybe this whole quest to the library was a bit foolish on her part. Maybe he wasn't entirely wrong.

"Yes, you do," he said, this time his voice grim. "Trust me, Princess. Things are changing in Oleanders, and I don't want you to get hurt."

Chapter Two

Kailyn

Benje was as good as his word—he guided her safely to the outside of the castle. Kailyn had grabbed a bunch of flowers growing near a statue of the Goddess by the library before they left so it looked like she had picked wildflowers.

She glanced behind her at the gate and saw Benje still standing there. He held up a hand in farewell and she nodded before turning and hurrying through the gate. Her thoughts were reeling from their conversation, and how strange and fascinating she found him, but she knew she couldn't think about it now. She had to get back to her maids.

The guards eyed her once more as she approached, but when she showed them her basket of flowers, they let her pass without comment. When Kailyn glanced over her shoulder to find Benje again, he was gone. She slipped unnoticed through the bustling courtyard, but when she entered the kitchen, she felt someone's eyes on her. She turned to look behind her but didn't see anyone.

The kitchen and courtyard were still filled with people, so she supposed someone had just looked her way before carrying on with their work. But the uneasy feeling didn't leave her as she made her way through the kitchen. She ran straight into

Myira at the staircase, who's eyes widened with relief when she saw Kailyn.

"Your hour is up, Ilia. Took you long enough." She pulled her onto the staircase and led her upstairs. "We must be quick, Your Highness," she whispered. "The potion should still hold, but I wouldn't put it past your father—" Her voice broke off and Kailyn immediately saw why.

Lord Shielen, a thin man who served as her father's top advisor and was as slick as a pulong's backside, marched past them with two guards, heading straight toward Kailyn's study.

"Stall him!" Kailyn whispered, but Myira shook her head. "Nea will, she's still at her post. But I don't know how to get you in, Your Highness. We'll just need to get you another change of clothes and fast."

"No time," Kailyn said. "You have to get Lord Shielen away from my study. If he finds Ilia . . ." Her voice trailed off. She'd heard of him throwing people out of the castle for less. Or sending them away to sea to die. She couldn't let that happen. Why did it have to be Lord Shielen?

Myira's eyes filled with concern, but she nodded. "I'll see if I can lead him away." She scurried up the staircase and took off toward the direction the men were headed. Kailyn could only pray that her maids could distract him long enough to let her slip past.

Steeling her nerves, she stood up from where she had been crouching and walked closer to the study. She heard voices; she recognized Nea and Myira and the oily tones of Lord Shielen.

"Move aside, girls, I need to see the princess," the man said calmly.

"Lord Shielen, the princess is in the middle of her lessons," Nea said bravely.

Myira added, "She is not to be disturbed until the evening meal."

"I don't care what your orders are, foolish girl. Her father ordered me to bring her to his study. Stand aside."

"I cannot."

She heard a growl and a slap, followed by her two maids screaming as they were flung from the door. Heart racing, Kailyn ran down the hall as fast as she could. Lord Shielen stood over her maids, sneering down at them. He reached for the door to turn the handle.

"Lord Shielen, wait," she called out, controlling her anger. The man stopped and turned toward the sound of her voice. His thin narrow face broke into a smirk.

"Princess, what a surprise. May I ask what you are doing in servant's attire?"

"I was exploring the castle undetected," she said, glancing at her maids on the ground for the briefest of instants. Myira shook her head, but Kailyn kept going. She had to protect her maids. Her friends. Her only friends.

"I simply wanted to see what it would be like to be a maid in my castle." She felt her face flush at the lie, but she hoped Lord Shielen wouldn't notice. If he ever found out she had left the castle, the punishment would be severe.

He studied her with his beady eyes, as if trying to find a weakness to her story. "You left your maids in front of your door so you could sneak about? Clever, Your Highness. But not clever enough. I've come to bring you to the king. Your father wishes to speak with you."

Kailyn's heart sank. Her father didn't want her even exploring the castle because he was so worried something bad might happen to her. If that were all she was punished for, then it would be worth it. Her secret was still safe. But why did she get the feeling something more was at stake?

"Well then," Lord Shielen said, addressing the maids. "I suppose you two should help her change into something more suitable to present her before the king. I will wait."

He gestured toward the princess's study. Mentally praying for the Goddess's blessing, Kailyn slipped into her study, her maids following behind.

Lord Don was still asleep, but so was Ilia. Nea woke her by touching her shoulder gently.

Ilia woke with a start, whirling around until her eyes landed on Kailyn. They went wide. "Y-you're back! I was staring at the book, trying to read like you said, but reading is so difficult, especially when the letters move. But I was trying! It got really stuffy in here and I fell asleep." She looked frantic and Kailyn's heart went out to her maid. She knew Ilia struggled with reading more than any of her other maids.

"It's alright, Ilia," she said, sending her maid a grateful smile. "I'm just grateful you were here in my place."

Ilia relaxed and offered Kailyn a tiny smile. "Thank you, Your Highness."

"*Ichla huffa.*" Myira shook her head. "We don't have time for this. Lord Shielen is waiting to take the princess to her father. We have to get her dressed."

Ilia's eyes widened even further than before and her face went pale. "Lord Shielen?" she squeaked. "He's outside?"

"Yes, and time's awasting," Myira grumbled, grabbing Ilia's arm and pulling her to her feet. Ilia brushed past the table on her way to her feet, bumping Lord Don. Everyone froze. He snorted and shifted in his seat, but his eyes were still closed. Kailyn exhaled, finding herself impressed—Myira's potion was incredibly strong.

"Let's leave him in the study," Kailyn said, motioning her maids toward the door that led to her chambers. They slipped in quietly and shut the door behind them, leaving Lord Don fast asleep.

The girls helped her change quickly. She could feel their anxiety hovering over them like a dark cloud. They all hated Lord Shielen.

"What does he want?" Nea cursed under her breath as she helped Ilia undo the stays of the pink dress. The maid slipped it off, revealing her servant's gown underneath. Ilia put the pink dress away while Myira brought forth another gown, a gentle green silk that Kailyn normally loved, but her heart was still tied in knots. They helped her slip off her servant's dress, and the parchment crinkled as Nea folded the dress over her arms.

The three maids stopped their work and looked at Kailyn curiously.

"The parchment," Ilia whispered.

"Did you get into the library?" Myira said as she picked up a brush to smooth Kailyn's tangled hair.

Nea brought the parchment out of the pocket of the brown skirt.

"Was it worth risking everything for?" she asked quietly, looking up at Kailyn, her blue eyes shining.

Kailyn stared at them, her heart heavy. She hadn't even been able to get into the library and now she had to go stand before her father, facing whatever punishment he'd decree. Her hands shook, but she took the parchment from Nea and spread it on the desk.

"I-I don't know," she said, steeling her voice. "I can't tell you now."

She stood, holding her hands straight at her side. She looked at her maids one by one. "Thank you for your help today. But now I must go face my father."

Her maids nodded, all three of them wearing worried expressions.

"Goddess be with you, Princess," Nea whispered.

Kailyn could only hope that she was. She'd need all the help she could get.

Chapter Three

Kailyn

"*Y*ou look resplendent," Lord Shielen said as Kailyn exited her rooms. Kailyn murmured her thanks, not daring to speak louder. She was already in trouble, and she didn't want to make things worse. He offered his arm to her. "Shall we, Princess?"

She kept quiet the entire way through the castle. She knew these corridors and staircases, as it was all she had ever known. But after seeing the glittering white expanse of the library, and the clear beautiful sky overhead, the stone seemed even more confining than normal.

Lord Shielen led her to the oaken doors that marked her father's study. The two guards who stood outside them nodded at the princess before letting them in. Kailyn sent a quick prayer for strength heavenward before entering the study, Lord Shielen following.

The white-gray stone of the walls shone brilliantly in the light of the high windows, bouncing off the tall bookcases filled with tomes Kailyn knew her father never read.

The king of Oleanders sat on a brilliant blue cushion that filled his entire lush chair. The cushion puffed at its seams, and golden tassels tangled over the ground. Lia, her father's newest dog, was pawing at a tassel but perked up when Kailyn entered.

"Stay, Lia," the king commanded. The dog lay back down on her paws. Kailyn could sense Lia's nervous energy. She'd always had a special relationship with dogs, but she couldn't focus on Lia now. Even though right now all she wanted was to stroke Lia's silky ears to calm her own racing heart.

She glanced at her father and curtsied. She hated looking at him. His white scalp reflected the bright light from the window, nearly blinding her. His swollen legs barely reached the floor. And a platter of the softest and juiciest fruits was just in reach of his chubby fingers.

"Daughter," he said, extending his fingers toward her. Kailyn rose.

"You wished to speak with me, Your Majesty?" Her heart hammered. Would Lord Shielen mention her excursion through the castle?

To her surprise, Lord Shielen remained silent, though he sent her a smirk that sent shivers down her spine. What was he up to?

"Yes, my flower. It is the matter of your betrothal. Lord Shielen and I have been discussing who your husband will be, and we've just finished the arrangements." He threw a purple fruit into his mouth which burst, the juice running down his white powdered chin.

Kailyn watched the juice trickle down, the dark purple stain cutting his pale chin in half, trying to register what he had said. "My . . . betrothal?"

The king nodded. "You are engaged to Prince Zolan of Oronia. He will be arriving in a month's time, at which point, we will throw the most glorious engagement ball Oleanders has ever seen. Then you shall be wed before going with him to his home country."

He snagged another fruit and popped it into his mouth.

Kailyn watched in sickening horror as more juice dribbled down his chin. Her father swallowed and continued. "It is a most auspicious day for our nation! The Goddess has bestowed her bounty on us, and you, my flower, will lead us into a period of prosperity like no other." He brandished his fingers toward her.

Kailyn stared in disbelief at her father's purple-stained fat fingers that more resembled sausages than human flesh. Her heart sank down to her slippers. It couldn't be true. He couldn't have said what she had heard.

"Have you mentioned the best news, sire?" Lord Shielen said, reminding Kailyn the snake was still there.

Her father's weak blue eyes brightened. "Ah, I was getting to that. With your marriage, Oleanders will finally have an heir, as Prince Zolan will inherit my throne upon my deathbed. You'll be taken care of forever, my flower."

It was too much. Tears gathered in the corner of her eyes. He was taking her away from Oleanders before she even got the chance to get to know it.

Her father took her hands in his sweaty massive paws. "I know it's overwhelming, my flower. But there is a recently arrived Oronian lady of the court, Lady Horia, who will be teaching you all you need to know about Oronia. I realize it's sudden, but it's for the best. You're dismissed, daughter." He smiled at her with what he likely thought was a kind, fatherly smile, but to her it looked like a gaping hole about to swallow her.

How had everything changed so quickly? Her mind thudded dully as she thought over and over about her father's words as she walked back to her apartments, escorted by a guard. She almost wished Lord Shielen had told her father about her excursion. This was worse than any punishment she'd been dealt before.

Engaged? To Prince Zolan?

She didn't even know anything about Oronia! Her father's limited library only mentioned it as their prosperous neighbor across the sea, nothing more. All she knew was what she'd learned from a book of folk tales. That wasn't enough to go to another entire new nation! She hadn't even been able to explore her own.

To her relief, it was only Nea and Ilia in her rooms when she got back. The mysterious Lady Horia—who Kailyn had never met—wasn't there.

"Your Highness!" Nea curtsied. "Are you alright?"

Kailyn closed the door with a thud. "I-I am well."

"Your father's not punishing you?" Ilia asked, her voice going higher.

"No—but . . ."

The door opened and Myira slipped into the study, her eyes wide. "Princess! Why is Lady Horia heading this way?"

She felt Ilia tremble next to her. "Lady Horia? She dismissed a girl for dropping a plate just this morning, after giving her ten stripes across the back! Oh, I don't want to get the sack!"

Kailyn rested a hand on Ilia's arm. "No one's giving you the sack, Ilia. I'll make sure of it. I'll need the three of you when I wed Prince Zolan." She tried not to choke on that last syllable. She had no idea what the prince even looked like, much less what marrying him would be like.

"Marriage?" the three maids said at the same time a knock sounded on the door.

Kailyn made shooing motions with her hands and her maids fell into their normal positions at her side.

Kailyn picked up the book by her table and donned her best demure expression. "Come in," she said. She opened the book and pretended to skim the pages while her heart hammered.

A tall, thin woman breezed into the room in a poof of gray silk, followed by two women dressed in identical blue robes.

"Ah. Princess," the woman said in a thin, reedy voice, drawing out the *s*'s. "What are you doing?"

"Reading, Lady Horia," Kailyn said politely. "It is my study time after all." She heard a quiet chuckle from Nea.

Lady Horia's eyes narrowed. "I see. And do you think this is the kind of appropriate behavior for an Oronian bride?"

Kailyn frowned. "I-isn't it?"

"Hyget non! Absolutely not! Oronian brides are much too busy to be reading. They are to govern the affairs of their household in everything. Give that book here please."

Kailyn stared at Lady Horia in horror. Books were her one source of freedom—the one thing her father allowed her.

"No, thank you, milady," Kailyn said, her fingers curling around the book. "I have much to study before—"

To her great astonishment, Lady Horia slapped her. The sting was nothing compared to the shock and the outbursts of her handmaids.

"How dare you strike the princess!" Myira snapped, then said something in her native Cyronian that Kailyn was pretty sure was a curse. "Get away from her!"

Lady Horia's mouth was open in a perfect O. Then her mouth settled into a thin line.

"Well. We're in worse shape than I thought. First thing that must be done is get rid of your maids. I can only imagine what kind of . . ." she eyed Myira coldly, " . . . barbaric influence they must have had on you, Your Highness."

Kailyn jumped to her feet, the book dropping to the floor. "Y-you can't! Don't!" She thrust out the book. "Here, take it. Anything. Just don't hurt my maids."

Lady Horia took the book, but her expression remained unchanged. "Nin, Pran, please clear away the princess's books. We have much to instruct her on."

Nea and Myira made to help the two new maids in blue, but Lady Horia held up a hand.

"As for you three," she said, her voice ice-cold. "You are dismissed. Leave the palace at once."

Horror shot through Kailyn. Her only friends were being taken from her. She'd be friendless. Forever.

"You can't do that!" Kailyn said, standing in front of the door. "You can't take them away."

"Non?" Horia arched her perfect brows. "Perhaps I shall have them killed? For disobeying the king's orders?"

The horror coiled in Kailyn's stomach. She thought she was going to hurl. "No! P-please."

"We will leave." Myira laid a hand on Kailyn's arm. Her voice was resigned. "Your Highness, we'll be alright."

"But—!"

Nea shot Kailyn a look, and Kailyn felt her shoulders drop. There was nothing she could do. Her friends had to leave. It was better they were alive and away from the palace than dead because of her.

"Al-alright," Kailyn stammered, watching her friends disappear out the door one by one.

Ilia waved a sad small wave as she closed the door behind her.

"Enough of these dramatics," Lady Horia said. "Come, my dear. We've much work to do."

31

Life with Lady Horia was utterly appalling. All of Kailyn's books were taken away, which she felt almost as keenly as the loss of her friends. All she'd ever wanted was to learn of the world and explore it. But with Lady Horia, a native Oronian, Kailyn's education was entirely different.

Lady Horia fed Kailyn a strict diet of Byun bread, a flatbread that tasted like chalk powder mixed with the bitter rind of an apple. Thinness was apparently a virtue of Oronian women.

As was fashion. Lady Horia got rid of all of Kailyn's comfortable dresses and instead brought in row after row of fabric to turn Kailyn into a traditional Oronian bride, bedecked in all the latest styles. Her entire wardrobe had to be replaced before the ball in four weeks.

And she had to memorize rules upon rules of etiquette and behavior.

"Smaller steps, Your Highness! Oronian women do not gallop," Lady Horia said about Kailyn's walk. "Sway gracefully. You're a walking tree."

Kailyn frowned. "But I'm not—"

"What have I said about talking back?" Lady Horia snapped.

Kailyn shut her mouth. Oronian wives did not speak unless spoken to, and they never spoke out of turn. Her only job as the wife of Prince Zolan was to look beautiful and provide him with an heir. So Lady Horia said.

Kailyn was shocked. She'd hoped that Oronia was more civilized than this. But what did she know? Her books never mentioned anything about the prosperous country, other than it was large and across the sea to the east. And mostly desert. But surely there was more to Oronian life than balls, parties, and endless fashion parades?

Kailyn dreaded the coming ball. If the prince was as bad as Lady Horia, then her life was officially over.

Her one consolation was thinking of her visit with the young man Benje. Before bed every night, she'd think about her visit to the library and their chance meeting. How his brilliant brown eyes had sparkled in the light . . . She'd never met a handsome man like him before. Someone kind too—he didn't have to go out of his way to escort her back. And knowledgeable. Surely he'd delight in talking about Old Alarian. Maybe he could even teach her how to read it better.

But as she drifted off to sleep, she'd remember that she was a princess, engaged to a foreign prince. And she had to do what she was told.

Chapter Four

Abrina

*P*rincess Abrina of Florryn never did what she was told. It's what had gotten her into this fight with the young frost giant in the first place. Thankfully, she was winning.

She stabbed at the beast's toe and it howled in pain, blowing freezing wind at her and driving her back. She held her shield to block most of the gust, but it was still frigid. Ice spread across her shield, coating her armor. She grimaced as she wrenched her arm back into a movable position, cracking the ice. Thank the Goddess the creature hadn't touched her. If it had, she'd be frozen and completely unable to move. And this beast was only an adolescent.

She dodged another chilly blast behind her ice-encased shield and twirled out of the monster's reach. Her shield was growing heavy and useless. She needed to dispatch the beast quickly.

"Princess!" Captain Wilen called out from a nearby rock. "What are you doing?"

"Helping you, Captain!" Abrina yelled back. She ran as fast as she could across the snow-covered rocky ground around the frost giant, ducking under its swing, and slicing her sword at its knee. The leg buckled and the giant went down on the rocks, bellowing the whole way and spraying ice everywhere. The blast caught two of her men, freezing them instantly.

Fury raged inside Abrina like a mountain gyon and she leapt through the air, dropping her shield and stabbing her blade in the beast's chest. The creature shuddered before going still, dissolving back into ice and snow.

Abrina stood up, panting. It was gone. For now.

If only it would stay dead.

One of her knights, Sir Tyir, a balding man wrapped in the blue fur cape of the Florrynian guard, waved his hands at her. Abrina had to squint to try and make out his signing in the snow that fluttered around.

"Brilliant move, chopping its leg off."

Abrina grinned and signed *"Thank you"* to the man. That was quite the compliment coming from him. Sir Tyir, even though he couldn't hear anything, was a marvelous tactician. He saw things others didn't and he'd taught her to watch for patterns and weaknesses. It's how she knew the giants' weak point was their legs.

She glanced at the two frozen men, their arms and legs covered in white ice. Her smile fell. She couldn't even tell if they were breathing. *"Will they be alright?"*

Sir Tyir waved over a medic. *"We will do what we can for them."* He and the medic headed over to the two frozen men.

Abrina was about to follow when Captain Wilen came up to her, his graying hair covered in a dusting of snow.

"Princess." His voice was barely civil and his eyes looked thunderous. He was not happy with her. Again. "You need to get back to the castle."

Abrina scoffed. "Mother will make me attend another meeting. They're as boring as snow. The action is out here, where the frost giants are." She gestured behind her toward the frosty foothills of the Rosstross Mountains where several of their guard were spread out, looking for more of the beasts. "We have to keep them back."

"It is not your job to fight them, Princess Abrina," Captain Wilen said, shaking his head. "Your mother will have my hide if you don't come back from a raid."

"That will never happen," Abrina said, brandishing her sword. Her fingers itched to swing the blade around, to cleave ice and snow and stop the frozen giants of the north from destroying Florryn. She had to destroy them first. It was the only way she could save her people. She spied the swirling particles of snow a few meters away, swirling into a vortex. She could make out the head and shoulders reforming. It was back.

She flexed her legs and took off running, ignoring the captain who called out her name behind her. She didn't care about going back to the manor. Out here was where she belonged.

The icy vortex solidified into a fully formed adolescent frost giant, who lumbered toward Abrina. She tensed, feeling the pull of battle, and swung her sword, lobbing off the beast's hand. But almost immediately, snow swirled around the stub, the hand reforming.

She ducked as the giant swung its other hand toward her, barely missing the blow. The ice from its breath however, crystallized on her armor, slowing her movements to a crawl and then a complete stop. She tried wrenching her arm free, but it was stubbornly refusing to move. The ice spread to encase her torso and her legs. Only her head was free to move, but who knew how long that would last?

She cursed as she looked up at the young frost giant, who raised its other hand, about to pound her into oblivion. She swallowed thickly and frantically tried to move her arms again, but the ice was too strong.

Maybe she didn't fully have this fight.

Fire suddenly materialized in Abrina's periphery and her eyes followed the launch of several dozen flaming arrows that all landed on the frost giant. It hissed in pain, and lumbered away from Abrina. A dozen more flaming arrows launched and the frost giant clambered back up the foothills, screeching at them as it did so.

Abrina tried to move, but she was still frozen in place.

The fire got closer and closer until she saw a woman in a long purple cloak, holding a torch aloft. She wore a fierce scowl on her face as she lowered her torch to the ice encasing Abrina's arms and legs. Abrina could already feel the cold retreat in the heat, but she almost wished the woman would just leave her there to her fate.

"Daughter," said the queen of Florryn. "What a fine mess you've landed in this time."

It took almost thirty minutes to thaw the ice on Abrina's armor. By the time she could move again, she was freezing, and still her mother kept lecturing her. Abrina wished her mother had stayed in the manor.

"This is the third time this week, Abrina!" her mother snapped, using her torch to lead the way back to the horses. Abrina was wrapped in three blankets, but her teeth were still chattering.

Her men looked at her sympathetically as she passed, except for the captain. He raised his eyebrows in an "I-told-you-so" kind of way. Abrina scowled at him.

"Do you have a death wish?" her mother demanded. "Abrina, I need you at the manor, not off chasing ice and snow!"

Abrina turned her scowl on her mother. "I don't know why you need me at the manor—it's not like I do anything there. Out here, my sword counts for something!"

"You are more than just your sword, Abrina. This is not behavior suitable for a bride."

Abrina snorted and then sneezed. "Well, that's good then. Because I'll never be a bride."

Her mother straightened her shoulders. "We'll discuss this back at the manor. Can you ride?"

Abrina held her chin up. "Of course I can ride."

Even if her fingers were so cold that gripping the reins would be a struggle. But she was Florrynian, through and through. A little thing like cold wouldn't prevent her from doing what needed to be done.

Besides, her horse, Beri, knew the way home.

The whole way, as the wind whipped around her and she held onto the reins the best she could, Abrina thought about the frost giants. They were getting bolder. Three months ago, the frost giants had started coming down from their mountains, invading Florryn. They'd already taken a five-kilometer radius from the mountains.

Florryn had already shrunk thanks to the treaty after the civil war ended a year ago—a third of their land went to Lord Tera to make up the new kingdom of Terarryn to the east, and a third went to Lord Mita to make up the new kingdom of Mitarryn to the west. And now their country was shrinking again, thanks to those cursed frost giants. They had to beat them. What other choice did they have? It's not like they could ask Oleanders for help.

Abrina shuddered, and not just from the cold. Oleanders. Their long-sworn enemy who lived to the south, beyond the Rosstross Mountains. Even though the war had been over for twenty years—before Abrina was even born—she could never forget the stories of how Oleanders had terrorized her nation, how their superior navy had shelled their coasts.

She'd seen the scars in the crumbled ruins and villages, which had fallen again with the civil war. She firmly believed the civil war wouldn't have happened had they not lost the war with Oleanders.

And that wasn't the worst part.

Oleanders had killed her sister.

She clenched her fists. She'd never told anyone. She'd kept it in the family, like her mother asked when she'd told her all those years ago. But the rage that filled her heart . . . she itched to fight every last Oleanderian and make them pay.

That they could ever be allies was unthinkable. There was no way that Florryn would ever ask Oleanders for help. They'd rather freeze.

At the rate things were going with the frost giants, they might end up freezing. There wasn't any way to prevent them from reforming. Fire was effective, but only temporarily. Even now, it was likely that the frost giant Abrina had just fought had already reformed.

She eyed her mother's figure as she raced ahead. She was grateful her mother had shown up with the fire. Even if it meant she was going to get lectured even more at the manor. Her mother wanted her to stay safe and warm, and wanted to prepare Abrina for marriage.

Abrina made a face. There was no way she was ever getting married. She'd rather fight the frost giants all day everyday than marry some bratty prince of a foreign land.

Florryn was home. And she was doing all she could to save it.

Back at the manor, after taking a long bath to soak away the cold, Abrina sat in her mother's parlor, wrapped in warm furs and polishing her sword. Her mother had insisted on talking as soon as Abrina was warm again.

"This reckless behavior needs to stop, Abrina," her mother demanded, narrowing her fierce brown eyes. "You were frozen this time!"

"It was just an adolescent, Mother." Abrina shrugged, examining her blade. Had she missed a spot?

"An adolescent may not freeze you permanently, but you are endangering your life." Her mother sharply exhaled. "Abrina, this is serious. It is not your job to protect the border. It's the guards'."

Abrina set the sword down and turned to glower at her mother. "I know it's their job. But how many of our men must freeze and die before we pitch in and help? Or should we abandon Florryn to the frost giants?"

Her mother was a crack shot with her arrows, as she'd just demonstrated. If she helped them fight, they'd get more of those giants down. Maybe even find a way to *keep* them down. Their tendency to reform was unnerving. And concerning. What if they wiped out Florryn? No. Abrina had to do everything she could to save her people.

"I am helping them, Abrina," her mother said, then sighed, her anger deflating as she put her head in her hands. "What am I to do with you? I can't lose you too."

A pang echoed in Abrina's heart as she thought of her father.

She missed him with all her heart. He'd been killed five years ago during the civil war with Lords Mita and Tera. There wasn't a day that went by when she didn't miss him. She took after her father—in more than just their stocky builds. In temperament, she was also very like him. He'd tell her to use her strength to help her people—and he'd probably be fighting right alongside her.

But he was gone and there was nothing she could do to get him back. She could, however, defend her people against the frost giants. It's what her father would be doing if he were still here.

"You don't have to do anything with me," Abrina said softly, looking at the glitter of firelight on her sword. "I can take care of myself. And my people."

"Yes, but fighting the frost giants by yourself isn't the answer. You're going to get hurt. Even worse than being temporarily frozen."

Abrina shrugged. "I've been doing it for the last three months, Mother. I'm fine."

Though, she had to admit, being frozen wasn't exactly fine. But she'd survived, hadn't she? And now she knew that she needed longer range weapons. Maybe they should try flaming spears tomorrow. Or catapults. They just had to figure out a way to get catapults up on the rocky terrain. She should suggest it to Captain Wilen, if he was ever done glowering at her.

"You are most certainly not fine, Abrina." Her mother sighed. "While you are an excellent swordswoman, you are meant for more."

Abrina frowned. She didn't want to be anything more than a swordswoman, fighting alongside her men, protecting her people.

Her mother went on, changing her tone to the one Abrina

41

hated—the one that meant Abrina wasn't going to like whatever her mother was going to say. "Dearheart, there's something I must tell you."

Abrina fiddled with the furs wrapped around her. "You don't want me sneaking away again."

Not like that would stop her. Her people needed her.

"No, it's not that. I mean, yes, I don't want you sneaking away again. But it's more important than that." She locked eyes with Abrina. "An ambassador is arriving this evening. He should be here shortly."

"An ambassador?" Why under the Goddess's moon would an ambassador come here? Florryn's resources were limited. Her people were still trying to recover from the civil war, and now they were dealing with frost giants. What need did they have of an ambassador?

Abrina frowned. "Why?"

"I'm afraid I can't tell you that yet, Abrina." Her mother smiled sadly. "For your sake. But it's why I need you here."

Abrina's frown deepened. Her mother rarely hid anything from her. Sudden realization dawned, fury boiling inside her, even stronger than when she'd faced the adolescent giant. It was her worst fear. What her mother had been preparing her for her entire life. "You're sending me away to get married, aren't you?

Her mother sighed, walking over to Abrina and laying her pale white hand on Abrina's arm. "I know you want to fight your way out of everything, my *irrele*. And you'll get your chance to fight. I know you will. But please be patient. There is more to this than a simple marriage agreement with Tigahel."

"So you *are* marrying me off!" Abrina said, yanking away her arm and slamming her hand against the wall. It hurt, but it was also satisfying. "I knew it! I knew you didn't want me fighting the frost giants, but I never dreamed it was for *marriage*!" She spat the word. Marriage was utterly disgusting. She'd take a fight with a frost giant any day.

Her mother shook her head. "Dearheart, there is more at stake than even I thought. I need you to trust me on this. It will be dangerous. We may lose Florryn. But it's the only chance we have."

"Lose Florryn?" Abrina said, her anger curbed slightly by her confusion. "How is that possible?"

Before her mother could answer, a soldier entered the room and saluted them.

"My queen, my princess."

"At ease, Lady Signa," Abrina's mother said.

"The ambassador has arrived."

Chapter Five

Abrina

The queen sent Abrina to her room while she went to speak with the ambassador.

"Be at peace," she'd told Abrina when Abrina opened her mouth to protest. "You'll meet him in the morning, I promise. Rest now, my *irrele*."

Then she'd closed the door, leaving Abrina by herself.

Well, Abrina wasn't having any of that. She was fuming that her mother wouldn't let her meet the ambassador. The fire and furs had been enough to warm her up so she was no longer freezing. She didn't even need to rest anymore. So she did what she always did to control her emotions: find something—or someone—to fight.

Since she couldn't risk going to the front again so soon after her most recent attempt, she had to find the next best thing—battling a new recruit in the training room. Over her tunic she wore a breastplate made of one of the lightest metals in Almarryn, only found in the Rosstross Mountains, and she wielded a sword that was perfectly balanced. She had been maintaining the upper hand when the recruit feinted, then twisted around and landed his sword neatly on her shoulder.

"Nicely done, Zachry," called one of the guards watching, an older fellow named Byron.

"Beginner's luck," Zachry said with a shrug.

Slightly irked, Abrina brought her sword up again, knocking his sword away and shoving him back. Zachry stumbled and fell, ending up with Abrina's sword to his throat.

"Feel lucky now?" she taunted.

Zachry grinned. He had a boyish face, still whisker-free, and wavy black hair that came to his ears. "Ah, Princess," he said. "I feel the games are just beginning."

Abrina chuckled at that and offered a hand to help the boy up.

"And now you are officially welcomed to the royal guard," Byron said, smirking. "I think all of us have been bested by the princess."

"Hey now, I also need to practice," Abrina said as she loosened the straps that held her breastplate in place. She winced with the movement. Her arms were still sore from the battle earlier. "And you all are easier to fight than a bunch of frost giants."

Zachry chuckled. "Definitely wasn't prepared for this."

Abrina turned to him, cocking her head. "What, sparring with your princess?"

"And getting whooped? Aye. You're certainly not like most princesses, Your Highness."

Abrina smiled wryly. He had no idea.

It wasn't until the next day that Abrina first caught sight of the Tigahelen ambassador. She'd come back from a morning ride with Beri and was sneaking to her room when she'd spied him walking down the hall from her mother's study.

She had only one word to describe him—beautiful. He wore the white robes of Ligerthia, which she found strange, but they fit his muscled form well. He held a solid blue wooden staff that glowed slightly at the top. But that wasn't what drew her to him. The way his golden skin glistened, like he'd spent all his days in the sun. The curl of his golden locks, so irresistibly messy, but in such a charming way. . . and the brief glint of intelligence she saw in his eyes before she ducked out of sight.

Abrina didn't know how long she stood there after the ambassador left before she blinked. *That* was the ambassador?

He was not at all what she'd expected.

Abrina ran to her chambers, musing over what she'd seen.

Her maid, Yera, had pulled up another bath for her while she'd been out. Abrina smiled fondly, grateful for her maid's thoughtfulness.

Yera was old, but she'd been working for the castle for so long that Abrina's mother hadn't bothered to turn her away when they couldn't afford to pay servants anymore. Yera was like family.

Family. A word that had brought her no end of heartache. Abrina slipped out of her tunic and into the tub. The warm water was relaxing, and she rested her head against the towel placed on the edge, lost in thoughts of yesteryears.

Her father had been gone for five years now, but it still hurt to think about him. She missed him every day. He was the one who had encouraged her to pick up a sword and learn to ride a horse, despite the protests of her mother. He had taught her battle strategy when she was barely old enough to walk, and, more recently, had taught her unity as he attempted to bring Florryn's lost sisters home . He had died in a fierce battle at the border, giving his life for his family and his country.

He'd at least had a chance to fight for his own life. Not like her sister. Her poor twin sister who'd been brutally murdered.

Abrina scowled into the suds. How she wished she could

enact her revenge on Oleanders for what they'd done to her family. But no, they were at peace. She had to respect the treaty. It didn't mean she had to like it.

Yera came into the room, carrying a white woolen towel.

"Ah, Princess," she said, setting down the towel on the nearby stool. "I had wondered if ya were here, lassie. Or if ye'd gone off again."

Abrina smiled at the squat old woman. Her mother said that Yera was part gnome, and Abrina believed it. She wasn't as short as gnomes were rumored to be, and unlike full blooded gnomes, she had lived in the daylight for at least six decades, giving her dark brown skin and plentiful wrinkles.

"I had finished my morning ride, Yera," she said. "As always."

"And as always, these old bones are tired, lassie. Now hurry it up. I believe yer wanted in yer mother's study."

Abrina's heart quickened. Wanted? Was she finally going to meet the ambassador? Maybe she could talk her way out of the marriage agreement, insist that she was needed more here. Maybe she could duel the man. He was muscular, yes, but that didn't mean he was a warrior. If she could best him in battle, maybe she could win her freedom to stay in Florryn. She smiled at the thought.

"Come along now, time to get goin', lassie. Yer daydreamin' again." Yera motioned for Abrina to get out of the tub.

"I'm going," Abrina said, getting out of the tub and drying herself off. She slipped into soft woolen breeches and a purple tunic, wrapping a belt around her waist and tying a triple knot, like her father had shown her. She towel-dried her hair, combing the knots out with her fingers. When she finished, she jammed her feet into her boots and ran from Yera, who called out, "Yer hair, lassie! Ya look like a wind demon!"

Abrina didn't even look back as she ran to her mother's study.

She burst through the doors, fully intending to shock the beautiful man with her intensity and call off the marriage. But he wasn't there. Abrina sighed, combing her wet black hair with her fingers some more. Yera was right. She could have spent a few more moments on it.

"Abrina," her mother said, exasperated. "What's with your hair?"

"I hurried here, Mother," Abrina said as she twisted her hair into a very wet braid that dripped onto the bear rug below her mother's wooden desk. "You asked to see me."

"I expected you to be presentable." Her mother pinched the bridge of her nose and took a deep breath. "I suppose it's better than you sneaking off to fight frost giants. But you are going to be representing Florryn abroad. I need you to try and act the part."

Abrina crossed her arms and scowled. "What if I don't want to go?"

Her mother got up from her chair and started pacing in front of the large bookshelves behind the desk. The room had been her father's before he died, but her mother hadn't changed much since then.

"Abrina." Her mother's voice was hard. Firm. Warrior-like. "Our kingdom needs this marriage alliance. Your destiny is to go to Tigahel to marry Prince Henri. There's no room for discussion. You, like me, are to save your kingdom through marriage."

Abrina scowled and turned to the large window. She knew her mother had married her father for the good of Florryn twenty years ago, after the treaty was signed with Oleanders. That was the story told, anyway. Her mother had hailed from Wyta, a tiny island nation that was deep in the Tigahel Archipelago. She had only been eligible for marriage to the mainland prince of Florryn because of her island's fierce warriors.

It was that alliance that had saved them when the civil war broke out between Lords Mita and Tera, who had each claimed, through violence, a third of the once-grand kingdom of Florryn. It was the Wyta warriors who had completely overwhelmed Mitarryn's forces the day her father was killed, giving Florryn a brief victory. That victory would not have happened had her mother not married King Wendol, then Prince Wendol, a man she had never met before their wedding day.

Abrina had known her whole life that her mother had never regretted it, even when King Wendol died and left her sole ruler of a dying nation.

But Abrina had never even considered that one day she would have to make the same choice.

"Abrina," her mother said, in a softer voice. "I know you don't think you're ready. But you are. You were meant to save our people. And this is how. Not through battling the frost giants. Your union will bring resources to help us survive. Please. We need this."

Florryn had been devastated by the wars, Abrina knew that. She hadn't realized how desperate they were for resources though. And it was all dependent on her? She swallowed thickly. Marriage still wasn't appealing. At all. But she did want to save her people. If she could.

"Will it even work?" Abrina whispered, still gazing out the window, wishing she could face the frost giants of yesterday. What if she went across the sea to marry this foreign prince and her kingdom was still destroyed by ice and snow?

49

"It will," came a kind voice behind her. Abrina turned to see the beautiful man walk into the room, a brilliant smile making his golden face shine like the sun. How was he even more handsome now?

"This marriage will bring your kingdom the resources it needs to survive the frost giants," the ambassador said. "And you will be a hero."

A hero. For a moment, visions of glory danced around Abrina's mind as she saw herself single-handedly saving her people by returning with resources and using them to defeat the frost giants.

Then the visions faded as she remembered she would have to marry for those resources. And she'd likely never come home. Her mother had never returned to Wyta after her marriage. Her heart sank. She was leaving home. Forever.

"We'll need an escort," the ambassador said, like Abrina's world hadn't just come crashing down around her. "We leave tomorrow."

"I'll pick out my ten finest men," Abrina's mother said, inclining her head toward the ambassador. "Thank you."

He smiled another brilliant smile as he left.

Abrina scowled at his back. He was too perfect. What was his prince going to look like, an ugly old pulong? Or like the wind demons Yera was always talking about?

She could only hope this marriage would save her people. Even if she didn't like it. At all.

Chapter Six

Abrina

Abrina stared at the monolith that marked her father's grave.

"I'm leaving today," she whispered.

"Mother is sending me away to Tigahel to marry a prince I've never met to save our kingdom from frost giants. I-I don't want to go. But Florryn needs help. The frost giants . . ." Her voice trailed off as she remembered the fight two days before. "They can be hacked to pieces, lit on fire, or blasted with rocks. And still they reform. I worry they'll destroy us. Destroy Florryn."

She traced the curling letters of her father's name, wishing she could hear his voice again, comforting her, assuring her that all would be well, and that he'd fight her battles with her to the end.

Every warrior needs a loyal wolf at their back, he'd frequently tell her, reminding her of the stories of the great Alarian wolves, the ancient symbols of Florryn that were believed to have once roamed the Rosstross Mountains. Even though no one had seen one in centuries.

"I wish you were here," she whispered softly. "We'd find a way to stop the frost giants together. We'd save Florryn."

Tears pricked her eyes as she remembered her mother's words the day before, and she pushed her palm against the cool black stone. "Mother says this might not be enough.

We may lose Florryn to the frost giants. I don't even want to imagine that."

She shuddered. If all of Florryn were overcome with frost . . . it would spell their end. She'd merely been frozen by the proximity to the giant's ice. If everyone were permanently frozen . . . they'd fall. Just like Ligerthia.

"But if I can give us a fighting chance," she said, tracing his name again. "Then I have to go."

Even if the thought of marrying a complete stranger filled her with revulsion. She couldn't picture this Prince Henri's face. She'd never even seen his portrait.

It did not help that all she kept picturing was the golden face of the ambassador. He was too handsome for his own good.

But none of that mattered. She had to fulfill her duty.

Even if she never saw her people again.

A tear fell from her eye and landed on the cold, empty ground near the monolith. Spring had been delayed by the frosts, but if the frost kept spreading, their growing season would never come. Perhaps she'd have to relocate her entire nation to Tigahel.

The thought filled her with a lonely emptiness.

She had to try though, didn't she? Florryn wouldn't go down without a fight.

And she supposed this was a fight, just not like any she'd ever experienced before.

She rested her forehead against the cool stone and breathed in the earthy, crisp smell of the garden, wishing she could see her father's kind eyes and gentle smile one more time.

But he was gone. And she had work to do.

Squaring her shoulders, Abrina turned and faced her future.

Her knights—Captain Wilen, Sir Zachry, Sir Byron, Sir Tyir, and six other knights she'd served with before—stood waiting with the ambassador and his two escorts outside the front of the manor. Beri was saddled up, ready to go.

Yera, a handful of servants, and the royal guard stood at attention as Abrina and her mother walked to Beri.

"Abrina," her mother said, looking at her, eyes filled with a deep sadness. And a deep love. "I know this is going to be hard for you. But you're the only one who can do it."

Abrina nodded once, solemnly. "Thank you for your trust in me, Mother."

"Take this," she said, slipping a necklace over Abrina's head. Abrina looked down at it quizzically. She didn't wear jewelry— her mother knew that. But the simple chain held a bronze stone etched with a wolf. An Alarian wolf, the symbol of Florryn.

"My mother, the queen of Wyta, had this made for me before I came to Florryn to marry your father. I think it only fitting that you carry it with you."

Abrina stared at her, not sure what to say to such a gift. So she embraced her mother, hugging her tight.

"May the Goddess protect you always, my fierce *irrele*," her mother whispered, placing a kiss on her brow.

When they parted, Abrina mounted and raised her fist in salute to her people. They saluted back. Bolstered by their courage, Abrina turned Beri and followed her men into the unknown.

Chapter Seven

Kailyn

The fanfare started as soon as Kailyn arrived at the ballroom entrance. She held her breath, which the tight cinch of her ostentatious gown made difficult, but she slowly counted to ten, as Lady Horia had taught her, until the royal guard opened the doors and her name was announced. She took a deep breath—as much as her cinch allowed—and entered the room.

Lady Horia had done her job well—Kailyn glided delicately across the floor to meet her father, holding her head high to keep the heavy headdress she wore from falling. The headpiece was a massive golden tree with ruby birds attached to its branches. Her dress was equally jeweled—the many black layers were decorated with bold red flowers studded with rubies, and blood-red ribbons encircled her neck, her hemline, and each ruffle of her skirt. The effect was stunning. She knew it.

She hated everything about it.

She curtsied deeply to her father, who was sitting triumphantly on the raised dais, clothed in lush purple robes that looked infinitely more comfortable than her gown. Standing next to him was a man she knew without a doubt was the prince.

He was a dark-skinned man dressed entirely in black, except for the red decorative sword at his waist. A thin gold crown rested on his head. His gaze was thoughtful as he watched her, but there was something almost predatory about his dark eyes that roved across her appraisingly.

She swallowed and curtsied to him. He gave her a tiny nod, but his mouth remained impassive. He lacked the warmth she'd seen in Benje.

No, she couldn't think about him. The prince was her life now.

Her father stood from his throne and made his way over to Kailyn, taking her hand.

"You look exquisite," he whispered as the musicians struck up the chords for the first dance of the evening. A waltz. Kailyn murmured her thanks, though she definitely didn't feel exquisite. She was starving, but Lady Horia had forbidden her from feasting as she still wasn't "thin enough" by Oronian standards.

She tried to shove those thoughts aside as her father twirled her across the floor. Due to her father's bulk, they didn't go very far, which she was grateful for as she was feeling faint. The weight of the headdress didn't help. She was aware of the dozens of eyes upon her, the murmurs about how lovely she looked, but she didn't let herself pay them any attention. She couldn't. Her fate was already sealed and no one could change it now.

After the waltz, her father led her back to the prince, who still stood at the dais.

"This is my daughter, Princess Kailyn," her father said, collapsing back onto his throne, wheezing from the exertion. "Kailyn, this is Prince Zolan of Oronia." The prince took her gloved hand and kissed it.

"Charmed, Princess," the prince said, gazing at her with those midnight black eyes, which flicked to her face, to her dress, and then to the surrounding courtiers, like Kailyn wasn't interesting enough for him. She bit her tongue, swallowing the revulsion that coursed through her before curtsying to him, keeping the heavy tree balanced on her head.

"May I have this dance?" he asked almost lazily as he offered his arm to Kailyn. She nodded and he led her onto the dance floor. He spun her around perfectly in time to the music, but he kept gazing around like she wasn't even there.

"Oleanders is a beautiful little nation," the prince said after a while, his voice deep and rich, but still sounding bored. He extolled some of the virtues of her kingdom—its fountains and silks mostly. He seemed amused by their culture and called it "quaint" several times.

It grated on her nerves. He found her nation small? It was the wealthiest trade center in the world—people came from all over for their silks and pearls. And the architecture was unmatched. True, she'd only seen a snippet of the architecture, but she'd read books. Her nation was more than beautiful. And their navy was unparalleled. At least it had been, twenty years ago after the war with Florryn had ended.

"And you are its very pretty princess," the prince went on. "I see why your father has kept you closely guarded. You are a beloved treasure. Oleanders should be proud." He pulled her closer as the dance picked up, placing his hand on her bare shoulder. The touch shocked Kailyn and she trembled. No one had ever been so forward with her before. She preferred the prince's aloofness to this closeness. She wanted to run away and never come back.

But he was almost her fiancé. The fiancé she'd never wanted.

"Scared, Princess?" he asked, sounding amused. "You needn't be. Your future is in good hands. Oleanders will be the jewel of the Oronian empire."

Kailyn nodded mutely, though inside she wanted to scream. Oleanders wasn't part of any empire! She wanted it to stay that way and send this prince packing and rule her kingdom herself. But Lady Horia's warning to be seen and not heard was pounding in her ears. She swallowed her words. She didn't think the prince would appreciate anything she had to say anyway.

"Oronia is beautiful too, but I'm afraid in a much harsher way, my abera." The word was Oronian and unfamiliar to Kailyn. She shivered again. She didn't want to be his abera, whatever that was. She didn't want to be a part of the Oronian empire. She didn't want any of this.

She could never be happy married to this man.

But this was her role, her duty. She had a part to play, and she had to embrace it, no matter what it entailed. There wasn't anything else she could do. It wasn't like she could fight her way out of the marriage—she didn't even know how to use a sword.

When the dance ended, the prince returned her to her father's side. "Until later, Princess," he said, kissing her gloved hand again. Kailyn hoped that moment would never come.

Kailyn watched from the dais as other couples twirled across the dance floor. Her father was going to officially announce her engagement before the banquet. Now that she had met the prince, she didn't know what to think. What would marriage to him be like? Especially if she was denied her books, like Lady Horia had insisted on for the past month. Did no one in Oronia read? Kailyn's heart ached at the thought. If only she could barricade herself inside the sealed doors of the Goddess's Library and never leave.

A movement near the wall attracted her attention. She spied a young man dressed in a soft forest brown tunic with horns attached to his head, which wasn't all that strange considering the outrageousness of Oronian garb that graced their halls tonight, and certainly less strange than her golden tree. There was something about him though . . . he looked . . . familiar. If only he'd turn his head . . . she felt for sure she'd seen him before. It couldn't be Benje . . . could it? How would the blacksmith even get into a royal ball?

Kailyn watched the man curiously. He didn't dance, but he was watching the partygoers intently, as if waiting for something. Kailyn wished he would catch her eye, but he never did. Who was he?

After a few more dances, her father stood up and the music quieted. The prince stood silently next to her father, though he offered Kailyn the tiniest of smiles. Kailyn's throat constricted. He wasn't a bad sort, not really. Just not . . . the man she'd have picked for herself.

Unbidden, her eyes sought out the young man she'd spied earlier, but he was gone. She frowned. Where did he go?

Her father cleared his throat. "Tonight, we gather to celebrate the engagement of my daughter, Princess Kailyn Tryana Yalan of Oleanders to Prince Zolan Crion of Oronia. We welcome our visitors from Oronia and thank you for your support of this alliance. We look forward to a long and prosperous future together."

The attendees in the room burst into applause. Kailyn felt like she was going to be sick. It was done. She was officially engaged to Prince Zolan.

The prince smiled at her and offered her his hand. Her heart thundering, she let him take it and lead her to a seat on the dais, right next to his.

Her father continued, his large arms outstretched. "To celebrate the occasion, let us have some Oronian entertainment, the likes of which you have never seen before!"

As the audience applauded again, a strange girl walked into the ballroom, wearing a costume made of blue and bright orange triangles. They flared around her like multicolored flames. An orange jewel-studded mask hid the top half of her face. Five masked men walked behind her, each carrying an instrument. The girl curtseyed for the royals with a grand flourish.

"The entertainment has arrived." Her voice was surprisingly deep, but very elegant. Kailyn's curiosity was piqued, despite her heart's despair over her engagement. What kind of entertainment had Oronia brought?

"Very well," her father said. "Let the entertainment begin!"

The girl cued the ensemble she had brought with her, and they struck up an energetic tune. She started dancing, kicking her legs up high and twirling her bright skirts around her. The fabrics swirled in a frightening display of color, whipping around her like wind gusts. The music grew faster as her dancing sped up.

The audience oohed as she flipped into the air and landed on her feet. The prince was cheering right along with everyone else, and even her father seemed to be enjoying himself, tapping his leg in time to the music.

When she finished, the audience burst into applause. The girl grinned, bowing again toward the royalty. Kailyn was stunned. She'd never seen anything like that before. Where had the girl learned to dance like that? Kailyn had so many questions. But she was to sit there and observe, like Lady Horia had taught her.

"Thank you, Your Majesty, Your Highnesses, and my lords and ladies. For my next act, I will dance in darkness!" The girl threw a bag onto the floor, which flashed a brilliant light until the world was suddenly encased in darkness. The girl's dress lit up, each tier of her skirt glittering orange or blue. The musicians struck up a slow, somber tune and she twirled slowly in the dark.

Kailyn was mesmerized by the pattern of the skirt, which sparkled like flames, the oranges and blues blurring together as the girl's tempo increased. Her mind drifted away from her fiancé and the fate she was now bound to as she thought about the colorful skirt and the dance. She wanted to learn about it, explore the customs. Was all of Oronia this magical?

The girl danced closer and closer to the dais, spinning faster and faster. Kailyn blinked, trying to focus on the colors, but the dancer was moving away again. She moved forward and back several times, ebbing and flowing like the tide, before she slowed down, the two colors sparkling in the dim light.

She struck a pose before the candles started flickering to life throughout the room.

As the lights glowed again, Kailyn glanced at her father to see what he thought of the display, but to her horror, her father was slumped over in his seat unnaturally, a knife sticking out of his chest.

She screamed.

The ballroom erupted into chaos.

"The king's dead!"

"Who killed him?"

"Where'd that dancer go? It must have been her!"

Kailyn felt herself get yanked off her feet by rough hands, a blade pressed to her throat.

"No one move or the princess dies!" came a deep throaty voice.

Kailyn froze. Her eyes flicked to the prince, who hadn't moved from his seat. He fingered his decorative sword at his belt, staring at her uncertainly. Was he going to do anything?

"What do you want?" she whispered to the man holding her, her voice sore from lack of use. Had the man even heard her?

"The people of Oleanders want to be heard! Your rich fat king is dead. The rest of you will be next unless you listen to us!"

"That's not going to happen," came a silky-smooth sneer. Lord Shielen strode into the room, flanked by dozens of guards.

The man holding Kailyn shook, his knife vibrating against her throat. A thin dribble of blood dripped down her neck. She closed her eyes, wishing the nightmare would end.

Acrid smoke filled her nose. She sniffed, wondering what was going on when the man holding her suddenly released her and someone else was dragging her away. She opened her eyes to see the young man with the antlers from before. Her heart leapt as she recognized him. It was Benje!

"Benje . . ." she whispered. "What's going on?"

"No time to explain, Your Highness," Benje said solemnly. He pulled Kailyn down a staircase, out into a smaller courtyard where a horse stood waiting. He offered his hand to Kailyn. She stared at him.

"What am I supposed to do?"

"Take my hand."

Kailyn hesitated for a split second before placing her gloved hand in his warm one. Benje pulled her close and hefted her onto the horse. She gripped the horn in front of the saddle, struggling to stay upright.

Moments later, she felt Benje's warm presence at her back, preventing her from slipping.

"I've got you, Princess," he whispered.

Then they took off into the night, the castle flickering with firelight behind them.

Chapter Eight

Kailyn

Kailyn had no idea how long they'd been galloping. Had it been hours? Days? Weeks? She'd watched the scenery flash by—first the city streets, then the woods. Now, she had no idea where they were—everything was trees and darkness. She couldn't see the castle anywhere.

Benje—no longer wearing his antlers—helped her off the horse, setting her down on a stump. She felt numb and her head hurt terribly from the crushing weight of the headpiece. It was as if a hammer were pounding under her skull.

"Let me help you with that," Benje said softly, kneeling next to her so he could undo the straps of the headdress. He pulled it off gently, unwinding her hair from its inner workings. As soon as it was disconnected, Kailyn breathed a massive sigh of relief. Her head felt freer than it had in days, despite the fact she was still emotionally drained and exhausted from the evening. Her father . . . the prince . . . the ball.

Kailyn frowned. "Benje. What happened? My father . . . is he de. . . ?" She couldn't bring herself to finish her question, grimacing as the silver glint of the knife flashed in her memory. Then the tears came.

She sobbed for several minutes, letting the tension of the last few hours drain out of her. Her father was dead. The prince—her fiancé—hadn't done anything. The man with the knife who'd held her. The smoke. The screams.

Her kingdom in chaos.

And she'd left them all, following a man she barely knew to escape.

"Shh, Princess, it's alright." She felt Benje's steady presence beside her, his arms encircling her. She leaned against his solid chest, taking deep calming breaths until her tears subsided. Her head ached, her eyes hurt, and her throat was scratchy. Benje handed her a canteen filled with sweet water that she drank greedily until her throat felt better.

"Wh-what happened?" she asked again, handing him back the canteen.

Benje put both the headpiece and the canteen into bags on his horse's saddle before he answered, his words slow and methodical. "A rebellion. The people have been unhappy with your father for years, and the alliance with Oronia was the final straw. So they rebelled."

Kailyn stiffened as she remembered the man's words. *The people of Oleanders want to be heard! Your rich fat king is dead. The rest of you will be next unless you listen to us!*

She shivered. Her own people had killed her father. "And Lord Shielen?"

"Is likely in charge now. His guards were putting out the fire and putting down the insurrection as we escaped." He looked as serious as he had that day at the library.

She eyed him shrewdly. He owed her nothing, yet he was risking life and limb to help her. Why? Wouldn't it have made more sense for him to abandon her as he fled for his own life?

"Why did you help me?"

"I didn't want to see you hurt, Your Highness." He offered her a hand. "Are you alright to ride? We need to get going before Lord Shielen comes after us."

Kailyn tensed. Something about his story wasn't adding up. But he had saved her life. And, if she was honest with herself, she wanted to be as far away from Olean as possible. She had a feeling that if she stayed, Lord Shielen would make her marry the prince of Oronia anyway. At least now she had a chance of escaping and finding her own path, whatever that might be.

She stood up, feeling lighter than she had in weeks.

"Alright, Benje. Lead the way."

Hours later, Kailyn woke up ravenous. Sometime during the long ride, she'd fallen asleep. She groaned in the daylight that was starting to stream through the trees. The horse's gait was more uneven now as the ground was getting rockier.

Benje handed her an apple. "Here. Breakfast."

Kailyn took the round pink-colored fruit and held it to her nose. It smelled divine—of sunshine and sweetness. She took a bite and groaned. It was delicious. It had been weeks since she'd had anything other than Byun bread. She ate the apple as fast as she could, relishing the sweet taste and the juice that trickled down her fingers.

"I didn't realize they were starving you," Benje said quietly when Kailyn had finished the apple and had thrown the core into the trees. It was unladylike of her, she knew. But there was something satisfying about throwing it.

Kailyn quirked an eyebrow. "You don't know much about Oronian wedding customs, do you?"

She felt Benje tense behind her.

"They're a brutal people, Princess," he said softly. "Believe me—it's better that Lord Shielen is in charge than Oronia."

Kailyn wasn't so sure about that. The prince, while uninterested in her, didn't seem like a tyrant. Unlike her father's loyal advisor. What vile plans did Lord Shielen have in store for Oleanders now that her father was gone?

For that matter, what exactly was Benje's plan? Oleanders was her home! Her people! She had to do something to help them, but with every hoofbeat, they were getting farther and farther away.

"Where are you taking me?"

Benje sighed. "To the gnomes. We'll take their caverns to Tyloan where we'll board a ship to Tigahel."

Kailyn frowned. She'd seen the Tigahel Archipelago on maps. It was across the ocean, nowhere close to Oleanders. "Why are you taking me to Tigahel?"

"We'll need allies to take back Oleanders."

Kailyn hadn't thought about that. She'd supposed they'd use their military might to take back Oleanders, but if Lord Shielen was in control of the military, then she had no support. Oronia wasn't officially their ally. They couldn't depend on them to save their kingdom either.

Cyron, their neighbor to the east, was practically an Oleanderian colony. She knew Lord Shielen had holdings there. It wouldn't surprise her if Cyron refused them aid.

And Florryn wasn't an option.

Which meant that Tigahel might be their only choice for help to take Oleanders back from Lord Shielen.

All because her people had revolted against their king.

"I wish I had known," she whispered. "I wish I could have helped."

"Princess," Benje's voice was sorrowful. "There was nothing you could have done. Trust me. You will be helping your people by going to Tigahel."

She only hoped he was right.

They lapsed into silence, Kailyn lost in thought. She noticed the birdsong for the first time. She hadn't ever heard the birds before she'd left the castle. There were no trees that reached her chambers, and she hadn't been paying much attention the day she'd met Benje at the library. Here, the birds called to each other between the dappled light of the trees. It was as if it were an entire new world. The golden glow of sunshine—tinted green by the leaves—filled Kailyn's soul. For a moment, it felt as if all the darkness of the past few weeks hadn't happened. These trees felt like they were blessed by the Goddess herself.

Benje didn't speak again until they emerged from the trees to a rocky clearing. The Rosstross Mountains were much closer here—they were practically at the foot of the mountains. Pink-gray rocks the size of horses littered the countryside, dusted with snow. It was serene, especially in the light of the sun. But frigid. Kailyn shivered and rubbed her arms. It was late spring. Why was it so cold?

"Princess, we're here."

A gleam of light caught Kailyn's eye. Benje dismounted and then extended his hand. It took effort to slip off in her cumbersome dress, but after a moment, they both made their way to a crevice in the rocks. To Kailyn's astonishment, a thin line of metal shone around the rock on both sides of the crevice—making it look rather like a door.

She made to go in, but Benje stopped her.

"We should make our offering first," he said, slipping his hand into his pocket and grabbing a small package. He unwrapped it and it caught the gleam of the metal from the crevice. The ground rumbled around them, and the crevice grew bigger, big enough that they could enter. She looked at him and he nodded, slipping the strange trinket back into his pocket.

Where had he gotten that offering? What even was it? Had he made it at that forge where she'd first met him?

She had so many questions about this man. All she knew about him was that he'd rescued her—twice. He'd helped her when no one else had. And she felt safe around him.

So when he offered her his hand, she took it, following him into the darkness.

The first thing Kailyn noticed was that they were in some sort of tunnel, and strangely enough, she could see. It was also significantly warmer inside than it was outside the mountain. She glanced up at the walls and noticed a faint glow coming from them.

"What's that?" she asked, squeezing Benje's hand nervously.

"It's a luminescent metal," Benje said, gently squeezing her hand back. His hand was rough, but comforting in this unfamiliar place. "The gnomes use it to mark entrances to their caverns."

Gnomes! She'd never met any gnomes before. Were they as short as her books described?

Both she and Benje had to hunch to walk forward, as the ceiling wasn't very tall. They followed the tunnel as it sloped downward. A few times Kailyn glanced back to see if they could see the light from where they had entered, but it grew farther and farther away until it disappeared entirely, and they only had the dim light of whatever was in the rock leading their way.

"Is this where the gnomes live?"

"They're further down, Your Highness." He guided her through another turn in the tunnel. It felt like they were walking into the belly of the earth. It was an odd place to still be called by her title. Especially by the man who'd rescued her twice already.

"Kailyn," she said. "You saved my life, Benje. You can call me by my name."

Benje was silent for a long moment. She only knew he was there because he was still holding her hand.

"Your Highness," he began. "There's something I must tell you—"

"Look!"

A pulsing light caught her attention. Up ahead, the tunnel curved upward, leading toward somewhere that held more light than this tunnel. They increased their pace, her back aching from bending over so much. They were forced to crawl to get to the top of the incline. There, to Kailyn's amazement, stood what was unmistakably a gnome.

Chapter Nine

Kailyn

The gnome's head barely reached Kailyn's shoulder, but Kailyn still felt intimidated by their leather armor that concealed a stout muscled form and the short sword that hung from their belt. The gnome's eyes glowed golden in the light cast by a small lantern carved from the wall.

"*Egle grun oo?*" the gnome grunted in a deep gravelly voice, sounding distinctly male to Kailyn. He peered at them curiously but didn't move to attack them, which made Kailyn breathe a little easier. She looked back at Benje, wondering what he was going to do.

"*Grun Benje e agh ta grangos.*" Benje showed the gnome the metal thing he'd removed from his pocket. "*Eer ag geren.*"

The gnome gasped and put away his sword. He grabbed the trinket and examined it in the light of the carved lantern. His eyes roamed its surface like he was a nobleman appreciating a fine piece of art. Kailyn watched him, sure that this creature, this gnome, understood beauty. And whatever Benje had made, the gnome clearly thought it was precious.

"*Geren ge alk?*" The gnome stared at Benje in wonder.

Benje got down on one knee to be at eye level with the gnome, though Kailyn wasn't sure why. "*Alk de geren. Golth.*"

The gnome looked again at the metal sculpture—which Kailyn could see resembled a legendary jawk—and nodded. He motioned for them to follow and led them further through the tunnel.

"What was all that about?" Kailyn whispered, confusion tumbling through her thoughts.

"It'll allow us passage."

"But a jawk? Where'd you learn to make that?" She'd only ever seen descriptions of the legendary birds in her books—no one had seen one in a thousand years. It was rumored there had been one in Ligerthia, but of course there was no way to prove that now.

Benje stayed silent, and Kailyn frowned in the darkness. His secrets were unsettling.

They followed the gnome up the tunnel until they reached a strange door. It was made out of the same glowing metal that had been in the ceiling, but it was now looped, forming intricate circles that were linked together. There were runes that Kailyn had never seen before wrapped around the looped circles. The gnome slid his finger into a hidden hole and twisted. The runes glowed brighter and brighter until the door rolled up into the rock. Kailyn gasped.

Inside lay an enormous cavern. It was bigger than the castle of Olean, maybe bigger than the entire nobility district. Intricate walkways passed over each other and some wound around the cavern. The whole place was lit by the same glowing material that had formed the door. But what amazed Kailyn the most were the gnomes. They were everywhere. Some were wheeling wheelbarrows laden with strange metal-colored roots. Some were carving and tinkering in little stalls cut straight into the rock of the cavern itself. But all of them stopped to stare as they entered.

The gnome that had guided them called out, "*Enje sav-ter fueren ti! Ee sawine ol gurtha!*"

Kailyn had no idea what he had said, but the gnomes in the cavern let out a cheer. Their gnome guide led them through a maze of pathways. Her hand found Benje's again and she grasped at its familiarity in an alien land. Even if she was still so confused by Benje's backstory, he was the only thing even semi-familiar here. Her books hadn't prepared her for anything like this.

Eventually, their gnome guide led them to an even more ornate door than the last. Two other gnomes, dressed in some sort of gold tunic, bared spears at their approach.

"*Ech lik oo Eurintidz?*" one of the gnomes said in a clearly threatening tone.

Their gnome guide made what Kailyn assumed was a pleading gesture by bowing so low, he looked like he was going to fall over.

"*Enje sav-ter fueren ti!*" the gnome repeated. "*Sawine ol fier gurtha.*" He held out the relic Benje had given him. The guard grabbed the piece, his eyes roaming its surface greedily.

"*Ee entri,*" he said to his companion, who nodded and slid his finger into the door. It too slid up into the ceiling and another cavern greeted them.

This one was far grander than the one they had left. Columns lined the sides, carved from the rock. Intricate gold and silver murals covered the walls, depicting gnomes fighting a war. They fought alongside humans who were dressed in silvery armor, swords glinting. The detail was exquisite—she could make out the individual plates of armor, the texture of the banners, the shafts of arrows. She'd never seen anything like it.

Kailyn was so distracted by the mural that she didn't see the throne at the end of the cavern until a booming female voice said, in pure Almarrynian, "Benje! You've returned!"

She turned to see a stout female gnome in red and gold silk robes seated on a silver dais.

Benje dropped down into a bow. "Your Majesty."

The queen tutted and dismissed the guards behind her with a wave of her hand. The guards bowed and left the room, along with their guide.

"Your skills are getting better," the queen said, gazing at the relic Benje had made. "Master Barholow would be proud."

Kailyn blinked. Who was Master Barholow? For that matter, how did Benje know the queen so well?

"Rise, Benje," the queen said. Benje rose from his bow and stood next to Kailyn.

The queen turned to face Kailyn and blinked her wise golden eyes. They were like miniature suns that radiated light and Kailyn found herself relaxing in the queen's presence. "You must be Princess Kailyn of Oleanders."

Kailyn nodded and swept into a curtsy, grateful she was still clothed in a fine gown, despite having traveled on horseback over the course of the night. "Yes, Your Majesty. It's a pleasure to meet you." Though she was confused how the queen knew who she was.

"Likewise," the queen said. "Come. Walk with me, Princess Kailyn."

Kailyn glanced at Benje, who nodded. Kailyn approached the rotund queen, who was even shorter than the first gnome Kailyn had met. As they walked along the chamber, Kailyn's eyes drifted to the murals again. As she examined them, she could make out the gnomes helping the knights battle what looked like a creature entirely made of white.

"What is this?" Kailyn wondered.

"This is a depiction of the fall of Ligerthia," the queen said simply. Kailyn's eyes widened. The fall of Ligerthia! It's what she'd always wanted to learn about, and how she'd met Benje in the first place. And here it was, arrayed in glittering stone.

"B-but . . . how?" Kailyn stammered. "No one knows how Ligerthia fell."

The queen bowed her head. "Alas, very few do. I was one of the survivors."

Kailyn gaped. "You were there?"

"Yes, child. I was there the day the queen of Ligerthia took fate into her own hands and attempted to use Forging to control the frost giants. I was there the day everything became encased in ice and snow and all of Ligerthia lay barren. I was there the day the queen escaped to Tigahel. Yes, child. I was there."

Kailyn looked at Benje, who was standing at attention, watching them.

"But . . . why are you telling me this?" As nice as it was to know how Ligerthia had fallen, it didn't help her save her kingdom now. Her own people had revolted, and now Lord Shielen was in charge. She needed an army to take back Oleanders. An army she didn't have.

The queen sighed. "Ligerthia's fall . . . it will come again. It will destroy all of Almarryn. Even now, the frost giants attack Florryn. They're already in our mountains."

Kailyn's eyes widened. The unearthly chill she'd felt—that was the frost giants!

"But they will not stop," the queen continued. "They will destroy Oleanders, Cyron, and everything on the continent. The only way to stop them is to go to Tigahel. This is why Benje brought you here. You are meant to stop the frost giants."

They locked eyes, and Kailyn sensed her ancient wisdom in the gnome queen's many wrinkles and deep dark eyes. She swallowed nervously. Frost giants were not what she'd signed up for. Her kingdom was under threat from greedy politicians, not giant monsters made of ice and snow.

As if she'd read her mind, the queen laid an old wrinkly hand on Kailyn's sleeve. "I know you don't yet see it. But if you want to save your kingdom, this is the only way. We don't have much time. The ice is spreading. Soon even Olean will feel the touch of the frost giants."

The queen looked over at Benje. "You have my blessing to traverse the tunnels. Please be safe."

Benje clasped his fist to his chest. "By my sword, I swear it. The princess will arrive at Tigahel safely."

Kailyn stared at him, open-mouthed. He looked so serious. All he'd mentioned was getting allies by going to Tigahel. But clearly he knew more than he'd let on.

"Good." The queen of the gnomes motioned for an attendant, who stood by her throne. "Summon Yulks. Before our friends leave, we must prepare them a feast."

Kailyn's head was reeling. She'd wanted to know how Ligerthia had fallen. But she'd never have guessed frost giants. And not only were the giants now invading Florryn, their frost already touched their side of the mountain. She shivered. Frost giants were deadly—she'd read accounts of them freezing thousands of soldiers with only their breath. Even Oleanders' bitterest enemy didn't deserve death by icy monsters.

How long did Oleanders have? The Rosstross Mountains protected them, but snow already touched the rocks of the mountains. How long before Olean too succumbed?

She sighed. All she wanted to do was save her kingdom and avoid marrying the prince of Oronia. She'd wanted freedom. Maybe a chance to get to know Benje better. Not these cryptic warnings about ice and snow destroying everything.

She hadn't seen Benje since they'd met the gnome queen. The gnome queen had motioned for her attendants to take Kailyn away, and she'd been led to a room to freshen up. None of the gnomes spoke her tongue, but they were all kind. They offered her a simple gown that was much more comfortable than the black and red silk she'd been wearing since the ball the night before, though the color was a bit unusual. The murky silver wasn't at all like the bright blues, pinks, and greens back home. But Kailyn wasn't at home anymore.

While a gnome attendant was doing her hair, Kailyn thought about what the queen had revealed. Ligerthia's fall would come again . . . She'd been right to look into that parchment. But was there anything they could do to prevent it?

The queen and Benje were both insistent she had to make it to Tigahel. But why? It was more than for allies, of that Kailyn was positive. How was Tigahel connected to Ligerthia's fall? And why did they need her to go there? The problems were here in Oleanders. She sighed. Nothing made sense.

Kailyn's thoughts were a mess, but she did at least feel presentable when her gnome attendants guided her to the queen's dining hall. She thought it strange that the gnomes hadn't given her any new shoes, but considering they were all barefoot, she supposed it made sense. She had slipped on her slippers from the black dress because she didn't like the feel of dirt on her bare feet. Hopefully it wasn't rude of her to do so.

She walked into the queen's dining hall and tried to hide another gasp. These walls were also inlaid with grand mosaics, depicting the gnomes harvesting roots of gold and silver. A beautiful woman whose dress seemed to be moving—though how that was possible with stone, Kailyn didn't know—was in the middle of the depiction, raising her hand as if to bless the gnomes.

"Ah, yes, that's the Goddess blessing the harvest," the queen said from the head of the table. Glancing around, Kailyn saw that she was the only one standing as both the queen and Benje were seated. Sheepishly, she took her seat.

"I'm sorry, I got lost in the majestic work of your murals, Your Majesty," she said.

The queen laughed and waved away her apology. "Don't apologize, my dear. We gnomes love to have our work admired. It shows that our talent is appreciated, which is a fine thing, don't you think, Benje?"

Benje, who looked rather dashing in a silvery white shirt with a copper cravat, met Kailyn's eyes. "It is a beauty to behold, Your Majesty."

Kailyn felt a blush creep onto her cheeks. She was fairly sure he wasn't just speaking about the murals. But then she forced herself to look at her plate. Benje was hiding things from her. He wasn't telling her everything. For all she knew, he'd helped stage the takeover of her country. Might he be a spy?

"Now, let's feast!" The queen clapped her hands and a bunch of gnome servants scurried in, carrying platters stacked high with foods Kailyn didn't recognize, but that smelled delicious, even with her stomach tying itself in knots.

"We are herbivores, my dear, so there won't be any meat available," the queen said as she passed Kailyn a dish laden with odd copper-colored roots. They smelled earthy, and as she tried one, she was surprised at how rich the flavor was. It was far superior to any meat she had ever had, and a far cry from Byun bread.

"Thank you, Your Majesty, for your hospitality," Kailyn said as she served another root, this one mustard yellow, onto her plate.

"My dear, we are grateful you made it in one piece," the queen said. Her leathery face softened. "We heard what happened in Oleanders, and we are sorry for your kingdom's trials. But we're grateful you made it. We will gladly light your way to Tigahel."

The root curdled in Kailyn's stomach. Everyone had everything planned out for her. She'd thought she could find freedom outside the castle. But even the gnome queen and Benje had expectations for her. Even here her life was not hers to live.

Kailyn nodded mutely and ate the rest of the meal in silence.

Chapter Ten

Abrina

The farther they traveled from Heria, the more damage Abrina saw. No trees, no villages, no creeks or streams. Even the vast River Hane was now no more than a mere trickle. All Abrina saw were empty fields with no one to tend them.

It sickened her.

Only hours after leaving the manor, they passed a deserted village blackened by fires. Her heart hurt seeing the collapsed roofs, their beams sticking out like broken bones. Ash and soot covered everything, and the dead fields looked like they hadn't been tended to in years. Everything was covered in a dusting of snow too, another sign of their impending doom by the frost giants. But what hurt worse was not seeing a single living soul.

She'd known the damage was bad, but she'd had no idea it was this bad.

"Are they all dead?" she asked the captain who rode next to her—the same man who had been with her at the front. Her mother had called Captain Wilen and his best back and sent another squadron in their place. She wanted them to be with Abrina in her quest, though Abrina was pretty sure Captain Wilen preferred the front. He was still icy toward her.

He grunted. "Flina fell in the war with Mitarryn. The people who survived are in a refugee camp somewhere."

Abrina set her jaw. It was difficult to imagine her people languishing in a refugee camp. "Couldn't we house the refugees in Heria?"

The captain shook his head. "I wish we could, Princess. But we simply don't have the resources. We barely have enough to protect the manor." He gazed off toward the Rosstross Mountains behind them for a moment. "And with this new threat of the frost giants . . ." His voice softened. "There's not much we can do."

Abrina swallowed the dread that rose in her throat. Her people were on the brink of extinction. Unless she went through with this marriage, Florryn would end. She glanced behind her at the golden ambassador, who was laughing at something Sir Tyir had acted out and gritted her teeth. She had no idea what this prince of his would be like. But she would marry him. For the good of her people.

If she didn't, her kingdom would collapse.

Abrina knew it was only a few days' journey to the coast, but every night, her nerves were on edge as she listened to the complete silence that encapsulated the burnt and frozen Florryn ground. No insects chirped and no birds called out to each other. It was as if the land itself was dying.

"It's uncanny, how quiet it is," Sir Zachry said to her, as if voicing her thoughts. They'd camped by the edge of a running stream two days into their journey, and while she'd barely known the knight before they'd left, she had taken a liking to him. He was a good sport about losing their fight and was always quick to help them set up camp. The two of them were gathering firewood for the night.

"The land . . . it's so still," Abrina murmured.

"But Florryn lives on in its people, doesn't it, Princess?" Sir Zachry said, picking up another piece of wood. "No matter what happens to us, we'll endure. That's the spirit of Florryn."

Abrina thought about his words as she picked up more fallen wood. She'd always believed Florryn was in the hearts of its people. But, just in the last seventeen years, they'd lost her sister and father, and then their kingdom split in three because of the civil war.

Now these cursed frost giants. Florryn may live on in the hearts of her people, but if all her people were destroyed, there'd be nothing left of Florryn to endure.

It was a bitter thought. She tried to stuff it to the edge of her mind while she and Sir Zachry walked back to camp.

The company already had a glowing fire lit. One of her knights had managed to catch two small hares, the only living things she'd seen since they left Heria. She set down her sticks by the fire, catching the tail end of the ambassador's story.

"And then we swooped into the sky with our pilfered golden fruit, escaping those pesky tree snakes and climbing higher on the cajuna."

Sir Byron scoffed. "Flying horse creatures with six limbs? I don't believe it."

The ambassador grinned, his brilliant white teeth flashing in the light of the fire. "Aye, the purple beasts fly around the isles of Tigahel. We use them to travel across the archipelago. They're also used for races." He winked at Abrina and she felt her cheeks blush.

She shook her head. Let him tell his foolish tales. It was a far cry better than dwelling on the state of her kingdom.

Sir Byron was also not easily convinced of the truth of the ambassador's stories. "But beasts that fly? You can't be serious."

"Ah, they're real, Sir Byron. You'll see."

Sir Byron folded his thick arms and frowned at the ambassador while Sir Tyir and Sir Zachry started skinning the hares and skewering them.

Only the captain hung back. Abrina walked over to him, curious why he wasn't joining in the evening meal preparations.

"Captain? Everything alright?"

The captain stared thoughtfully at the fire. "I'm troubled, Princess. Why hasn't aid been offered from Tigahel before? Why now, when we're at our weakest?"

Abrina watched as the ambassador laughed with her men. Almost as if he sensed her watching, his eyes met hers, making her blush again. She scowled and turned away. He was an attractive man, that was all. She couldn't get close to him—she was supposed to be marrying someone else. Someone else who could help her save her kingdom.

"Because we need it, Captain." As much as she was loathe to admit it. Florrynians did not rely on outsiders' help—not at all.

But if they didn't take Tigahel's offer, then her land would never recover.

A day later, they were attacked by bandits.

They were heading to Jeru's Keep, traveling on a road that wound through rocky cliffs on its way to the coast. Abrina spied the glint of the gray-blue ocean. It filled her with a deep dread—mountain people did not belong on the ocean—but she squashed it in favor of determination. She was doing this to save her people. It didn't matter if the prince looked like a troll—she would marry him.

But it was there along the cliffs, while traveling single file that bandits popped out of the rocks, dressed all in black and brandishing swords and spears.

Beri neighed underneath Abrina. She pulled at the reins with one hand and reached for her sword with the other, her hand clutching its comfortable grip. But she didn't unsheathe it. Not yet. Perhaps these men could be negotiated with. The tight quarters weren't ideal for sword fighting anyway. Maybe negotiation—her mother's tactic—was a better fit here.

"Stand your ground!" she called.

"Well, well, if it isn't the princess herself," sneered one of the robbers, coming up to Abrina's horse. He was too thin, but he brandished the jagged dagger he held in a way that told Abrina he meant business.

Beri neighed in protest and Abrina wished she could let her mare run as fast as she could and knock the foul man over. But she would need to act like her mother for this. She closed her eyes and pictured her mother's face. Courage. She could do this.

She opened her eyes. "What can we do for you, good sirs?" she asked in what she hoped was a passable imitation of her mother.

The man glowered. "We want Florrynian silver. Hand over your weapons."

Abrina tried not to wince. Florrynian silver was the rarest metal in Almarryn and only found in the Rostross Mountains, though most of it was now in the hands of King Tera. The only silver she had on her was her sword.

Abrina would *not* part with her sword.

"I am sorry, but I cannot give you Florrynian silver."

The man unsheathed another knife and pointed it directly at her, narrowing his gaze. "Then perhaps you can give me my brother back."

Abrina stared at him. She had no idea what the man was talking about. "Your brother?"

"He was killed by a frost giant! After fighting for Florryn for five years in that terrible civil war!"

Abrina ground her teeth. The cursed frost giants again. Couldn't they just leave everyone alone until they had the resources needed to dispatch them?

"Sir, we are on our way to stop the frost giants—"

"How?" the man demanded, stepping closer and brandishing his knives. "You're running away! Same as every Goddess-forsaken noble Florryn's ever had. You're abandoning us!"

That did it. She did not have her mother's patience. Abrina brought her sword up and smashed the man on the head. He crumpled to the ground at the same moment fighting broke out between the other bandits and her men. One bandit tried to grab her horse, but Beri reared and kicked him, sending him flying into a rock. Abrina grinned. This was fun.

"Stop this madness!" came a booming voice. A blue light rippled from the back of the caravan, and everyone dropped their swords. The ambassador held his glowing blue stick and stood regally, looking for all the world like a Ligerthian Knight of legend.

The bandits gaped at him, astonishment filling their eyes.

Abrina scowled. What was he doing? They'd had the men on the run!

"You'd really fight your own comrades, over silver?" the ambassador continued, his deep voice washing over the crowd.

He dismounted, his brilliant blue staff glowing like a star from the heavens. He strode over to a man Abrina had knocked over and helped him to his feet. The man looked warily at the ambassador.

"Who-who are you?" the man stuttered.

"I am escorting Princess Abrina to the Tigahel Archipelago where she will seal an alliance with my nation to provide resources for yours. I suggest you let her pass."

The man glowered. "Florryn is not beholden to outsiders like you!"

Abrina dismounted and pointed her sword at the man. "If you want to survive, I suggest you do as he says and let us pass."

The man's eyes went wide and he nodded. "Very well. You and your retinue may pass."

He whistled and the rest of his men vanished into the rocks, leaving Abrina, her guards, and the ambassador behind.

She sheathed her sword before whirling on the golden ambassador. "Why did you step in like that? I had it well in hand!"

"Princess." His voice was quiet. "More violence will not help. Take a look around. Your country is dying. Your people are starving. They are desperate for anything to help them survive."

Abrina sighed, exhaling some of her anger. "Let's just get to Lord Jeru's Keep. We still have a long way to go until we can help my people."

The ambassador nodded. "Lead the way, Your Highness."

Chapter Eleven

Abrina

_L_ord Jeru's Keep was perched on the edge of the cliffs, over-looking the sea. They reached it before sunset, with thankfully no more delays. Abrina's shoulder had been throbbing ever since she'd bashed the bandit on the head, but she gritted her teeth and stayed vigilant.

She kept thinking about what the ambassador had said—how her people were desperate. The devastation she'd seen . . . She knew he was right.

She hated that he was right.

Florryn had once been a proud and prosperous kingdom, profiting off the silver in their mountains and trading their boun-teous harvests with the world.

Until Oleanders had invaded 120 years ago, trying to expand their borders.

Abrina cursed under her breath. Oleanders was behind all their suffering. Not that there was anything she could do about it other than marry the prince of Tigahel.

Which is why they were heading into the white keep to meet Lord Jeru.

The keep was a shining building made out of the white rock of the cliffs. Miraculously, the keep hadn't been taken in the civil war, despite Mitarryn's best efforts to control all of Florryn's seaports. It stood as a proud monument of Florryn's triumph.

One of the few things that stood as a monument to Florryn's triumph.

The entire household had assembled to meet the princess, including Lord Jeru himself. Abrina was surprised. She had expected to meet him in a sitting room, the way her mother greeted guests. But the great bearded man bounded up to her and shook her hand joyfully.

"Your Highness, thank the Goddess you made it alright! I was worried something might have befallen you on our roads. They're home to thieves and brigands, you know. Welcome, welcome to my keep!"

Abrina quirked an eyebrow. Thieves and brigands indeed. Still, she couldn't help marveling at the energy of this man. He looked younger than her father would be, but she knew he'd been in possession of the keep since long before she was born.

"Thank you, Lord Jeru. You are most kind."

"Come, come, a fabulous feast awaits!"

The feast was indeed fabulous. Abrina hadn't seen so much food since before the civil war. Her mother tended to be conservative in the kitchens, insisting that they only eat what their people ate, which was a humble fare at best. But this was a feast fit for a queen.

There were roasted birds covered in creamy sauces, jams and jellies, and golden loaves of bread. The herbs smelled much stronger than what Abrina was used to. She recognized the potatoes and other vegetables piled sky-high on shining golden plates. She recognized some of the fruits too, even though there were some Abrina was pretty sure only grew in the Oronian colonies. She stared at a bright orange star-shaped fruit in wonder. How did Lord Jeru come by so much wealth?

Her knights feasted with great abandon, likely because they hadn't seen so much food in so long. Sir Byron, who was already more drunk than Abrina had ever seen him, kept relating loudly how he'd bested a frost giant single-handedly just the other day. Abrina shook her head, smirking slightly. None of it was true, of course, but it did gladden her heart to see her men laugh a little. They'd all been so serious since they'd started this journey.

Even the captain looked slightly less tense—he toasted Abrina with his glass when he saw her look his way. Abrina raised her glass at him in return. The captain was a good man. He had fought alongside her father during the civil war and let her fight with him and his men, even if he protested sometimes. He'd been the one to encourage her to keep practicing her sword fighting skills after her father died.

Abrina turned to her food again to distract herself, but it wasn't any use. The creamy potatoes in front of her were replaced by her father's image in her mind, his strong chiseled jaw that in later years was covered by a full black beard. She pictured his graying hair that fell into his piercing green eyes. His powerful arms that lifted her up on his shoulders when she was younger. He had been a lion of a man in life. And in death, he had left a hole that no one else could fill.

"Are you alright, Princess?" came the ambassador's gentle voice to her right.

Abrina blinked, her food coming back into focus. She scowled at her potatoes. "I'm fine."

"Ah, Princess Abrina!" Lord Jeru called out jovially, holding up a wineglass. "A toast to you on your recent engagement to the prince of Tigahel. We are all wishing you well on your journey."

Abrina bit her lip. "Yes, thank you, Lord Jeru."

She glanced down at her plate, but none of the sumptuous food looked the least bit appetizing anymore. "If you'll excuse me."

She ignored the looks thrown her way—particularly the ambassador's—and left the dining hall.

She found herself wandering the tapestried walls of the keep, which felt more like a fortress than her family's manor.

The tapestries were rich works of art that depicted the life of the Goddess. Abrina hadn't known Lord Jeru was so faithful. The tapestries told of the Goddess's miraculous birth and her humble journey to enlightenment, stories Abrina was familiar with even though she wasn't practicing.

But what surprised Abrina the most were the depictions of fantastic creatures—creatures that Yera had only ever told her about in bedtime stories. There was the legendary jawk, a bird so big that the Goddess could fly on its back. There were depictions of water spirits, woman-like creatures that lived in the seas and streams, said to appear during thunderstorms. There was even a depiction of what Abrina assumed was a troll, a monstrous creature made of hulking rock, but it looked . . . peaceful.

All the creatures looked peaceful, even the monstrous ones. The thought was strange. How could monsters be peaceful? She shuddered, remembering the ice of the frost giants. Those creatures were anything but peaceful. They had to be destroyed.

Abrina made her way to the courtyard, where they had arrived an hour before. The sun was setting, bathing the world in deep shadows. They felt eerie to her, in this stark land on the edge of her barren kingdom.

Had it only been a few days ago that her mother had given her a necklace and wished her farewell? It felt like a lifetime ago. Abrina clutched the pendant, wishing she could gain strength from her mother simply by touching it.

I will make you proud, Mother. I will save Florryn.

No matter who she had to battle to do so. Even if that battle was to accept marriage to a man she didn't know.

She made a face. Marriage. Of all the things she had to do to save her kingdom, why did it have to be marriage?

Something glimmered in the light of the dying sun. Abrina saw a shining white pathway, inlaid with gleaming silver at the back of the courtyard.

Curiosity piqued, Abrina hurried down the path, which led to a shrine. A single lantern hung from the post, which was what had caught her eye. The shrine was open to the elements, with five pillars, symbolizing the five lifetimes of the Goddess, supporting a curved roof. At the edge of the shrine, a white statue glittered in the hollow of a golden tree. Abrina had to give Lord Jeru points for taste. The small sanctuary was far more elegant than her family's shrine. The whole place sparkled in the light of the setting sun.

"It's beautiful, isn't it?"

Abrina turned to see the ambassador standing there, holding his deep blue staff, which was, thankfully, no longer glowing like it had been during the bandit attack.

Abrina scowled at him. "What are you doing here?"

"Seeking you." His blue eyes twinkled mischievously. "You ran off so quickly, I didn't get a chance to ask you how your potatoes were."

She rolled her eyes. "They were delicious, and you know it."

"Do I?" He smiled at her, and her heart leapt. She scowled

again. The man was too charming for his own good. She needed to change the subject.

"You didn't need to interfere back there, you know." She glared at him. "With the bandits. I had it well in hand."

"You mean well in sword?" The man quirked an eyebrow. "You cannot fight your way out of everything, Princess."

Her lips curled into a snarl. "Can't I?" She whipped her sword toward the ambassador, who simply dodged it. She twirled, pressing her attack, but he dodged every blow but the last, which he caught on his staff, then sent her sword flying across the shrine with a single yank.

The ambassador shook his head. "Fighting in a shrine, Princess? How very disrespectful of you."

Abrina took a great big gulp of air, letting her breath settle into her lungs. Infuriating man. She glowered at the ambassador. "I'll fight you anywhere. Name the time and place."

The ambassador sighed. "There are some fights you cannot win, Your Highness. The sooner you learn that, the happier you will be."

She scowled. She wanted to lunge at him again, but he was built like a wall. Brute force would not be the way to fight him.

And . . . if she was honest with herself . . . she didn't really *want* to fight him.

"Why are you here?" she asked again. "And don't give me any of that potato nonsense."

He laughed. "I did come seeking you. To make sure you were alright."

She scoffed. "Why would you care?"

"You're marrying my prince. I want to make sure you arrive there safely."

The prince. Everything was about that wretched prince. A man she'd never even met.

But the ambassador . . . *he* had met him. Maybe there was an angle she could work here.

"What . . . what can you tell me of the prince?" she asked, surprising herself with the question.

The man's eyes sparkled. "His people find him kind. Agreeable. Fair. Some say he's charming, and has a delightful sense of humor. I've known him to be a capable poet and a good hand at riding cajuna."

She quirked an eyebrow. "A competent warrior?"

"Fighting isn't everything, Princess."

It was to her.

She turned away from him, walking along the edges of the shrine, staring at the fine carvings in the columns, though not registering what they depicted. Maybe if she ignored him long enough, he'd go away. His prince sounded insufferably stuffy. Someone she would never choose to marry. But he was someone she was going to have to get used to. For her people. For Florryn.

She felt a hand on her shoulder and stiffened.

His voice came from behind her. "I hope you'll find that the prince is . . . or at least, he'd like to be, your friend, Your Highness. If you'll let him." His voice was soft, hopeful.

She turned to see him smiling at her with that charming smile. Her heart quickened again.

Then she registered what she'd just heard.

"Wait a moment—"

Bells clanged overhead. Screams sounded from somewhere nearby. Abrina tensed, her hand reaching for her sword.

"Your Highness, wait—"

But she was already gone.

Chapter Twelve

Abrina

Abrina barreled down the path back to the keep and to the dining hall. She shoved past a few servants to find Lord Jeru shouting something to a guard.

"—tell them there's nothing for them here!"

Abrina frowned. The man's jovial face was drawn tight in worry. It made him look years older. "Lord Jeru. What's going on?"

Lord Jeru's eyes widened. "N-nothing, Your Highness. Merely a disagreement with the locals."

"Princess." The captain's clipped voice came from behind her. Sir Zachry, Sir Tyir, and Sir Byron stood next to him, grim looks on their faces. "You better come see this."

"*Far worse than we imagined,*" Sir Tyir signed, his kind face drawn out in a deep frown.

Abrina's heart leapt within her as she ran with her men down to the gates of the keep where several of Lord Jeru's men wielded swords and shouted threats through the gates. Behind the iron bars stood an army . . . a strange army. They weren't armed with swords and shields, but rather rakes and shovels. And they were thin. Skeletal thin.

"Let us in!" a woman at the front of the crowd cried out. "Jeru's Keep is supposed ta be open ta all!"

"Me child be sick," another woman said, cradling a small sack of cloth where a tiny hand peaked out. "Please! He needs food."

"Lord Jeru has forbidden anyone to trespass on his grounds," one of Lord Jeru's guards said, a big burly man wearing a shiny helmet. "Be gone with you!"

Abrina stood there in horror. Her people.

She drew her sword and brandished it at the burly guard.

"What's going on here?" she demanded.

The guard turned to face her, and his gaze was cool, unfazed.

"These locals have come demanding provisions. But Lord Jeru is the overseer of the ports. He makes sure the people have what they need."

That was a load of pulong dung! These people clearly didn't have what they needed—the evidence was right in front of them. Abrina yelled out and kicked the man between the legs, then smashed him on the head with her sword. The man crumpled while the crowd cheered.

Several of the other guards turned to Abrina, brandishing their blades, but she hefted her sword and licked her lips. Finally, a battle.

She heard her knights behind her unsheathe their swords.

"Let these people in!" she cried.

The guards looked at each other nervously and shook their heads. "We've got orders, Princess."

"Lord Jeru feeds my family," another guard said apologetically.

"And what right does that give you to keep everything yourselves?" Abrina swung her sword a few times, knocking the blades from the guards' hands. The crowd cheered louder.

Abrina grinned and pointed her blade at the man she'd just disarmed, whose eyes went wide with alarm. "As princess of Florryn, I order you to open that gate."

The guards scampered away. Cowards. The whole lot of them. She turned to the captain. "Where's the extra food stored?"

He frowned. "In the pantries, I'd assume. But Princess—"

"Find it. Now. Byron, Zachry, go with him. Help distribute the food and whatever else these poor people need." She turned to Sir Tyir and signed "*You're with me. Guide the people where they need to go.*"

She held up her sword and turned to address her people.

"We will help you! We will provide you food and whatever else you need. But form a line by Sir Tyir."

She clashed her sword against the gate, shattering the lock. The people surged through, more or less in a line, Sir Tyir directing people where to go. Good. Sir Tyir was a master at logistics and infinitely more patient than she was. He'd take care of them.

She sheathed her sword and took off to find Lord Jeru.

Traitorous selfish pulong. He was starving her people and keeping everything for himself!

After all they'd been through, he was denying them basic sustenance. For what? So he could feast day in and day out in his hideaway while the rest of his kingdom fell?

Not if she had anything to say about it.

She found him in the great hall, feasting like nothing had happened. Notably though, there wasn't anyone else in the hall. Just Lord Jeru. Abrina bristled.

"Ah, Princess!" Lord Jeru said, wiping his face with a napkin. "I was just—"

"Save it, Lord Jeru," she snarled, whipping out her sword and brandishing it at the fat man. Lord Jeru's face went pale and he scampered back.

"Your days of gluttony are at an end," she continued, stalking after him.

"Princess, that isn't fair," Lord Jeru said, holding up his hands as Abrina slowly approached. "Our kingdom is dying. I merely wanted to help those who wanted to escape—"

"Escape?" Abrina spat, her grip tightening on her sword. "You were going to abandon your people and leave? Taking everything with you and letting us starve? No. That makes you a traitor to Florryn and its people."

She pointed her sword at his neck and he yelped, diving under the table, quivering like a leaf.

"Alright, yes, it was selfish of me! Redistribute it, yes, fine, I don't care! But p-please, Princess, don't kill me."

Abrina's blood thrummed in her ears. Pitiful. He was absolutely pitiful. How dare he hurt her people more than they'd already been hurt? He was worse than the frost giants—he was abandoning ship and sending hundreds to starvation.

She'd make him pay for his treachery.

She swung her sword toward Lord Jeru, but it was stopped by a familiar blue staff before it could hit its target.

Abrina glowered at the ambassador, who stood there, a quizzical look in his eye. "Princess."

"What are you doing?" she hissed. "I had him!"

Lord Jeru chose that moment to scamper from under the table. But he didn't get very far—the ambassador turned, yanking Abrina's sword from her hand so that it skittered across the stone floor, and picked up the simpering, sniveling Lord Jeru. With one hand, he pinched a nerve in the noble's neck and the next second, Lord Jeru was out cold.

Abrina scowled as she went to retrieve her sword. "He is an enemy to the state! He deserves death!"

The ambassador shook his head. "No. He deserves a chance to right this wrong. Killing him won't change anything, Princess."

Abrina clenched her hands into fists. "Look around you! My kingdom is dying. He—" She pointed at Lord Jeru's unconscious form. "—was speeding that death along. No one would have missed him!"

The ambassador's eyes glinted coldly. "You have every right to be angry at him. He was harming your people, yes. But to solve every wrong with another wrong . . ." He picked up his staff and strode from the room, carrying Lord Jeru over his shoulder like a sack of potatoes.

Abrina kicked the nearest table, fuming. Of all the insufferable men . . . she'd had Lord Jeru in her grasp! She'd have dispatched him swiftly, and he'd never have plagued her people again.

She glowered at the door and stomped off, in search of a post to slash.

Chapter Thirteen

Kailyn

Kailyn glanced over at Benje yet again. He was, not surprisingly, silent.

He had been ever since the gnomes had shaken their hands farewell and led them to the tunnels that would take them to Tyloan.

Kailyn's head was spinning. Benje was keeping things from her. Why was it so important that she go to Tigahel to solve the frost giants' secrets? Her kingdom had been taken over! Why wasn't that their priority?

True, she didn't really know a lot about her kingdom. Under her father's orders, she'd been kept in her rooms most of her days. She knew her father hadn't wanted anything bad to happen to her, but she yearned to understand her people. What made the people of Oleanders... Oleanderian? That wasn't something she could learn from her books.

She snuck another glance at Benje, who was staring stoically ahead. She couldn't get a read on his expression, though it was admittedly difficult in the dim light of the luminescent metal overhead. Was he leading her to her doom? If so, he was hiding it well.

But what choice did she have, other than to follow him? She couldn't marry the Prince of Oronia.

And if her kingdom really was under threat from the frost giants . . . then perhaps this was the right way?

Still. Something didn't sit right with her. As she walked through the cold and narrow tunnels, she was starting to feel like she was walking into the belly of a giant beast.

After what felt like hours, they finally paused for a moment.

"Here, Princess." Benje offered her a stone flask. She took it, barely glancing at him before guzzling the cool water. It tasted slightly earthy, but was rejuvenating.

She handed it back to Benje when she'd finished, and got up to go, but Benje grabbed her arm. She jerked away.

"What is it, Benje?"

"Princess, we need to talk," he said, his voice calm.

Kailyn sighed. "I suppose we do. Where are we really going?"

"To Tigahel. Like I told you, Oleanders needs allies."

She frowned at him. "But the gnome queen said that Tigahel will help us against the frost giants. Who aren't even a threat." Though she did keep thinking about the unearthly chill on the mountains she'd felt when they'd arrived at the caverns of the gnomes. Was that from the frost giants?

"They're a threat," Benje said quietly. "That snow we saw earlier was only the beginning. It will get worse. Trust me—Tigahel has the answers."

"Answers and allies?"

"Yes." Benje's voice sounded tired. "But there's more to it than that."

She furrowed her brows. "What do you mean?"

"Tigahel. Their queen. She . . ." he hesitated, clearly struggling to find the words.

He finally breathed out a big sigh. "I'm working for the queen of Tigahel."

Kailyn froze at his words. "You're not Oleanderian?"

"No, I am. But I have an allegiance to her . . . She's the one who commanded me to take you to Tigahel."

He sounded so pained that it sent waves of confusion spiraling through Kailyn. "You . . . you're an agent of a foreign nation? A s-spy?"

In the soft golden glow of the metal in the ceiling, Benje nodded.

Kailyn's stomach churned. She was walking into unknown territory . . . with a spy?

No. *No!*

She took off running down the tunnels, away from Benje.

"Princess!" he called out.

She ignored him. She had to get away.

Kailyn didn't know how long she ran, but she ran until she couldn't breathe anymore before curling up on her side and sobbing, letting the tears wash away the remains of the tiny plant of affection she had started to feel for Benje. He was a spy for a foreign nation, and he was taking her to his queen.

Why?

And to think she'd let herself feel things for him.

She couldn't trust him. She couldn't trust the gnome queen—who was equally insistent she get to Tigahel. She couldn't trust Oronia. She couldn't trust Lord Shielen. She couldn't trust anyone.

She was well and truly alone.

Alone, came a voice into Kailyn's mind. Startled, she sat up, wiping away her tears.

"Hello?" she called out. "Who's there?"

Alone, came the voice again. It sounded low and gravelly, but she could somehow feel the emotion in the single word. The person, or creature, or whatever it was, was alone. Achingly alone. She knew that pain—it was her own.

She stood up, taking a few deep calming breaths. Someone was here in the tunnels with her. Perhaps they needed her help.

It's not like she had any way to get home.

Home? came the voice again, as if echoing her thoughts.

She marveled. Whoever this voice belonged to was clearly magical. Was it the gnomes?

But no, they hadn't been able to project thoughts when she'd been in their presence. So what was it?

Was it foolish to go in pursuit of a voice in her head? Most definitely. But she couldn't go back to Benje, and she had nothing else to lose. So she headed off into the caves, letting the gentle glow of the ceiling light her way.

After a while, Kailyn felt the presence even stronger in her thoughts. It wasn't saying anything, but she knew that this presence was waiting for her. And she was drawing closer to it.

The tunnel ended in a round circular room, if one could call it a room. It was a cave with little niches set into the wall. It wasn't tall, and Kailyn found herself crouching. It took a moment for her eyes to adjust to what was lying on the floor. When she recognized it, she froze.

It was a *wolf*. A great white wolf lay on its side, its sides rising and falling with its breath. Slashes covered the hindquarters of the wolf, and its white fur was matted with red blood. Kailyn shuddered. It looked like it had been in a fight—and lost.

After a tense moment, she realized that the wolf wasn't attacking her. Maybe it was asleep. She turned around, fully intending to leave while she still had the chance.

Alone, came the voice again, this time much louder and clearer in Kailyn's mind. She turned back to the wolf, looking for the source of the voice. The wolf was staring at her. It had bright blue eyes that sparkled in the dim light of the ceiling. Kailyn swallowed. Hard.

The wolf was talking to her.

"Are . . . are you alright?" she asked the wolf. Those slash marks looked recent, and they looked brutal. Kailyn knew it was a foolish question. The wolf was probably dying.

But then why bring me here?

The wolf just stared at her. *Alone,* came the voice again.

And then the wolf laid its head down. For a moment, Kailyn thought the wolf had died, but then she heard another sound—a small yipping sound. The sound tore at her heart.

She had heard it once before, back in Olean. Her father had loved dogs, and she remembered when his beloved Maie had given birth to four little pups, one of which was his last dog Lia. It was one of the few times she had really bonded with her father as they snuggled with the puppies.

She was certain that the wolf had just given birth. Curious, she crept closer. The wolf eyed her but didn't say anything. Kailyn had the distinct impression that the wolf wanted her to approach. So she did.

There, lying next to the wolf, was a small pup. "Only one?" she asked the she-wolf. The thought was strange. Dogs rarely gave birth to only one puppy at a time.

The she-wolf said simply *Alone* and then laid her head down. Kailyn watched the wolf's side rise and fall, rise and fall before it rose no more. With a sickening jolt, she realized that the she-wolf had called her there—somehow—to save her pup's life.

She knelt down next to the wolf's body and tentatively reached a hand to the small pup. It turned its head toward her, sniffing blindly. The moment the wolf's nose connected to her palm, a glow spread up her arm from where the pup had touched her, tingling like little fireflies on her skin. And she heard, or more accurately *felt* the thoughts of the pup. She felt his fear, his hunger, his sorrow. And she felt his name.

Canis.

Chapter Fourteen

Kailyn

Kailyn snuggled with the small wolf pup until he started to yip.

"I bet you're hungry, aren't you?" she asked Canis.

Food? The thought was accompanied by an image of a young pup suckling his mother's milk. Kailyn glanced at the still form of the she-wolf and sighed. Canis would not get any of his mother's milk.

But she had to do something, otherwise the poor creature would starve. And he had no one else to care for him, just like she didn't.

She didn't have any supplies though. She was going to have to find Benje again.

The thought made her stomach churn, but she tried to brush her fears aside. It didn't matter if Benje was a spy. He was the only one in the tunnels who could potentially help her. She had to find him.

"Can you help me?" she whispered. "I'm trying to find Benje. He's in these tunnels."

Food?

Kailyn laughed. "He's not food, but he does have food. Help me find him?"

Canis yipped again and put his tiny snout in the air, sniffing before he bounded from her arms and took off down the tunnel.

"Hey, wait!" Kailyn called out, before running after him. Canis yipped loudly ahead, turning his little white head to look back, as if waiting for her.

Kailyn caught up to the pup. "Don't . . . run off without me. Anything . . . could be lurking . . . in these tunnels."

Canis yipped again and took off once more, though this time he wasn't quite so fast.

Kailyn followed him for a while, wondering if she'd gotten completely lost in the tunnels when she'd run from Benje. Was he still there? Had he gone back to the gnomes? Or was he even now trying to look for her?

Food!

"Did you find—" Kailyn collided with a warm body, nearly tumbling to the ground before comforting arms encircled her, helping her find her feet again.

Benje.

"Are you alright?" he asked. She could see the worry in his eyes. And it needled her. Why was he worried about her? He was using her for his own purposes!

She yanked away from his grasp. "I'm fine, thank you."

Food?

Kailyn looked down to see Canis looking up at Benje, the pup's bright blue eyes sparkling in the light of the ceiling.

"What's this, Your Highness?" Benje asked.

"A wolf cub. His name is Canis. I-I found him after his mother had . . ." She swallowed, not sure Canis would understand that his mother was gone.

Benje raised an eyebrow. "You found an Alarian wolf in these tunnels?"

She frowned. "A what? He's just a wolf cub."

"He's communicating telepathically with you, isn't he?"

Food?

Kailyn reached down and rubbed the soft head of the wolf cub, not sure how Benje knew Canis was communicating telepathically with her. She wasn't sure she wanted to know how he knew that right now. "Do you have any food to give him?"

Benje reached into his pack and pulled out a root from the gnomes. "Though I'm not sure how much good it'll do. He's a wolf." He placed the root in front of Canis, who sniffed at it curiously. He took a tiny nibble, yipped, and started gobbling the rest of it.

"Well, I guess that answers that question," Benje said, setting down another root for the pup.

Benje turned to face Kailyn and she saw the deep pain in his eyes. "Princess . . . I am deeply sorry for any hurt and mistrust I caused you."

She narrowed her eyes at him. "You're a spy for Tigahel. I think that means that by definition, I cannot trust you."

Benje shook his head. "You don't understand. I . . . I don't trust the queen of Tigahel. She's planning something, something that involves you."

Canis yipped loudly and started on the second root. Kailyn watched the wolf cub eat as she pondered Benje's words. "Why don't you trust the queen of Tigahel?"

"My master didn't. He told me that the queen was ruthless at getting what she wanted. The only way I can guarantee that you are safe is to be with you."

"But why do what she asks in the first place?" Kailyn frowned. "If she's ruthless, then she's not to be trusted at all. So why are we going there?"

Benje stared at his hands for a long moment. "Because the frost giants are a real threat. They're already in the Rosstross

Mountains. And they're spreading. The queen of Tigahel knows something about it—and the gnome queen confirmed it. The secrets to stopping the frost giants lie in Tigahel. We just have to get you there safely."

He ran his fingers through his black curls that reflected the dim light of the cave. "The queen of Tigahel told me to make sure no harm comes to you and that you arrive safely. She has promised allies and any resources you need to get you there."

Kailyn frowned in the darkness. *Food?* Canis rubbed his soft body against her leg. She reached into the pack Benje had left open and grabbed another root for the cub.

"I still don't understand. Why does she need me?"

Benje shrugged. "I wish I knew, Your Highness. But I swear to you, that is all I know."

She looked at him and saw the sincerity shining out of his brown eyes. But then she remembered the ball and the rebellion and Benje's cryptic warning that things were changing in Olean.

"That's not all you know," she said, staring at Canis, who was still nibbling on the third root. "You knew of the rebellion."

Benje hung his head. "Yes. I did." Each word sounded heavy.

"So you were part of the plot to assassinate my father?" Kailyn's eyes went wide as she pictured the knife sticking out of her father's chest. "Did you kill him?"

Benje shook his head. "No, I did not kill him. I was only there at the ball to protect you. As I told you, the queen of Tigahel ordered no harm to come to you."

Kailyn felt tears prick her eyes. "So you weren't part of the rebellion to overthrow the king?"

Benje pounded his fist to his chest. "I swear. I was only ordered to protect you and escort you to Tigahel. The queen is . . . up to something. That's all I know."

Kailyn looked down at the wolf cub, who apparently trusted Benje as he curled up by Benje's boot, eyes closed.

Benje reached down and stroked the wolf cub's fur while Kailyn watched. He didn't have to look out for the wolf cub. He didn't have to be so genuinely kind.

But she needed to know she could trust him.

"How do I know you're not going to lead me to Tigahel to assassinate me?" she asked, staring at the ceiling overhead.

Movement grabbed her attention. Benje stepped gently away from the sleeping cub before he unsheathed his sword and got down on his knees. He held up the blade to Kailyn. She could see the fine etchings in the silver blade, the detail glinting in the light from the ceiling. She frowned. It was an exquisite work of art. Why was he offering it to her?

"*Hayisha Telyir Hyera, helia intra yundi. Gyond de dolwo, fyeria sheld onno. Lyfe en de, yielo shyn.*"

The Old Alarian words hummed with an ancient power and Benje's sword glowed softly. The words swept into Kailyn's body and found a place in her heart. Somehow she knew, with every word he spoke, that he would give his life for her, and that he meant what he said. The words enveloped her in a cocoon of warmth, soothing her doubts. Her soul felt anchored.

She blinked, swallowing hard as his eyes focused on hers. "Will that suffice, *yiera?*" he said softly.

Kailyn nodded, still reeling from the powerful words. "What did you say?"

"The Ligerthian Knight's vow. It roughly translates to 'I give my vow on the five lives of the Goddess that I will let no harm come to you. I will do everything in my power to protect you from the darkness and evil that may seek to destroy you. If I live and break this vow, my sword will claim my life.'"

"Goddess above," Kailyn whispered. She had to be the first person in fifty years to hear such a vow. And she believed, no, she *knew*, he meant every word of it.

They journeyed together again, but the feeling had changed between them. Kailyn trusted him more, and Canis seemed to trust him too. The small pup had already grown since Kailyn had found him, which was baffling as she knew the pup was only just born. Then again, he also communicated telepathically, so she shouldn't have been surprised that he grew faster than a normal wolf.

Still, even with his small growth spurt, he fit inside Benje's pack, his small head peeking out to see the world. Every so often, thoughts of *food* or *home* flashed through Kailyn's mind from the pup's, making her smile.

Somehow, with Benje and Canis, she didn't feel so alone.

After what felt like hours, they saw a glimmer of light in the distance, far brighter than the luminescent metal overhead.

Light! Canis yipped.

"That must be the exit," Benje said. He offered Kailyn his hand and she took it, eager to escape the darkness.

The light grew brighter and brighter until they emerged into the sunshine. The warmth blasted Kailyn from head to toe, a stark contrast from the mountain. She closed her eyes, smelling grass and flowers and listening to the twittering of strange animals perched in the trees. She opened her eyes a crack and saw Benje watching her, a crooked smile on his face. Canis was still yipping in excitement.

"What?"

"I feel the exact same way." His lopsided smile broadened, and Kailyn's stomach lurched. He really was quite handsome. "Come, Princess. Tyloan awaits."

They heard Tyloan before they saw it. Loud cries of merchants and bellowing animals came to them as they crested the hill that led to the city. From the top of the hill, Kailyn saw brilliant-colored banners hanging from rock-hewn buildings, flapping in the breeze that blew from the sea. People in all sorts of colorful outfits bustled between booths, though from her vantage point, she couldn't make out any of their wares.

In the distance, great big ships filled the harbor, frigates and schooners and vessels she'd never encountered in her studies before. In the light of the sun, the bustling town seemed to sparkle.

"It's . . . beautiful," Kailyn whispered.

Food! Light! Colors! Canis yipped happily from Benje's pack.

Benje chuckled and rubbed Canis's head affectionately. "It is quite breathtaking. Tyloan is known as the jewel of the Cyronian trade routes. Come on, let's find a ship."

As they walked into town, they were hailed by dozens of merchants offering wares from brightly colored dyes, to rugs they insisted really flew, to magical foreign creatures trapped in cages.

"Four kinyas for the pretty bird. Four kinyas!" cried a large fat merchant in an odd combination of purple, green, and golden tunics draped over his rotund belly. His long beard snaked toward his knees and Kailyn could tell the man hadn't bathed in quite some time. He was pointing to a cage that held a large bird with black and red plumage that looked far better on the bird than it had on Kailyn at the ball.

But the cage was too small and the bird looked at Kailyn sadly.

Its beak was bright red and opened up and down and sideways, letting out a long weary note that reminded Kailyn of the days she had been trapped inside the castle, of the night her father died, of being unbearably alone, cut off from everything. A tear trickled down her face as the bird let out another mournful note.

Sad? came Canis's inquisitive yip. Kailyn shook her head, trying to clear her melancholy, but it felt like dark clouds of sorrow blanketed her soul. She'd never felt so heavy.

"Keep moving," Benje said, grabbing her arm and pulling her from the fat merchant. The bird echoed another soulful cry, and Kailyn's heart echoed it. She wanted to free the creature.

"What was that bird?" she asked as he led her to a marketplace square. Dozens of booths were set up, all displaying vibrant colors. Benje led her to a large decorated fountain in the middle of the square, setting down his pack. Canis's head popped up, his bright blue eyes seeming to be filled with the same sadness that flowed through Kailyn.

"A warbblier, sometimes known as the evening sun bird. It's said that its cry makes people feel powerful emotions. It's dangerous that he had one."

"Why? The bird didn't look dangerous."

Sad? Canis yipped again. He projected an image of a lone wolf among plains of snow, crying into the storm. Kailyn stared at the pup. She didn't realize how much the bird's cry had impacted Canis.

"It may not look dangerous, but it is," Benje said. "There aren't very many of them left in Alamarryn, partially because of how dangerous they are. It's no easy task acquiring one. He probably smuggled it in."

Kailyn's eyes went wide. "Smuggled?"

But before Benje could answer, loud music started playing.

A band had struck up a quick tune and soon all the market-goers were dancing, holding hands as they circled the fountain where Kailyn, Canis, and Benje sat.

"Come on," Benje grumbled, picking up the pack with Canis and pulling Kailyn away from the marketplace and down toward the dock. But it seemed like everywhere they went, the whole town was in celebration. Kailyn saw streaks of colored powder burst up in the sky above the crowds, dusting them in brilliant blues, purples, golds, and pinks.

People pressed spicy warm rolls into their hands and called out "Arrea! Arrea!" as they passed.

They finally found another more deserted courtyard that had a much smaller fountain, though they could still see the color rockets explode above them.

Food?

Canis poked his head out and Kailyn fed him bits of a spicy warm roll as she realized what was going on.

"It's the festival of color," she said in awe, wandering around the courtyard to look at the colors. "I'd never actually seen one in person, but I'm willing to bet five kinyas that's what it is." She watched another color rocket explode, showering a dazzling green upon the people below.

Food! Canis munched happily on the roll.

Kailyn smiled as she watched the colors explode. She had seen the famed color rockets a few times before in Oleanders, but only ever from her quarters. She had begged her father for years to let her go and see the celebrations, but he had never given in.

She wished he had. The rockets were incredible. And being there with both Benje and Canis made it even better.

"This is amazing," she whispered, wishing she could stay there forever.

Danger! Canis's thoughts projected a feeling of abject terror that made Kailyn gasp out loud.

Benje jumped to his feet, whirling out his sword as footsteps approached.

Five guards, dressed in the gold and purple plumes of Oleanders, had entered the courtyard, their swords drawn.

"Your Highness," one of them said. "You're coming with us."

Chapter Fifteen

Kailyn

"Stay back, Princess," Benje said, his tone even and cool as he bounced on the heels of his feet.

Danger! Kailyn wanted to stroke Canis's soft fur and reassure him that it would all be alright, but he was still by the pack. She had no idea how they were going to get out of this. Or if they would.

Oleanders had caught up with them.

The guard laughed at Benje. "Do you really think you can take down all of us?" His cronies laughed with him.

Kailyn saw Benje's grip tighten on his sword. What was he going to do?

"Don't make us use force, Princess," the guard said, his tone dripping with condescension. "I'd hate to see you come to harm."

Another rocket sounded right above them, squealing angrily before it burst into a swirl of yellows, oranges, purples, and blues, sending the powder directly onto them.

Color! Canis cried happily. Kailyn couldn't see him, as she'd left him at the pack on the fountain, but the little pup's yips sounded closer until she felt a ball of fluff curl up by her feet. She scooped him up and tried to make her way toward where she'd last seen Benje and the guards, but everything was a blur in the brilliant splash of color.

A hand grabbed her. Kailyn screamed as the hand yanked her and Canis down an alley, away from the cursing guards.

When the air was clear again, Kailyn found herself in a dim alleyway that smelled strongly of fish. She finally got a good look at her rescuer and gasped.

Her lady's maid Myira was looking at her with concern mixed with the colored powders on her dark skin. "Are you alright, Your Highness?"

"Myira?" she whispered. "What are you doing here?"

Danger! came Canis's voice, reminding Kailyn that she'd left Benje behind with the guards. Her heart clenched with fear. "Benje! I left Benje!"

Myira frowned. "The young man with you?" she shook her head. "Against that many guards . . . I'm afraid . . ."

She trailed off as someone scaled down the walls above them.

Canis yipped as the person landed in front of them and dusted off the bright colored powder. Kailyn stared. It was Benje! But how did he escape unscathed?

Benje smiled at the pup before he peered out the alleyway, glancing around.

"We should keep moving," he said. "The guards won't stop searching now that they know you're here."

"My place isn't too far away," Myira said, recovering faster than Kailyn did. "Come on."

She led them down the street, which was crumbling compared to the stone buildings they had seen earlier on the other side of town. Fewer people frequented these streets as they were all probably still at the color festival. They passed a few beggars, who looked at Kailyn with such wide pleading eyes, they reminded her of the warbblier she had seen earlier. Despite the celebration, Tyloan was clearly suffering, and she wished she could help. Canis's feelings echoed the sadness in her mind, and she had to blink back tears multiple times. She had to stay focused.

Myira pulled them into another alleyway, this one lined with staircases cut directly into the rock of the buildings. She led them up a stairway to a small door.

"It's not much," she said, "but it should keep you away from the guards for a bit." She opened the door.

Kailyn didn't know what she had expected. It definitely wasn't seeing a young man wrapped around a young woman, the two of them practically glued together.

"Mirnabad Trinche!" Myira yelled sharply. Canis yipped. The couple suddenly sprang apart. "You have some nerve coming back here, especially with one of your . . ." She spat out a word that Kailyn hadn't ever heard the maid speak before, but guessed it was foul. "Get out!"

The young woman smiled coyly at them, pecked the man on the cheek before scampering past them out the door, her skirts swirling behind her. She smelled strongly of fyir.

Poison, echoed Canis. Kailyn had to agree as the smell was sickening. The pup nestled in her arms, his white fur dusted with different colors from the rockets. He needed a bath. Kailyn glanced at her own arms and grimaced. So did she. Those rockets were incredible, but far from clean.

The man named Mirnabad got to his feet, a sheepish grin on his face. "Ah, come off it, Myira. I was just having a bit of fun with the festival."

Kailyn couldn't stop staring at the strange man. He was as dark-skinned as Myira, with a glistening golden tattoo that curled around one ear. He was dressed in a sailor's costume of rich plum trousers and a white shirt that exposed his muscular chest.

He grinned at Kailyn when he noticed her staring. "And who might you be?"

She blushed, feeling Benje tense beside her. Canis's yips were drowned out by Myira's curses.

"You will leave her alone, you good for nothing *tyadal. Gyor impa Hussin*!"

"*Ze ben*, watch that tongue of yours, Myr." Mirnabad laughed, putting his hands behind his head as he lounged on the couch. "I'm only in town for a few days and then we'll be off to distant lands again."

Myira pressed her fingers into her temples and muttered more under her breath. "Fine. But stay away from my friends, you hear? I don't need them mixing up with your pirate ways."

Mirnabad held a hand to his heart, looking offended. "Pirate? *Ze ben!* You exaggerate, sister."

Myira frowned at him. "Go! I don't want you to bring another girl around, you hear? I'm only letting you sleep here because Maman made me promise. Leave before I regret it."

Mirnabad tilted his head rakishly. "Ah, but can't you introduce me to your friends first?"

"Leave!"

Mirnabad pouted but wisely didn't say anything else as he grabbed his hat. He winked at Kailyn, ruffled Canis's fur, and saluted Benje before disappearing out the door.

Food? Canis yipped excitedly. Kailyn rubbed the wolf's soft muzzle, sending him thoughts of calm. They had to figure out what was going on first before she fed him.

Myira let out a loud sigh then ushered Kailyn and Benje deeper into the house. "I'm so sorry you had to see that, Your

Highness. My brother is . . ." She muttered another curse in her tongue. "I'm sorry. If I had known, I would never have brought you here. I don't think it's wise you should stay here with him."

Kailyn blinked, trying to shove the image of Mirnabad from her mind, and continued stroking Canis's muzzle. "We can find other lodgings until we find a ship. It's alright, Myira."

Myira shook her head. "No, it's not alright. That *tyadal* should know better! How many times have I told him not to bring his *fyirin* here, but does he listen?"

Benje spoke for the first time since they had arrived. "Princess, it might be best if we find a ship as fast as possible." His words were completely calm—the exact opposite of Myira's fury. "Myira, did your brother say he worked on a ship?"

"He's technically the captain of one, if you call piracy a living." She swore again. "Goddess curse the day that *tyadal* was born!"

"Do you think he'd take us on his ship?" Again, Benje sounded so calm. Though it took a moment for Kailyn to register what he'd said. Go with Mirnabad on his ship? Was that a good idea?

Myira echoed Kailyn's sentiment. "What? Go with him on his ship? No, no, the princess can't go! Not with him. He's a filthy, lying, no-good *vyko*! And you can't mix with him, Princess. Oh, this is all my fault. I should never have brought you here."

Kailyn put her hand on Myira's, holding Canis with her other arm. The wolf cub was still sending her thoughts of food, but this was more important.

"If you hadn't rescued us, I surely would have been taken back to Oleanders tonight, and Benje . . ." She glanced at Benje, still wondering how he had gotten free from the guards and crowd to follow them. It seemed he had a host of skills she didn't know about. But he was right—they needed to leave Tyloan as soon as possible.

"You can't stay here. You can't," Myira's voice broke. "My brother…"

"Is a filthy lying no-good *vyko*. So you've said. We will leave as soon as we can."

Canis yipped in agreement.

Myira shuddered. "It's worse when you say it, Princess."

At that, Kailyn burst out laughing. Oh, how she had missed her friend.

Myira told Kailyn to stay as far away from her brother as possible. "And if he does agree to take you to Tigahel, then I'm coming with you!"

Canis, who had settled in with a bone to gnaw, looked curiously at Kailyn, who was chopping vegetables, before going back to his dinner.

Kailyn frowned. As much as she loved Myira, she didn't want to inconvenience her further. "Don't you have work here?"

Myira shook her head. "I haven't worked since I was dismissed from the palace. And from what I hear with Lord Shielen taking over, it's a good thing too. The only reason I came back here is because of my mother. My brother has been paying for this place since she died."

"Oh, Myira." It was all her fault Myira and the others had lost their positions when she'd snuck out to find the library. She hadn't ever wanted them to suffer because of her. But they had. And still were. She sighed. But was there anything she could do about it now? The thought reminded her of what else Myira had mentioned.

"What's this about Lord Shielen?"

Myira made a face. "He's put Olean under martial law, he's forcing everyone to work for him, and anyone he finds in the resistance, he removes."

Kailyn's eyes went wide.

Aru? Canis's mind nuzzled against hers, sending her comforting images of other wolves snuggling together burrowed deep in dens for the winter.

She smiled and blinked to focus her mind.

"Well, a good thing we're on our way to Tigahel for reinforcements then." *And some way to defeat the frost giants.* She didn't voice that thought aloud though—she still wasn't sure the frost giants were even a real threat to her kingdom.

Myira flashed a bright smile. "That's the spirit, Princess. Besides, once we get to where we're going, I'll be rid of that *lyfin* brother of mine for good."

Kailyn laughed. "Alright. I don't suppose it would hurt to have you along. What do you think, Benje?"

Benje had been standing guard by the window, his hand resting on his sword. He merely grunted agreement and continued his vigil. She knew he was looking for any signs of trouble, but he still kept himself distant from her.

Kailyn sighed and turned back to the vegetables. They were in the middle of preparing supper, a corned meat stew that smelled spicy and delicious. Myira had initially protested to Kailyn's help, but when she needed an extra set of hands for chopping the vegetables so she could prepare bread dough, Kailyn had volunteered. Myira had shown her how to cut the roots in half and then in smaller bite-size bits. Myira was incredibly fast at the task, but Kailyn was slow. So far, she had only cut one of the roots into bite-sized pieces and there was still a stack of five to cut.

Myira dusted her hands, having finished the bread. "Ah, Princess, your hands aren't meant for this kind of labor," she clucked, taking the knife from Kailyn and cutting the roots in quick succession. Kailyn's heart sank as Myira finished chopping and dumped the roots in the stewpot. She really was unprepared for the world. All she had was knowledge from old books, and a wolf pup not even a day old.

She glanced at Canis, who was still gnawing on his bone. He was now twice the size he'd been when she'd found him earlier. If he kept eating, how big would he grow?

"Maybe it would be a good idea for you to come along," Kailyn said as Myira stirred the stewpot.

Myira chuckled. "If only to cook for you and your pup? I'll gladly take you up on that one, Princess." She started muttering about how terrible of a cook her brother was and how Kailyn would likely starve if she relied on his cooking.

Kailyn felt her mind wander as she looked solemnly toward Benje, who hadn't even moved from his stance. His hands were held behind his back, his feet wide. He was still covered in colors from the rockets, which bothered Kailyn. That stuff itched terribly which was why she and Myira had scrubbed themselves—and Canis—off as soon as they could, but Benje didn't seem fazed. She ached to talk to him alone again, to ask him more questions. It was almost like he'd become a different person once they'd arrived at Tyloan.

She sighed. Just when she thought she had figured him out, he had yet more secrets for her to discover. He was like a book that was constantly being written, even though she thought she had already reached the ending.

"Princess?" Myira's voice brought her back to her maid.

"Oh, apologies. I was distracted."

Myira followed her gaze and raised an eyebrow. "I can see that."

Kailyn blushed and wondered if Benje was listening in on their conversation, but he continued to stare stoically out the window, constantly on alert. Kailyn frowned. He was taking his vow way too seriously. Weren't they fine for the moment? She turned back to Myira. "Is there anything else I can do to help prepare supper?"

Myira shook her head. "It'll be done momentarily, Your Highness."

Kailyn bit her lip, thinking. She'd tried to get Benje to call her Kailyn in the caves, but he'd stubbornly refused to do so. Would Myira do the same? "I think it best if you call me Kailyn," she said. "I'm not a princess out here."

Myira shook her head. "No. You are still my princess. It's you who deserves to rule Oleanders, not that flyl Shielen." She shuddered. "He's had guards posted everywhere trying to find you."

Kailyn grimaced, remembering the steel of the guards they'd only just avoided. Maybe Benje standing guard was for the best after all.

Dinner was deliciously homey and reminded Kailyn of the gnomes. She hoped they were alright under the mountain. Though it troubled her to think that even the gnomes were sending them to Tigahel. Would they really find all their answers there?

"Your Highness? You look troubled," Myira said as she cleared away the dishes. "Are you alright?"

"Well . . ." Kailyn wanted to trust Myira with everything that had happened since the ball, but she'd been avoiding her questions all throughout dinner. So much had changed since she'd last seen her. And she still wasn't sure what to make of them going to Tigahel. "I'm just worried about finding a ship and sneaking past the guards."

"I've been thinking about that," Benje said quietly. He had finally joined them for dinner at Kailyn's insistence, but he kept glancing at the window every few moments. "I think our best bet will be to disguise ourselves as sailors and go with your brother aboard his ship."

"But he doesn't take women sailors," Myira said, before her eyes widened. "No! I refuse. I will not pose as his *fyirin*!"

At that moment, Mirnabad came through the door. He still looked as flamboyant as he did before, but he was covered in the colored dust from the festival, and he swayed drunkenly on his feet. Benje tensed next to Kailyn. Canis growled. Kailyn told the wolf cub to calm down, but Canis's distrust of Mirnabad put her ill at ease. If her wolf cub didn't trust him, she definitely wouldn't either.

Myira swore again as she went to guide her wobbling brother to a chair and bolted the door behind him.

"Is he alright?" Kailyn asked.

The pirate glanced at her with dilated eyes. He blinked as he focused on her. "Ah, pretty siebald. Have you come to take me home?"

"He's just drunk, Your Highness," Myira said, washing the dishes from the meal with more force than they warranted.

"I'm not that drunk," Mirnabad said, his voice definitely slurring now. "Just a little faint for the love of women." He winked at Kailyn as if they were sharing some secret.

"Keep your paws to yourself, *vyko*," Myira snarled. Kailyn saw Benje's hand inch toward his sword. She blinked. Were they going to fight Mirnabad in front of her?

But she needn't have worried. Mirnabad rolled his eyes before passing out cold.

"How in all of Almarryn did he make it here safely?" Kailyn wondered. Canis padded over to her and laid his head down by her feet. It was comforting to have him near.

They heard a distant crash outside and Kailyn jolted, a spike of fear filling her heart. "What was that?"

Benje stood up quickly. "Stay here, Princess." He slipped out the window.

"Why does he keep doing that?" she mumbled.

Myira laid a comforting hand on her shoulder. "It'll be alright, Your Highness. But you should probably rest if we're sneaking out of here with that one." She jerked her thumb at her snoring brother. "If they followed him here . . ." She cursed again. "I'll personally kill him for you, Princess."

Canis yipped, sounding like he agreed with Myira.

Kailyn's thoughts focused on Benje. Was he fighting the guards by himself? What if he got himself killed? What if she never got to talk to him again? Her heart was pounding ferociously in her ears. Even if she did lie down, she didn't think she would be able to rest.

"Come, Princess," Myira said, tugging her arm gently. "To bed with you."

"But Benje!"

"He can take care of himself. You need rest."

Myira led Kailyn to the small bedroom. "Rest here."

Canis followed, bounding on the bed with a single bounce and curling up on the mattress. Kailyn watched him for a moment, smiling softly. Then she realized there was only one bed.

She turned to Myira. "Where will you sleep?"

"I'll be alright, Princess. Please stop worrying. Everything will work out."

Myira helped Kailyn slip out of her dress so that she could

sleep in her shift. It felt like old times, back at the castle. Back before everything had come crashing down on her. Back before Benje. The gnomes. Canis. Before everything.

After Myira had left, Kailyn stared at the dark ceiling for hours worrying about Benje. It was Canis's presence and his soft fur that finally lulled her to sleep.

Chapter Sixteen

Abrina

*B*eing on a ship was one of the most unnerving things Abrina had ever done. The boat swayed with every wave, bobbing along like a cork in a tub. She felt ungrounded.

It didn't help that she was in close quarters with the ambassador.

She scowled, tossing on her bed, trying to find rest. But all she saw was the ambassador's disappointed eyes as he carted Lord Jeru away.

She sat up, cursing at him. He'd locked Lord Jeru in a room, then had gone to help distribute the stockpiled food. She'd followed, wanting to continue the fight. But the ambassador was stubborn. He'd even gotten the captain on his side—asking what they could do to help these people. The look he'd given Abrina . . . it still haunted her.

So she'd let the captain send several of her men to escort Jeru back to her mother's manor for trial. Sir Tyir and two others had been left in charge of redistribution of Lord Jeru's massive pile of goods. Only Sir Zachry, Sir Byron, and the captain himself remained a part of Abrina's retinue, along with the ambassador, his two guards, and the crew of the small vessel.

Abrina knew she'd done right in opening the stores of Jeru's

Keep to the people. The looks of gratitude she'd seen as people had left, clutching fruits or sacks of flour, would stay with her forever. Her people needed that food.

But why did she feel so agitated about the ambassador?

After tossing and turning for a few hours, she headed up to the deck. The ambassador's ship was small and barely had space in the bulkhead for everyone—all the men had to share a cramped barracks. She and the ambassador had their own quarters, which were tiny rooms that contained only a bed and a washstand. Belowdecks also contained the captain's quarters, the tiny galley, and a small storage space.

Abrina hated how claustrophobic the ship made her feel. On deck she could at least see the waves and the sky and could breathe a little easier.

Up on deck, there was the helmsman and a watch. To her surprise, the ambassador was standing guard tonight, his blue staff glowing like a beacon.

She scowled at it and headed to the gunwales, leaning on the railing to look out at the sea. Somewhere, beyond those clouds, lay her new home.

And a prince . . .

She cast an eye at the ambassador, who was still scanning the ocean around them. His posture was relaxed, but he glanced her way every so often, letting her know he was aware of her presence. She turned away to gaze at the vast indigo expanse, which reflected the stars above.

She kept turning over in her mind the line he'd said two nights ago when he'd mentioned that the prince wanted to be her friend. She had a sneaking suspicion that kept bouncing in her thoughts.

"Trouble sleeping?" His calm voice made her scowl deepen.

"For some reason, yes."

"Ships can take some time to get used to."

She huffed. "It's not the ship."

"Then I imagine you're worried about your knights."

It wasn't that either. She shook her head tersely. "My knights can take care of themselves. They'll help the people and make sure Lord Jeru gets to my mother."

She swallowed the lump in her throat. She still thought that the traitor didn't deserve a trial. He'd betrayed her people. There was nothing to judge about that—he deserved the heaviest punishment.

"So you're not worried about the knights or the ship. I can only assume then you're worried about your upcoming marriage?"

She snuck another glance at him and saw he was smirking.

That did it.

She wheeled from the railing to face him, pointing an accusatory finger his direction. "You're the prince, aren't you?"

He gave a sweeping bow. "Prince Henri of Tigahel, at your service, milady."

Abrina snarled and her hand went to her waist for her sword, but she'd left it in her bunk. "Why?"

It was the only question that really mattered.

"You're not the only one who didn't want to marry a perfect stranger." The prince's voice was soft. His face looked thoughtful as he gazed at her. "I wanted to meet you before my mother made everything official. I wanted to see who the next queen of Tigahel would be."

His words were gentle, but they irked Abrina. She didn't want to be the queen of Tigahel. She was Florryn's princess. All she wanted was to help the people of Florryn, not rule an island nation she didn't even know.

She slammed her fist against the railing behind her. "You lied to me."

"I didn't lie," the prince said, his voice still soft. "I just . . . withheld certain truths."

Abrina closed her eyes, wishing she could dismiss the man in front of her as easily. *This* was her betrothed? A man who didn't even fight? What kind of warrior was he?

And to think she'd felt something for him.

No. She shoved those thoughts away. She'd marry him, but no one said she had to feel things for him. He'd lied to her, pretending to be someone he wasn't just to get to know her better.

"I . . ." She clenched her fist. Unclenched it. Clenched it again. "I don't understand," she said finally, releasing her fist. "You came all this way, in disguise, just to meet me?"

The prince smiled that brilliant smile at her and Abrina felt her heart skip a beat. "Is that really such an outrageous thing to do?"

She swallowed thickly. He was enchanting. And he had come all this way to meet her. If she was honest with herself, she felt a little bit . . . flattered.

She locked eyes with his deep blue ones and saw a tenderness there that surprised her. She took a step toward him, and he reached out a hand to her. The moment their hands touched, Abrina felt a thrill race down her arm, filling her with a cascading warmth she'd never felt before. She cracked a shy smile at him.

"There," he whispered. "That wasn't so bad now, was it, Princess?"

She licked her lips as he kissed the back of her hand. A pleasurable tingle radiated from the spot. She didn't know what she was supposed to do here. All she knew was that she was starting to really appreciate the fact that she'd had extra time to get to know her intended—and that her heart was secretly pleased that he wanted to get to know her too.

Then something rocked the boat violently and Abrina jumped aside, straight into her battle stance, her hand reaching for her absent sword again. "What was that?"

"Don't be alarmed." The prince raised his hands, one still holding his staff. "It's just Vergyl."

Abrina tensed as the boat rocked again. "Who or what is Vergyl?"

The prince smiled again. "A sea monster."

Abrina cursed and took off to find her sword.

She found it quickly, strapped it on, and ran into Sir Byron and Sir Zachry on her way back to the deck.

"Princess? What's going on?" Sir Zachry asked, rubbing sleep from his eyes.

"Did we hit something?" Sir Byron asked. He held an apple in his fist like he was about to throw it at something.

Another shudder rocked the boat. Abrina gritted her teeth and charged toward the deck. If there was a sea monster about, then she was going to fight it.

But when she got to the deck, she stopped in her tracks.

The prince stood calmly at the prow, holding his glowing blue staff high in the air. A giant snake head with teeth as long as her sword was only a few meters away from him, rapidly closing the gap.

Abrina's gut clenched. Was it going to swallow him whole? No. She couldn't have that.

She let out a battle cry and launched herself across the deck.

But the prince caught her with his strong arms. "No, Princess. Don't attack. Vergyl will destroy us if he's provoked. Only the light of a Forged staff will keep him at bay."

Abrina struggled in his gentle but firm grip as the sea monster got closer. To her utter astonishment, the prince tapped the nose of the sea monster with his glowing blue staff and the creature nodded its large head before slithering back into the sea.

The prince released Abrina and she whirled to face him, her heart hammering.

"You-you led us to a sea monster!"

"Vergyl protects the Archipelago. He's more an over-grown guard dog than a monster." He sounded amused. Curse him.

Abrina turned from him and stomped down the deck, blowing past Sir Byron and Sir Zachry and their concerned expressions, heading back to her quarters.

She sat on the bed, thinking about everything that had happened. The prince's touch . . . how he'd wanted to see her. Then that wretched sea beast.

She'd wanted to fight those giant scales, see if they were impervious to her blade and her wrath. But the prince hadn't even given her the chance. He'd tapped the thing on the nose, sending it slithering away like it was nothing.

There was far more to him than he let on. She scowled in the darkness. How could he be so pleasant and so irritating at the same time? It perplexed her.

She unsheathed her sword and started polishing it to settle her nerves.

The next morning, the boat pulled safely into the harbor of the main island in the Tigahel Archipelago. Abrina stood on deck, her nerves only slightly settled. Her knights stood next to her.

And the prince stood nearby. He sent an easy smile toward her, but she scowled. She wasn't sure she wanted to marry him, despite the attraction she definitely felt. She'd spent half the night reliving the moment his lips had touched the back of her hand. No amount of sword polishing had banished that feeling from her memory.

She mentally scolded herself. She was acting like a foolish girl instead of a princess. It didn't matter if she liked him or if she hated him. Marrying him was the only way her people could get Tigahel's resources to defeat the frost giants.

And what resources did they have to offer! From her viewpoint on deck, she could make out lush green trees everywhere on the island. They pulled toward a dock that was crowded with workers hauling fish and fruit. She could make out other vessels from the Oronian colonies, and a few from the isles of Wyta, laden with rice, silks, metals, and other goods.

Her heart thumped loudly when she spotted the gold and purple Oleanderian flag. She clenched her fists and tried to soothe the anxiety bubbling inside her. *Oleanders.* She wanted to light the boat on fire.

She exhaled deeply. These islands were prosperous. They had good trade going on, even if they did trade with her enemies. That didn't mean *they* were her enemies. They were going to help Florryn.

She just had to marry the prince. The infuriating man who kept sending smiles her way.

The moment the ship came to port, a queue of people formed up on their dock. The prince saluted them, and they cheered.

Her stomach twisted itself in knots. What was she getting into?

"You alright, Princess?" Captain Wilen asked. She shot him a look. His weary pewter gray eyes looked quizzically at her.

She squared her shoulders. Enemy ships or no enemy ships, handsome prince or no handsome prince, she was the princess of Florryn. Her people could face anything. She could do this.

"I'm alright, Captain," she said. She didn't have time for distractions.

She followed the prince to the dock.

An older dark-skinned man dressed in the same white robes that the prince wore greeted them at the end of the dock. He held a silver staff that seemed more to keep himself propped up than to do anything magical.

"Prince Henri," he said, bowing low. "Welcome home."

"Klaius." The prince nodded his head toward the man. "May I present Princess Abrina of Florryn. My bride-to-be." He motioned his hand toward Abrina, and she nodded toward the older man, though her stomach lurched. She was really here in Tigahel, about to cement this alliance. She swallowed thickly.

Klaius bowed to Abrina. "Princess Abrina, welcome to the island of Elandel." He swept his hands, gesturing toward the darkening trees behind him.

For half a moment, Abrina wistfully thought of exploring those trees to fight monsters like the sea serpent. But then her eye caught the prince's and she remembered the real reason she was there. The duty she had to fulfill.

She took a deep breath, standing as straight as an arrow.

"Thank you, Klaius, for the kind welcome." She hesitated for a moment, unsure what to say next. Her mother would know what to do in this situation, but Abrina hadn't exactly been the best student on international relations. She'd skipped class multiple times to find someone to spar with.

Thankfully, the prince stepped forward. "We're ready to report to my mother, Klaius."

Klaius nodded. "Your Highnesses, if you'll follow me." He motioned for them to follow along the dock. At the end of it was a rather typical carriage, though Abrina had never seen a green one with a golden insignia before. The whole thing glittered in the sun. It was a handsome vehicle, but she much preferred horseback.

Her eyes wandered to the six horses attached to the carriage and she took a double take. They were the strangest horses she'd ever seen. They were purple, or at least looked that way in the morning sun. Shorter than a normal horse, with a squashed jaw, and six legs each, the creatures stared at her curiously with large yellow eyes. And she was pretty sure those long folded things along their sides were wings.

"Um . . ." she swallowed. "What are those?"

The prince had the audacity to laugh. "Those are cajuna. Weren't you listening to my stories, Princess?"

"They're real?" Sir Zachry whispered next to Abrina. "The flying horse creatures?"

"I thought he made them up," Sir Byron grumbled.

"Ready to ride one?" the prince asked, his eyes twinkling merrily.

Klaius cleared his throat. "Your Highness, your mother insisted that you all are to arrive in the carriage. Less danger of broken bones."

The prince sighed. "Very well. If Mother insists. I suppose she has a point for a first ride." His eyes glinted with challenge as he looked at Abrina. "Though I'm sure we'll have plenty of chances to fly solo later."

Abrina swallowed again as her cheeks heated up. Why did he do this to her?

The prince waved a hand. "Right this way!"

Abrina frowned as she followed the prince to the sumptuous green carriage. "Does it have room for all of us?" Including Klaius, there were six of them. The carriage didn't look big enough.

"Don't you fret about us, Your Highness," Sir Zachry said with his usual enthusiastic grin. "I'm sure they'll find someway to transport us up to the castle."

The captain frowned at him then looked at Abrina. "I don't want you to leave without an escort, Your Highness."

"Ah, but there's plenty of space for everyone," the prince said, motioning toward the carriage. "Mother uses it to carry her entire retinue. There's room, trust me."

Abrina felt his eyes on her when he said those words, but she ignored him and climbed into the carriage.

The interior was a dark forest green with golden thread lining the cushions. It was far more spacious on the inside than it seemed on the outside. Everyone settled in, the prince right across from her. Klaius closed the door after Sir Zachry and then they were moving.

"Are we really going to fly?" Sir Zachry asked excitedly.

Abrina couldn't help but feel a little of that same thrill. She'd always wanted to fly. Even if she still wasn't fully on board with the circumstances.

"Hang on, everyone. And Princess." The prince's eyes twinkled again. "Look out the window. You won't want to miss the view."

Despite herself, Abrina glanced out the window right as they picked up speed. Before she could see anything, the carriage jerked, sending Abrina, Zachry, and Byron to the floor. Abrina glanced up to see the captain clinging to his seat for dear life, but the prince looked as comfortable as could be.

"I did say to hang on." He grinned, offering Abrina an arm. As she tried to grab it, the carriage bounced forward and Abrina's head crashed into the seat. Dazed, she tried to right herself, only to get Byron's boot to her thigh.

"I'm so sorry, Your Highness," Byron said, struggling and failing to right himself. When the carriage finally felt smooth and safe again, Abrina took the prince's hand and sat on the bench, feeling completely disgruntled. It didn't help that the carriage was still swaying, worse than the boat had on the open sea.

"What in the name of the Goddess was that?" Abrina demanded, her face red and her thigh throbbing.

The prince's grin—if possible—grew even wider. "Take-off. Look out the window, Princess."

Face still red from embarrassment, Abrina glanced out the window. Her breath caught. They were flying above the massive deep green trees of the island. Occasionally, she spotted people in the trees. Other cajuna flew by, some with people on their backs, some with wagons attached and some without any load at all. The people who saw the carriage waved at them before flying back below the trees.

The clouds were above them, dazzling pure white in the gleam of the sun. The brilliant blue sky looked like it stretched to the end of the heavens—even to the Goddess's Palace of Stars. "Goddess's eyes," she whispered. She glanced back at the prince, who chuckled.

"It's breathtaking, isn't it?"

She nodded mutely, too stunned by the grandeur—and the sheer fact that they were flying—to say much more.

They approached a mountain, which Abrina hadn't noticed upon her initial arrival to the island. They neared the top, approaching four massive trees, all twined together to create one great tree. Abrina wondered what they were doing here. Did the royal family live in trees?

The cajuna touched ground, and the carriage bounced roughly to a stop. Abrina braced herself this time and managed to stay in her seat, though Byron and Zachry still fell to the bottom of the carriage. Both of them stood up shakily, Byron cursing at the landing, though Zachry just grinned.

"That's quite a rush!" he said good-naturedly.

"This is only the beginning," the prince said, flashing yet another smile. Abrina shook her head. Did he ever get tired of smiling? It hurt her cheeks if she smiled too much.

When they exited the carriage, Abrina was surprised to see stairs carved into the mountain that led from where they had landed up to a door carved directly into the giant tree.

The branches extended far into the sky, all of them thicker than a man's body. Vines hung from the branches, covering the trunk. Abrina couldn't tell if there was a building in the tree or if the tree itself was a building, but the four massive trees did resemble a building of some sort. Stairs wound around the outside edge of the trunks, going high into the canopy. The trunks were carved with openings that were flooded with light, rather like the windows on Lord Jeru's Keep. The memory sent a stabbing pain through Abrina's heart. Her people deserved better than Lord Jeru.

Klaius cleared his throat. He had moved to stand before the steps. "Princess Abrina," he said. "Welcome to the Great Tree, home of the royal family."

She looked over at the prince, who was still grinning. "You live in a tree?"

"The Great Tree, Princess. It's perhaps the most unique palace you will ever see."

If it was where golden prince boy was born and raised, Abrina had no doubt about that.

Chapter Seventeen

Abrina

Abrina was amazed at how open and spacious the tree was. Klaius led them down a smooth hallway that was carved directly into the trunk. It opened into a throne room inlaid with gold and green sparkling carpet on the floor, though when Abrina glanced at it again, she saw that it was made up of golden flowers inlaid with precious gems and green grass.

Her attention was drawn to the end of the room where a woman with delicate features and raven-dark hair sat upon a throne made of both green and golden vines and branches, looking for all the world like it was grown from the tree itself, though it too was inlaid with precious gems.

The woman was dressed in resplendent blue robes, wearing a twisted golden crown set with deep blue jewels. She looked younger than Abrina's mother, except for her eyes. There was an ancientness to her deep black eyes that was troubling to Abrina. But she didn't think much of it as the woman rose from her throne as they approached.

"Princess Abrina, welcome to Elandel. I am Queen Leilana."

Abrina bowed to the queen, opting not to go for the clunky curtsy. She'd never particularly liked them.

The queen lifted her dainty eyebrows, but merely turned to address her son. "Henri, thank you for escorting her."

"My pleasure, Mother." The prince moved to stand next to his mother on the small dais. Seeing the two of them side-by-side, Abrina was struck with how different they looked. The prince didn't look at all like his mother. They didn't share a single feature, which she found a bit odd. *He must take more after his father,* she thought. *Like me.*

The queen addressed Abrina again. "We are so glad to see you've arrived safely. I hope the journey wasn't too terrible?"

Abrina thought of the bandit attack, the raid of Jeru's Keep, and the sea serpent. "Not at all, Your Majesty."

The prince quirked an eyebrow at her, but Abrina ignored him. Besides, it wasn't a total lie. She was just . . . omitting some of the details. Just like he had. She bit her lip to keep herself from smirking at the irony. Perhaps she and the prince were more alike than she'd thought.

"Indeed. Well, let me be the first to say that I am glad you are here and that we look forward to this alliance so that we can assist your kingdom in their time of trial."

Abrina's good humor melted away at those words and the painful reminder of her duty. She was there to save her people. She didn't have time for flirtation. It was time to jump into action, doing all she could to save Florryn. Even if she never saw her country again. She shoved the thought aside and forced herself to bow again to the queen.

"Yes, Your Majesty. Shall we begin the wedding plans?" Even if she knew next to nothing about planning a wedding, and only slightly more about the prince she was marrying, she needed to move this along. The sooner everything was complete, the sooner her people had the help they needed.

The queen smiled, though Abrina noticed it was a little forced. "Princess, with all due respect, you've only just arrived.

I'm sure you and your retinue are exhausted. Let us reconvene tomorrow morning, shall we? There's much I wish to discuss with my son."

The prince looked regretfully at Abrina, but she stiffly nodded. And stifled a yawn. Perhaps a rest was in order.

"Very well, Your Majesty."

Abrina bowed once more before following Klaius out of the room. She could have sworn the prince's eyes followed her as she left.

After a night in the most luscious bed she'd ever slept in—even if it was nestled in gold and green tree branches—Abrina woke up eager to get wedding preparations underway. She was here on a mission and she needed to complete it. Her people were counting on her.

She hastily donned her tunic and leggings, ignoring the light pink robe that had been laid out for her, before heading down to breakfast.

She was not expecting to come into the middle of an argument with the prince and his mother.

"We need to send supplies to Florryn as soon as possible, Mother. The conditions there were appalling. The people are starving."

Abrina stopped in her tracks outside the door. The prince sounded angrier than she'd ever heard him. Even the night he'd stopped her from killing Lord Jeru.

"I know Florryn is in a spot of trouble, son. But we must wait. The wedding must be completed first before we send aid."

The queen sounded odd, her voice both cold and considerate at the same time. But what made matters worse was that she was refusing Florryn aid. And that simply could not stand.

Abrina burst through the doors. "Your Majesty, my people cannot wait."

The queen, dressed in glittering black robes this morning, though still wearing her blue and gold crown, frowned at Abrina.

"This is a private affair, Princess Abrina. I suggest you go wait in the dining hall where we will join you shortly."

Abrina shrugged off the dismissal. "No. You are discussing the future of my people. And I agree with Prince Henri—my people need help. Now."

She linked eyes with Henri for a moment and saw that they glittered with warmth. His name felt very pleasing on her tongue. She forced herself to focus on her mission at hand.

"We can be wed tonight with little ceremony and send aid tomorrow." She surprised herself with the words but barreled on anyway. "All that's needed to cement the alliance is a marriage contract. We fulfill that, you fulfill your end of the bargain, everyone is taken care of."

The queen's eyes hardened. "This is not a battle to charge into, Princess Abrina. There is a way things must be done to prepare for a wedding of this magnitude. It will not be done tonight, tomorrow, or even in a fortnight. Perhaps a month, if everything is aligned properly. The preparations are underway, but it takes time to plan."

Time? Her people didn't have time! Abrina clenched her hand into a fist, wanting to punch something. But she locked eyes with Henri, who shook his head ever so slightly. She sighed. He wanted her to wait.

She stared at the queen, who had turned away from them to look at a painting on the wall Abrina hadn't seen when she'd barreled into the room. It depicted a woman who looked very similar to the queen, only with fair hair and lighter eyes. The queen stared at the painting for a long moment.

Abrina sent another look at Henri, but he was staring at his mother, waiting. Abrina's foot itched and she longed to scratch it, but perhaps silence was the call of the moment. Would the queen change her mind? Florryn needed aid, there was no argument about it. Abrina was willing to get married in the next five minutes if that's what it took to help her people.

The silence stretched on for a few more minutes, Abrina anxiously wishing she could smack something or at least scratch her foot. But she stood still. Or at least tried to. Goddess above, she hated waiting.

After what felt like an eternity, the queen spoke again. "But I cannot let innocent people suffer. You are both right. The people of Florryn need relief now. I will send Klaius to the docks with orders to begin the humanitarian aid effort."

A thrill zinged down Abrina's arm and she flashed a brief smile at Henri, who merely nodded in return. His eyes looked troubled.

"Very well, Mother." His voice was as calm as ever, but there was an undercurrent of frustration to it.

Curious, Abrina followed him to the dining hall where her knights were already feasting.

Sir Zachry looked up from a cornucopia rainbow of fruits and vegetables, most of which she'd never seen before. Florryn wasn't exactly known for its produce.

"Good morning, Princess!" Sir Zachry called out. "Come try this fruit! It's delicious."

She walked over and sat next to her knights, eyeing the strange purple star-shaped fruit on his plate. "What is that?"

"The locals call it yilnel fruit," Byron said, taking a bite of his own. "It's quite the delicacy, apparently."

The captain eyed Abrina and the prince curiously. "Everything alright, Your Highness?"

"Just fine, Wilen, just fine," Henri said, picking up a purple star-shaped fruit. He sounded nonplussed, which was odd considering his behavior in the throne room. What was going on with him? "Come, Princess, try some. Tigahel is known for its rare fruits."

Abrina eyed the fruit suspiciously. She was craving some rich meat sausages, and she didn't even care if they were from a pulong. She hadn't gone without a hunt this long since her father died. But her knights seemed to be enjoying the fare. As did Henri.

She took a bite of the fruit to clear her head. The fruit startled her taste buds with an explosion of tartness. She made a face and hastily gulped some water. As soon as she swallowed, the aftertaste mellowed into something that reminded her of Yera's sugar cakes. She took a huge gulp of water to clear the taste of the strange fruit from her palate.

"What in the Goddess's palace was that?"

Zachry and Byron burst out laughing.

"That was my reaction too," Zachry admitted, popping a smaller orange fruit into his mouth. "It grows on you though."

Abrina took another gulp of water and glared at the strange purple fruit. "I think I'll decline that offer."

Prince Henri inclined his head toward her. "Princess, would you be willing to take a walk with me after breakfast?"

She looked into his deep blue eyes, surprised by the sadness that sparked in them. Maybe he wasn't as carefree as he appeared to be. "O-of course. I can go now."

He nodded. "Follow me."

Prince Henri led her to a courtyard inlaid with sparkling blue and gold marble. Bright purple and white flowers grew in bunches around the courtyard. A gurgling fountain stood in the middle. Abrina took in the scene, curious as to why he'd led her there. She turned to look at him and saw that he was frowning, which didn't look like it belonged on his face.

"Prince Henri?"

He glanced at her, and his face broke into a brief smile. "Apologies. My mother . . ." He glanced at the fountain then back at Abrina. "I feel like she's stalling."

Abrina looked at him quizzically. "Stalling? Stalling what?"

"The wedding."

Abrina frowned. The queen had sounded rather dismissive of their pleas to send aid to Florryn earlier. "Do you really think she'd keep aid from Florryn? She promised she'd send help." Her hand went instinctively to her sword. Did she need to knock some sense into the queen? She wasn't afraid to fight royalty.

"And she will. Of that I have no doubt. But it's odd. She's been planning the wedding for months."

Abrina's heart lurched. "Months?" She'd only just heard of the wedding the day the prince had arrived at the manor. "How is that possible?" Had the queen and her mother been planning a wedding this whole time? Surely her mother would have told her.

Then again, it's not like she would have listened. Perhaps they had been planning it for months without her knowledge.

He shrugged. "I don't know. All I know is that she's stalling for some reason." He shook his head. "I don't know what to make of it."

Abrina didn't either. Perhaps it was nothing—perhaps Tigahelen weddings just required a lot of work. It's not like she'd spent much time preparing for a wedding before.

All that really mattered was that Florryn got aid. As long as her people were taken care of, it didn't really matter when she and Henri got married.

"I know what we need," Henri said, his eyes brightening. "Would you like to see one of the hidden treasures of Tigahel?"

Something about the gleam in his eyes made her heart quicken. She didn't hesitate. "Of course."

He smirked. "Then let's go find a cajuna."

"Oh, Goddess's eyes!" Abrina swore when she saw the creature the prince wanted her to mount. It was a deep dark blue, unlike the purple of some of the other cajuna she'd seen, but it was shorter than a horse. It eyed her warily, like she was going to attack it. Which was tempting. The thing didn't look at all like Beri, her beloved mare. A horse was so much easier. With only four feet, and walking securely on the ground, where you could see where you were going, it was preferable in every way.

How was she even supposed to mount the thing? There was no saddle anywhere.

The prince laughed, looking far more relaxed than he had in the courtyard. "Don't tell me you're scared of poor Hyna here? She's a sweet young mare. She won't bite."

"She looks like she wants to," Abrina muttered, which made him laugh again.

"Here, it's easy to mount a cajuna. All you have to do is put your hands on their front shoulders and hoist yourself up. It's much like mounting a horse, but you want to sit between their front and middle shoulders. They don't take kindly to people sitting directly on their joints. It hurts them."

"Don't you have saddles for the cajuna?" Abrina said, wishing more than ever that they had horses here. "They'd be so much simpler."

"Saddles are troublesome with the cajuna. They prefer to be ridden bareback. I'll show you how to mount. Have a little faith, Abrina."

He locked eyes with her and she swallowed. It was the first time he'd used her given name. She liked how it sounded in his deep tone.

"Alright, Henri," she said, relishing how his name sounded aloud. "Show me how."

He was holding the mane of a taller deep purple cajuna, who Abrina could tell was a stallion. Henri grasped the beast behind the front shoulders and hoisted himself up, swinging his leg over. He settled into his seat and smiled down at her.

She scowled at him. He'd made that look easy.

His smile morphed into a smirk. "Scared, Princess?"

Her scowl deepened. "Absolutely not."

She glared at the cajuna who was still eyeing her warily. She could do this. It was just like mounting Beri. Only a purple colored horse who had an extra set of legs and a pair of wings.

"Here goes nothing."

She placed her arms on both sides of the cajuna and pressed them into the creature's fur. It felt like feathers, but she supposed that made sense as cajuna were creatures of flight. She pushed all her weight into her hands and hoisted herself onto the cajuna's back. But something felt wrong. Instead of the smooth seat she held whenever she rode Beri, she felt like she was sitting on a hump.

"You might want to adjust your seat, Princess!" Henri called out, but it was too late. The cajuna reared onto its back legs, its wings flapping against the breeze. Abrina tried to clutch its neck, like she did with her horse, but she overcompensated and fell face-first onto the ground.

The creature was still squealing, pawing the air with its four front paws. Abrina scrambled away from it, worried she would get hit. Henri jumped down from his steed and grabbed the mane of the cajuna. He spoke quiet words in a language Abrina hadn't heard before, but they somehow calmed the beast.

Henri held out a hand toward Abrina. "You sat on its shoulders, Princess."

She slapped his hand away and got to her feet, her face hot with embarrassment. Henri looked amused.

"Place your hands before its shoulders, like this, alright? Then hoist yourself up between the two sets of shoulders. Don't sit too far forward or you'll end up on the ground again."

She nodded, not eager for a repeat performance. Henri stood at the cajuna's head, holding the creature steady. Abrina placed her hands before its first set of shoulders before hoisting herself up. This time, she made sure to settle between the shoulder blades. The cajuna squealed a little as Abrina adjusted herself, but it stayed on the ground this time.

"Good work," Henri said, nodding encouragingly. "Do you think you can stay on Hyna's back while I mount Gyor over there?"

Abrina nodded. Her hands were holding onto the mane like a bridle. She thought it rather foolish of the islanders to not have saddles when riding their beasts in the sky. If she had fallen while airborne . . . well, marriage would have been the least of her concerns.

Which would have been a shame, she thought while watching Henri mount his steed. He did it so effortlessly despite his stature. He looked so regal, his blond curls wafting in the breeze.

He smiled at her. Her heart fluttered and she shook her head, trying to clear her mind of his brilliant smile and gentle eyes. She was acting foolish. If they were to fly on these beasts, she needed to focus.

"Ready, Princess?" Henri asked.

Abrina wanted to say no. She wanted to back down. She didn't want to be in the air at the mercy of these creatures. But she was curious as to where he was taking her.

She met his blue eyes that shone with excitement. Here was a man ready for an adventure. A man who cared for her people as much as she did. She suddenly felt grateful she got to spend the afternoon with him. "Ready, Prince Henri."

He grinned wickedly, looking rather boyish. "Then hang tight. Here we go! Hyut!" The cajuna started running, their lopping gait reminding Abrina painfully of her horse, though not near as comfortable. It was a little awkward, but she thought she could get used to it. Then she saw their wings spread, and her stomach lurched as they launched into the air.

They sailed away from the Great Tree, and as the wind rushed by, blowing her hair behind her, Abrina felt the knot in her stomach unravel and let out a joyful cry. *This* was a way to travel—and far better than the carriage! Henri had been right. Why had she been so terrified?

She let go of the cajuna's mane, her arms held out at her side, laughing from the exhilaration.

Henri glided close by. "Do you find this more enjoyable, Princess?"

She laughed again. "Lead the way, prince boy!"

He whooped and took off into the distance. Abrina dug her heels into the cajuna's side, and the beast's speed increased.

Chapter Eighteen

Abrina

They flew across Elandel, the vast jungle canopy spread out below them. Abrina could make out more cajuna flying, like she had seen when they had arrived, but she could also see furry creatures in the trees, and people peering out of homes nestled in the branches.

She smirked. It figured that if the royal family lived in trees, so would everyone else.

Flying the cajuna was freeing. With the wind in her face, the sky at her fingertips, and the ground below, Abrina felt more alive than she'd ever felt, even in the heat of battle. There was something inherently freeing about being on the back of such a noble beast.

They reached the end of the island and kept going across the sea. A few minutes later, they passed an island filled with sandy beaches. But still Henri kept flying.

"Where are we going?" She had to yell to make herself heard over the wind.

"We just passed Isle Carna," Henri yelled back. "Isle Nyx is the next one, which is our destination."

They flew over the island of sand quickly and within moments, were sailing over the open ocean again. Abrina was amazed at the speed of the cajuna. She wondered how far they could travel before they got tired. Could she fly all the way to Florryn on one? She'd have to ask Henri. She much preferred cajuna to taking a boat. Less chance of meeting a sea serpent that way too.

A dark speck appeared below them. From what Abrina could tell, there wasn't anything other than black rock interspersed with some trees. Compared to Elandel though, this island was a desert. What in all of Almarryn did the prince want to show her?

"This is it!" Henri called, circling his cajuna lower as they approached. Abrina followed suit.

He led them to a clearing that was entirely made of black rock. The ground got closer and closer, and for a moment, all of Abrina's fears about flying returned. How was she supposed to land this thing?

But a slight jostle was all that she felt as her cajuna touched down on solid rock.

Henri dismounted and offered a hand to Abrina. Again, she slapped it away, but this time it was more playful. She jumped down and petted her cajuna affectionately on the nose. The creature squealed quietly and nuzzled her hand.

"What did you say her name was?"

"Hyna. She's my mother's favorite."

Abrina could see why. Hyna was a sweet creature, once you got to know her. Perhaps more like Beri than she'd originally thought.

"Well, this is the place," Henri said. "Isle Nyx, one of the first colonies to be settled by Tigahelens. It's abandoned now though, thanks to a volcanic eruption a hundred years ago."

Abrina scrunched her brows. The island was mostly black rocks and sparse trees from what she could tell. Not exactly the jungle paradise of Elandel. "Why'd you bring me here?"

He smiled. "This island is home to one of the very first Ligerthian temples outside of Ligerthia."

Abrina raised an eyebrow. "So?"

Henri shook his head, scoffing. "You can't be serious. It's an ancient and powerful source of knowledge, sacred to the Goddess. All Ligerthian Temples are, though this one is older than most. But I've never been able to get in."

He sounded dejected about not being able to see a bunch of books. It wasn't exactly her idea of a romantic getaway, but to each their own, she supposed.

Still, the idea of exploring a lost library did not sound appealing to her. "You took me here to see an abandoned building full of books . . . that you can't enter?"

Henri huffed. "Well, when you put it like that . . ."

Abrina tilted her head. "You said it was an adventure. A locked building doesn't really count as an adventure."

"You got to fly on the cajuna to get here."

He had a point. She patted the nose of her cajuna, who nuzzled into her hand. "Fair enough. That alone was definitely worth it." She moved back to Hyna's side, ready to mount again. "Well, this is a lovely rest area, but let's get going, shall we?"

Henri shook his head. "The cajuna need a little rest before we fly back. Besides, don't you want to explore?"

She glanced at the barren landscape. There really wasn't much there . . . other than a black mountain.

She squinted as something sparkled in the sunlight. What on Almarryn could possibly be sparkling on this barren rock? "I think I see something!"

She took off sprinting, trying not to slip on the loose scree.

"That's what I thought," she heard Henri say behind her.

She chose to ignore him.

It took nearly an hour for them to reach the glittering summit of the island, where the gleam was coming from. Abrina, despite her training and daily exercises, found herself out of breath. She sat down on a rock to rest for a moment.

Henri sat down next to her and handed her a canteen.

"Thanks," Abrina said, taking a swig of the earthy-flavored water.

She handed it back to him when she'd slaked her thirst. "What is this place?"

Before them stretched a wall of black stone that had a portion fallen like a crumbled door to reveal a structure made of glittering white rocks unlike anything else on the island. Thick columns lined the front and intricate relief sculptures were carved into the surface. The structure was at least as tall as the Great Tree on the main island, if not taller. Two white stone knights stood at each side, long staffs crossing in an X. What was most peculiar was that there wasn't a door anywhere to be seen.

"This is the Ligerthian Temple I told you about." Henri took a swig from the canteen.

"But there's no door."

"I told you, it's locked." He grinned. "I've tried for years to get in, but all that ever happens is that the knights tell me to train more."

Abrina frowned. "The knights . . . you mean the stone knights?" That was impossible. Stone didn't talk.

"Of course. They're the spirits of Ligerthian Knights. Like me."

Abrina blinked slowly. "You're . . . a Ligerthian Knight?"

Henri bowed his head, clasping his fist to his chest. "At your service, milady."

Abrina couldn't help it—she started laughing. She wasn't sure if it was from the shock of traveling with the prince who happened to be her intended—whose presence she was enjoying immensely—or finding out that he was a Ligerthian Knight. Everyone knew the Ligerthian Knights had been wiped out fifty years ago when Ligerthia fell. No one had seen one since.

"You can't possibly be . . ." she wheezed when she'd stopped laughing. "They're all dead."

"Not all of us," Henri said, folding his arms. He didn't sound amused. "I'm one of the few that remain."

She eyed him shrewdly. He didn't seem to be joking. "You're not Ligerthian though, are you?"

He shook his head. "My mother was. She escaped The Fall and came to Tigahel where she met my father, the king. She wasn't able to have me until twenty years ago though."

Abrina blinked, processing that information. "Your mother doesn't look a day over forty summers."

Henri chuckled wryly. "She's much older than that. She'll never tell me how old though."

Abrina raised an eyebrow. "Probably because it's a nosy question."

"You asked it first."

She laughed again. "Fair point."

They lapsed into silence, Abrina looking out over the barren black landscape below them. The ocean sparkled in the distance, a brilliant jewel against the blackness of the island.

"So you're really a Ligerthian Knight?" It didn't seem possible.

"My mother, the last queen of Ligerthia, knighted me on my twelfth birthday, making it official." His expression grew sad. "It was my father's dying wish. I-I wanted to honor him."

"Oh." Abrina bit her lip, wanting to lay a hand on his knee. Was that appropriate here? She didn't know. All she knew was that she wanted to comfort him somehow. How did one comfort their intended? Was it the same way one comforted a comrade?

Well, Goddess take her, she didn't have experience comforting anyone. So she decided to share a little of her own pain.

"I lost my own father five years ago."

Henri nodded. "I know. I'm deeply sorry for your loss. There's nothing like losing a father."

There really wasn't.

Abrina stared at the stone soldiers. "Do you think they'll let us in?" It seemed a foolish question. Stone didn't move. Or talk.

Henri shrugged. "Maybe this time will be different. Come on. Let's bow to the stone."

Abrina laughed again. "Bow to stone? Be serious, prince boy."

"I am serious. It's a Ligerthian Knight ritual. Treat everything in the temple with respect, including the rocks that form the building. You never know how blessed something may be."

She raised an eyebrow but stood up and followed his lead. He approached the statues—which she could now tell were wearing the same kind of robes he was, holding the same kind of staff he'd used on the trip—and knelt.

Nothing happened.

"Princess." Henri inclined his head toward her.

Sighing, Abrina got down on her knees next to Henri.

Immediately, Abrina felt a presence with them.

"*AT EASE*," a deep voice called. It sounded older than the land, possibly even as old as the stars. Abrina looked around for the source, but she didn't see a living soul.

"Who's speaking?" she asked warily, her hand inching toward her blade.

"*WE ARE THE GUARDIANS OF KNOWLEDGE, PRINCESS ABRINA OF FLORRYN. WE GUARD THE LOST TOMES OF THE AGES. YOUR DESTINY LIES IN OUR VAULTS.*"

Abrina blinked. "My . . . destiny?" She shot a look at Henri, who shrugged.

"*THE FATE OF ALL ALARIA LIES IN YOUR HANDS, PRINCESS. IF YOU DESIRE TO LEARN YOUR DESTINY, YOU AND THE PRINCE MAY ENTER. OTHERWISE, DEPART THIS PLACE AND NEVER RETURN.*"

"Ominous," she mumbled. But something thrilled within her. A destiny? More than coming to Tigahel and marrying Henri? As delightful as he was . . . she'd always hoped to do more for her people. She glanced over at Henri again. He had a thoughtful look on his face.

"What do you think?" she asked.

"I've never been this close," Henri said, sounding awestruck. "I thought all the libraries were locked fifty years ago. Do you know what this means?"

She rolled her eyes. Of course he'd be interested in the books. "Henri, I'm talking about my destiny. Didn't you hear the statues?"

Henri nodded. "Yes, but the sheer knowledge that must be in those walls! So much about everyone's destinies!"

Abrina smirked at him. Prince boy liked his books apparently. It explained a lot.

If she was honest with herself though, she was intrigued by what the statues had said. What did this library have to say about her destiny?

"We wish to enter," she called out in a loud clear voice.

The ground rumbled as the statues lifted their crossed staffs. A door suddenly appeared between them, opening inwardly on a hidden seam.

"*ENTER.*"

The darkness was all-encompassing. Abrina couldn't see the walls, any shelves, or any sunlight from the world outside. It was as if the building had swallowed the sun.

Her hand reached for her sword, but instead she bumped into Henri's arm.

"Henri?" she whispered.

"I'm here, Princess." His voice was reassuring, though she'd never admit it to anyone.

A light gleamed in the distance. It glowed white, almost a blindingly bright white. It approached, washing over her. Suddenly the room became flooded with brightness, and she could see Henri again. His mouth was open as he stared at the room in front of them.

Abrina followed his eyes. "Goddess's breath," she whispered.

Floor-to-ceiling shelves filled the brightly lit space that was as big as the Great Tree. The shelves were carved out of solid white stone and filled with hundreds and hundreds of scrolls and books. Statues graced the corners of the room, though Abrina couldn't make out what they depicted from where they stood. Something glittered on the ceiling far above. Looking up, Abrina thought she saw stars twinkling on the dark dome. The whole place felt eerie, even chilly. Like a tomb.

"We're probably the first living creatures here in decades," Henri said, his voice soft.

Which was an incredible feat by any warrior's code, Abrina had to admit. But they had to stay focused on their mission. She looked at Henri. "Where might information on destinies be?"

Henri shrugged. "Your guess is as good as mine." He reached out to touch the volumes gracing the nearest shelf. "Maybe just look at what's here?"

He pulled a volume down and stared at it, a look of euphoria on his face. "This is the most beautiful thing I've ever seen," he whispered.

Abrina shook her head and reached out to pull a tome from a shelf. But when she stared at the words, she couldn't read it.

The letters looked like scribbles looping over one another in some ancient font. It was baffling.

"Henri? What does this say?"

Henri pulled the book close. "*The Goddess's Ascent to the Palace of the Stars by Van Vinderbrook.*" He glanced up at her. "You can't read Old Alarian, can you?"

She shook her head, scowling. "No one but Ligerthians can, prince boy."

He chuckled softly. "I had forgotten the world had given up the tongue of the ancients. I don't think you'll be able to read any of these tomes, Princess."

Abrina made a face at him. Of course she wouldn't be able to. If they were written in a dead language, then none of this knowledge the statues had spoken about would be accessible to her. How was she supposed to find anything about her destiny if she couldn't read anything here?

"Fine. You read your dusty books. I'll scout out the library."

"You do that," Henri said, pulling down another book, this one leafy green with swirling silver handwriting on the cover. "*The Collected Works of Alin the Wise.* I don't even know why they have this one. Alin wasn't very wise at all. His philosophies about the nature of Forging are opaque at best. I wonder if they have Malev's counterproposal to Alin's work. I couldn't ever find that one in Mother's library . . ." He started muttering to himself as he reached for other tomes.

Abrina stared at him for several seconds, shook her head, and turned to walk down the aisles of books. Henri was turning out to be far more . . . book-learned than she'd imagined. Maybe that explained how he had in Jeru's Keep and on the boat with the sea serpent.

For half a second, she wished she could read the ancient tongue like he could. Maybe there were things in the books that would be helpful to her.

Then she shook her head again and continued walking down the aisles to the distant statues.

She reached the first one, which towered over her. It depicted the Goddess in one of her many lives, though Abrina didn't know which one. She had six arms, each bearing a different fruit. Abrina noticed one of the fruits was the same shape as the purple fruit she had eaten for breakfast. She grimaced and moved along. The fruit was unappetizing to the extreme. That statue most certainly didn't have anything to do with her destiny.

The next statue showed what must have been an actual Ligerthian Knight. He also towered over her and held a staff in his hand. The knight wore the same flowing robes Henri wore with an insignia carved over the right breast. It looked like a flower merged with a sword. He was wearing a helmet, so she couldn't make out his face, but he looked fierce. A warrior.

If they all looked like that, then why did Ligerthia fall? She shook her head and kept walking.

The next statue was of another Ligerthian Knight, this one carrying a sword in a defensive position. The next five statues afterwards were all different Ligerthian Knights, all wielding different weapons. She gave each a glance before moving on to the next one. She saw a spear, a mace and chain, a shield, and a battle-ax, but nothing called to her. Where was the destiny the statues outside had promised?

In the middle of the library, she found a statue that depicted another woman, but this one wasn't the Goddess. For one, she only had two arms. For two, she was wearing the same robes as the Ligerthian Knights, but with a flowing cape and a thick belt. She had a circlet set on her brow, held a staff with a diamond cut into the top, and clutched a book in her other arm. A large wolf rested by her feet.

Abrina stared at the wolf for several moments. The wolf looked suspiciously like the Alarian wolves that graced the art of Florryn's manors. There was even a wolf on the Florrynian coat of arms. Why did this statue have one?

She blinked and her eyes caught on the two identical swords strapped onto each hip of the statue. They were short blades, but the grips were carved in the shape of a dragon, the tails curling around the pommels with the heads facing the blades, which were etched in swirling fire.

There was something about the swords that drew her in. She reached her hand to touch the hilt and felt an engraving. Peering at it, she tried to discern what it said, but it was in that strange loopy script she had seen on the book cover. Old Alarian, Henri had called it. There was something about the swords . . . she had to know what they said.

"Henri?" she called out.

"Abrina?" his voice came from the front of the library. "What is it?"

"I think I found something. Come look at this."

Within moments, Henri appeared by her statue. For a large man, he sure moved quickly.

His eyes widened. "The First Queen." He bowed to the statue.

"Look at her swords," Abrina said, still bewildered by his bowing to statues. Ligerthian Knights made no sense.

Henri glanced at the dragonheaded swords. "Their craftsmanship is unique, Princess, I'll give you that, but I'm not sure why you called me over."

"Look at the blade. There's something engraved there, but I can't read it."

Henri ran his finger over the engraving, tracing the loopy letters. "Old Alarian! *Hilka e dyoin—*"

"Translate it, please," Abrina interrupted. She didn't want to hear it in the strange tongue—it sounded like gibberish.

"Alaria's hope and salvation."

"Well. That's helpful." Abrina glared at the swords. She was expecting something more. And with the wolf . . . that had felt like a clear indicator of her destiny.

She walked around it a few times, trying to see if there was something the statue was hiding, but there wasn't anything there. Maybe she'd been wrong and there was nothing special to this statue.

"Abrina, look at this," Henri said. "There's a word here on the wolf's nose."

"What?" Abrina looked where Henri was pointing and sure enough saw a tiny bit of the loopy script on the wolf's nose.

"*Eryon,*" the prince whispered.

A sudden thud sounded, startling Abrina into her battle-ready stance. She whipped her sword out, ready to fight . . . the moving statue.

The statue vibrated, the wolf's jaw opening like the lid to a chest, revealing a brown leather-bound book, tied with a golden ribbon. The statue thudded again, but the wolf's jaw remained open, the book gleaming at them.

"What in the Palace of Stars?" Abrina muttered, sheathing her sword.

Henri grabbed the book. Brilliant golden letters spun across the surface.

He turned to face her, his face alight with wonder. "Princess! This is the First Queen's diary!"

Abrina's heart started to pound. There was something about that book. Something that filled her with dread.

"Read it then," she said softly.

He smiled a reassuring smile at her before untying the ribbon, flipping the book open, and beginning to read.

"*They do not know why I did it, and they never will. But for the future of Alaria, it had to be done.*

"*My brothers have left the kingdom, breaking my parents' hearts. The Goddess will look out for them, but I worry. They both left with their armies and followers. I know they won't be back.*

"*But they will one day need to be reconciled. They will one day need to reunite, even if they can't now see past their hatred for each other. Their descendants will all be destroyed unless they do. I've foreseen it.*

"*I cannot yet tell my parents about the Forged Dragonblades. They will only be saddened further. They do not think it is possible for my brothers to ever be reunited.*

"*But the Goddess has warned me. The Dragonblades will be the salvation of Alaria. She showed me how to make them. They are her design. But their power can only be accessed by blood descendants of my brothers. I doubt they will be able to set aside their pride. I doubt the Goddess, though I know I shouldn't. She is wise, she is just, and she is all-knowing. Her prophecy is the only safeguard protecting the future. I only pray that it works.*

"*I fear for my descendants. They will not know how to access the power of the Dragonblades. But they must guard them. Alaria's only hope resides in the power of these swords. They must be kept safe. They must be preserved.*

"*I know not who shall read these words, but if you are a descendant of my brothers, I leave you a warning. Do not seek to use the Dragon-*

blades for glory. They will only work when wielded with pure love. The Goddess has shown me that this must be so. I cannot deny her word."

Henri paused and looked at Abrina. "The dragonblades," he whispered in awe, before pointing toward the twin swords that were strapped to the sides of the First Queen statue. "That must be what those are."

Abrina's heart was pounding even fiercer. There was something in those words that unsettled her. "She said their power can only be accessed by the descendants of her brothers. Who were her brothers?"

Henri looked at her quizzically. "Princess, haven't you read your history? The First Queen was the elder sister to King Flor and King Olean."

No. *No.* Not Oleanders.

She shuddered. "You can't mean Oleanders!" she spat out. "They're liars, thieves, and betrayers, every one of them. They take whatever they can get. If there hadn't been a treaty twenty years ago, they'd have driven us from our home too."

Henri looked at her sadly. "Princess. Perhaps you misunderstand them. There must be wisdom to what the First Queen is saying. Don't you see? Perhaps this is your destiny!"

Abrina's fists clenched in fury. This was not her destiny. "Henri, they hate my nation. They've slaughtered thousands of my people over the last one hundred years. They pushed us beyond the mountains. They refused trade with us for centuries before that. How can the First Queen expect me to get along with a descendant of *them*?! They're the spawn of the fiery python!"

Henri shook his head again and glanced back at the book. He flipped through a few more pages. It irked her. Why couldn't he understand? Florryn had never gotten along with Oleanders. And they never would. If not for the treaty twenty years ago, they'd still be at war.

"Oh, Princess," Henri said, his voice so soft Abrina barely caught it.

"What?" she snapped. Then she swallowed, allowing a little of her anger to dissolve. It wasn't Henri she was mad at.

She tried again. "What did you find?"

Henri looked at her with a deep sadness in his eyes. "Listen to this."

"Darkness looms, ice storms approach.
Devouring the land, Alaria encroached.
The end of days will soon be nigh,
All will be frozen and left to die.

But a spark burns within this night,
Two royal hearts can set this right.
From nations at war, yet with shared royal blood,
Only they can stem the flood.

Only together will they be strong,
Only together will they right this wrong.
Else the world will fail, and life will cease,
The end of hope, the end of peace."

"Shared royal blood?" Abrina repeated blankly. "What do you suppose that means?"

Henri shook his head, frowning. "I-I don't know. But this isn't good. Abrina . . . I have a bad feeling about this. We need to go tell my mother."

Abrina wasn't so sure about that, but she couldn't shake the sense of dread that filled her as she stared at the book. Was this her destiny?

If it was, she definitely didn't want it.

Chapter Nineteen

Kailyn

Kailyn awoke the next morning to a loud crash accompanied by a male voice swearing in the front room.

Aru? Canis sounded sleepy, but he padded after her as she hastily threw on her dress and ran out to find Mirnabad had tripped over Myira sleeping on the floor. Both siblings were tangled up and looked murderous.

"Princess!" Myira said, scrambling to get herself back to her feet. "How did you sleep?"

"Well enough," she said, glancing around. "Is Benje back?"

Myira shook her head. "He was gone all night."

Kailyn sighed, her heart clenching in worry. She hoped Benje was alright.

Safe. Canis sent her an image of Benje with his sword on his back and she smiled softly. She knew the pup was right. Benje could take care of himself—he'd already proven that. But she missed his companionship.

"Don't you worry, siebald. Any worries you have, you can tell me." Mirnabad winked at her only to be slapped by Myira. Canis growled at him.

"Knock it off, lyir," she snarled.

Mirnabad cursed. "Really, Myira? It's too early for your claws this morning."

"Well, it's too early for you to be drunk, yet here we are."

Mirnabad put his hand to his heart. "*Ze ben*! Sister, I'm offended! I'm only mildly intoxicated at best." He put his hand to his head and swooned dramatically onto the couch.

Myira sighed and nudged Mirnabad's boot for good measure. Mirnabad had started to snore, but Kailyn couldn't tell if it was real or fake.

"Come on, Princess," Myira said. "Let me do your hair."

She grabbed Kailyn's hand and led her to the back room, where she fixed Kailyn's dress and started combing her hair. Canis curled up by Kailyn's foot.

Kailyn glanced at the wolf cub thoughtfully. "Do you think your brother will take us on his ship?" She wasn't sure she wanted closer proximity to Mirnabad, but they did need to get to Tigahel.

Myira paused combing. "I think he will, though if he had his way, he'd want us to do tricks to get onto his ship."

Kailyn wondered why Myira sounded so angry about her brother. He seemed a decent sort, even if he did like his drinking and the company of women a bit too much. "What happened with you and your brother anyway?"

Myira sighed and resumed combing. "It's a long story."

"I'm not going anywhere," Kailyn said with a smile, which quickly faded. She wasn't going anywhere until Benje got back, and if he didn't get back soon, she'd personally go out and search for him, even if there were guards looking for her. He'd been gone far too long. "Please, Myira. I need something to distract me from Benje."

"Oh, very well. I suppose a story would be a good distraction." Myira kept combing. "My brother has always been a more . . . adventurous soul. And he wanted to make his way early in life. So at the tender age of fourteen, he left to travel the far reaches of the known world. But his ship was besieged by pirates, and we didn't hear from him. Months went by. We thought he was dead. My mother was heartbroken."

"Ah," Kailyn said, starting to realize where this was going. It sounded like one of her stories. "But he didn't die by pirates."

"No, he joined with them, if you can believe it! He became a pirate and was so well-liked by his crew that he became captain! And *then* he sailed home to see his family."

Kailyn frowned. "I can't imagine your mother was very happy about that."

"She was livid! She wanted to skin him alive for worrying her down to her sickbed! She was angry that he hadn't come home for five years. I've never seen her that angry."

Kailyn was still confused. "But how did that affect your relationship with him?"

Myira tugged a little harder on Kailyn's hair and Kailyn winced.

"Sorry, Princess. Sorry. He, the ungrateful *vyko* that he is, started coming to town more frequently and bringing his . . . his foul women with him! Maman kicked them out, and he respected her wishes, until she died. But now he keeps bringing them here, even though he knows I hate it."

Kailyn frowned. "Why doesn't he go anywhere else?"

"He used to. Before Oleanders came to Tyloan. But with their frequent patrols, and him being a wanted criminal in Oleanders, fancy that, he has to keep a low profile."

"It's a miracle he hasn't been discovered yet," Kailyn mused, thinking about the guards they had run into the night before.

"Yes. It is." Myira's tone got sad. Kailyn's heart went out to her maid. She had no idea her life was like that.

Aru? Canis nuzzled against her leg.

I'm fine, Canis, she thought, projecting an image of her and her maids laughing together. She wished Myira could have stayed at the palace. If only she'd had the good sense to stay put that day with the parchment. Sure, she wouldn't have met Benje then, but maybe Myira's life would have been better.

"I'm so sorry, Myira." The words weren't enough, but they were all she knew.

"It's alright, Princess. It's not your fault my brother is the way he is." Myira's well-trained hands kept twisting and tucking Kailyn's hair until she pronounced her finished.

"Now, if you wear a Tyloan scarf, it should be harder for you to be recognized," she said, grabbing a silky blue scarf from a drawer and tying it around Kailyn's hair. "Though it is such a shame to hide your pretty hair."

Kailyn smiled sadly. "Yes, but I'd rather not be immediately recognized if we have to sneak out tonight to get to your brother's ship."

At that, Mirnabad poked his head into the room. "Sorry to disturb you, ladies, but your friend has returned."

Kailyn's heart quickened and Canis perked up his head again. *Safe!* Canis padded his way out of the room, and Kailyn quickly followed.

Benje was back! Benje, despite being covered in colored dust again, smiled when he saw Kailyn and Canis, who'd run up to him and was rubbing his face against Benje's leg.

"I'm glad you're safe, Princess. The guards are everywhere. They've been searching all the buildings, and it was all I could do to convince them you were seen at the other end of town. We don't have very long."

"What are you talking about?" Mirnabad said, his hand holding a bunch of ice to his head. Kailyn wondered where he had found the ice, because she was confident ice didn't keep well in the Tyloan heat.

"We wanted to ask if we could come with you on your next adventure," Kailyn said with as much confidence as she could muster. Mirnabad unnerved her.

"With me? On my ship? I'm flattered, truly I am." Mirnabad said, a smile splitting his face. He looked far more charming with the smile, but Canis kept sending her thoughts of *danger*. Mirnabad was not a trustworthy soul. She'd have to be on her guard around him on his ship.

"But we have one slight problem," Mirnabad went on. "As your friend has mentioned, guards are everywhere. They won't exactly be happy to see me either." He scratched his gold tattoo. "If they were Cyronian guards, I could simply bribe them and be on my way. But Oleanders . . ." He sighed. "We'll have to wait until dark."

"They might have searched here by then," Benje said, crossing his arms across his chest. "We can't wait that long."

Canis scampered back to Kailyn and she picked the cub up in her arms, stroking his fur to calm her raging heart.

"We'll have to stay in hiding here." Mirnabad shrugged. "I can't convince them in the day that I'm a sea-faring merchant. But at night, ah, the magic of the night!"

Myira shot him a look. "We can't wait until night, Mirnabad. If we're discovered. . ."

"You'll be executed for treason?" Mirnabad said, quirking his eyebrow. It sounded like he was joking, but Kailyn knew he wasn't talking about them. But it was far more serious than he knew.

"I'll be taken back to Oleanders and forced to marry the prince of Oronia," she said quietly. "My people will be under Oronian rule, a part of their glorious empire." She felt tears prick her eyes as she stroked Canis's fur. "And I'll be powerless to stop any of it."

Aru? Canis nestled in her arms, sending her calming images of snowy landscapes, but they only reminded her of the frost giants and the reasons they had to get to Tigahel.

Both Benje and Myira shot her quizzical looks. Mirnabad's eyes widened.

"*Zen badin*! Princess Kailyn!" He saluted her awkwardly. Kailyn didn't know what to think of that. She wasn't anyone's princess out here.

"Shhh!" Myira said, looking around as if guards lurked in the shadows of her apartment.

Mirnabad scratched his tattoo again. "Of course, if I take the princess, I expect to get paid for my troubles."

Benje narrowed his eyes at Mirnabad. "You will get your payment, pirate. But first we need to get to your ship. The sooner the better."

Mirnabad smiled, his eyes growing calculating, causing a shudder to go down Kailyn's spine. "I have just the plan."

They decided to wait until the heat of the day, when the guards were the most tired by the unrelenting sun. Mirnabad was confident that this was their best time to sneak past the patrols. He advised them on what attire to wear and how to act to sneak past the guards as they made their way to his ship.

Kailyn wasn't so sure his great plan would work, but she knew that if they were discovered, she would never get the chance to go to Tigahel and never be able to help anyone ever again. She'd be brought back to Oleanders and forced to marry Prince Zolan.

That is, if Lord Shielen didn't lock her up until the end of time for escaping Oleanders. Or Oleanders froze first.

So, saying a prayer to the Goddess, she donned the costume Mirnabad had acquired for her. It was a brilliant orange gown, covered with sequins and feathers. The neckline was a little lower than comfortable, but the skirts were layered and full. Mirnabad liked how Myira had done her hair, but he insisted that Myira add make-up. Kailyn had only worn the colored powder a handful of times back home, and only ever to her father's festivities, but the way Myira applied it this time was different. She added pinks to her cheek and spread cream on her lips. She finished with a fine white powder that tickled Kailyn's nose.

She replaced Kailyn's blue silk scarf and nodded once. "There."

Kailyn reached for the hand mirror but Myira shook her head. "Trust me, Princess. You don't want to see."

Kailyn quirked an eyebrow. "That bad?"

"You'd look lovely in anything. But I despise my brother for this plan. Come on, they're waiting for us."

When they left the backroom, Benje was standing by the window again. He had changed into all black clothes, his sword strapped onto his back in the style of the Cyronians. It suited him. Canis peeked his head over Benje's pouch.

Color, the pup sent Kailyn's way. Kailyn felt like a walking painting, which wasn't a flattering feeling.

Mirnabad whistled appreciatively when he saw them, tipping an extravagant black hat at them. Kailyn wasn't sure where he had gotten it. It had at least fifteen feathers of all different colors stuck into it and had the floppiest brim she had ever seen.

"Good, good! You'll make excellent distractions. Are we ready?"

Benje's eyes locked with Kailyn. He was quiet, but his brown eyes spoke volumes. Kailyn blushed under his gaze. She felt exposed, despite the many layers of the dress.

"This better work, Mirnabad," he said, his voice low.

"Tut tut, we discussed this, my good sir. It's *Captain* to you."

Benje growled but didn't say anything.

"Yes, it'll work." Mirnabad said with a twirl of his hat. "Let's go."

At first, everything went according to plan. Benje had told them there were guards stationed by the docks and guards who patrolled the streets searching for the princess. They followed Benje past the buildings where Myira's apartment was toward the docks.

Danger!

Kailyn stiffened as she spied the shining silver armor of two guards on watch. She hoped Canis would stay safe.

Then again, the pup was with Benje. She knew he'd be safe.

Mirnabad placed his arms around both Myira and Kailyn and swayed drunkenly. Kailyn felt a slither of revulsion crawl up her spine.

"Laugh like this," Myira hissed, and then let loose a simpering giggle that made Kailyn's stomach churn.

But they had to act the part. So she pretended to giggle in the same way Myira had and tried not to cringe. She hated the sound that came out. She sounded like an idiot, the kind she had read about in some of her father's books.

The two guards eyed them but smiled when Kailyn waved at them.

"What's your business, citizens?" said the taller and thinner of the two.

"Ah, my good sirs," Mirnabad said in a drawl. "We're here to see my beauty of a ship!"

"And what ship is that, citizen?"

"*The Raven Queen,* good sirs. She's the finest ship on the waters!"

The other guard checked his papers. "That's registered to a man named Tobis Relen. Is that you, citizen?"

"Ah, yes. Captain Tobis Relen at your service," Mirnabad said, tipping his head in their direction. "These ladies are to accompany me on my next voyage."

The first guard lifted an eyebrow. "And their names are?"

Myira giggled. "Nyia Holtis and my cousin Nea Thander," she said.

Kailyn had picked her fake name based on Myira's suggestion it be something she could remember. This whole adventure reminded her of her other maids. She missed them dearly.

The second guard scribbled down their names on his paper. "Very well. Do you have their papers to travel out of Cyron?"

"Papers? Papers, my good sir, we don't need papers to travel!" Mirnabad sounded offended.

"We have our orders, citizen."

Kailyn's heart plummeted. Mirnabad hadn't mentioned anything about them needing papers. He only said they would distract the guards with their feminine charms. She was starting to realize how terrible a plan it really was.

"Ah, but how about another favor, good sir?" Mirnabad said, reaching into a pouch at his side.

"Unless it's their papers, you may not proceed," said the first guard, an ice-cold edge seeping into his voice.

Suddenly, a knife appeared in the man's chest.

"What the—" the other guard said before a second knife appeared in his chest. They both dropped dead at the trio's feet.

"Mirnabad!" Myira screamed.

Mirnabad raised his hands. "It wasn't me this time! I swear on Maman's grave!"

Benje stepped out from the pier where he'd been hiding, Canis's white head still poking out of the pack, but the pup was quiet. With a start, Kailyn realized Canis had fallen asleep.

Benje calmly walked over and picked up the two knives and cleaned them on a guard's tunic before sliding the bodies into the sea.

"We don't have much time," he said as way of explanation.

Kailyn's blood pounded fiercely in her ears. What had happened? He'd killed two men like it was nothing! With Canis asleep in his pack! She shook her head, trying to grapple with the different versions of Benje she'd seen. What kind of man was he?

Without any other complaints, the group followed Mirnabad onto his ship, *The Raven Queen*. It was a smaller ship, not as big as some of the Oleanderian cargo vessels, but Kailyn could tell it was fast. There was a small crew manning it that waved when they saw Mirnabad.

"Ahoy, Captain!" one of them cried out. "How was your leave?"

Mirnabad's voice turned business-like. "Nevermind that, Pierr, we must weigh anchor!"

"But Captain—"

"No! We must leave Cyron at once!"

The crew didn't further protest and soon had the ship launched into the harbor. Kailyn wondered how long they would have until the dead guards were missed. She was still trying not to think about how suddenly the knives had appeared. How quick Benje had been to kill. Was he an assassin in addition to a spy? She sighed. There was more to Benje than he let on.

She was jarred from her thoughts when Mirnabad grabbed her hand. "Princess, you should probably be belowdecks until we've reached the open ocean."

"But—" she started to protest, but Mirnabad held a hand to her lip.

"No protests. Please. This may get ugly," he said seriously. Behind him, Kailyn could barely make out a small ship at the edge of the harbor. It flew the colors of Oleanders. She swallowed. They could very easily get caught. And they didn't have time for that.

"Come on, Princess," Myira said, tugging Kailyn gently. "I'll take you down to the galley."

"Not there, Myira." Mirnabad shook his head. "Follow me, both of you."

He led them belowdecks through a twisting maze of corridors. There was a slightly fishy air to the ship, which didn't help Kailyn's nerves. She wished she could remove the uncomfortable orange dress and wear her outfit from the gnomes again, but they had left her old gown behind because Mirnabad had told them they needed to be convincing in their roles. She was regretting that decision now.

Aru? Canis sounded like he'd just woken up.

Kailyn stopped and turned. "Wait, Canis!" she said.

"The pup will be fine with your friend topside," Mirnabad said. "Come. This way."

He led them down to a room filled with crates and opened a hatch in the floor that blended in seamlessly. If she hadn't seen Mirnabad open the hatch, she never would have known it was there.

Kailyn eyed the hole warily, still hearing Canis in her thoughts. She didn't like the look of that square dark hole or being separated from her pup and from Benje. For all she knew, Mirnabad was throwing her into the open ocean.

"Princess, please. It's a smuggler's hold. They won't find you down here. Myira will stay with you, won't you, sister?"

"Yes." Myira squeezed Kailyn's arm, the touch reassuring, but Kailyn still didn't want to get in the hold. Who knew what horrors lurked down there?

"Good. Get in!" Mirnabad gestured to the hatch.

Kailyn hesitated. Should she trust Mirnabad? His first plan hadn't turned out so great. If Benje hadn't been following them, they would have been turned over to Lord Shielen for sure.

"Princess, please," the captain pleaded, sincerity shining in his golden eyes. "We can't have them discover you. It would be bad for business."

Kailyn sighed and went down the hole. It was more spacious at the bottom than she had considered, although she could barely stand up straight. She felt the waves outside the boat and wobbled, leaning on the wall for support. Myira came down the ladder and stood next to her, holding onto Kailyn's arm.

"You'll let us out, won't you, brother?"

"When we're clear of them, yes." Mirnabad closed the lid of the hold, and they were thrown into the darkness.

"Myira?" Kailyn winced, hating how creaky her voice sounded.

"I'm here, Princess."

"Do you think they'll find us?"

She squeezed Kailyn's arm. "My brother may not be the most intelligent human in Almarryn, but he has succeeded as a pirate for years. I think we'll be alright."

But Myira's words didn't reassure her. She wondered what was happening above deck. Were they moments away from being discovered? Would the guards kill them all on sight? Including Canis and Benje?

Her heart clenched with fear. She couldn't imagine a world without either of them. Even if Benje had been very distant since they got to Tyloan, he'd rescued her so many times already. And Canis trusted him.

She bit her lip to stop it from trembling. She couldn't bear if something happened to them. She prayed with all her might that the Goddess would see them out of this. They had to make it to Tigahel. They had to. No one else could save her people.

Chapter Twenty

Kailyn

Kailyn didn't know when she had fallen asleep, but she woke up when the hold opened and Mirnabad called down that it was safe for them to leave. Kailyn got up, her legs shaky. She clutched on to Myira's hand for support before grabbing the ladder. Her stomach roiled. She felt sicker than she ever had before.

"Are they gone?" she heard Myira ask as she clutched the ladder. The ship swayed again, and her stomach lurched.

"Yes. They searched the entire ship, but they didn't find the smuggler's hold, like I knew they wouldn't. They didn't even hear about the murder of the guards. We're in the clear."

Kailyn nodded mutely, trying to keep her stomach clenched. She'd barely made it halfway up the ladder.

"Princess?" Myira's voice was soft behind her. "Are you alright?"

Kailyn kept climbing, afraid of answering. She reached the top of the ladder and grabbed Mirnabad's hand. She swayed again with the ship before vomiting the contents of her stomach.

"I think she's seasick," Mirnabad said, with what sounded like concern, but Kailyn couldn't have been sure. Her ears were ringing.

Aru? came Canis's voice to her mind. *Sick?*

Kailyn didn't even have the energy to send calming thoughts to the pup. She clutched her stomach as she heaved again.

"I think she should lie down," Myira said, having climbed out of the hole and was now helping Mirnabad support Kailyn.

"Follow me," Mirnabad said. Kailyn was barely aware of anything as they carried her to a soft bed. She fell asleep almost instantly.

Kailyn's dreams were troubling. She saw massive sea creatures burst through the waves, devouring her ship. She saw herself dancing with Mirnabad, while Benje's head was stuck on a pike and Canis was chained with bright colorful feathers, howling mournfully. She saw herself being chased by guards across the Frozen Wastelands until her limbs froze in place by the frost giants' breath.

When she woke up, the lurch of the ship sent her stomach's contents into a bucket placed nearby. A cool cloth was placed on her forehead. Warm fur tickled her fingers, the presence calming. Soothing voices spoke to her, sending her back into troubled dreams.

When at last her stomach felt less queasy, Myira was sitting in front of her with a bowl of soup. Canis was curled up next to her on the bed, sleeping peacefully. Kailyn stroked his fur thoughtfully, trying to make sense of her situation. Last thing she remembered was the smuggler's hold.

"How long have I been asleep?" she rasped. Her voice sounded strange to her ears, like she had a bunch of colored powder stuck in her throat.

"Nearly a week, Your Highness," Myira said, offering her

a glass of water. Kailyn sipped the cool refreshing liquid. It soothed her throat. "We're well out of Oleanderian reach. We're nearly to Tigahel."

"Benje?" she asked, still stroking Canis's fur.

"He's been serving as a lookout. I don't think he trusts my brother or his crew."

She couldn't blame him. She glanced around the strange golden room. "Where am I?"

Myira made a face. "My brother's cabin."

Kailyn jerked forward, nearly spilling water on her sheets. Canis chuffed softly in his sleep and Kailyn's hand found a gentle stroking rhythm again, even though her thoughts were churning.

"What?"

Myira sighed. "He said it was the only place on his ship even slightly suitable for a princess. He's been staying belowdecks with his crew."

"He doesn't need to do that. I'm well enough." Kailyn swung her feet to the edge of the bed and tried to stand, but the sway of the ship sent her back onto the bed next to Canis.

"That's enough of that, Princess," Myira said, helping Kailyn get settled again. "You're not to move from this bed until I give the all clear."

Kailyn sighed and settled back onto her pillows, looking around the room. Mirnabad may be a scoundrel, but he did have a nice room. Gold seemed to be a favorite. There was a golden wheel attached to one wall, next to a golden sword. There was a golden rug draped over a table that held many small chests. Kailyn wondered vaguely what was in them. He even had a bookshelf filled with many tomes, some of them gold-bound.

"How rich is your brother?" Kailyn asked, amazed at the wealth around her. Not even her father had had such grand displays of gold in his home.

179

"Richer than he should be. Would you care for some soup?"

Myira nursed her back to health for another two days, Canis never leaving her side. By that point, Mirnabad said they were hours away from the Tigahel Archipelago. They hadn't spotted any other ships since they had left Tyloan, which was reassuring. Kailyn had thought Oleanders would be scouring the seas for her, but it seemed for the moment, they thought she was still in Tyloan. Which was just as well for her.

She had perused the tomes in Mirnabad's cabin and was pleased to discover one was in Old Alarian. She wanted to study it in depth and ask him where he'd gotten it from, but she only saw the pirate captain briefly. It was slow going without her notes, and with Myira constantly checking in on her. She loved her maid, but she was starting to feel a bit crowded. She longed for some quiet with her and Canis, who had grown again in the week of being on the ship. He was nearly twice the size he'd been when she'd found him.

Myira was humming and stitching something when Kailyn closed her book with a snap.

Aru? Canis perked up his head. Kailyn scratched his ears absently.

"Myira, is it alright if you take your leave of me tonight?"

Myira looked up from her stitching, her face full of confusion. "But Princess, what if you collapse again?"

Kailyn made a face. "Really, I'm not as soft as you think. I've been feeling better for the past few days. I think I could do with some fresh sea air."

"But my brother!"

"Has been leaving me alone the entire time we've been on board. I think I'll be alright. Besides, I'll have Canis with me."

Myira sighed. "If you're sure, Princess."

Kailyn raised an eyebrow. "You don't have to keep calling me that. I've told you—you can call me Kailyn."

Myira shook her head. "I dislike being so informal with the last princess of Oleanders. You're the only royalty left, and you deserve to be reminded of it."

Myira's words resonated with Kailyn's heart. She was the last royal of Oleanders. The thought made her sad. Even though she knew her father wasn't the best of kings or the best of fathers, she still missed him. She missed home.

Kailyn nodded once, clearing her mind of her sad thoughts. "Alright, you can call me however you wish. But I do ask for some time to myself, just for tonight."

Myira stood up, clutching her sewing. "Alright. But let me know if you need anything."

"I will, Myira."

Myira was reluctant to leave, but at last she did so. Kailyn wrapped a robe around herself and set off to the top deck to find some air, Canis padding along behind her. She was rather ashamed she'd gotten so sick. She'd always wanted to explore the ships in her father's harbor, but she'd never had the chance. Now that she was actually on a ship, she was wobbly and seasick. Fate was cruel.

Stars!

Kailyn gasped as the stars came into view. She could see the whole expanse of the heavens from here. Canis howled softly up at the glittering expanse and she smiled. She echoed his sense of wonder.

She hadn't seen the stars in such clarity before. In Olean, there were always lights on at night. She never saw the stars like this, so bright and clear in a sea of midnight black. She wondered if the Goddess saw her from up in her palace in the stars and prayed that she would guide them to Tigahel. They needed help. They needed to take back her kingdom. And to stop this threat of the frost giants. If they were on their own, they would fail. She had already failed on her own. She wasn't cut out for these types of adventures.

"It's a beautiful night out, isn't it?" came a silky voice behind her. Kailyn's heart jumped. Mirnabad.

"Yes, it is, Captain." She stared resolutely out to sea, pointedly ignoring him. Canis was still softly howling at the stars.

"Ah, come now, Princess. No need to be so formal with me."

He wrapped his arm around her. Shivers went down her spine and she jerked away.

"Captain, please. I was just enjoying the stars. I'll be going now."

Aru? Canis bounded over and growled at Mirnabad. *Poison.*

Mirnabad eyed him. "I don't think your dog likes me."

"He's a wolf," Kailyn said, her heart swelling with gratitude toward her pup. "Leave us alone, Captain." She turned to go, but Mirnabad somehow trapped her hands in his larger ones.

"Don't leave, Princess," he crooned. "I was just thinking how much more delightful this night would be with a lovely woman at my side, and you appeared! *Ze ben*, it is almost like the gods sent you to my little corner of the universe tonight."

Kailyn struggled against his grip. "I'm not here for you, Mirnabad. Please let me go."

Canis pounced on Mirnabad's foot. The captain shook the pup away, but Canis kept bashing his head against Mirnabad's leg.

Kailyn had to give the pup credit. Even if he was still small, he was fierce. She tried to yank her arm from Mirnabad's grip again and this time she succeeded, but only for a second. Mirnabad snarled and grabbed Kailyn, hoisting her off her feet.

"Put me down!" Kailyn cried, smacking her fists against Mirnabad's arms. But they only tightened around her.

Aru! Canis's voice sounded panicked.

"We'll just have to go someplace more private, siebald," Mirnabad whispered in her ear. "Somewhere without any dogs." His breath smelled strongly of fyir and the sickening smell made her stomach lurch again.

"Unhand the princess," came another voice. Canis yipped and Kailyn's heart swelled. Benje.

"'Tis my ship, man! She's a woman on my ship!"

"She doesn't belong to you, Mirnabad. Unhand her, or I'll make you." Benje's voice was as cold as steel.

Mirnabad laughed, the sound reverberating right through Kailyn's ear, and she winced as he made her sway in the air. She missed the semi-stable ground of the ship.

"Make me, then. Go on."

Kailyn saw a flash of silver before the captain suddenly released her. She wobbled to her feet, wheeling around to see Benje facing the captain, a steely look on his face.

"You alright, Princess?" he asked without looking at her.

Canis bounded up to her and started licking her face. Kailyn patted him on the head. "I'm fine, Benje." Her arms still trembled, but she was at least back on somewhat solid ground.

Danger!

She looked up to see Benje, who had sunk into a ready stance. The captain was holding his injured hand, which was bleeding. Kailyn glimpsed a sheen of silver sticking out of the railing behind him. One of Benje's knives.

Her heart hammered. The look Benje was giving the captain worried her. Was he going to kill Mirnabad, like he had those two guardsmen at the port? Part of her admired his bravery, but part of her knew that they might be thrown overboard if he succeeded.

"Benje, please!" she said. "Don't kill him."

"I'm not going to, Princess," he said, though his voice suggested otherwise.

Mirnabad snarled, having managed to wrap his injured hand with part of his sleeve. He unsheathed his sword and ran at Benje. "You can't best me from my woman!" Benje merely dodged, Mirnabad running right past him.

Mirnabad turned around and swung again, but lost his balance and toppled to the deck.

Benje hadn't even drawn his sword. He looked down at the captain. "Leave the princess alone."

Mirnabad looked confused. "But she's on my ship."

Benje drew his sword and clubbed Mirnabad on the head, knocking the captain unconscious. Canis howled again, almost like he was cheering.

Aru! Safe!

Kailyn blinked. The whole thing had happened in less than two minutes. "Benje . . . what did you do to him?"

Benje inclined his head toward the captain's prone body. "He was going to hurt you, Princess. I swore to protect you."

"He's not . . . dead?"

"I told you I wasn't going to kill him. He's going to wish he was dead when he wakes up though. Come on. Let's leave him."

He offered Kailyn his arm, which Kailyn took. She tried not to think about how nice and firm his arm was—and how safe she felt, especially compared with Mirnabad—as he led her away from the captain's slumbering body toward the portside of the ship, Canis following. They passed one of the watchmen, who eyed them curiously.

"The captain has had too much to drink again," Benje said, gesturing toward where the captain slumbered.

"Goddess's eyes, again?" the man grunted. "That's the second time today he's passed out on deck." He walked over toward the captain, grumbling the entire way.

Kailyn raised an eyebrow at Benje. "The second time today?"

"This was the first time I'd knocked him unconscious. Earlier he really did pass out."

Kailyn laughed. "That I can imagine."

They lapsed into silence as they stared at the distant stars, Canis nuzzling his head against her leg. He kept sending her images of the two of them together, which helped calm Kailyn's racing heart.

She found herself sneaking repeated glances at Benje. There was so much to this man. He had rescued her, multiple times, he had lied to her, then he'd saved her again. Canis trusted him—said that he was safe. And Kailyn couldn't forget the Ligerthian Knight's oath he had given her. Yet his skills. He was far more than a simple blacksmith.

Benje caught her staring. "Something on your mind, Princess?"

She blushed. He was also incredibly observant. "I was thinking about . . . everything that's led us here."

Benje gazed toward the horizon. "There's still much more to come."

"Tigahel."

"Yes." His voice sounded strained.

"Do you think they'll help us?" she whispered quietly. Canis had curled up by her feet again, content now that the danger was past.

"I honestly don't know," Benje said, his voice low. He gazed silently out into the distance for a moment. "I wish my master were still alive."

"Master Barholow?"

Benje nodded. "He was a master Forger—he could have made anything. If he were here, we wouldn't need to go to Tigahel. I'd never have sworn allegiance to their queen . . ." He clenched his fists. "I've failed Oleanders, Princess." That second part he said so softly it took a moment for Kailyn to parse out his words.

She sighed. "Benje . . ." She reached her hand to gently rest it on his, feeling elated at her moment of bravery. Benje flinched, but he didn't move away. "You said the frost giants are a real threat. We saw the snow in the mountains. The gnome queen said they were spreading rapidly, and that Tigahel holds answers to defeat them. If that's the case, then you've done the only thing for Oleanders."

"But the queen should never have requested you." Benje looked pained. "I don't know what we're walking into, but I don't like it."

Kailyn didn't like it either, but they had no choice. She couldn't retake her country without help. And she had nowhere else to go.

They fell into silence again, their hands still clasped. Kailyn wished there were some kind of book she could read that would help her understand Benje better. He was such a mystery to her.

Her eyes widened as she realized something. Wait a moment. The tome! Benje could read Old Alarian. Maybe he could help her translate it!

"Benje, I found a book in Old Alarian," she said. Benje turned to face her, his eyebrows furrowed.

"Here?"

"In the captain's quarters."

Benje's face hardened. "You can't keep staying there. Not after tonight."

Kailyn nodded. "Alright. But my things are still in his room."

"We'll retrieve them. Right now. The man can't keep his hands to himself and the sooner you're removed as far from him, the better."

Kailyn sighed and followed Benje down to the captain's quarters, Canis following. Snoring reached her ears as they reached the door. Her heart quickened. The crew must have moved the captain into his room again.

Benje held his finger to his lips and quietly pushed open the door. The door slid open. Mirnabad was passed out on the bed, his foot hanging off the edge. His snores filled the cabin.

He doesn't look threatening asleep, Kailyn thought.

Danger! Canis sent her way, with an image of her in Mirnabad's arms. She shuddered, remembering how helpless she'd felt. He was right. The man was dangerous, even if he was passed out from fyir overindulgence.

"Where's the tome?" Benje whispered.

"On the table there." Kailyn pointed toward the thick gold-bound book she had been trying to read earlier that day. Benje nodded before sneaking in and grabbing it. He was back so quick Kailyn didn't even have a moment to panic.

"Is there anything else you need, Princess?"

Kailyn thought of her orange gown that lay draped over the chair and shuddered again. "No. Nothing else." She wrapped her robe closer around her. She wished she had her travel gown from the gnomes. She'd be stuck with either the orange dress or the robe the rest of the voyage, and neither option appealed to her very much.

"Come on, Princess." Benje pulled her away from the captain's quarters toward another door, this one leading to a smaller, but well-kept cabin. Benje's pack from the gnomes lay by the bed. Canis sniffed the pack and fished out a root.

"I'm surprised you had any left," Kailyn remarked, sitting down next to Canis to stroke his fur.

"They keep a surprisingly long time. Besides, Canis has been fed by Myira in the kitchens, when she hasn't been taking care of you."

"Is this your room?" Kailyn asked.

Benje nodded. "But you will stay here the rest of the voyage. I'll get Myira to stay in here with you. Anything to keep that brute away from you."

Kailyn nodded. "Alright." She felt safer already, especially with her two protectors nearby.

"Now. The tome." Benje opened the volume, scanning the first page. His eyes widened.

"Breath of the Goddess!" he swore. "This is a volume of holy scripture from a Ligerthian temple!" He scowled at the door. "Where did he get it from? All the libraries have been sealed for the last fifty years."

"I don't know," Kailyn said, stroking Canis's fur.

Her mind was filled with wonder at the idea of an actual volume from the Ligerthian temple. All that knowledge about the Goddess, available right here. If only she could read Old Alarian as well as she could read Almarrynian. For at least the hundredth time, she wished she'd actually been able to get into the sealed library that day. Now she might not ever have that chance.

"What does the book say?"

Benje scanned a few pages quickly. "Well, it mostly talks about the Goddess's fifth life, before she ascended to her palace in the stars." His eyes widened. "It tells of how she gave the Ligerthian Knights Forging! This . . . this is a priceless tome!"

"The actual process of Forging?" Kailyn looked at him curiously, remembering the little jawk he'd made for the gnomes. "Is that what you do?"

Benje nodded. "Forging is like regular metalwork, only imbued with magic. That was what made the Ligerthian Knights so formidable. Sadly, their secrets have been lost since Ligerthia fell. But this . . ." He lifted the book up with his hands. "This holds the answer to knowledge long forgotten!"

Kailyn smiled at his enthusiasm. Then a darker thought surfaced in her mind. Benje had killed two men before their escape. And he probably would have killed the captain too. Even if Canis thought Benje was safe, he had still killed people. It didn't align with what she knew of the Ligerthian Knights. She tried to snuff out the thoughts, but Benje, ever the observant one, tilted his head at her.

"What is it, Princess?"

"Did the Ligerthian Knights promote killing innocent men?" Her voice was quiet as she continued stroking Canis's fur.

Benje frowned. "No, of course not. Why would you—oh." Understanding dawned in his brown eyes. He smiled sadly and sat down next to her on the floor. Canis perked up and padded closer to Benje so he was equal distance away from them.

He took her hand in his, and a small zing raced up her arm. She tried to ignore it and focused on his words. "Princess. Those men weren't innocent. They were trained soldiers working for Lord Shielen. If they had known who you were, they would have turned you in. We needed to escape, and Mirnabad's fool plan wasn't working."

He gently rubbed his thumb along her palm, sending more tingles up her arm. "I am sorry you had to see that, though." His eyes locked with hers. "I did many things with the rebellion that I regret," he continued softly, continuing to trace Kailyn's hand.

"But I don't regret leaving them. And I swear by my sword that I will only ever kill to protect you."

Swear by my sword. The words reminded Kailyn of the oath he had given her back in the gnome caverns. She knew he meant it. If her life were in danger, Benje would be there. Protecting her.

"Benje, I . . . I don't know how to thank you," she whispered.

He smiled sadly. "You don't need to, Princess." He tenderly kissed her hand. Tingles shot up Kailyn's arm at his touch and she stared at him in surprise before smiling back, gazing at those warm brown eyes. Eyes that hid so much pain, but eyes that shone with a devotion to her. Eyes that she never wanted to be without.

A sudden jostle to the ship sent her tumbling onto her back. Benje got to his feet and extended a hand to her, his face serious once more.

"What was that?" Kailyn asked, taking Benje's hand and getting to her feet.

Benje frowned. "I don't know."

Danger! Canis yipped, scrambling away from them and out the door.

"Canis!" Kailyn took off after him, Benje's footsteps echoing behind her.

Chapter Twenty-One

Kailyn

The top deck was in chaos. The whole crew was close to the railing, looking for something in the water, Canis yipping loudly.

Myira rushed up to them, throwing her arms around Kailyn. "Oh Princess! I was so worried! I thought you had gone over the edge when the ship was hit!"

Kailyn frowned at Myira's worried expression. "I was with Benje and Canis. What's going on?"

"I'm not sure. My brother seems to be missing."

"He's asleep." Benje sounded stiff.

"What?" Myira furrowed her brows. "With all this noise? How?"

"I'll tell you later." Kailyn gestured to the crowd of men. "What do they think is attacking us?"

Another loud jostle caused Kailyn to lose her balance. She slid to the railing, Myira following suit. Kailyn looked over the edge and saw the biggest head she'd ever seen. Its mouth was as big as half the boat, its slimy pink throat glistening up at her. Kailyn screamed in terror. A sea serpent! They were under siege by a sea serpent!

"Princess!" Benje called, grabbing Kailyn and Myira and pulling them away from the edge.

"Canis!" Kailyn cried out in panic. "Where's Canis?"

Aru! Canis bounded over the deck, weaving under crew-members who cursed at him.

Benje scooped him up and handed him to Kailyn. "You might want to keep ahold of him, Princess."

Kailyn held Canis tight as one of the crewmembers hollered "FIRE!" and shot harpoons into the sea serpent's mouth. The beast hissed and snapped at the ship, taking half the railing with it.

"FIRE AGAIN!" the crewmember yelled as the crew ran scrambling to get more harpoons. Benje unsheathed his sword.

"Benje, no!" Kailyn cried as he ran off. Her lip started trembling.

Danger! Canis echoed in her mind. She bit her lip to stop herself from crying. The pup was right—there was so much danger all around them. What if something happened to Benje? What if the sea serpent got him?

"What are we going to do?" Myira wailed. "A sea serpent! We're all going to our watery graves!"

Mirnabad came stumbling up to them, his hat on crooked, a look of pain crossing his face as Canis bared his teeth at him. "Ah, girls—and dog. What show is going on?"

"Your ship is being attacked, you pirate!" Myira screamed at him. "Defend the princess!"

Canis growled, as if echoing the sentiment.

Mirnabad grimaced at them before turning to his crew. "Attention, lads! We need to kill this here beastie before she swallows us all!"

The men, who had paused when the captain addressed them, cheered but that cheer quickly turned to screams when the head of the monster burst through the ocean on the other side of the ship and picked up three of the crewmembers in one fell swoop.

"Fire the cannons!" Mirnabad yelled. There was a scrambling as the crew raced to their positions.

Kailyn stood at the edge, holding Canis, and trying not to get flattened. She tried to see where Benje had run off to, but the whole deck was chaos. There had to be something she could do!

A loud shot echoed through the night and the creature screamed at them. The serpent twisted its body around the mast of the ship and, with a loud snap, it came crashing down, barely missing Mirnabad.

Which wouldn't have been such a loss in Kailyn's mind—or in Canis's echoed sentiment—but Myira was screaming as loud as the creature was. The sea serpent was going to get all of them. There was no way they could overpower it. But maybe . . . maybe they could outsmart it.

"Myira!" Kailyn shuffled Canis's weight in her arms to reach out her free hand to grab her maid. An idea dawned in her mind. "We can outwit the creature! We've got to get it away from the ship!"

Myira stopped screaming and stared at Kailyn.

"Is there any fish on board?" Kailyn continued, grateful that Myira had at least stopped screaming. "Any fish at all? This whole place smells like one, it must be why the creature is attacking."

As if to prove her point, Canis flooded her mind with an image of a massive pile of fish. *Food!*

Not the time, Kailyn thought.

Myira swallowed hard. "There's some fish in the galley."

"Then let's get it. If we can throw it overboard, perhaps we can distract it away from the ship so the cannonballs do their job. Come on."

Kailyn felt her blood rush as she grabbed Myira's hand and led her belowdecks, still holding Canis. She didn't want the pup to get lost in the chaos on deck.

The screaming of the men still echoed in her ears, but it wasn't as intense down here. Myira directed her to the galley, which smelled fishier than the entire ship.

Food! Canis squirmed in Kailyn's arms and burst free to grab some fish on the floor.

"Canis!" Kailyn reached for the wolf pup, who was scarfing another fish. Myira had grabbed two big buckets.

"Grab your pup, Princess!" Myira called.

Kailyn managed to scoop up Canis, who was still eating.

She reached to grab another bucket and followed Myira as quickly as she could up the stairs, Canis grabbing a few fish with his teeth.

When they got back up to the top deck, they found that all three masts were broken off and a third of the crew was missing.

Kailyn and Myira ran to the side of the ship.

"What do we do now?" Myira asked.

"Throw it overboard, as far from the ship as possible!" Kailyn called, still trying to keep Canis away from the fish in the bucket she carried. It was difficult to hold both the bucket and the pup.

Food. Canis sounded glum, but Kailyn tried to tune him out.

"Stay put," she urged the pup, who stilled only slightly in her arms. "Myira, throw it now!"

Myira threw the contents of both her buckets and then Kailyn's bucket overboard. The serpent raised its head in their direction before snatching up the fish in its jaws in one gulp.

"It's not enough!" Myira screamed.

Kailyn watched as the sea serpent raised its head once more, staring them down with its big yellow eye.

Big eye, Canis projected.

Kailyn couldn't help but agree as the eye got closer and closer. Would this be the last thing she'd ever see? A massive eye about to swallow her and her friends whole?

Benje popped out of nowhere and launched one of his knives at the beast. The creature squealed in agony before disappearing into the waves. Kailyn stared down into the murky water, expecting to see its massive head again, but it had disappeared.

"Well done, Princess," Benje said, smiling at her in the silence that followed.

Danger!

"LOOK OUT!" a crewmember yelled. But it was too late. A loud crunch echoed as the ship jolted, wood crunching.

"What did we hit?" Kailyn asked, whirling around before she saw it. Massive dark rocks stuck like teeth out of the ocean, blending into the dark night sky. The sea serpent had led them to their deaths after all.

Danger! Canis sounded frantic in Kailyn's mind. She held the pup tightly. She didn't know how they'd make it through this.

As the deck cracked apart, Kailyn, holding Canis, and Myira next to her held on to the railing for dear life. Benje yelled at them to jump in the waves.

"Are you daft? That beast will eat us!" Myira screamed.

"I don't think so!" Benje called. "I think its mission is to prevent anyone from getting past the rocks. If we can swim past the rocks, I think we'll be safe! Jump!"

Kailyn looked at Canis, fear pounding in her heart. "Can you do it?"

Canis yipped. *Water!* And he wriggled from her arms, jumping into the ocean below.

"Canis!" Kailyn squinted her eyes shut and jumped into the freezing ocean. The water was so frigid it felt like her joints froze on impact. The weight of the water made her robe heavier and heavier. Frantically, she tried to move toward the surface, but her arms burned.

Aru! Canis's voice was panicked. *Swim!*

Kailyn flailed her arms. She'd never been in water before. She had no idea how to swim.

She felt something brush past her and saw a white blur. Canis projected an image of a wolf paddling with its legs in the water. Kailyn shifted her arms and legs, trying to follow along.

She burst through the water, gasping. The rocks were somehow behind her. But she couldn't see any islands.

She kept swimming in that paddle stroke Canis had shown her until her arms gave out and she sank beneath the waves.

Aru! Canis called out frantically.

But she couldn't struggle anymore. Everything was too heavy. And she was too tired.

She was going to die, far from home, drowned in the depths of the endless sea.

Aru!

She felt something grab her arm and drag her through the water. Suddenly, her feet touched sand and her head broke through the surface of the water again, and she gasped, inhaling great mouthfuls of air. She was only a few yards from shore. Canis was right there, nudging her with his nose.

Land!

Renewed, she struggled with all her might toward the shore, finally collapsing on the sandy surf, too tired to move further as waves pounded her body. She felt Canis lick her face, but she couldn't move any more. Dazed and confused, she stared up at the stars until she fell asleep.

"Princess! Princess!" A familiar voice pulled her from her sleep. She tried to pry her eyes open, but they seemed crusted shut. Something licked her face.

"Canis?" She could feel the wolf's soft, but still damp fur. She wrenched her eyes open and, blinking forcefully, saw a black blurry outline in front of her. The more she blinked, the more the shape formed into someone she recognized.

"Benje?" she rasped, her mouth tasting like sand.

"Oh, thank the Goddess, I thought you were dead." Benje pulled her into his arms and rocked her back and forth. Kailyn wanted to protest, but his chest was comfortable and solid. It felt real.

"Wh-what happened?" she stuttered as her eyes started to come into focus. She noticed that Benje's black attire was completely shredded. He had seaweed in his hair and a deep scratch along his arm, but otherwise seemed unhurt.

"Canis led me to you," he said. Canis curled up next to them, his thoughts filled with images of sand and Kailyn's prone form.

She blanched. "Canis saved my life."

She stroked the wolf's fur, once again grateful that she had this magical pup as a companion.

"He's a good wolf," Benje said softly. "We need to get you both out of here though. The sun's not going to help anything once it reaches its zenith. Can you stand?"

"I . . . I think so?" Kailyn wasn't sure if she could crawl, let alone walk, but Benje helped her to her feet. She wobbled before crashing back into the surf.

Aru! Canis licked her face again and she rubbed his nose affectionately.

"I guess not," she said, trying to laugh, but it was painful. Her legs hurt and her mind was still spinning. Were they the only survivors? Where was Myira?

"Come on, we need to get you cleaned up and dried off. Let's see if we can find anyone around here," Benje said, scanning their surroundings. It was barely morning. Kailyn gazed toward the watery horizon, trying to see if she could see anyone else out there, but there was nothing. She couldn't even see the rocks where they'd crashed.

"Where is everyone?" she asked, her throat scratchy.

"Dead in the sea," Benje said, his voice tinged with sadness. "Those rocks were deadly."

Everyone? Her heart hammered. "Myira?"

His face crumpled. "She hit a rock with her head. I don't think she made it."

Gone. Canis projected an image of Myira's still form suspended in the water.

"She's . . . gone?" Kailyn blinked back tears with her crusty eyelids, shoving the image from Canis away. Her oldest friend . . . gone. And it was all because of her.

She blinked mutely at the waves, wishing she'd never gotten on that boat. Or at least insisted Myira had stayed home. She didn't deserve death.

Benje knelt next to her on the sand. "Come on, Princess, we need to get you to safety."

Kailyn nodded mutely, letting Benje carry her out of the surf, but never taking her eyes from the horizon. Myira was gone. Her one last friend from home was killed by the merciless ocean. Tears pricked her eyes. She was gone, and it was all her fault.

Danger! Canis, who'd been padding along the shore ahead of them, stopped, growling at a blurry shape that was moving toward them.

"Ahoy, friends! Ahoy!" an eerily familiar voice called out. For the first time in her life, Kailyn cursed.

It was the captain. He was caked in sand, and his clothes were torn in multiple places. He pulled a squid from his arm and tossed it back into the sand. "*Ze la ben*! I thought I was alone! Ahoy!"

"Stay away from the princess, Mirnabad." Benje's voice was tight.

"I won't harm her." Mirnabad gestured to the state of his ripped clothes. "Look at the state of me, would you believe that sand does get everywhere?" He laughed. "I wish Myira could see my state."

"Myira is dead!" Kailyn yelled, surprising herself with the ferocity of her words.

Aruuu! Canis howled as if agreeing with her.

Both men stared at her. But Kailyn wasn't done yet.

"She's dead because of your incompetence, you lazy no good *vyko*!" It felt good to say the words.

"Princess." Benje carried her further up shore, but Kailyn wasn't done yet. She tumbled out of Benje's arms and marched up toward Mirnabad, her anger carrying her as she raised her finger in righteous indignation, Canis bounding on the sand next to her.

"You promised you would get us here! You promised you'd keep her safe—"

Mirnabad held up his hands. "Actually, I never promised such a thing—"

"And you got yourself drunk! I wish the sea serpent had eaten you!"

Food, Canis agreed, sending her an image of the sea serpent eating Mirnabad. Served the man right.

"Don't you think I wish that too, Princess?" Mirnabad said, all the pomp and circumstance drained from his voice. He sounded hollow. "I searched for her, right when the ship went down. I searched and searched, but by the time I found her, she was already dead." His eyes looked misty, but Kailyn wasn't sure he was going to cry. He couldn't be remorseful. Not him. He wasn't capable of feeling remorse. It wasn't in his nature.

"Goodbye, Mirnabad," she spat out, turning around. "Let's go," she said to Benje and Canis, who followed her further up the shore toward the tree line, leaving Mirnabad behind.

They walked for a half hour until Kailyn ran out of energy. They sat under the canopy of trees, resting. Kailyn's bare feet hurt. Her head hurt. Her heart hurt. Kailyn didn't want to think about anything, but she knew they needed a fresh change of clothes and a bath. Canis too—his fur was matted from sand. She had sand in places she didn't think sand could get into and her robe was falling to pieces. Her shift was in tatters. She knew she looked a state, but part of her didn't care.

Myira was gone. The loss was a hollow hole in her chest. Myira had always been there, even longer than her other two maids, Nea and Ilia. She didn't know if she'd ever see her other two maids again. Myira had saved her from Lord Shielen, and what was her payment? Dead at the bottom of the sea.

Canis pushed his nose into her arm. *Alone.*

Yes. Kailyn was alone again with only Benje and Canis.

"We need to keep going," Benje said after a while, getting back to his feet again. "Can you walk, Princess?"

"Yes," Kailyn said, getting to her feet. She was still wobbly, and her feet throbbed, but she knew she could keep walking. For Myira, she would.

She marched off into the darkened trees, Benje and Canis close behind. She knew Benje wanted to ask her how she was feeling, but right now she didn't want to talk about it. She didn't want to feel anything.

After a while, Canis stopped, his nose pointing at some

branches. She stopped, Benje next to her. "Is anyone there?" she called out.

A rustle of leaves told her someone was. Benje leaned into the bushes and caught something. He brought it out. It was a creature that was short and fluffy with bright blue eyes, and it was staring right at Kailyn. The effect was unnerving.

"Who are you?" Kailyn asked, but the creature didn't respond. Just as well. She didn't know if she could handle another talking animal just then.

Benje released it and the creature hopped into the bushes.

Food? Canis asked hopefully.

"Go ahead," Kailyn said. The wolf yipped happily and bounded after the creature. She turned to Benje. "He's probably starving."

"Poor cub needs meat," Benje agreed. He reached his hand toward her and she let him take it. She was grateful for some assurance of normality in this wilderness.

Another rustle of the bushes caught her attention.

"Benje?" she asked. It wasn't Canis—their mind link showed the pup munching on the fluffy creature from moments ago.

Benje went to go investigate, but before he could, three people burst through the shrubbery, armed with spears. They were taller than the gnomes but not by much. Their hair was silver and went past their knees. They wore long green robes tied with a darker green sash. They were glaring at the newcomers.

"Who are you?" demanded the middle one, who was fatter than the other two.

Benje held up his hands. "I am Benje Thornsid. I'm an agent of Queen Leilana, here to escort Princess Kailyn of Oleanders to her court."

Kailyn's heart lurched. Benje's mission. She'd nearly forgotten.

The tallest of the three, a man with a beard almost as long as his hair, squinted at them. "An agent of the queen? Why haven't you arrived at the docks?"

"Our ship was wrecked offshore," Benje said. "We were attacked by a sea monster."

The man pointed his spear at them, eyeing them suspiciously. "Vergyl attacked you? Did you not have the staff of the Ligerthians with you to make peace with him?"

Benje grunted. "I am not a Ligerthian Knight. But I am a servant of the queen." He knelt on the forest floor, clasping his right arm to his chest again. "Please. Take us to her."

Kailyn stared at him, wondering if it would work. Would the strangers believe them? Would they take them to see the queen? Or would they run them through right then and there?

The man withdrew his spear, nodded, and whistled at the other two islanders. They turned to follow him through the shrubbery. Kailyn gave Benje a skeptical look, but he took her hand again and they walked through the bushes, the branches grabbing at Kailyn's arms and clothes. Moments later, Canis bounded after them. The strangers eyed the wolf, but they didn't say anything.

They followed the strangers for what felt like hours. Kailyn's feet started to throb, and she had to lean on Benje for support. But the strangers didn't slow down. How did they walk at such an energetic pace for so long? Surely they'd reach their destination soon. It must be nearing midday as the day was growing warm, and Kailyn was drenched in sweat from walking so far. She missed the cool tunnels of the gnomes.

Hot, Canis agreed. He had to be even warmer than she was with his fur.

An hour or so later, they emerged in a clearing in front of a massive tree. Well, four trees that wound together into a massive tree. Stairs carved into the tree led up to a giant front door.

Thousands of windows graced the structure, and the tree seemed to almost glow from within.

"What is this place?" she wondered aloud.

"The queen's palace," said the tallest man. He saluted the two of them. "Here's where we leave you."

Benje nodded as the men turned and slunk into the shrubbery.

Food? Canis wondered.

"I'm sure they'll have food here," Kailyn said. Her feet hurt from all the walking, but now at least they were here.

Benje offered her his arm. "Shall we?"

She reached for Benje's hand and found his comforting fingers interlaced with hers once again. "Onwards."

Standing inside the entrance, Kailyn gawked at the architecture of the giant tree structure.

The branches grew around one another to form walls. The floor had actual marble forming intricate patterns that twisted like the tree branches. Light streamed in from the openings in the tree that she had mistaken for windows. Vines draped from the branches like drapes. It was surprisingly cool inside the tree, which struck Kailyn as strange considering the tree was open to the elements.

Shade, Canis agreed, padding along the marble floor. He kept sending her images of ice, so she guessed the coolness of the marble was soothing to his paws.

It also struck her strange that there was furniture inside the tree. She traced the design of a small round golden table and noticed it felt more like a flower than wood. This island was very odd.

A man met them at the door. He was dressed in a brilliant white robe that made Kailyn ashamed of her tattered attire. He had long white hair, like the leader in their rescue group had, and his robe was even in the same style, but with embroidery over the sleeves and chest of the robe.

"My name is Klaius," he said with a deep low voice that immediately put Kailyn at ease. "How may we assist you?"

"I'm here to report to the queen," Benje said, saluting Klaius with his right arm over his chest.

The man's eyes widened. "One of our order. Yes, the queen mentioned she'd been expecting you."

Klaius led them down a tree corridor that was wide and well lit. Kailyn noticed there were bright splashes of color, like paintings on the walls, but they seemed to be growing there rather than mounted like the paintings in her father's castle. She wanted to ask Klaius what they were, but she hesitated. She had no idea what the etiquette was for arriving bedraggled to a foreign queen's court.

They reached an elaborate door carved with ancient runes that Kailyn guessed were probably Old Alarian. She turned to ask Benje what they said, but he shook his head. His face was still stony. She'd have to ask him about the runes later.

Canis pressed his face into Kailyn's leg. *Food?*

"Not yet," Kailyn whispered. They first had to meet this queen, where hopefully everything would be resolved. "Though maybe you should stay outside? Just in case?"

Aru! Canis pressed his face even harder into Kailyn's leg.

Benje chuckled. "I don't think he's staying behind, Princess."

Kailyn nodded. "Alright then." She looked to Klaius. "Shall we?"

Klaius inclined his head and opened the large ornate door. Loud voices echoed back to them.

"—seen this before? It's a prophecy of the First Queen."

"How dare you sneak around behind my back! It was not yours to seek!"

"Why were you hiding this? How is this my destiny?"

Klaius banged his deep green staff on the tiles.

"Your Majesty, Your Highnesses, may I interrupt your meeting for a moment? I'm afraid something urgent has come up," Klaius said. The voices stopped instantly. He motioned for Kailyn to follow him.

It was a pleasant room, wide but cozy. A table was laid for tea. An elegant woman with raven-black hair, wearing deep purple robes, sat at the table, looking shrewdly at the newcomers. Standing in front of Kailyn was a young woman with dark hair, wearing a tunic that was belted at the waist, a sword buckled at her side, holding a book.

Standing next to her was a broad-shouldered man, roughly the same age as Benje, but he had more of a scholarly air to him. He was dressed in white robes with a blue sash, holding a blue staff. Blond curls swooped over his forehead. The company assembled widened their eyes with shock when Kailyn and Benje entered the room.

Kailyn curtsied, but sand fell from her shift. Canis pressed his face into her legs.

Strangers. She agreed. The room was filled with strangers who were staring at her.

"I'm so sorry, Your Majesty," she said, her cheeks reddening. This was not at all how she had wanted to meet the queen of Tigahel.

The woman in the purple robes lifted an eyebrow. "And you are?"

Benje strode forward and knelt, clasping his right fist to his chest. "Benje Thornsid of Oleanders, escorting Princess Kailyn of Oleanders to Tigahel, as requested."

The queen nodded, her features settling into something that vaguely resembled a smile. "Thank you, Benje—Princess Abrina, what are you doing!?" she shrieked.

Kailyn yelped as a sword point was thrust in her face. The black-haired girl was staring at Kailyn down the blade, her dark eyes glinting dangerously.

"Who are you," she said in a low threatening voice. "And why do you look like my mother?"

Chapter Twenty-Two

Abrina

$\mathcal{A}$brina glowered at the newcomer, who, despite her rags and crusty blond hair, looked the spitting image of her mother. She'd recognize those blue eyes anywhere, the angle of her gaze, despite the terror written across it.

But before the girl could get out a peep, the man who'd been kneeling before the queen whipped out his sword and deflected Abrina's blade. Abrina turned into the attack, but he stepped forward, twisting his sword and disarming her, her sword skittering across the marble floor.

"Take Princess Abrina outside, please," the queen said, her tone hard. Abrina felt firm hands on her shoulders guiding her out of the room. As soon as the door was closed, she twisted and burst free.

"Abrina?" Henri asked, his face a mix of confusion and concern. "Are you alright?"

Abrina only glowered and started to pace. Who was that girl? Why did she look like her mother?

The man who'd disarmed her had called the girl a princess . . . of Oleanders. She clenched her fists. *Oleanders.*

But why did she have an Alarian wolf cub with her? Only Florrynians had that blessing from the Goddess.

A line from the prophecy ran through her head. *Two royal hearts can set this right. From nations at war, yet with shared royal blood.*

A chill went down Abrina's spine. If the girl looked like Abrina's mother, that could only mean one thing . . .

No. There had to be another explanation. Trickery? Forbidden magic to make her look like her mother? But who would do such a thing?

And if she was her sister, how in the three hells did she end up here?

The door opened softly and Klaius stuck his white wizened head out. "Prince Henri, you are needed."

Abrina could feel the prince's eyes on her, unanswered questions hanging between them, but she ignored him.

"Will you watch her?" the prince asked after a moment. Abrina thought he was talking to Klaius, but was surprised when a different voice answered.

"We will," Byron said. The familiarity of his voice pulled her briefly from her spiraling thoughts. Zachry, Byron, and the captain were back, and there was a strange man with them.

For a moment, Abrina stopped pacing to stare at the newcomer. He was dark-skinned, bald, and had a glittering golden tattoo that curled around his ear. He had a floppy hat in his hands that he kept twirling. His golden eyes landed on Abrina and his mouth curved into a sly smile.

"*Ze ben!* What have we here?" he said, his voice soft. He spoke with an accent she didn't recognize, but she didn't like the way his gaze made her feel. She glowered at him.

"Leave the princess alone, Mirnabad," Byron said, nudging him sharply. The man named Mirnabad had the audacity to wink at her. Actually wink.

"Touchy, touchy." He twirled his hat again. Abrina grunted. The man was irritating, and he was *this* close to getting a fist to the stomach. She supposed it was better to ignore him though.

She turned to leave, but heard Mirnabad sigh dramatically

behind her. "You princesses are always guarded by strong men, no?"

"What?" Abrina whirled on him, wishing she still had her sword, but her fists would do in a pinch. She grabbed his arm and twisted it back. "You dare insinuate that a princess of Florryn needs protecting?"

"Ah, ah!" He squealed in pain. "Of course not, dear Princess!" Fear shone in the man's golden eyes.

"Princess," the captain said, his tone icy. "Unhand the man."

Abrina scowled and released the stranger, who wobbled away, rubbing his arm.

"*Ze ben*, she's an angry one. The other princess was much sweeter."

Other princess. The *Oleanderian* princess. Who looked like her mother. *Two royal hearts . . . from nations at war, yet with shared royal blood . . .*

Abrina thought she was going to be sick. She raced down the hall, needing to find air, needing to breathe. This couldn't be happening. It couldn't be true.

She burst into the courtyard where Henri had taken her merely hours before. Had it only been a few hours since they had left the island? Discovered the book of the First Queen?

And then the princess of Oleanders showed up here! It was too much of a coincidence.

Curse the Goddess, she thought savagely. *Curse the prophecy!*

There was no way that blond-haired island girl was her sister. Absolutely none. Florryn had no dealings with Oleanders. Oleanders had killed her sister seventeen years ago. Her mother had told her the story so many times—they'd found a body outside the castle, wrapped in the blue and silver blanket of Florryn.

But what if . . . somehow . . . a tiny voice whispered in Abrina's mind.

She squashed it. No. There was no way in all of eternity that that larnel-flower-headed princess was her sister. She'd rather the world froze over than somehow be related to *Oleanders*.

Byron found her out in the courtyard hours later, where she was still pacing, obsessing over the princess from Oleanders.

"Princess Abrina?" he called quietly.

Abrina looked up and glared at him. "Why are you here?"

"I might ask you the same question. Why are you so angry?"

"That . . . that . . . larnel wench looks like my mother," she finally managed to say.

His eyes widened. "Mirnabad mentioned he had traveled with a princess, but she abandoned him on the beach. That's the girl you speak of?"

She gritted her teeth. "Yes." Unless there was another princess wandering about Tigahel.

"Are you saying she's . . ." He paused. "Goddess's eyes. Is she the lost princess of Florryn?"

"She is *not*," Abrina hissed, making a rude gesture Sir Tyir had taught her a long time ago before making a fist. "She's the princess of *Oleanders*."

Byron's eyes glinted harshly in the sunlight. "Are you saying Oleanders stole our princess and then raised her to be their own?"

Abrina's fist grew tighter, her fingernails digging into her palm. Who knew what treachery Oleanders was capable of?

"I don't know. I don't know anything. All I know is that she's not my sister."

Byron's eyes softened for a moment. "But what if . . . what if she was?"

Abrina clenched her teeth. "*No.* There's no way."

Byron tilted his head. "The Goddess has done surprising things before. Maybe . . . maybe there's a reason for this."

Abrina glared at him. "Oleanders nearly wiped us out twenty years ago. Then they killed my sister three years later. There is no way this impostor is the lost princess of Florryn. She's just a look-alike."

Byron nodded, his gaze hardening once more. "Very well. But somehow, we've got to get to the bottom of this. You have to admit the whole thing is suspicious."

Abrina concurred. Why did that girl show up now? And what did that wretched prophecy mean? *Two royal hearts . . .* She scowled. She wished they'd never found the cursed thing.

At that moment, Sir Zachry came running into the courtyard, breathless.

"Your Highness!" He saluted Abrina. "The queen requests to see you."

Abrina grunted. "Fine. Lead the way." This was not going to be a pleasant conversation.

"I am very disappointed in the both of you," the queen said when Abrina reentered the room. She glanced around and quickly noted that the ragged island girl with her mother's face was missing. But the man in black who had disarmed her stood quietly in the corner, his dark eyes never leaving Abrina's face. There was something . . . fierce about that man. He had incredible reflexes, like he'd been trained all his life for combat, but he didn't wear armor. He reminded Abrina of herself actually. She scowled at the thought. As if she'd ever have anything in common with those Oleanderians.

Henri stood in the middle of the room, looking ashamed. His eyes briefly met Abrina's, worry clouding his beautiful blue irises. Abrina felt a pang. She wished she could go flying with him on the cajuna again and forget about everything that had happened.

"Your Majesty," Abrina said tersely, bowing.

The queen narrowed her purple eyes at Abrina. "You call yourself a princess, yet you attack our guests with savagery. I cannot condone that behavior. I have half a mind to banish you right now."

Abrina glared at the queen. "She's the princess of Oleanders," she hissed. "The sworn enemy of my people. Why is she even here?"

The queen's eyes glinted coldly. "She is here for a reason. As are you. And unless you can control that temper of yours, you are not to have your sword the remainder of your stay on our islands."

Abrina bristled. Even Henri gasped. "Mother—"

"No. If she is to be queen of Tigahel, she better start acting like it."

She leveled her cool gaze at Abrina. "Is that understood, Princess?"

Abrina clenched her fist, then looked at Henri, who looked worried.

She bowed her head, forcing herself to submit. At least on this. "Yes, Your Majesty."

"Good," the queen said. "We will discuss this more tomorrow. You need some time to cool your head, and your sister needs time to refresh herself."

Abrina glared at the queen. "She is *not* my sister."

The queen raised an eyebrow. "Is she not the princess of Oleanders?"

Abrina gritted her teeth. "Yes."

"Then she is your sister."

Henri sucked in a breath. "Mother. What have you done?"

The queen's eyes remained impassive. "What I needed to. For the good of Ligerthia. And the good of Almarryn."

Abrina's mind churned. What was the queen talking about? And why did she sound so . . . cold?

Once again, Abrina itched for her sword so she could point it in the queen's face. Maybe then she'd start explaining what was going on.

"Tell us," Abrina spat. "Tell us about the prophecy. And why the princess of Oleanders has my mother's face."

The queen stared at Abrina. "All will be revealed tomorrow. I suggest you rest. You are dismissed."

Abrina glowered at the queen, wanting to throttle her, but once again, felt the gentle, firm arms of Henri guide her from the room.

Chapter Twenty-Three

Abrina

That evening, Abrina was locked in her room. She'd half expected it. After her irrational behavior earlier that day, she should have known they would keep an eye on her. But it only left her alone with her thoughts about the impostor and her family.

Her family. She traced the pendant from her mother. What would her mother say to the impostor? Her entire kingdom hated Oleanders.

The whole thing felt like some cruel cosmic joke.

A soft rap sounded at her door, startling her from her thoughts. She hurried to it. "Hello?"

"Abrina?" Relief washed over her as Henri's gentle voice came from behind the door. She had hoped to talk to him again.

"Henri?"

"I can't stay long, but I needed to speak with you. May I come in?"

"Yes."

A key rattled in the lock before the door opened. Henri stood there, looking grim. He walked in, closing the door behind him and stood awkwardly in the middle of the room. Abrina motioned to the chair she'd sat in.

"Would you like to sit down?"

"I . . . yes." He sat down and stared at her for a moment. She sat down on the bed across from him.

He ran his fingers through his curls, sighing heavily. "I don't blame you, you know."

She raised an eyebrow. "For what?"

"Pulling a sword on the girl."

She cocked her head, almost amused. That wasn't what she'd expected. "Would you have done the same?"

"Had I met someone with my parent's face? Likely. It would be unnerving."

She smiled wryly. "Yes. Well. Your mother was definitely unnerved." And acting highly suspicious. How did his mother play into all of this?

"Yes." His face hardened. "I don't like this, Abrina. I'm afraid of what my mother's planned."

Abrina's heart skipped a beat. Henri was afraid. That wasn't reassuring. "What do you think she's got planned?"

He sighed. "From the looks of things, I'd say she manipulated you and the other princess here to fulfill the prophecy we found this morning."

A cold wave of dread washed over Abrina. She'd been thinking that very thing, but she hadn't wanted to voice it aloud.

"Why?" Her voice was barely a whisper. "Why would she do such a thing?"

Henri raised his giant shoulders in a shrug. "I don't know. But somehow . . . you, her, this prophecy, my mother . . . it's all connected." He blinked his brilliant blue eyes at her and Abrina felt her cheeks heat up. His tenderness and kindness surprised her.

"Er . . . yes." She swallowed thickly. "Thank you, by the way."

He quirked an eyebrow. "For?"

"For today. The library." And the freedom . . . before this new disaster had unfolded.

He smiled. "Anything for you, *fyrrel*."

A delightful shiver went down Abrina's spine. "What does *fyrrel* mean?"

"Dear one of my heart."

Her own heart skipped a beat. "But . . . you barely know me."

His eyebrow quirked again. "We're engaged to be married, aren't we?"

"Yes, but . . ."

He raised a finger. "Do you want to know the real reason why I came to Florryn?"

"You wanted to meet your bride-to-be." She shrugged. "You told me that already."

Henri nodded. "But more than that. I wanted to see if it was possible for me to love someone my mother had selected for me."

His mother. Abrina made a face. "Your mother is a meddling nuisance."

"She is still my mother." He looked sad. "And she has experienced much loss in her life."

"So?" Abrina demanded. "What right does that give her to go meddling in other people's affairs? Arranging marriages? Plotting and scheming? The only way that she could know that the other princess could ever possibly be my sister is . . ." She stopped herself, not wanting to finish that thought.

"If my mother did something. Yes," Henri said softly. "Abrina . . . I am sorry. I can't even imagine how confusing this must be for you."

Abrina scoffed. He had no reason to be sorry. Unless . . . had he tricked her into finding the prophecy? Was he obeying his mother's orders? How was Abrina to know she could actually trust the man she was engaged to?

She narrowed her eyes at him. "How do I know that you're not simply following her orders?"

"Because of this." Before Abrina could blink, he'd reached for her, and without thinking, she reached for him, allowing him to pull her into his arms. Their lips met and it was a kiss unlike anything Abrina had ever imagined. He tasted sweet and salty, tame, yet with a wildness lurking underneath. She wanted to be lost in him forever.

"Henri," she whispered, breathless, when they pulled back, her mind reeling from the intensity of that kiss. "What was that?"

He quirked an eyebrow at her, and this close, she could see the flecks of gold in his eyes. "A declaration of intent. I love you, Princess Abrina." He gently traced her face with his hand. His touch was soft, gentle, and yet longing all at the same time. Abrina had never felt anything like it.

She blinked, stunned at his quiet but fierce words. "Why?"

"Because of your fiery spirit. Your passion for your people. Your leadership skills. Your determination." He smiled. "You're fearless. Nothing intimidates you."

Abrina bit the inside of her cheek, mulling over that. "But you stopped me. With Lord Jeru. Why?"

Henri's eyes glinted with sorrow. "Because your fiery passion sometimes needs to be directed for the right things."

She made a face. "He deserved it though! He was a traitor—"

"Abrina." He kissed her again, which effectively shut her up. "There are more ways to win a fight than by wielding a sword."

She didn't know about that, but then again, he had managed to defeat a sea monster with only his glowing stick.

"I don't know what tomorrow holds," he went on. "But can you try to keep an open mind? The Goddess has a hand in all things—even things we don't like."

Abrina wanted to protest. She still didn't think he was right about Lord Jeru, and she definitely didn't think the Oleanderian princess was her sister. But maybe . . . maybe she could try to keep an open mind. At least for Henri.

"Alright," she agreed. "I'll try. But I don't trust your mother."

He smiled wryly. "Neither do I." He pressed a kiss to the top of her head and stepped back. "Rest well, my fyrrel."

But after he left, rest was the last thing on Abrina's mind. She continued to pace the room, thinking of the girl who shared her mother's face.

It didn't make sense. Her sister was dead. She'd heard the story—one of her father's guards had found the body, and her family had gone into mourning for the next six months. Abrina grew up an only child as her parents were never able to conceive again.

The lost princess of Florryn. She was *lost*. Killed by Oleanders.

But what if somehow her sister had survived and been spirited away?

To their ancient enemies?

It was ludicrous.

Unease kept her pacing long after the shadows stole across the blankets on her bed. A candle was the only light in the darkened room, but Abrina's thoughts were a mess as she grappled with the pieces of her shattered world.

Chapter Twenty - Four

Kailyn

Kailyn's head was spinning as she sat in a golden-green tub, washing off the grime of the last few days. *Princess Abrina . . . of Florryn.* She shuddered. Florryn was known for their fierce warriors. Oleanders was superior on the water, but Florryn was superior on land, especially in the mountains. And their ferocity was legendary.

There was something about the steely glimmer in Princess Abrina's gaze, how natural the sword looked in her hand . . . She closed her eyes, wishing she could wash away the terror she'd felt.

Aru? Canis perked his head up. He was curled up on the bed, already clean. One of the maids had helped Kailyn give him a bath before drawing one for her.

"I'm fine, Canis," she whispered.

But she wasn't. Her heart was still hammering wildly. *Who are you and why do you have my mother's face?*

Kailyn didn't know why she looked like the other princess's mother. She hadn't gotten the chance to ask any questions, as Princess Abrina had been forced from the room by the scholarly giant next to her.

Then Kailyn had spoken to the queen. She sighed, sinking into the water as she remembered that conversation.

"I am sorry for such a rude introduction," the queen had said, a frown crossing her elegant face. "Princess Abrina has . . . temper difficulties."

"She pulled a sword on Princess Kailyn," Benje had scoffed, sheathing his sword on his back, but his face was still hard. "She could have killed her."

"She will be dealt with." The queen's voice had been as hard as stone.

"Why did she say I have her mother's face?" Kailyn asked, her voice still shaky.

The queen looked at Kailyn and her eyes softened. "All will be explained tomorrow. You and your pup must be eager to freshen up."

Canis yipped and sent her an image of wolf cubs frolicking in a stream, which had made Kailyn smile.

Kailyn had nodded, still feeling self-conscious in her dirty tattered robe. "Yes, Your Majesty."

The queen had smiled radiantly then, her smile like the sun coming out. It was like she'd become a whole different person. "Of course, my dear. I'll have my maids help draw you and your pup a bath."

Kailyn leaned against the tub, trying to sort through the memories. Benje had looked furious when Kailyn and Canis had left, but the queen had said she'd had more to discuss with Benje, who she called Apprentice Thornsid. She'd also summoned her son—who apparently was the big scholarly man.

Kailyn sighed. Her heart was conflicted about Benje. And it ached over Myira's loss. For yet the thousandth time, she wished she hadn't sneaked out to go to the library. She might have still had the engagement ball to Oronia, but at least her maids wouldn't have been sent away. Would Myira still be alive had she stayed put?

When she finished her bath, she wrapped herself in a warm pink robe and curled up next to Canis on the comfortable bed, hoping that everything would make more sense in the morning.

At breakfast the next day, Princess Abrina hastily left the room, scowling when Kailyn and Canis entered.

Three knights clad in Florrynian colors clustered around the long table. Kailyn's heart hammered. She'd never been so close to Florrynians before.

Benje, who'd been eating some strange, purple-colored fruit, came to her side in an instant.

"Princess." He bowed. "Are-are you well?"

"I feel better," she admitted. A bath and sleep had helped her heal. But her heart still ached.

Food! Canis yipped, reminding Kailyn of his presence. She laughed and fed him some of the cooked jerky laid out on the table.

"Is that . . . an Alarian wolf?" one of the knights whispered. He had silky black curls and shining green eyes. His pleasant face was filled with an eager curiosity.

Kailyn nodded. "His name is Canis."

Food! Canis chomped on the bits of jerky happily.

"He's incredible," the knight whispered in awe. "Where did you get him?"

"Zachry," snapped one of the other knights, this one with a ruddy complexion, flaming red hair, and a deep scowl. "Leave the impostor alone."

"Impostor?" Kailyn frowned. "What are you talking about?"

221

"Don't play games with me, Oleanderian wretch. Your family killed our princess!"

Benje hissed and moved into a protective stance in front of Kailyn. Canis looked up from his jerky and growled at the knight.

Kailyn stared at him. He was battle-hardened, she could tell from the scars that crossed his arms and face. And if looks could burn, she'd be as crispy as the jerky she'd fed Canis.

"Byron. Enough," said the third knight, a silvery-haired man with weary eyes. "We are all guests of the queen of Tigahel. Let's not disturb the peace." Though Kailyn noted the man wouldn't meet her eyes either.

She sighed, grabbed some fruit and jerky, and left the room.

Benje and Canis followed as she headed down a marble path to a quiet courtyard. A fountain burbled merrily in the center. Kailyn sat on the edge, throwing some of the jerky at Canis, who was quite happy munching on it.

"Princess." Benje inclined his head toward her. "What's on your mind?"

"They hate us," Kailyn whispered. "Because we're Oleanderian."

Benje set his jaw. "Don't let that bother you. I could take all of them in a duel. But they won't dare harm you. Not while we're here on neutral territory."

Kailyn shook her head. "Don't fight them. I just . . ." She sighed, mulling over the conversation from the breakfast room. "What did they mean that I'm an impostor? I have no idea what they're talking about—I have no connection to Florryn. I was born and raised in Oleanders."

Benje inclined his head. "That may be. But the queen . . . She told me yesterday that she has another mission for me. And for you." His deep brown eyes were filled with pain.

Kailyn's heart skipped a beat. "Another mission?"

Benje nodded, his face grim. "She said she'd reveal everything today."

Kailyn's head was spinning again. The queen had a further mission for Benje . . . and for her? Was it not enough that they'd come to Tigahel to seek aid? What about the answers the gnomes had promised them? Kailyn felt like she was back in the ocean, trying desperately to stay afloat, but the water kept crashing over her, sending her back under.

Water? Canis sent her an image of the ocean surf, pounding the shore relentlessly.

"No, Canis. We're not going to the beach today," Kailyn said, feeling overwhelmed. So much had happened since they'd left Tyloan. And now . . . she was being accused of being an impostor of Florryn? What sort of madness was this?

Goddess, please. Help me find answers.

It wasn't until mid-afternoon that the queen summoned them to her throne room.

Kailyn, Benje, Canis, Princess Abrina, and the queen's son— Prince Henri, Kailyn had been informed—were gathered before the queen's throne. The queen was dressed in a resplendent deep blue robe and holding a silver staff, a golden crown on her head.

"Thank you for coming," the queen said, gesturing to the assembled company. "We have much to discuss."

"First and foremost being why this impostor is here," Princess Abrina spat. Kailyn stiffened. There was so much hatred dripping from the girl's tone. Yes, their kingdoms had long been enemies, but that didn't mean *they* had to be, right? Couldn't they at least be civil? At least until they figured out what was going on?

"Princess Abrina," the queen said stiffly. "You will hold your temper."

The Florrynian princess merely crossed her arms and glared at the queen. "What's this about, Your Majesty?"

"I'd like to know that as well, Mother," Prince Henri said, though sounding far less angry than Princess Abrina. "Why is Princess Kailyn here?"

"Because you two," the queen gestured to Kailyn and Princess Abrina, "are to fulfill an ancient prophecy to stop the frost giants once and for all."

Kailyn blinked. "A p-prophecy?"

"Yes." The queen then proceeded to read a sheet of paper. With each word, a greater sense of dread pounded in Kailyn's heart.

"Darkness looms, ice storms approach
Devouring the land, Alaria encroached.
The end of days will soon be nigh,
All will be frozen and left to die.

But a spark burns within this night,
Two royal hearts can set this right.
From nations at war, yet with shared royal blood,
Only they can stem the flood.

Only together will they be strong,
Only together will they right this wrong.
Else the world will fail, and life will cease,
The end of hope, the end of peace."

"The end of days," Kailyn whispered. *"All will be frozen and left to die."*

Benje looked at her sympathetically and extended his hand to her. But Kailyn shook her head, finding instead the safety of Canis's fur as the pup rubbed his head against her leg. What did this mean? What did any of this mean?

"The prophecy we found at the Queen's Library," Prince Henri said slowly. "You already knew about it. How long?"

The queen set her lips in a line. "That is none of your concern. All that matters is that Princess Kailyn and Princess Abrina are here now. They are the sisters of the prophecy. They must seek the ancient dragon on Wyrm's Isle to start their quest. All of Almarryn's fate lies in their destiny."

Kailyn staggered back at the words, holding Canis's fur to ground herself. "S-sisters?" She looked over at Princess Abrina, who was furiously not looking at her. What did she have in common with this fierce warrior princess from Florryn?

"A dragon?" Princess Abrina scowled. "You mean *we*," she pointed at Kailyn, "have to face a dragon together? No thank you. Just look at her! She couldn't fight a dragon if her life depended on it."

Kailyn lowered her head, stroking Canis's fur. The thick fibers were comforting.

Aru? Danger?

No danger, Canis. Kailyn thought. *Just sad.*

Sad? Canis sent her an image of a wolf pup frolicking in snow. Kailyn shook her head. He meant well, but he was only a wolf cub. He couldn't understand what was going on. Kailyn barely understood what was going on. All she knew was that she suddenly had a sister. And they were destined to save the world together apparently, according to the prophecy from the Goddess. Her heart sank.

"Your Majesty," Benje began. "What do you mean these two are sisters? They look nothing alike."

The queen raised her head to look haughtily down at them. "They are sisters. I know because I was there."

"Mother." Prince Henri's grip tightened on his staff. "What did you do?"

The queen looked at each one of them in turn. She spoke calmly, but each word rang like a death knell in Kailyn's ears. "Princess Kailyn was taken from Florryn shortly after she was born. She was brought to Oleanders as a miracle because the queen and her golden-haired babe had died that same day. Kailyn's destiny was always to be princess of Oleanders. And now that you two are together at last, as representatives of both kingdoms, we can finally begin the quest to save the world."

Princess Abrina snarled. "You stole a princess of Florryn? And placed her in the heart of our enemies?"

The queen merely raised her eyebrows. "It does not do to discuss the details of how Kailyn came to Oleanders. All that matters now is that she is the Oleanderian princess, and you, Princess Abrina, are the Florrynian princess, and that you are sisters. The conditions of the prophecy have been met. '*From nations at war, yet with shared royal blood.*' You are from long-time enemy nations, yet you share the same blood. Only together can you stop the frost giants and prevent the end of days. Now that you've been brought together, you can fulfill the prophecy."

Arguing broke out among the group.

"How did the Florrynian princess get stolen?"

"Why would she be taken to the enemy?"

"How is this supposed to save anyone?"

Kailyn didn't say anything, as she was still trying to process everything she'd learned. All her life, she'd been told she was a miracle, her father's flower child, a blessing from the Goddess. It's why her father had kept her sequestered in the castle. She'd never suspected that she was actually stolen from a different home. What would it have been like to be raised in Florryn's climes, to hear their legends and stories, to explore their side of the mountains? Would she be a fierce warrior like Abrina?

But no. It didn't do to dwell on what-ifs. She was a princess of Oleanders.

"Enough!" The queen slammed her staff down on the tiles, and sparks flew from the top, ending the argument. "You two will go to the dragon. Today. You must go. The world is counting on you."

"This is foolishness," Prince Henri said. Benje murmured his agreement. "You cannot send these two to save the world. Why does this centuries-old prophecy suddenly matter, Mother? You've never believed in prophecies before. Why now?"

Everyone was silent as they stared at the queen. She blinked, took a deep breath, then sighed. "Because it's my fault."

The silence that rang throughout the room was deafening.

"How is it your fault?" Kailyn whispered.

The queen looked right at Kailyn. "Because the ice and snow are the result of a mistake I made. I tried to fulfill the prophecy with my sister to contain the threat of the frost giants in Ligerthia. But I failed. And I lost everything." She hung her head.

"So what right does that give you to meddle in our lives?" Abrina demanded. "You stole the other princess from Florryn!"

The queen blinked slowly. "Yes. I did. But I did so to protect the world."

"You did it to satisfy your own guilt," Abrina spat, clenching her hand in a fist. "We're done here." She turned to leave, but the queen banged her staff on the ground again. Abrina was suddenly frozen.

Kailyn blinked, horrified. "What did you do?"

"A temporary freezing charm. She needs to hear this without doing anything rash. Only the two of you can fulfill this prophecy. But if you don't trust me, and I understand if you don't, seek out the dragon on Wyrm's Isle. He will confirm the truth of what I'm saying. Dragons cannot lie."

"But you can, Mother." Prince Henri sounded deeply disappointed. Kailyn didn't blame him. She was disappointed in the queen too. How could she have done this? To her? To Florryn?

But then you'd never have been an Oleanderian princess, a part of her whispered. *You'd never have met your maids. Or Benje.*

Kailyn took a deep breath and exhaled, trying to quiet her mind. What was done was done. Now all they could do was move forward.

"The danger is real," Benje said quietly. "The gnomes have seen it. It's already in the mountains."

"It's very real in Florryn too," Prince Henri added. "The frost giants will spread over all of Almarryn."

"Which is why I need you, my son, to deliver supplies to Florryn."

"What?" Prince Henri looked up at the queen, confusion etched on his face. "Why?"

"Because I made Abrina a promise. Florryn will receive aid while they're off questing to defeat the frost giants."

Prince Henri looked at Abrina, who was still frozen in place, but Kailyn could see the scowl etched in her face. She didn't know what the prince saw in the other princess—her sister?—but he nodded. "Alright, Mother. I will go."

"Good." The queen looked at Benje. "As for you, Apprentice Thornsid. I need you to ready the cajuna for the princesses and their small retinue. Pack warmly. Princess Abrina will want her knights, who are all experienced soldiers."

Soldiers would be helpful, Kailyn thought. Even if they didn't like her very much, at least they had more knowhow than she did.

She wouldn't be very helpful in fighting frost giants at all.

"Be warned, Princesses," the queen said. "If you don't complete this quest, the world will end."

Kailyn swallowed. That was it then. They were going to visit a dragon.

Chapter Twenty - Five

Abrina

Cursings! Cursings be upon the Goddess, upon the prophecy, upon the queen, upon the Oleanderian princess!

Abrina couldn't move, not even to make the worst swear signs with her hands that she so desperately wanted to, but she could listen, and her heart was growing ever more sickened by what the queen said. She had *stolen* the Oleanderian princess— Abrina still couldn't think of her as a Florrynian princess—and then arranged for them all to be here at Tigahel so they could go on a quest together and save the world?

Abrina didn't want to. She didn't want to go anywhere with the larnel-headed girl, who looked near tears. They might be related by blood, but she was still the enemy. She'd been indoctrinated by Oleanders her whole life. They were not sisters.

But Abrina did want to save Florryn. And if these mystical swords could defeat the frost giants once and for all, then she'd pursue them to the three hells and back to save her people.

Even if that meant traveling with the enemy.

When the queen lifted the charm, Abrina headed to her room to pack her bag with her supplies—including a winter coat that had been laid out on her bed—and headed down to the stables. The apprentice—Benje—had several deep purple cajuna at the ready.

Henri was also there. The two men appeared deep in conversation, but they looked up when Abrina approached.

"Princess." Benje inclined his head stiffly. "Preparations are almost complete."

"Good," Abrina said, equally stiff. She didn't trust the man. "The sooner we get this done, the sooner we save Florryn."

"And all of Almarryn," Benje said, staring at her darkly.

"Yes. That." Abrina moved to one of the cajuna, then looked around. "Where is that blasted girl?"

"She's coming," Benje said. "She needed a moment to herself."

Abrina scowled. "We don't have a moment. If the queen is right—"

"You can wait a few moments, Abrina," Henri said softly. "Give her some time. She just found out her whole world is a lie."

She huffed and turned to face the gentle giant. His expression was morose.

"Abrina . . ."

She shook her head. "I can't believe your mother."

"Don't be too hard on her."

"Your mother?" She rolled her eyes. "She deserves it! She caused the ice and snow in the first place and now we're going to fix her mess."

"Not my mother. She has much to atone for." His eyes glinted in the light. "No. Don't be too hard on your sister."

Abrina sighed, thinking of the Oleanderian princess. It wasn't the girl's fault she'd been raised in enemy territory. But that didn't mean Abrina would trust her. She couldn't. Oleanders was not their friend. Never would be. Even if she'd been born in Florryn, the other princess had been raised by Oleanders. But she would try to keep an open mind. *Try* being the operative word here. She couldn't guarantee anything.

231

"Alright," she said softly. "I'll try."

He kissed her forehead gently. "That's all I ask. I'll do what I can to aid Florryn."

Abrina's heart swelled with gratitude for this man who cared for her kingdom as much as she did. "As will I."

At that moment, the other princess and her wolf cub, along with Captain Wilen, Sir Zachry, and Sir Byron, approached. The other men looked ready for action, but why were they arriving with the other princess?

Sir Zachry saluted Abrina. "We're ready, Princess."

Abrina nodded. "Good."

She watched as the Oleanderian princess struggled to get on her cajuna. It would have been comical if Abrina didn't feel the rush of time. They needed to act now. Now that they had a plan—even if it was all orchestrated by the queen of Tigahel—Abrina wanted to complete it. She had to do something to help Florryn. And this was it.

Finally, Benje and the other princess were situated.

She looked at Henri, who handed her a map. "Head straight east. Wyrm Isle will be the last island in the archipelago, the one just past Nyx."

She nodded, taking the map and stuffing it into her saddlebag.

"And I thought you might want this." He pulled out her sword from his robes. Abrina gasped, unable to help herself. The Florrynian silver sparkled in the sun as she clasped it around her waist, feeling complete once more.

"Thank you, Henri," she whispered.

He smiled sadly. "Just be safe. And remember what I said. Keep an open mind."

Abrina nodded. She looked back at her knights and the two

Oleanderians, who were all assembled on their respective cajuna, and clucked her tongue. "To the skies!" she cried.

Together, their retinue took to the air, flying above the Great Tree and leaving the queen behind.

The flight was longer than any of the other flights that Abrina had taken. They flew over the island she had been at earlier with Henri. Faintly, she could see the top of the wall that hid the majestic stone library. She glowered at it. What they had found there had given them more questions than answers. They needed answers. They needed to defeat the frost giants so they all could go on their merry way.

Though Abrina didn't know what awaited her after this. She was supposed to be getting married, but would Henri even be back when she returned? She felt a pang at leaving him behind. Just when she'd started to think they could have a future together, it was ripped mercilessly away.

The other girl also seemed lost in thought. Abrina didn't want to talk with her. If the queen was to be believed, they were sisters from war-torn nations, specifically selected to fulfill a prophecy.

But that still made her Oleanderian.

When they arrived at the dragon's island, the girl from Oleanders fell from her cajuna onto the black sandy beach. The wolf, who for some reason never left the girl's side, nudged her with his snout. Benje, the apprentice, helped her to her feet. Abrina eyed them shrewdly. The girl had obviously never ridden a horse before. Not much Florrynian in her at all.

Abrina dismounted much more gracefully and gazed around

the island. All she saw was black sand and black rocks, much like Isle Nyx.

"It doesn't look like there's a dragon here," she said.

"Look up there," Sir Byron said, pointing toward a mountain rising in the distance, with smoke blooming out of a cave. She shuddered. That was the home of a dragon. A great killing beast.

She glowered at the mountain. She was a princess of Florryn. She would not be scared by some overgrown lizard. "Alright. Onward."

"Princess," the captain said, inclining his head toward her. "Some of us should stay with the cajuna."

She nodded. "Very well. Who volunteers to go with us to the dragon?"

Both Byron and Zachry raised their hands instantly, but the captain shook his head. "The two of you will remain with the cajuna. I will accompany the princesses."

Benje clasped his right fist to his chest. "As will I."

Abrina rolled her eyes at the apprentice's over-eagerness. "Alright then. Let's go conquer a mountain."

It took another three hours for them to reach the cave. The other princess slipped and fell multiple times, but both Benje and the captain helped her to her feet. Abrina rolled her eyes again. Maybe they should have left the girl behind with the others. She clearly had no idea how to travel uneven terrain.

Even her wolf cub was nimbler than she was—he practically bounced on the black rocks.

"Princess Abrina," the captain said after the girl had fallen yet again. "Perhaps we should slow down."

Abrina sighed and sat on a rock, fidgeting with her sword. The other princess nearly collapsed on a rock next to the white wolf and Benje.

"You-you're quite the . . . the adventurer," the princess hazarded. Her voice was breathy from the climb.

Abrina shrugged. "We should keep moving. The sooner we get to this dragon, the sooner we save the world."

The other girl frowned. "If we really are the children of the prophecy. What if . . . the queen was lying?"

"She's not exactly been honest," Benje said, handing the Oleandarian princess a canteen. Abrina grabbed her own from her pack.

"You do share my mother's face," Abrina said softly after taking a drink. "Which adds credibility to her story."

The girl nodded. "You mentioned that." She sighed. "Everything's so confusing right now."

It was. But there wasn't much they could do about it sitting around. They needed to keep going. They had a country to save.

"Come on," Abrina said, slinging her canteen back into her pack. "Let's keep moving."

They finished the climb in silence, other than the Oleanderian princess stumbling on the mountain. When they reached the top, the girl's robe was darkened from the dirt and her hands were scratched up, but she'd made it. Abrina was half impressed.

The girl sat down on a rock, holding her side. "I'll need a moment before we face the dragon." The wolf cub bounded over and started licking the girl's face.

Abrina found herself smiling, but then scowled. Why did the Oleanderian princess have an Alarian wolf? Her people had longed for that blessing for generations, and now the princess of her enemies got it? It was cruel. Yet another reminder of the treachery of Oleanders.

Abrina turned toward the cave, where the smoke was thick. It sank into her lungs and made her cough. It smelled like roasted pulong. She squared her shoulders. They had arrived.

"Dragon!" she called out. "Dragon, we have questions for you!"

A laugh filled Abrina's mind. It sounded like clanging bells, pealing in mirth.

"*Princess Abrina. I've been expecting you.*"

"Expecting me?" Abrina repeated blankly. She'd known dragons were all-knowing, but it still surprised her.

"*Your prophecy is well-known to me. Do come in, both of you. Though the rest of your company should stay outside, including the wolf pup. This is not a meeting for them.*"

The other princess looked straight at Abrina—Abrina could see the fear in her wide blue eyes. "Did you hear that?"

"Hear what?" The captain frowned. "I didn't hear a thing."

"Nor I." Benje crossed his arms. "You alright, Princess?"

The girl from Oleanders nodded. "He wants you to stay here."

Benje set his jaw. "But it's a dragon."

"I don't like it either," the captain said. "Hearing strange voices is . . . suspicious."

The other girl pulled herself up to her full height—which was still shorter than Abrina—and put on a look that Abrina had seen her mother wear several times. "The dragon asked to see us alone. And I trust him."

Abrina half-admired the girl's gumption. Then she shook her head. What was she doing? The girl was not Florrynian. They couldn't be friends. Not even allies. No Florrynian had ever been allied with an Oleanderian and who was she to break with tradition? Oleanders had wronged her people for generations. Even if this girl was her sister, she was still the enemy.

The wolf pup yipped.

"Yes, you too, Canis. I'll be back. I promise." The other girl locked eyes with Abrina. "Ready?"

Abrina nodded tersely. Best get this over with.

They walked into the cave together, though Abrina took

the lead. She saw mounds and mounds of gold spreading as far as she could see. There were jeweled chests with diamonds as large as her hand bursting out of them. There were swords from every era piled about. But mostly there was gold. It spread all the way to the back of the cave. She almost didn't see the dragon until she found the source of the smoke. The dragon was the same color gold as all the mounds piling around him. It was the perfect camouflage. His face was as big as two cajuna, and his jaw, lined with saber-long teeth, could swallow a horse whole.

Abrina took a deep smoke-filled breath, then coughed. It did little to calm her racing heart. This was a dragon. An actual man-eating dragon.

But, as Henri had told her, she was fearless. She could do this. She was a princess of Florryn. She could do anything.

The dragon blinked his round ruby eyes slowly as she approached.

"So confident. So sure of yourself. Surely you, proud princess of Florryn, do not come to beg a humble dragon for aid?"

Abrina swallowed. His voice was sharper now, like a sword point. "We have questions for you," she repeated, though her voice wavered slightly. He was still terrifying.

"Questions are best served warm, Princess. Speak your queries."

She pointed at the other princess, who was gaping at the treasures in the room. "Who is she and what is her connection to me?"

The dragon chuckled. *"Such a bold question. I expected nothing less from the princess of Florryn. Surely you know already who she is?"*

Abrina felt her heart tighten. They had told her, but she was struggling to believe it. Just because she shared her mother's face didn't mean they were sisters.

The dragon sounded thoughtful as it blew another plume

of smoke. "*Ah yes, I can sense your doubts. But Princess Kailyn of Oleanders, heir to the throne, is your twin sister.*"

Abrina clenched her fists. "So it's true then."

"*Yes, Princess. It's true. The queen of Ligerthia stole your sister away from her rightful home, weeks after the two of you were born.*"

"Does that mean . . . I'm a Florrynian princess, Lord Dragon?" the other girl whispered.

"*Lord Dragon?*" The dragon sounded amused. "*That is not a title I've heard in a long time. You know the title of dragons?*"

The girl nodded. "I've read about you. You're more glorious than I had imagined."

Abrina rolled her eyes. The girl was a flatterer. And a reader, apparently. She'd get along well with Henri.

She scowled at the thought. They were *not* sisters.

The dragon continued. "*A truer compliment was never spoken. But still you doubt?*"

The Oleanderian princess frowned. "Yes. I mean . . . no? I believe you when you say she is my sister. Dragons cannot lie. And the queen confessed that she took me . . . but why?"

The dragon snorted. "*You are correct, dragons cannot lie. Your mother is Queen Jullee of Florryn. You and your sister were separated shortly after your births, and you were brought to Oleanders as a babe by Queen Leilana of Ligerthia.*"

Abrina scowled. "Why? What right did the queen of Ligerthia have to steal away a child of Florryn?"

The other girl nodded, her eyes wide. "Why did she take me from my home?"

"*Oh, Princesses.*" The dragon's voice grew sad. "*I speak prophecy according to the commands of the Goddess. It is she who orchestrated this prophecy, not the queen of Ligerthia.*"

"But the queen is behind it," Abrina scoffed. "She told us."

"*The Goddess works with the weakness of mortals. The queen made a mistake, princess of Florryn. Decades before you were born, she thought she and her sister were the children of the prophecy. Ligerthia had been fighting off the frost giants for months. The queen attempted to control the frost giants with staffs Forged by her Ligerthian Knights. Together with her twin sister, she meant to banish them from her realm forever. But instead, the staffs broke, her sister died, and the frost giants overtook Ligerthia.*"

"Its fall," the other princess murmured. "The queen's behind the fall of Ligerthia."

The dragon grunted. "*Yes. And to make amends for her wrong-doing, she swore she would do the prophecy right. So after she came to Tigahel, she sought for the next set of royal twins and planned to separate them.*

"*Thus, six weeks after you were born, the queen of Ligerthia took the babe Kailyn to Oleanders, replacing the dead Oleanderian child as if it had come to life again. The Goddess did not command her to do so. This was all the queen's design. But you are the children of the prophecy, regardless of how it came about. Only you can defeat the frost giants raging in the north of Almarryn and save your kingdoms.*"

"But the queen manipulated everything," the other girl cried, sounding anguished. "Did she manipulate the takeover of my home country too?"

The dragon let out a long spew of smoke. "*No, little one. She did not. Your people made that choice themselves. But something tells me you will be the one to reclaim Oleanders.*"

"So what is she?" Abrina demanded, caring little about Oleanderian politics. "Is she a Florrynian princess or an Oleanderian one?"

"*She is both,*" the dragon said. "*Though she is the only remaining heir to the Oleanderian throne.*"

Abrina looked at the other girl, who nodded stiffly. Abrina looked away. If the girl was heir to the throne of Oleanders . . . Abrina set her jaw. The other girl was the enemy. She eyed the gleaming swords in the treasure. *I bet she couldn't even wield one. Coward. How in Almarryn did Oleanders ever win against us? I could even the score right now . . . look at all the swords in this collection. She wouldn't stand a chance . . .*

"*Princess Abrina,*" the dragon chided. "*Your thoughts betray you.*"

Abrina gritted her teeth. "She is an enemy to my people. It doesn't matter that she was born in Florryn. Her allegiance is to her country, which makes her an enemy to mine."

At that, the great dragon growled, a sound more ferocious than anything Abrina had ever heard. It was ten times louder than the screams of the frost giants, more gut-wrenching than the cry of Vergyl the sea serpent. And its rage was entirely directed at her.

"*YOU CALL HER AN ENEMY?*" the dragon roared. "*SHE HAS NOT WISHED YOU ILL SINCE YOU STEPPED ONTO MY ISLAND, YET YOU HAVE IGNORED HER, REVILED HER, AND INSULTED HER IN YOUR THOUGHTS, ALL BECAUSE SHE IS FROM OLEANDERS!*"

Abrina cringed, but the dragon wasn't finished.

"*IF ANYONE IS AN ENEMY, IT IS YOU, PRINCESS ABRINA OF FLORRYN. AND UNLESS YOU CAN CONTROL YOUR TEMPER, YOU WILL FAIL THIS QUEST AND PLUNGE THE WORLD INTO AN ETERNAL WINTER.*"

Abrina bristled. How dare he! He called her an enemy? He knew nothing! "You call yourself a great dragon, but you know nothing of the horrors my people have faced at the hands of the Oleanderians! She is nothing but an enemy. Even if the same blood flows through our veins, she was raised in enemy territory. She is nothing less than—"

"*SILENCE!*" the dragon roared and Abrina found her tongue glued to the roof of her mouth. She couldn't say anything even if she wanted to. She felt the eyes of the other princess upon her, but Abrina ignored her.

"Lord Dragon?" the other princess said softly. "Please spare her. I understand why she's angry. My people have wronged hers, for centuries. We nearly destroyed Florryn in the last war. It's not her fault she's angry. Please don't eat her."

Eat her? Abrina was aghast. There was no way she was going to be lunch. Not if she could still move. Her hand inched toward her sword. Maybe she could surprise the dragon?

But then the dragon surprised her. His voice softened. "*Little one, your knowledge has saved her this time. You know her history. You have a hope of loving your enemy.*"

"She is not my enemy," she said softly. "Not any longer. The war with Florryn is over. And these frost giants threaten us all—Oleanderians and Florrynians alike."

"*You are correct, little princess,*" the dragon said. "*Your bravery does you credit.*" He locked eyes with Abrina, whose hand had grasped her sword's handle. She froze under his gaze and found she could not move. Again. Curses.

"*Unfortunately, your sister has not learned the true meaning of bravery. And it will be her undoing.*"

The Oleanderian princess shot Abrina a look of pity, which made Abrina glare at her. Her eyes were about the only thing she could move. She did not need pity, least of all from her.

"Is there any helping her?" The other princess's voice was soft.

"*She will have to cross that bridge herself. But I can assist you.*"

The dragon raised a great claw from the pile of gold, sending a cascade of shining coins to the floor. Something shimmered in his claws. Abrina would have gasped if she could have moved.

It was a sword. And not just any sword. It was one of the twin dragonblades she and Henri had seen on the statue of the First Queen. How did the dragon have it?

"*Ah, you recognize the sword,*" the dragon said, nodding at Abrina. "*It is indeed one of the swords of the First Queen. You will need it if you have a hope to succeed on your quest. This blade is the only thing that can stop the frost giants.*" He lowered his claw but extended it toward the other princess, not Abrina.

Abrina wanted to scream as the girl took it. How could he do such a thing? That Oleanderian princess couldn't even wield a sword! Abrina glared at the dragon but the dragon shot her a piercing, red-eyed look.

"*The time is not yet right for you, Princess,*" the dragon said sharply. "*Nor is the set complete. You must journey to the ruins of Ligerthia and unearth the second sword. Only then can the frost giants be defeated.*"

"The ruins of Ligerthia?" the other princess repeated. "But isn't it encased in ice?"

"*You will need to move quickly.*"

Ligerthia. Of course, it made sense. In a bizarre sort of way. If the book with the prophecy was from the First Queen of Ligerthia, and the people of Ligerthia had fled to Tigahel, then of course their quest would lead them in the reverse direction back to that frozen wasteland.

"Thank you, Lord Dragon," the princess of Oleanders said, bowing to the beast. "I appreciate your wisdom."

"*You are welcome, little princess. But a word of caution before you leave. If you fail, your kingdom will fall. You are the last hope of Oleanders. Your people will die if you do not follow through on this quest, do you understand?*"

The princess looked ashen-faced. "Y-yes, Lord Dragon. I understand."

"*Good.*" The dragon's claw emerged from his pile again, this time holding a glowing vial. "*I foresee that you will need this too on your journey.*"

The girl stared at it, her face awash in the golden glow. "What is it?"

"*Dragon's fire. It can mend even the fiercest of breaks. Remember, little one. There is always a way back. Always.*"

The dragon locked eyes with the Oleanderian princess, who dropped into a curtsy far more elegant than Abrina would have given her credit for. And far more elegant than anything Abrina would ever be able to do. "Thank you again, Lord Dragon."

She turned to leave, taking the intricate dragonblade and the glimmering vial with her. Abrina tried to follow, but she still couldn't move her limbs.

"*Princess Abrina,*" the dragon said, his voice still sharp, but at least he wasn't growling at her anymore. "*Of all the routes you have traveled, this will be the most dangerous. And the most important. You must set aside your pride. If you do not, you will fail.*"

Abrina nodded mutely. She wished she could move her tongue again. And her limbs.

"*The effects of the spell will wear off once you leave my island. But know that I am watching. If you seek to destroy Princess Kailyn, you seek your own destruction.*"

Her own destruction? Traveling with that princess—a traitor to Florryn—would bring her own destruction.

The dragon breathed a small stream of fire near Abrina. The heat made her face swelter and she found she could move. She scurried back quickly.

"*DO NOT TEMPT ME FURTHER!*" the dragon hissed, a column of smoke filling the cave. "*I have spared you thus far because I know how crucial you are to the success of this quest. The First Queen gave me sanctuary here, and I will not fail her. Set aside your pride, Princess Abrina, or you will fail. You will fail us all."*

Abrina was steaming the entire way down the mountain. Literally and figuratively. Her tunic smoked from the dragon's fiery breath, but she was also furious with the Oleanderian princess.

Abrina barreled right past Benje, the wolf cub, and the captain, ignoring their quizzical looks as she headed back to the cajuna. The sooner she got off this rock, the better.

The other princess kept throwing her cautious looks, but she seemed much surer of herself than she had when they'd first arrived, picking her way down with greater ease as she held the golden dragonblade. She'd stashed the gleaming vial somewhere.

Good. Abrina didn't want to see the girl's blessings. It was aggravating. Why did she get the sword? She couldn't even wield one!

The knights were still waiting for them when they got back to the beach. "Princess Abrina!" Sir Zachry saluted them. "Princess Kailyn! Are you alright?"

"We are well," the Oleanderian princess said. "The dragon has confirmed that we are the ones the prophecy speaks of, and we've acquired a blade. The second is in Ligerthia."

"Goddess's eyes," Byron whispered. "May I see that sword, Princess?"

The girl nodded and handed him the blade. Byron examined the exquisite workmanship on it and whistled appreciatively. "It's a wonder."

Abrina grunted. It still irked her that the other girl got the sword while she ended up being frozen and made mute.

Sir Byron eyed Abrina. "Princess? Dragon got your tongue?"

She glared at him. Terrible joke.

The wolf cub nestled into the other girl's side as she answered for Abrina. "Princess Abrina has been temporarily deprived of speech."

"Due to her temper, no doubt," Byron said acerbically.

Abrina glowered at him.

He shrugged. "What? It's not like you haven't offended every single foreign entity we've encountered since we've left Heria."

"Byron, be respectful," the captain snapped. He turned to face the other princess. "So we're headed to Ligerthia?"

The girl nodded. "The dragon said the frost giants must be defeated at their source."

"Hmm." He looked at Abrina. "Didn't the prince give you a map?"

Abrina nodded, grabbed the parchment from her saddlebag, and handed it to him.

The captain spread it out on the ground. He pointed to the frozen lands of the north. "That's the giant's homeland. Are you sure we shouldn't go there? That would make more sense as the source of the frost giants."

"It's so far north," Zachry whispered. "Good thing we packed warm."

"Better there than Ligerthia," Byron muttered. "That land is filled with ghosts."

Benje stared at the two of them. "If the princess says it's Ligerthia, then we're headed to Ligerthia."

The two of them grunted. "Fine," Byron said.

"Good." Benje inclined his head to the captain. "When do we leave?"

The captain turned his head to look at Abrina. "When the princesses are ready."

Abrina shook her head, pointed to the cajuna, then to her throat, using the sign for speech Sir Tyir had taught her. Her knights nodded in understanding, but the Oleanderian princess translated anyway.

"Princess Abrina cannot speak until we leave the island," the other girl said. "I suggest we leave as soon as possible."

For once, Abrina agreed with her.

Chapter Twenty - Six

Kailyn

She really is my sister. As they flew over the ocean, Benje behind her on the cajuna and Canis in the knapsack, Kailyn kept replaying the dragon's voice in her mind. The Florrynian princess—Abrina—had seemed utterly confident when she had walked into that cave, but when she had challenged the dragon, Kailyn had been completely terrified. She thought the dragon would swallow them right there on the spot.

But she had remembered from her readings that dragons were vain creatures, even if they were gifted with foresight. They liked being complimented, and their titles were as elegant as they were. And it had worked. They hadn't been eaten. Kailyn felt her heart swell with pride at the thought. Myira would be proud of her. Which was more than she could say of her sister.

Abrina was as different from Kailyn as the Goddess from the Sun King the Oronians worshipped. While the Goddess was kind and compassionate, the Sun King was strict and stern. Unlike Kailyn, Abrina was not scholarly. She'd not come from a prosperous nation. She was a survivor who had survived more destruction than Kailyn could even imagine. She was a warrior.

And she hated Kailyn.

Aru? Canis's voice came into her mind again. *Fear?*

Kailyn shook her head.

It's alright. I'm just . . . trying to sort this out.

"You alright, Princess?" Benje asked as the cajuna flew on.

"I . . ." Kailyn sighed. "The dragon said we were the last hope of Almarryn. That only Abrina and I can defeat the frost giants. But she hates me."

Benje's arms stiffened around her. "She's Florrynian. They're all born with vengeance coursing through their veins. Why else were they the instigators of every single war with Oleanders?"

"But we've hurt them too, Benje." She gazed out at the endless blue ocean beneath them. "I understand where their hatred comes from."

"Still. If she tries to come after you, I will be there."

Kailyn glanced at the cajuna in front of her, where Abrina rode like the proud warrior princess she was.

She sighed again. How were they going to do this? Her thoughts drifted to the sword that Benje had buckled onto their cajuna. How was she even supposed to use it? Until the dragon had given her the blade, she'd never even touched one.

Not like Abrina. Kailyn had seen the jealous look that had lit up the Florrynian princess's face when Kailyn had gotten the blade. Abrina was a natural with the sword. A born warrior.

Kailyn wasn't. So why did the dragon give her the blade? What power did it have?

She wished she could fly back to Oleanders and hunker down in her study to figure out the history of the dragonblade, but the dragon's voice haunted her thoughts. *If you fail, you will not have a home to return to.* She'd thought she would be saving her people from Lord Shielen by coming to Tigahel, but with the imminent threat of the frost giants, she had to complete this quest with her twin sister, otherwise her people would be destroyed. It was all so very confusing.

They camped the first night on one of the small islands in the Oronian colonies. Kailyn's heart hammered fiercely as they landed, worried that Oronia might come after her, but there was nothing there other than birds and some spongy marsh. The birds spooked when they landed, but Kailyn was so relieved to get off the cajuna. Her legs hurt worse than they had when she had ridden with Benje. She stretched them out shakily before slipping the dragonblade from the saddle. What was she to do with the sword?

Canis bounded out of the pack and scampered across the marsh, sniffing at different plants and flowers.

Benje was looking at Kailyn with concern. "You must be tired, Princess."

"I'm fine," Kailyn said, wishing he'd give her a little more space. She knew he was protective—and she appreciated it, and his support, more than she could say. But she still wasn't sure how she felt about him, nor his role in getting her to Tigahel in the first place. They hadn't really had a chance to talk about it.

Benje looked at her again before heading off to help Captain Wilen and Sir Byron set up tents. Sir Zachry got a fire going while Abrina went off alone, probably looking for small game, though Kailyn had no idea what her sister filled her spare time with. Fighting probably.

Canis scampered back to her, sniffing her dress. *Food?*

She rummaged in the pouch on the cajuna and handed him some jerky. "Here." Canis sniffed at it, chomping at the jerky before bounding off to go exploring again.

She stood there, watching his white fur shine against the green marsh. Everyone seemed to be busy, even the pup. She was useless at this whole questing thing.

She sighed and sat down by the snapping fire, setting the dragonblade in her lap. Sir Zachry had a small knife out and was carving into a stick. Kailyn watched, fascinated as he slid off a few slivers.

"What are you doing?"

"Whittling." He glanced up at her, a perplexed expression on his young face. "Have you never seen anyone whittle before, Your Highness?"

"No," she said. "I'd never even seen a sword at close range until this morning."

Though she had seen a knife at close range before . . . buried in her father's bloated belly. She blinked, forcing the grisly image from her mind. It didn't do to dwell on ghosts. Not when she had to figure out this blade.

The young man's brown eyes widened. He motioned toward the sword in her lap. "The dragonblade. It's stunning."

It was. She fingered the inscription on the blade. It was in Old Alarian, the intricate swirling letters curling around each other. She still didn't know what it meant and hadn't gotten around to asking Benje. All she'd been able to pick out was the word *Alaria*. A carved dragon curled around the handle, its mouth pointed toward the blade like it was breathing metal instead of fire. She'd never seen anything like it.

"Not that I know how to use it," Kailyn murmured.

Zachry looked at her, a curious look on his face. "I'm sure you'll figure it out, Princess. After all, you are Florrynian. And Florrynians were born for the blade."

Not me, she thought, watching as he continued to whittle his stick. *I'm not even Florrynian.*

At that moment, the other princess arrived with a few small furry rodents in hand. She tossed them before Zachry.

"Dinner," she said as she pulled out a knife.

Kailyn watched, horrified, as the princess hacked off the fur, slicing the rodent into clean hunks of meat. She made it look effortless.

"You finished that spit yet, Zachry?" Abrina asked.

The young knight handed the thin stick to her. Kailyn watched as her sister skewered the meat from the rodents and placed it on two other sticks hanging over the fire.

"Ah! Fresh hyn rats," the ruddy-haired knight said as he approached, leaving the tents standing spotless behind him.

"Actually, I think these are marsh rats," Abrina said, watching the fire. "They looked close enough though, so I imagine they'll taste the same."

Sir Byron inclined his head. "Well, you have my thanks, Princess."

Princess Abrina grunted and poked the fire with another stick. Kailyn sat there, staring. Her sister could do everything. Ride a horse, wield a sword, hunt and skin animals. She wouldn't have had any problems had she been on the run from her kingdom's guards. She'd probably drive them all back single-handedly.

Kailyn blinked, forcing the angry tears from her eyes. She would not be jealous of her sister. It would only cause Abrina to hate her more.

Canis came bounding up to her, a large rat in his mouth. *Food!* He sounded way too happy as he chomped on it.

Kailyn averted her gaze, squeamish at the sight of the wolf gnawing on the rat.

"Are you alright, Princess?" a quiet voice whispered behind her. Kailyn turned, seeing Benje there. Having finished putting up the tents, he was polishing his sword, but his eyes were fixed on hers and they were filled with concern.

She sighed. He was way too observant.

"I . . . I think I'd better go for a walk," she said, standing up. Benje stood up, sheathing his sword.

"I'll go with you."

He was also too overprotective.

Aru? Canis looked up from his meal, his face covered with remnants of the rat.

Kailyn tried not to gag. "Stay there, Canis. We won't be gone long."

"Oh, if you two are going to walk around, could you collect more firewood?" Zachry said, eyeing the flames. "We'll need a bit more to fuel the fire after dinner is cooked."

Kailyn nodded and followed Benje away from the camp.

She didn't know where she was going, but she knew she needed to get away from her sister. Florrynians could do everything. She knew full well that Abrina couldn't stop the frost giants on her own, at least according to the prophecy. But at least Abrina was more prepared to face the frost giants. Way more prepared than Kailyn was.

All she wanted was to go home to Oleanders. But even that was denied her, as her kingdom was going through civil unrest and Lord Shielen was at the helm.

"You're troubled," Benje said, the fire a speck behind them. "What's on your mind?"

That was the other thing.

She whirled on him. "Why did you obey the queen to take me to Tigahel? Why?"

Benje held up his hands in a non-threatening gesture. "I did what I had to, Princess."

"Will they even give us allies?"

"Yes." He didn't even blink. "Prince Henri will be going to negotiate with Lord Shielen after he distributes aid to Florryn."

She stared at him. "He will?"

Benje nodded. "He's the ambassador for Tigahel. He can negotiate with Lord Shielen and the rebellion to try and bring peace to Oleanders."

She bit her lip, thinking about that. Henri was more of a diplomat than she'd ever be. She'd never even gotten the chance to see her kingdom before she was roped into this quest.

"But it's not his mess to clean up," Kailyn whispered. "It's mine. I need to do all I can to fix it."

"You are," Benje said, bending down to pick up some firewood. "You're on this quest, aren't you?"

Kailyn made a face. "After *you* brought me here on the queen's orders. And now we're here in the middle of nowhere with the Florrynians who are barely civil toward us, least of all Abrina!" She threw her hands in the air. "She's so . . . so Florrynian. More than all of them. She's hurt and bitter about the war, and even though the dragon said we're sisters, I don't think she'll ever treat me like one."

Kailyn took a deep breath, her side heaving as she leveled her gaze at Benje. "I wish you'd never brought me here."

Benje set down the sticks he was carrying and walked toward Kailyn, extending his hand. Kailyn, reluctantly, took it.

"Breathe, Princess," he said as he softly traced circles on her hand. "You're overwhelmed."

She took a shuddering breath and then glared at him. "You never answered me. Why did you do it?"

Benje was silent. In the stillness, Kailyn could hear Canis yipping.

Food! At least one of them was happy.

"She came to my master's," Benje whispered, his voice tense. "He'd been training me in the ways of the Ligerthian Knights, teaching me their creed. But only the queen of Ligerthia has the power to make apprentices knights."

A night bird called out, but Kailyn focused on Benje's words.

"I was fourteen. The queen asked my master to serve her once more. But Master Barholow refused. He said the queen had done terrible things in the past, and he didn't trust her decisions anymore."

"What happened?" Kailyn whispered.

"She left. But, shortly after that, a fire burned Master Barholow's forge and his house to the ground, killing him in the blaze."

"Oh, Benje." Kailyn squeezed his hand. "I'm so sorry."

"That's not the worst of it. She came back the next day and said that if I wanted to be a Ligerthian Knight, if I wanted to keep making a decent wage, then I'd need to serve her faithfully and she'd make me a Ligerthian Knight when the time was right. She made me spy on the rebellion, send her messages, keep her informed of the goings on in Oleanders." He sighed. "She even made sure I had a place at the Library's Forge, where other Ligerthian Knights-in-training worked. It was the job of my dreams. All I had to do was obey her orders.

"I'd known I was to take you to Tigahel for three years." His voice was growing softer and his shoulders shook with repressed tears. "I swore I'd do it, like I'd sworn I'd do all the other tasks. But Princess . . . when I met you, that day at the library, something changed. I knew the queen was wrong. Master Barholow hadn't trusted her. I'd only followed along because she promised I'd be a Ligerthian Knight. She promised me everything I'd ever dreamed. My mother and sisters are well looked after from her monthly payments. The other knights helped finish my training. So I became the queen's spy." He shuddered again.

"But you . . . you were innocent in all this. And when I met you, I knew who deserved my allegiance. It wasn't the queen of Tigahel. It was never her. But I was afraid."

Kailyn squeezed his hand again. "She killed your master, didn't she?"

He shook his head. "I could never prove it. But she kidnapped you, didn't she? Pretended you were the Oleanderian princess revived. She caused the fall of Ligerthia. What other things is she capable of?"

His shoulders shook even worse. "And I served her. I served her orders."

Kailyn felt a tear stream down her own face at Benje's confession. "Benje, she tricked you. She needed a spy, and she created one in you. But you don't have to continue working for her."

Benje nodded. "And I won't. This is the last mission I do for her. I don't care if I never become a Ligerthian Knight. No Forging power is worth sacrificing everything." He squeezed her hands softly. "I will protect you, Princess. You have my word."

"I know." Kailyn smiled, though she didn't know if he could see it in the fading light. "You already have."

She mulled over what he'd told her and frowned. "What do you mean this is the last mission you'll do for her?"

Benje grunted. "I'm seeing you to the end of this. Whatever *this* is. And then I'm breaking all ties with the queen. Her son is a much better ruler, but Ligerthians live a long time. It will be decades before Henri gets to rule."

Kailyn nodded, gratitude filling her heart. She was grateful Benje had told her, that he trusted her enough to open up. And now that he'd explained, his pain and conflict made more sense.

She remembered the words that he had given her in the gnome caverns, the words she'd repeated in her mind a million times since she'd heard them. His declaration of loyalty. To her.

"You don't need to become a Ligerthian Knight, Benje," she whispered. "You already are one." She slipped her free hand into her pocket and pulled out the glimmering crystal vial of dragon's fire.

Benje's eyes widened. "Princess . . . is that . . . dragon's fire?"

She nodded. "The dragon gave it to me. I want you to have it. As a reminder that you already have the fire of the Ligerthian Knights within you."

Benje pocketed the vial before he pressed a gentle kiss to her forehead. Tingles raced down Kailyn's spine at the touch. "Thank you, Princess."

"Kailyn. Please, Benje. You don't need to call me by my title. Besides," she smiled wryly, "there are two princesses now."

He chuckled softly. "Alright. Shall we finish gathering the firewood then?"

Aru? Canis called out. *Home?*

She laughed. *We're coming, Canis.* "We'd better. Canis is wondering where I am."

"He's a good boy." Benje squeezed her hand. "A fierce protector."

Kailyn smiled. "He's not the only one." She linked her fingers with his. "Let's get some firewood."

Even though the Florrynians—other than Sir Zachry—remained distant from Kailyn and Benje when they got back, Kailyn felt better. Benje was fully on her side. She knew why he'd done what he had.

And she trusted him. With her life. Together, they could face anything. Even her extremely ill-tempered sister.

Abrina flat-out refused to talk to Kailyn all throughout dinner and at the fireside. Kailyn saw her sneak glimpses her direction every so often, but then she'd jerk her head away, scowling.

As she prepared for sleep, Canis curled around her, Kailyn only hoped that she could work things out with Abrina like she had with Benje. Otherwise, this quest would be over before it really began.

Chapter Twenty - Seven

Kailyn

It took them another two days to get to Ligerthia. They camped in Cyron one night, which was already getting chilly. But as they flew over the bay from Tyloan, and over the Cyan Mountains, the weather got bitterly cold, filled with snowflakes. It snuck in past the warm furs Kailyn had wrapped herself in and stung to the bone. She tried pulling the furs closer, but they didn't seem to do much against the stinging wind.

Canis though seemed content that there was snow all around. *Snow!* He kept sending her images of flurrying flakes. Kailyn shivered, pulling her fur cape closer around herself.

She'd never been this cold in her life, and they weren't even there yet.

"We must be getting close," Benje whispered in her ear. She was grateful he was behind her, as he was helping her stay warm.

An hour or so later, they'd flown over the mountains to a vast whiteness that extended as far as the eye could see. Tufts of ice blew in the wind, gusting around like her father's court in full promenade. The cold was a sharp bitter blue that threatened to eat her. There was something wrong with the very air of Ligerthia itself.

The cajuna landed near some rocks, and the knights quickly

bound their wings. The creatures shrieked in protest, but the sound was carried away by the bitter wind. Prince Henri had told them before they left that the cajunas' wings would need to be bound to protect them from the cold climate. Kailyn still thought it was a risk that they were even traveling to Ligerthia by cajuna, but it was the fastest way there. They had to find the sword and stop the frost giants soon—before everything froze over forever.

Abrina signaled for them to gather around. "Our first objective is to find the second dragonblade. Sir Benje, I believe you mentioned the Ligerthian Temple?"

Benje nodded and pulled out a book. He'd told Kailyn last night that he'd gotten it from Prince Henri. The wind gusted its pages, but he held tightly to it to prevent it from being blown away. "The map points that way." He pointed off in the distance, but Kailyn couldn't see what he was pointing to.

Abrina frowned. "That doesn't look like the right direction."

"Trust me, it's that way." Benje stared down at the princess of Florryn, who stared right back at him, her eyes narrowing in anger.

A sudden strong gust of wind covered them with a dusting of ice particles. The cajuna shrieked into the gale, the sound eerily ripped away by the wind.

"We should seek shelter!" Captain Wilen called out. "We don't want to be caught out here by the frost giants. They could use this weather to surprise us!"

Kailyn had to agree with him. If it got any colder, her very bones were going to freeze.

Princess Abrina had them tie the cajuna together so they wouldn't lose any of them. Kailyn held onto the rope as she struggled to put one foot in front of the other. Canis walked by her side, practically floating on the snow. She wished she had fur like he did—she was freezing.

A looming shape emerged from the bleak white landscape. For a moment, Kailyn thought it was a giant about to leap at them, but it turned out to be an outcropping of rocks. Benje was leading them toward a cave.

The cave wasn't big, but it connected to a labyrinth of tunnels. Abrina insisted they stay close to the opening, as she said, rather vehemently, that she distrusted the secrets of caves. Kailyn could only think of the dragon incident from a few days ago. Abrina clearly held onto grudges for a long time.

But to Kailyn, the dim cave reminded her of the gnome caverns, minus the glowing rock on the ceiling.

Home, Canis agreed, curling around Kailyn's feet, resting his muzzle on his paws.

Byron had somehow found firewood—he'd likely packed it—and soon had a merry little fire going. The bright crackles and pops were the only sound accompanying the howl of the wind outside, and the occasional yips from Canis.

The cajuna were huddled near the back of the cave, nickering softly in the dim light. Kailyn felt sorry for the poor creatures. If they couldn't find them any food, they would starve. And after they had carried them all this way. It seemed like such a waste.

Food? Canis perked his head up again. Kailyn rolled her eyes. The pup was nearly the size of a full-grown wolf now, but he certainly still acted like a pup. She dug through her saddlebag to find him another root.

Benje and Abrina were arguing about where to go to find the dragonblade. Kailyn was tired. Tired from traveling, tired of the snow—though she had only ever been in snow today— and tired of their bickering.

Kailyn remembered the fascination with Ligerthia that Benje had demonstrated when she'd first met him. He had a deep longing to be a knight, as he'd told her that night on the marsh. What must it be like for him to be near where the knights originated? What sorts of secrets did this land hold? It was a shame that everything Ligerthian was frozen.

Well, not everything. She took the sword out of the scabbard attached to her side. The weight was uncomfortable. She would have preferred to leave it on one of the cajuna, but she was going to have to get used to it. Somehow, this blade was to help her defeat the frost giants.

"The Temple is in the center of Ligerthia! Crossing the frozen river takes us directly there," Benje insisted, pointing to the map.

"But have you noticed the lack of frost giants? They will be upon us the moment we try to get to the Temple. We'll be too exposed! We have to go an alternate route," Abrina snarled, her voice spitting sparks like a fire.

"We may not have time to go an alternate route, Princess! This storm might very well freeze us if we can't find a way through it."

Canis perked his head up. *Danger!*

"Quiet, the both of you," Captain Wilen hissed, holding up his fist. "There are frost giants outside."

Chapter Twenty - Eight

Abrina

Abrina tensed, slipping into battle mode, reaching for her sword. She'd been on edge since they'd set foot on Ligerthian soil. There was something *wrong* about the land. The very air felt deadening.

Now here was a chance to let loose some of her pent-up emotions. She glanced at the cave's opening, where all she could see was swirling snow. But the smell . . . the deep earthy, minty smell could only mean frost giants.

She knew how to beat frost giants. Or at least knock them on their backs. The magical dragonblade would just have to do its job and eliminate them for good.

She glowered at the Oleanderian princess and her wolf cub who stood there, holding the dragonblade, an expression of horror on her face. "Well, come on then. Let's go put that blade to use."

Captain Wilen shook his head. "No. Princess Kailyn is untrained. We can wait out the storm here."

Abrina scoffed. "With what? We've only got some meager rations from Tigahel. Once those are gone, we're done for. There's nothing here in this frozen wasteland!"

And yet they'd come here, all to fulfill a wretched prophecy.

She cursed. She wanted to be back in Florryn. Or with Henri back at Tigahel. Anywhere but here.

Suddenly, the dragonblade started glowing, the surface of the blade filling with a gentle golden light.

Abrina stared at it. "What's the blade doing?"

The other princess stared at the sword as it pointed toward the back of the cave where the cajuna were huddled. "It wants us to go there."

"But that's ridiculous," Abrina said. "The walls are solid stone. There's no way we can get through them."

The wolf cub perked up his head and started sniffing toward the wall.

Abrina raised an eyebrow. "What's he doing?"

"Canis says there's a tunnel back there," the other princess said, following the pup to the back of the wall. "Come on!"

"It's just a wall," Abrina grumbled.

Then she heard the howl of the frost giants outside and stiffened. She'd rather go fight them out there than hunker down in this cave.

She felt an arm on her shoulder. She looked up to see Captain Wilen, his pewter gray eyes filled with concern. "Princess. Perhaps it is wise to seek further shelter from these giants. There are more of them here than there ever were at the front. You cannot defeat them all."

Abrina clenched her teeth. She wanted to. She wanted to take on all the frost giants. But the cursed things reformed, and unless she could harness the power of the dragonblade, she'd be fighting until she was frozen, and then where would they be?

"Fine," she ground out. She followed the company to the back wall of the cave.

To her surprise, there was a carving of a dragon, curled around a book. The carving looked old—like it belonged more to the temple on Isle Nyx than to a rock wall in the middle of nowhere.

More of the looping script Henri was so fond of curled around the dragon.

The apprentice—Benje—knelt down and traced the curling script with his fingers.

"What does it say?" the other princess asked.

"It says this tunnel offers passage to the Ligerthian Temple." He exchanged looks with the girl. "It's quite possibly a direct route there."

The wolf cub howled as if he was agreeing.

Abrina shrugged. Well, this wasn't what she'd had in mind, but if there was a direct route underground away from the frost giants, it might get them to the other blade faster.

"Well, how in Almarryn do we get there?" Sir Byron scowled. "If it's a door, it sure ain't opening."

As if to prove him wrong, the carving started to glow the same golden color as the sword. The cave rumbled, the cajuna cried, and the wolf cub howled. When the rocks settled, there was a gaping black hole where the wall used to be.

"What in the Palace of Stars . . ." Abrina breathed.

The Oleanderian princess smiled at her. "Shall we?"

Abrina harrumphed. "Fine. Lead the way."

After grabbing torches and putting out the remainder of the fire, the company headed down the long tunnel. At the front of the pack was the Oleanderian princess and her guardsman. He and the wolf cub rarely left the girl's side. Abrina followed, walking alongside Sir Zachry. Byron and the captain walked behind them, leading the cajuna.

"Do you think the frost giants will get us in here?" Zachry asked tentatively. Abrina shot him a look. She'd forgotten that he hadn't been there at the front with Byron and the others.

"They shouldn't be able to," Abrina said. "They need ice and snow to reform. And there's none of that in here." Though it wasn't exactly warm either. She pulled her fur cape tighter around herself. They needed to get another fire going soon.

"Look at this carving!" the other girl exclaimed ahead of them. "It's magnificent!" Abrina rolled her eyes. This was the fourth carving she'd stopped to examine.

"Let's keep it moving, shall we?" she called. "It's just another carving." And she'd had enough of statues to last her a lifetime.

"It is magnificent though," Zachry said next to her. "You have to admit, who knew that so much of the Ligerthians' work was still preserved? I have never seen such exquisite workmanship."

Abrina pursed her lips. He sounded like Henri. She missed him. She hoped he was helping her people, wherever he was.

"It's beautiful, I suppose," Abrina muttered. "But it's not the other sword. We have to get that first. And then defeat the frost giants. We don't have time for carvings."

"The princess is right," Captain Wilen called from behind. "Keep moving, all."

They fell into a rhythm, following the glowing sword down the tunnel. The cave grew wider and the carvings more elaborate, but the other princess didn't stop to admire them anymore. Abrina nodded resolutely. Good. The girl was learning sense.

She scowled at the thought. Didn't mean the girl was competent. They were going this route because she didn't know how to use a sword.

"I wonder what the dragonblades do," Zachry mused after a few more minutes of walking. "I mean, besides glow, obviously. They must do something."

"They destroy frost giants," Abrina said grimly. "That's all we need."

"Yes, but how?"

She grunted. "I don't know. The dragon didn't say."

"He did say you're sisters though?" Zachry still sounded cheerful, but there was a sadness to his tone. "To think the queen of Tigahel stole the other Florrynian princess!"

"She is not Florrynian," Abrina muttered. "She can't ride, she can't fight, and she is completely clueless to the outdoors. She'd die on her own."

Zachry shot her a look. "You don't care for your own sister, do you, Princess?"

Abrina sighed. She was tired of the girl already. And her wolf cub. Her *Alarian* wolf cub—a clear blessing from the Goddess for Florryn. But the other princess *wasn't* Florrynian. So how'd she get a magical wolf cub?

Abrina rested her hand on her sword, drawing assurance from the comforting silver blade. She wanted this quest to be done with so she could forget it had ever happened. "She's Oleanderian. The enemy." It came out quiet. Deathly quiet.

Zachry was silent for half a beat. "But she was born Florrynian. That makes her your sister, and our princess."

"She is the heir to the Oleanderian throne. That does not make her Florrynian."

"Princess," Zachry sighed. "The war is over."

She glowered at him. "You may forget. You may forget how Oleanders ravished our homes, our villages, burned our fields, shelled our coasts. You may forget how they stole our silver, took thousands of prisoners to work in our mines, and then killed those prisoners when the work dried up. You may forget, Sir Zachry. But I. Will. Not."

She clenched her fists and stormed ahead of the group, bypassing the traitorous Oleanderians and the wolf.

"Princess Abrina," the other princess started to say, but Abrina ignored her and headed in front of the pack, holding one of the torches from the fire. She had to get the blade to end this quest. Because her patience was running out.

The tunnel emerged into a small underground courtyard flanked by giant statues of the Ligerthian Knights. They were made of the same shining white rock as the ones at the library on Tigahel. Each one had a different face, though they all carried staffs, crossing over those of their neighbors'. They stood proud, erect, their stone faces smooth. Abrina wondered, for half a second, if the statues were going to speak to her like they had at the library on Tigahel. But these were silent. Thank the Goddess. She didn't think she could handle talking statues right now. Especially without Henri. Goddess above, she missed that man.

"What is this place?" she muttered, looking around. The statues boxed in the courtyard. Other than the large round door she'd emerged from, there weren't any other entrances. She poked around some of the statues' legs, but the walls behind them seemed to be just walls. Had the glowing sword led them to a dead end? She glowered at the room, hoping something would appear that would make it all worthwhile, but nothing changed.

A yipping sounded behind her along with the sound of laughter and the soft cries of the cajuna. Abrina sighed. So much for a break.

"Well, this was useless," Abrina said when the others filed into the courtyard. "There's nothing here."

Byron's soldier-hardened eyes scanned the room. "No, but it's a good fortress. We should set up camp here tonight."

He had a point. Even if they were trapped, there was only one way in. It would be easy to defend.

"Very well," she said. "Captain Wilen?"

The man, who was holding one of the leads for the cajuna, saluted her. "Yes, Princess." He turned to his men. "Let's set up camp."

Within moments, the cajuna were nestled in a corner, and bedding was spread on the rocks. It didn't do any good to set up tents here. What elements would the cloth protect them from?

The guardsman Benje and the other princess were poring over the ancient book Abrina had found with Henri. *Henri.* She thought longingly of the prince, wishing he were there with them. But he was with her people and she was stuck here with the princess of her enemies. Sighing, she found a comfortable spot to curl up in and fell into an uneasy sleep.

Chapter Twenty-Nine

Abrina

$\mathcal{S}$he was standing next to Prince Henri, who was holding her hand. She glanced at him, her heart pounding fast at his nearness.

"*Fyrrel*," he said in that melty way of his that made her heart flutter. He smiled, his bright blue irises shimmering.

"Henri," she breathed, leaning closer toward him.

But before their lips could meet, a scream shattered the stillness. It was sharp, like daggers and as bitter as ice, cutting her to her core. It extended on into an eternity and she forced her eyes shut to block the sound out. When the sound finally stopped and she opened her eyes again, Henri was gone. In his place was her mother, covered in thick blue ice. Panic sounded in her ears, screaming as loud as the terrible sound.

"Mother?" She reached out a trembling hand toward the ice.

"Abrina! Don't touch it!" a familiar voice cried, but it was too late.

The ice pricked her finger. Her hand felt warm, blood flowing to the tips of her fingers, peeping through the pale surface of her flesh like flowers blooming through the snow in a Florrynian spring. But an ice shard dug itself into her flesh, and her finger turned cold, colder than stone, colder than ice, colder than death. The cold spread up her arms, shooting tendrils of ice deep into her skin, freezing her blood and slowly spreading toward her heart. So c-c-c-old . . .

Abrina gasped, awakening with a start. She glanced down at her hands. They were flesh, not ice. She heaved a sigh of relief, laying her head against the cold walls of the cave.

Her heart was still pounding from the dream. It had felt as real as when she'd actually been encased in ice by that adolescent frost giant. She shuddered, remembering how the giant's breath had caused ice to grow all over her arms. Were the frost giants spreading even further in Florryn? Were her people safe?

The line from the prophecy echoed in her mind. *All will be frozen and left to die.* How in all of Almarryn were they to fight that?

She glanced around the camp. The other knights were asleep. The girl and her guardsman were also asleep, though Benje's eyelids flickered back and forth in the dying light of the fire, like he was anxious in his dreams. She frowned. What sorts of things did he dream about?

Only the wolf cub was awake. His bright eyes, shining like blue stars, stared right at her as if he could see her soul.

Abrina swallowed. "Um, hello."

He chuffed softly. Abrina knew Alarian wolves were telepathic, but she wasn't sensing anything from the wolf. Her heart sank. Maybe she wasn't blessed with that gift like the girl from Oleanders was.

But the wolf still stared at her.

"I-I don't know what I'm doing," Abrina admitted, sitting next to him. The cub laid his head next to her hand. Tentatively, she touched his fur. The pup sighed, so she continued to stroke the soft fibers. He truly was glorious.

She knew the stories of Alarian wolves. They were one of the legendary creatures of Alaria, back before it had been divided into Florryn, Ligerthia, Oleanders, and Cyron. And though the Alarian wolves were thought to have retreated into the Rosstross

Mountains centuries ago, she had heard the story of the first king of Florryn being blessed with the ability to connect and communicate with them. It was said that only his descendants would inherit that gift.

And the other princess had been given that blessing.

"She has the Florrynian gift," Abrina mumbled. "She was somehow blessed with your companionship. But she isn't a true Florrynian. She's not my sister. She can't be."

The wolf whined and looked at her with those piercing blue eyes.

Abrina shrugged. "What? It's true. She was raised in Oleanders—the sworn enemy of my people. Even if we share the same parents, it doesn't mean we're family."

The wolf tilted his head as if questioning her.

Abrina scowled. "Why am I even talking to you?"

He poked her hand with his nose, then looked at one of the statues. Then back to her hand, which he licked.

"Quit that," Abrina grumbled. But he kept doing it. Sighing, Abrina, got to her feet and quietly walked to the statue.

Why was this one different from the other twenty-eight statues? She looked up at the face and blinked. It had the same face as the First Queen statue that she and Henri had found at the library on Tigahel. But she looked like a Ligerthian Knight, complete with the tunic, staff, and—

"The sword," she whispered. This First Queen statue had both blades buckled around her waist. Abrina felt foolish for not noticing it before. She looked back at the pup, who was staring at her inquisitively. "Did you know about this?"

He yipped again. Abrina rolled her eyes. Right. Magical wolf. What other things did he know?

She turned back to the statue. What was it guarding? Her

mind went back to that day where she'd flown on the cajuna for the first time with Henri to the library. How had they gotten the doors open?

Well, he'd bowed to them. And she'd followed suit.

She scowled. Bowing to statues. Utter nonsense.

But, because she didn't have any other option, she bowed.

A thunderous voice sounded in her head. It was neither male nor female, neither soft nor hard, neither kind nor severe. It reminded Abrina of the dragon who'd raged at her, but seemed older somehow.

"*WHO APPROACHES?*"

"It is I, Princess Abrina of Florryn," she whispered, still bowing. She touched her mother's pendant to steady herself. She would not lose her temper. There was something otherworldly about that voice. Something . . . ancient.

"*PRINCESS, WHY HAVE YOU COME?*"

"I come seeking the second dragonblade to fulfill the prophecy of the Goddess." *And save my people,* she thought.

"*DO YOU KNOW THE POWER OF THE DRAGONBLADE?*"

She scowled. No, she had no idea what the dragonblade could do. Other than glow in the dark and lead to courtyards filled with statues, apparently. As a weapon, it seemed kind of useless. It was much shorter than her regular blade and much more ornate. It wasn't very practical.

"*THEY ARE MUCH MORE THAN A WEAPON, PRINCESS.*"

The terrible voice was so loud, but Abrina didn't see anyone from the camp move. Were they all still asleep? How? The thunderous voice felt like it would split her skull.

"*THE DRAGONBLADES WERE FORGED TO HEAL A BROKEN BOND BETWEEN NATIONS. ARE YOU PREPARED TO REFORGE THAT BOND?*"

Abrina glanced behind her, where she could still see the white wolf cub staring at her. He motioned his head as if to say *go on.*

"Between my nation and Oleanders?" she asked the statue, her voice barely a whisper.

"*MEND THE BOND YOUR ANCESTORS RIPPED TO SHREDS. MEND THE MISTAKES OF THE PAST. DO THIS, AND YOU WILL ACCESS THE POWER OF THE DRAGONBLADE.*"

She grimaced. Make amends. That was what the prophecy was about. *Only together will they be strong. Only together will they right this wrong.* They needed the dragonblades to do that, and they needed the power. They didn't have a hope of defeating the frost giants otherwise. They'd just keep reforming and respawning and encase everything in ice. But to forgive Oleanders? That was unthinkable.

"I will do whatever it takes to save my country," she said, meaning every word. For the good of Florryn, she would do her duty. She'd work with this princess to stop the frost giants. But an alliance was all she could promise, and even then, only a temporary one.

"*BE WARNED, PRINCESS. IF THE SWORD FAILS YOU, IT IS NOT BECAUSE IT IS AN INFERIOR BLADE. IT WILL BE BECAUSE YOUR HEART IS NOT PURE. FAILURE OF THE SWORD WILL BE UPON YOUR OWN HEAD. DO YOU ACCEPT THESE TERMS?*"

A pure heart? She had wielded a sword all her life and never once was the purity of her heart called into question. She doubted whether her heart even was pure. With her record? She knew it wasn't likely.

But she needed that sword, pure heart or not. She bowed to the statue once more.

"I accept."

"*THEN PROCEED.*"

With a loud grating noise, the staffs slid apart, revealing a hidden door. It wasn't grand or carved with anything—like the door to the tunnel had been—it was simply a rectangle carved into the stone wall. It didn't have any handles from what Abrina could see, but when she touched it, it silently swung open.

Behind the door lay a carved stone staircase that descended into the gloom. She couldn't see any light source and wished for half a moment that she had the glowing power of the other drag-onblade. But that would require waking up the other princess.

She looked back at the wolf who had nestled his head onto his paws, blinking his blue eyes sleepily at her. For half a moment, she wished he could come with her. But then the pup closed his eyes, falling back into slumber.

She sighed and turned back to the tunnel. It was pitch black. All she could smell was earth. Gritting her teeth, she stepped onto the stairs and was not surprised when the door slid shut behind her, sealing her into the darkness of the tunnel.

Torches lit up along the walls as soon as the doors closed. They glowed an eerie blue that made Abrina feel like she was walking into Perthia, the lowest of the three hells. She shivered. Perthia was said to be where souls were consumed by blue fires for eternity.

Her fingers found her sword and wrapped protectively around the handle. She was here to find the dragonblade, so she'd carry on.

The staircase descended into the earth for what felt like an eternity. The tunnel was wide, and the white stones of the wall were gently illuminated by the pulsing blue light of the torches.

Abrina felt uneasy. What had the statue meant about reform-ing a bond? How was she supposed to do that? She would never claim that other princess as her sister. She couldn't. She'd be betraying centuries of her people's tradition. Oleanders was their foe. Surely working together, only temporarily of course, would be all that was required. Right?

Finally, the stairs came to an end and opened into what felt like a cathedral. Vaulted ceilings extended high above her. Warm alcoves of light lit up the stone cavern. And inside were treasures of a warrior age.

Her eyes widened at the trove. Weapons. Weapons of every kind. There were longswords, broadswords, short blades, multi-colored staffs, katanas, a strange, curved sword that looked like it could cut men down like wheat, thick clubs, maces, balls and chains, and even a wall full of glittering daggers.

Everywhere Abrina looked, there was a new weapon that she itched to try. A short sword that had an enameled handle carved from what looked like bone hung on a wall in its own alcove. The blade shone lovingly in the dim light and Abrina almost reached out to touch it, but she stopped herself. This didn't look like the other dragonblade. She sighed, cast another longing look at the blade, and walked on.

There was a giant battle ax bigger than she was on another wall. She thought about the adolescent frost giant she'd fought weeks ago and wished she'd had something like that ax to attack him with. Though it probably wouldn't have done them any good, considering how he'd just reform. If only there was something of a fiery nature that could keep the snow from reforming for good. She turned from the ax and kept going.

Row after row, she searched, weapons bringing back memories or forming questions. She found a thin knife that resembled more a stick than a blade, she found a sword as long as her leg encrusted with gems the size of philex eggs. She even found a pile of perfectly round rocks carved from what appeared to be gemstones. The brilliant colors blinked and twinkled in the torchlight. *How would these have been used?* she wondered, tracing the smooth surface of one. To her surprise, it was warm to the touch.

Strange. She went to heft it up and was surprised to find it heavier than she'd expected. She dropped the stone, and it rolled off into a far corner. She sighed, trudging after it. It rolled by a mountain of bows and a pile of arrows before settling next to a blade that sent a chill through Abrina.

She *knew* that sword. It wasn't the dragonblade—it was the sword her grandfather, King Selt, had wielded. It was a Forged blade, nearly as long as she was tall. She remembered the stories Yera used to tell of the blade that devoured all it touched, defeating armies in mere moments. It had gone missing when the king died in battle fighting in the Rosstross Mountains. How in the Palace of Stars had it ended up here?

The sword's power was legendary. With it, she could destroy the frost giants singlehandedly. She didn't need the other princess or anyone. Alliance be damned. She reached out tentatively to touch the handle.

A river of power surged up her arms, making her feel as big as a frost giant, as strong as a dragon. She was invincible. She could do anything. She could destroy—

"*PRINCESS ABRINA!*" roared the voice. "*UNHAND THAT BLADE.*"

Abrina hefted the sword. It was heavier than she'd expected, but she'd get used to it. With the kind of power swirling through her . . . nothing would defeat her. She'd lay waste to all her enemies. Starting with the frost giants.

"*DO NOT BE DECEIVED!*" The voice rushed through Abrina and she stumbled, gasping. She saw images of her grandfather wielding the same sword, cleaving through armies, decimating them. But she also saw how he was driven mad and brought his warriors deeper and deeper into the Rosstross Mountains, fighting anything and everything that crossed his path. Philexes. Mountain gyons. Even ugly beasts that were unmistakably trolls.

She even saw him battle a dragon, but the dragon proved mightier than his blade. Her grandfather died and his knights fought over each other to claim the sword. One by one, they all succumbed to the same madness.

She saw rotund creatures creep out of the earth and take the sword back to Ligerthia where the rulers tried to unmake it using their powers of Forging. But they failed and instead locked it in this very vault, never to be touched by human hands again, lest that same curse be unleashed on the world once more.

Abrina staggered from the weight of the images, her fingers slipping from the handle of the blade. It clattered on the stone floor and Abrina fell to her knees, clutching her head.

"*DO YOU SEE, LITTLE PRINCESS? DO YOU SEE?*"

Abrina gasped, wishing the tirade would cease. "Y-yes," she stammered. "It drives its users mad."

"*DO NOT RELY ON POWER TO DEFEAT YOUR ENEMIES! YOU HAVE ONE MORE CHANCE. FIND THE DRAGONBLADE. OR BE DESTROYED.*"

Abrina lay there on her hands and knees, trying to draw in ragged breaths. She saw her grandfather again, his men, all mad with anger, using the sword—that sword in front of her—to kill each other. If she wielded that blade, would she go mad with power? Would her people turn on each other, slaying one another with their bloodlust? Would the sword ever rest?

She scrambled away from the blade and gulped the stale air of the chamber. No. She would not be like them. She would resist the temptation.

A gleam of light caught her eye.

She blinked fiercely. There, not even a meter away, was the dragonblade.

It rested unceremoniously against a barrel filled with blow darts. But there was no mistaking it—it looked exactly like the sword the other princess carried. It was sheathed in deep green leather, golden dragons etched onto the surface. Whoever had crafted these swords was no ordinary swordsmith.

She unsheathed the dragonblade and felt its weight in her hands. It was perfectly balanced. She swished it around a few times and was amazed at how easily it flowed. Unlike her regular sword, which she used as an extension of her arm, this sword felt like it was part of her arm. It felt like if she just thought of the move, the sword would perform it on its own. She tested the sharpness and was surprised to find it as sharp as a brand-new blade. It was ornate, and the handle was a little bulkier than she'd have liked, but it was magnificent. It was a finer weapon than she'd originally thought.

"I like this blade," she said, struggling and failing to keep a grin off her face. She had found the sword! Now she needed to get back to the others so they could plan their attack on the frost giants and save the world, and she could get back to Henri. She'd done it!

Her heart sank as she saw the engraving on the other side of the blade. Despite the fact it was in Old Alarian, she knew what it said. *Alaria's hope and salvation.* She frowned as she stared at the loopy writing. For all its beauty, how was this blade, and its twin, going to be able to hew down fully grown frost giants? The other sword—her grandfather's sword—was far more powerful.

For half a second, Abrina imagined wielding that other sword in battle, defeating frost giants with a single stroke.

But that sword carried a curse. And Abrina couldn't afford to lose her sanity to a cursed blade. Besides, the dragonblade she held was what the dragon himself had told them to seek. She couldn't let herself get distracted. And this blade was elegant. It would do nicely.

"I suppose you'll have to do instead. You're a magic sword after all," she said to the blade fondly before sheathing it and attaching it to her hip. The weight was nearly familiar, almost as comforting as her own blade, which was strapped on her other side. She smiled, remembering how Henri had presented it to her from his robes, like it was a priceless treasure.

And he was right, in a way. It had been the last present her father had gifted her, and it was made precisely to her specifications. The dragonblade would take some getting used to, simply because it was new, but she was an expert swordswoman. She knew it wouldn't be a problem.

She cast one longing glance back at her grandfather's powerful sword before leaving the cavern.

Chapter Thirty

Abrina

*B*yron, Captain Wilen, the other princess, Benje, Zachry, and the wolf cub were all awake when Abrina re-entered the chamber. They were looking at the statues around the chamber, and both the other princess and Zachry jumped when Abrina emerged.

"Where have you been?" Byron demanded, crossing his arms. "We thought you ran off again."

She ignored that comment. "I found something." She unsheathed the dragonblade. Her knights stared at her, their mouths wide. Even the captain grunted appreciatively.

"It's the other blade," Zachry whispered. "You found it."

"Where?" Benje asked, his mouth set in a grim line. "There was no door."

"Yes there . . ." Abrina turned behind her, but the doorway was gone. ". . . was. Strange. It was here a moment ago."

"Maybe it wanted you to find it," the Oleanderian princess mused. The pup yipped happily. The girl looked at the fluffy creature, then at Abrina, her brows creased. "Canis said he showed you the way last night. What does he mean?"

Abrina shrugged. She was not going to tell them about her conversation with the wolf the night before. "He's a magical wolf. He knows things, I guess. Does it really matter? All that matters is we've got the blades."

"I hate to break it to you," Captain Wilen said sternly. "But we still don't know how the blades work."

"I've been thinking about that." Benje pulled out the book from the library and slapped it on a rock. He flipped to a page that showed a diagram of the two blades. "It says here that the First Queen Forged them with the intent that the wielders must use them with a pure heart to awaken their power."

Abrina made a face. Not this pure heart nonsense again.

"And then what?" the Oleanderian princess asked. "Do they glow?"

"Well, yes. But there's more to it than that. They glow a brilliant gold and shoot a beam of light at their foes." He looked up and shared a look with her. "It says that the wielder must trust in the blade implicitly or it won't work."

Abrina quirked an eyebrow. "So the sword does the work all on its own?" She rested her hand on the blade strapped to her side. "Feels rather like cheating."

Byron rolled his eyes. "It's a magic blade, Princess. What did you expect, you'd need to stab each giant in the heart?"

Abrina pictured flying through the air and plunging the gleaming golden sword into the giants' chests. She smirked, albeit grimly. "It would be effective."

"We've got to figure them out," Benje said, flipping through more pages in the book. "A few more days and we should know how they work."

"We don't have a few more days," Abrina snapped, growing annoyed again. They didn't have time to play with the swords. They had to fulfill this quest, get everything over with, so she could go back to Henri. Er . . . back home. "There are frost giants terrorizing the people of Florryn as we speak. We need to get this done now. I say we go out there and find a frost giant, defeat the beast with the magical blades, and move on to the rest of them."

The Oleanderian princess frowned. "It seems risky."

Abrina glowered at her. "War is filled with risk. But this is a necessary one. We have to know how the blades react to the frost giants, right? What better way than by testing them out against one?"

"Princess Abrina isn't wrong," Captain Wilen said, stroking his gray goatee. "It does make tactical sense. The sword reacted when we needed it in the tunnel. So I say we put it to the test."

"I don't like this." Benje crossed his arms over his muscular chest. "We take on a frost giant without knowing how the blades work, we could get killed."

The other princess laid her hand on his arm. "But the sword did work of its own accord in the tunnel. Maybe this is the same thing—it'll react as it needs to once we put it to the test."

The wolf pup yipped and rubbed his head against the other princess's leg.

Abrina raised an eyebrow. "The pup seems to agree."

The girl nodded. "Alright then." She looked at Benje, who frowned.

"I still don't like this," he said. Then he sighed. "But you two are the children of the prophecy. And if you're in agreement . . . then I guess we're seeking out a frost giant to test the blades."

They decided to leave Zachry behind with the cajuna before venturing out into the frozen wasteland.

"But, Princess Abrina," he'd tried to protest, but she raised a hand.

"We need someone to keep an eye on the beasts," she said, motioning toward the cajuna. "It doesn't make sense for us all to go."

"I agree with the princess," Captain Wilen said. He looked right at Abrina and nodded.

Abrina felt a swell within her heart. He was trusting her. He'd grown less and less cold the further they'd gotten from Florryn. And, despite his gruffness, he'd been instrumental in helping keep them together.

She only hoped they could get through this together.

Sir Zachry let out a breath. "Fine." He patted the nose of one of the purple cajuna. "I'll take care of them."

Abrina gave him a nod. "Good man."

But as Abrina, the Oleanderians, the captain, Byron, and the wolf emerged into the frozen landscape to the bitter wind, she couldn't help but wonder if they were making a grave mistake.

They trekked for hours across the snow, the wind blowing flakes in Abrina's face. She kept glancing at her dragonblade, withdrawing it from the scabbard and swinging it, but the thing refused to glow.

She cast a look at the Oleanderian princess, who was holding her sword like it was about to combust on her. Benje was trying to give her advice, but the girl looked as confused as a kitten with a knife. She fumbled the sword multiple times.

"No, that's not the way—" Benje took the blade from the girl and demonstrated some moves that made Abrina raise an eyebrow. He was an impressive fighter.

But she was overexerting herself. Every time. The girl was of a slighter build with a lower center of gravity than Benje. Her positioning would be slightly different.

She watched as the girl flailed with the sword again and

landed in the snow. Abrina bit back a laugh and crunched on the frozen ground to get to her side. Benje helped the girl out of the snow again.

"Hey map boy," she called to Benje, who scowled at her. "Give it a rest, will you?"

"Don't take a step closer to Princess Kailyn—"

Abrina rolled her eyes. "Relax. I'm not going to pull my sword on her. That was only the one time."

Benje narrowed his eyes. "You nearly took her head off."

Abrina looked at him. "She had my mother's face. What did you expect?"

Besides, if they were in an uneasy truce, at least until this quest was over, she needed to play the part. Maybe it would get the swords to work. The girl clearly needed help with a sword. Help she wasn't getting from her guardsman.

"Benje, it's fine. She's not going to hurt me," the girl said, dusting snow off her skirts.

Benje grunted but moved aside.

"Here," Abrina said, showing the girl the proper hold. "Don't be afraid of the sword. It's an extension of your arm. Hold it firmly but loosely so you can move." She demonstrated a few swings before handing it back to her. "Try that."

"You make it look so easy," the girl said, swinging the blade like Abrina had, but she overbalanced herself again and fell into the snow. The wolf pup, who'd been lightly walking on the snow near Byron, bounded to her side, licking her face.

"I'm fine, Canis, I'm fine," the girl spluttered. Abrina offered a hand. The girl stared at it. "What's that?"

"My hand," Abrina said, rolling her eyes again. Honestly, was she really that terrifying? She hadn't attacked anyone in days. "Come on, let me help you up."

Hesitantly, the girl took her hand. "Th-thank you."

The swords in both of their hands started to glow. Abrina and the girl stared at them for a long moment. The blade felt powerful in her hand.

Then Abrina heard the terrifying crunch of ice shattering. She whirled around, her glowing blade in ready position, as a wall of white suddenly rose up from the expanse they'd been walking on.

"Frost giants!" called the captain. "Blades at the ready!"

The white wall surrounded them, like the clouds themselves had descended on their location. Abrina couldn't see a thing, other than the glowing blade in front of her.

Her fist clenched around the sword, and she counted her breaths. There was a frost giant nearby. She could smell it.

Suddenly, a huge white hand loomed out of the wall, reaching right toward her. She turned and slashed it with the dragonblade, and it cut clean through. She smirked. *Good blade.*

The other princess screamed, Benje shouted something, and the wolf cub howled.

Abrina whirled, seeking her target. The frost giant loomed closer and closer, its hand already reformed.

A blast of light burst from somewhere nearby and smacked the frost giant. It bellowed and dissolved into particles of light.

"Goddess's eyes!" What had the other princess done? How did her sword do that? Abrina blinked, trying to process what she had seen when another shape lumbered out of the cloud, right in front of her.

"Princess!" Someone shoved her out of the way as a large white hand reached down. Abrina heard a deep crackle and whirled around to see Captain Wilen's flesh turn to blue ice, his gray pewter eyes staring, unblinking.

Abrina froze with horror. "No. No!" A leg lurched out of the white. She bellowed a war-cry and turned toward it. She shook her sword, demanding it to release the same kind of beam of light that the other one had. That the other princess had managed so effortlessly. She scowled. She was a better swordswoman. Shouldn't she be able to do this?

"Come on, come on," she muttered.

But the sword did nothing.

Abrina snarled. "Useless!" The glow had completely faded now, but she ran at the giant's leg anyway. She slid under the foot, turned, and reached up to stab the giant.

Only for the sword to break on impact.

Abrina stared at the three pieces of the blade in front of her in the snow. It broke? The wretched thing didn't even do what it was supposed to! Why didn't it shoot light for her, like it had the other princess? She clenched her fist around the broken hilt. Everything worked just fine for the Oleanderian princess.

Another blast of light burst from nearby and Abrina felt more than saw the frost giant above her dissolve. Once again, she could see the crystal form of Captain Wilen. She stared at it. It was so much worse than the ice that had temporarily frozen her back in Florryn. This . . . this had changed his flesh to ice. There was no way to thaw him. He was gone.

A wolf cry shattered the air. A hand grabbed her arm, but she yanked it free. It was the Oleanderian princess, her eyes wide. "We have to get out of here!"

"How?" Abrina demanded. "Captain Wilen is dead." Her heart throbbed at the words.

"Canis knows the way, but we have to go. Now!" The sword in the girl's hand emitted another beam of light, blasting another lumbering giant above her. The girl took off running, slipping and sliding on the snow, but continuing to move forward.

Abrina grabbed the pieces of her own sword and followed the wolf's cries.

Somehow—Abrina wasn't really keeping track—they made it back to the caverns. By the time they were safe inside, Abrina looked around to see who was still there. Byron had icicles hanging from his red beard, but otherwise looked unharmed. Benje looked grim, but unfrozen. The other princess still held her glowing sword. Captain Wilen was the only one of their company that they'd lost.

And it was all Abrina's fault. If he hadn't pushed her out of the way . . . Abrina would have been the frozen one.

She gazed at the pieces of her own dragonblade in her hand. How had the sword shattered? Why did it work for the other girl and not for her? Why did *she* get the blessings of the Goddess—first the wolf, then the sword? Abrina was the warrior here. Abrina was Florrynian.

So why was she failing miserably at being Florrynian?

Their company was silent until they made it back to the underground courtyard with the cajuna and Sir Zachry. He'd set up a fire and perked up when he saw them.

"Princesses, are you—" His face fell when he saw their expressions. "What happened?"

"Captain Wilen was killed by the frost giants," Abrina said bitterly. "And I broke the wretched blade." She threw the pieces of the sword on the ground, which skittered until they rested near Sir Zachry.

He bent down, picked up the handle, and frowned at it before staring at Abrina. "You broke the sword?"

"How did you break it?" Benje demanded. "Kailyn's works just fine."

Abrina whirled on him, her ire flaming. "Everything works

just fine for her! She gets the blessings, she gets the wolf, the sword. Nothing ever goes wrong for her." She glowered at the girl, who had taken a step back at Abrina's tone. "She's stolen everything."

"I've never stolen anything from you," the girl whispered. "I was trying to help—"

"How can you help when you've been nothing but a hindrance?" Abrina snarled. "If it wasn't for you, we'd never even be on this quest in the first place!"

"And the whole world would have frozen over," Benje said tersely. "Is that what you want?"

"No!" Abrina started pacing now, her anger fueling her momentum. Her hands were shaking, but she ignored them. The wolf pup howled, but she ignored him too. Her heart pounded with rage. Rage for the death of the captain. For the broken sword. For the larnel-flowered magical princess whose sword worked perfectly even though Abrina had practically been born with a blade. For having been forced on this infernal quest in the first place, forced to work with the enemy.

"It was a bad idea for Florryn and Oleanders to work together," she snapped. "It was never going to work."

"But we're . . . we're sisters," the other girl said, blinking her blue eyes at Abrina. "Shouldn't that be enough?"

Abrina glowered at her, blood boiling in her ears. That was the final straw. "You expect me to forget a thousand years of treachery simply because you're my sister? You know nothing of my people. Nothing! We have never been nor will we ever be sisters." She clenched her fists. "We're enemies. And we always will be."

"But, Abrina—" the girl started to say, but Abrina whipped out her regular sword from its scabbard at her waist and pointed it at the girl, whose face went white. The dragonblade fell from her hand.

But Abrina didn't care. How dare she use her name? What

right did she have? Hadn't she been listening? They had nothing in common, other than their birth parents. *Nothing.* She was Oleanderian. The enemy of Florryn.

"I'm done trying to work with you," she hissed, glaring at the girl. "You're nothing but a nuisance. Why don't you go back to Oleanders where you belong?"

Benje brought his sword up and clanged it against hers, sending her blade away from the other princess. She turned to face the guardsman, baring her teeth. Her anger seethed like a volcano about to erupt.

Benje's face was impassive as she pressed her attack. His positions were defensive, but he matched her strikes easily, move for move. She furiously attacked, and he dodged every single blow. Finally, he disarmed her, and pointed his sword at her. She fell to her knees, her breath coming in gasps. Her shoulders shook and she clenched her hands in trembling fists.

"Princess!" Byron called, but it was like through a fog.

"Don't ever attack her again." Benje's voice was low, but the threat was clear. The wolf pup howled and gazed at Abrina with a look of deep disappointment—if it was possible for wolves to look disappointed.

Byron held out a hand and helped her to her feet.

"We're done discussing this," Abrina snarled at the Oleanderian princess.

The girl shook her head and plodded along with her wolf, leaving the no-longer-glowing dragonblade where it had fallen. She sat down in a distant corner, her back to Abrina.

That was fine with her. She didn't want to hear anything more from the girl. She didn't know Florryn. She didn't know Abrina. And if Abrina had her way, she never would.

Chapter Thirty-One

Kailyn

The cold stung Kailyn's face as she flew high above frozen Ligerthia, leaving the quest—and her sister—behind. She squeezed her eyes shut to block the tears, but they streamed down her face anyway. Her mind kept replaying the hateful things her sister had said.

You expect me to forget a thousand years of treachery simply because you're my sister? You know nothing of my people. Nothing! We have never been nor ever will be sisters. We're enemies. And we always will be.

Kailyn sobbed up to the sky. Abrina was right. She didn't know her. She'd thought Abrina was opening up—she'd seemed, if not kind, at least more amicable since she'd retrieved the second dragonblade. She'd even shown Kailyn how to hold the sword.

But then she'd pointed a blade at Kailyn again, calling them enemies.

Kailyn wiped her eyes, but the tears wouldn't stop coming. She'd thought the best thing to save Oleanders and the world would be to go on this quest with the princess of Florryn, her supposed sister, but Kailyn wasn't cut out for this sort of adventure. And after the death of Myira, the queen's treachery, Captain Wilen's demise, and now Abrina's blatant hatred?

Kailyn couldn't do it any longer.

All she wanted was her books, her library. If the world was ending anyway, then she wanted to spend it surrounded by her books, barricaded in the one room she belonged. Not with the princess who hated her very existence.

Home? echoed Canis's voice in her mind. He sent her an image of a wolf pack, running through the trees, climbing over rocks, racing across the snow.

The wolf was in a bag that was attached to the saddle of the cajuna, like he'd been on the flight to Ligerthia. She was still surprised he had taken to it so well. His head stuck out of the bag, his tongue lolling to the side like he was having a good time. At least one of them was.

"We're not going to your home, Canis. We're going to mine," she said, stifling her sobs. *To see the world end.*

The wolf's nose sniffed the air, his ears perking up. *Safe! Follow!*

Kailyn wiped her eyes. "What?"

He sent her an image of a man on a purple cajuna. A man in black with a sword strapped to his back.

Her heart caught.

Benje.

She'd thought she'd given Benje the slip the night before. He'd come up silently while she'd been rearranging the few items in her pack in the dead of night while everyone else was asleep.

"Princess, what are you doing?" he'd said.

"Packing."

"There's no need to pack. We're settling into the cave for the night. Byron said we'll brainstorm a plan in the morning."

"What is there possibly to be gained from this quest anymore?" she had said, growing more and more frustrated. "It's a failure. *I'm* a failure." She fought the tears that threatened to burst. "I don't belong here," she had said quietly.

Benje had reached for her hands then. "You do belong here, Princess. You're a part of this quest."

At that, she had stood up, looking at him directly. "No, Benje. I'm not." She gestured toward Abrina's prone form that lay only a few dozen or so paces away. She had been staring at the wall so long that Kailyn knew she had to be asleep. "You heard what Abrina said. I'm a nuisance. I can't even wield a sword properly. The entire quest will be better off without me."

"You can't possibly think that we'd be better off without you, we need you here!" His voice had grown louder, and she felt the undercurrents of his anxiety. It had pained her to hear him sound so worried. But she couldn't stay. Not after . . . everything.

"No, you don't. Benje, I can't do it." She motioned to the dragonblade leaning against the cajuna. "It doesn't work as promised. It couldn't save the captain. It's not strong enough." She'd looked down then. "I'm not strong enough."

"No. You got the sword to work. You can do this, Kailyn."

Kailyn had started sobbing at that point. His confidence in her was too much. She hadn't done anything. It was the sword. It had acted of its own accord.

"You can't leave, Princess." His voice had practically become a plea at this point. "You have the only complete dragonblade. You saw the pieces of the other one. Princess Abrina's broke."

Kailyn pictured Abrina's brown eyes, so unlike her own, filled with hate and self-loathing as she cast the pieces into the middle of their broken, grieving circle. Abrina had broken the sword, yes, but then she had turned her fiery wrath on Kailyn. And the words hurt worse than anything, even watching her father die, and her kingdom overrun.

The words had hit too close to home. *How can you help when you've been nothing but a hindrance?*

Kailyn was as useless as Abrina's broken sword. But she couldn't bear to hear the hurt, the anguish, and the hate in Abrina's tone. It was more than she could bear.

"Not anymore," she had whispered, handing him her sword. The one the dragon had given her. "Here. Take this."

Benje had stared at the sword. Then he'd looked right at her. "Don't do this, Kailyn. Please."

Tears had built up in her eyes. "Benje . . . I-I can't stay here with her." She gestured toward Abrina.

Benje had nodded then, looking at the Florrynian princess, his mouth hard. The silence weighed heavy between them. "Where are you going to go?" His voice was soft, but the question was heavy.

"Home."

Benje had said that he had wanted to go with her then, but she had turned him down. She couldn't leave with him. She couldn't endanger him too with her lack of skills. So she had left while he was asleep. It had been the only way to make sure he wouldn't follow her. Canis had been her only witness.

Or so she'd thought.

Safe! Canis sent her another image of Benje on his cajuna, flying closer. Kailyn craned her head to see that he was only a few meters behind them. She sighed. She should have known it wouldn't have been so easy.

She bent over her cajuna and gently tapped the side of the beast so it would slow down.

"Kailyn!" Benje called when he was closer. "Please. Don't go."

293

"It's a little late for that, isn't it?" She eyed him, then burst into a relieved smile. It was good to see a friendly face. "What are you doing here?"

"Following you, of course. Did you think I was going to let you go off on your own? I gave you my oath."

She'd hoped he wouldn't have followed, but she should have known better—Benje had sworn he'd be her protector. And he was more faithful than any Ligerthian she'd ever met. Her heart beat wildly at seeing him, secretly pleased that he was there.

"What about the quest?" she called.

"There is no quest. Not anymore. Abrina's determined to fight the frost giants back at Florryn and live out the end of the world there."

"Without the swords?" Kailyn cried. Did Abrina want to die?

Then again, she'd been distraught over the captain's death. Maybe that was how she coped with loss—she threw herself into a fight.

Kailyn blinked, trying to clear her mind. She couldn't think of her sister. Her sister who wanted nothing to do with her. It did her absolutely zero good to think about Abrina. If she wanted to throw herself at the frost giants, that was her choice.

"She doesn't want it. She kicked the pieces away. I left the other blade with Sir Zachry to guard until she was ready, but I've got the pieces with me."

Kailyn raised her eyebrows. "Why?"

"Because I can fix it! With the dragon's fire you gave me. We just need to get back to my forge."

Kailyn's mind spun. She'd nearly forgotten about the dragon's fire she'd given to Benje so many days ago. She thought about what the dragon had said. *It can mend even the fiercest of breaks.*

She blinked, frowning. But why bother? Abrina didn't think they could work together.

And maybe she was right. Kailyn was incompetent with the sword. She'd only been able to use it when the sword magically started glowing by itself. She hadn't done anything.

Fire? Canis sent her an image of the sword blazing, Kailyn holding it aloft. She blinked in surprise. She looked powerful. Fierce. Almost . . . Florrynian.

She shook her head. No. He had to be wrong. The sword had acted of its own accord. She had nothing to do with it. All she wanted was to curl up with her books and let this whole thing blow over. Maybe the prophecy was wrong, and the world wasn't going to end in ice and snow.

"Princess Kailyn," Benje called out. "Please. We can't leave them. You know they'll die if we don't help."

She bit her lip. Benje really did have all the characteristics of a Ligerthian Knight. He was dedicated, studious, a master with the sword and the craft of Forging, and he was as loyal as Canis was.

Woof! Canis yipped in agreement.

She smiled. "Alright, Benje. Lead the way." At the very least, it couldn't hurt to try.

They rested a night somewhere in Cyron to give the cajuna some time to recover. And then they were off again. She watched the mountains and plains of Cyron fade behind them as they glided down into Oleanders, flying over Deri Lake and swooping through to Olean.

Kailyn felt her heart swell as she saw the glimmering white

spires of first the castle with its snapping purple and gold flags, and then the colorful banners that lined the merchant's level, then the gleaming silver-white library where they touched down.

Canis, who'd been asleep for the last several hours, perked up when they landed. Kailyn slid off the cajuna and landed on the cobblestones with a thump.

Food?

Kailyn laughed and got to her feet to dig through the knapsack to find something for him. She fished out another root and fed the pup, though he was definitely not really pup-sized anymore. "Here you go."

The air wasn't much warmer here in Olean than it had been in Ligerthia. Kailyn pulled her cloak around her even tighter. It was chillier than the mountains had been that day they'd visited the gnomes.

"I've never felt Oleanders so cold before," she whispered, looking around. Hardly anyone was out and about. What few people she did see outside the library courtyard all had thick furs on and scurried to buildings anxiously.

Canis's ears twitched, and he moved his head from side to side, looking everywhere. *Danger!* But Kailyn couldn't see anything.

"What's going on?" Kailyn whispered.

Benje frowned. "I don't know. But I don't like it." He extended his gloved hand to her and she took it, letting him lead her to his forge, which was . . . glowing.

Benje tensed and released Kailyn's hand to withdraw his sword. He motioned for Kailyn to stay back as he approached the open-air structure that was filled with the clanging of metal and piles of weapons.

"Benje Thornsid!" came a loud, raucous voice. "I should have known you'd be back."

Benje grunted and sheathed his sword. He turned to Kailyn and extended his hand again. "Don't be alarmed, Princess. It's only a knight-in-training."

Hesitantly, Kailyn followed, Canis right by her side, his ears still twitching. "Do you smell anything, Canis?"

Danger! But there was nothing specific associated with it. Just a vague sense of unease.

Kailyn nodded and set her jaw, like how Abrina had a thousand times. She shook her head. She was not going to think of her sister. But she adopted the same kind of authority she'd seen Abrina wield like a weapon as she pushed her way into the forge.

She saw a big, dark-skinned man—who wasn't wearing a shirt—stoking the forge. He looked up when Kailyn entered, and his face broke into a wide grin. "Princess Kailyn!" He bowed to her. "What are you doing here?"

She eyed him uneasily. Who was he and why was he here? "I could ask the same about you."

Benje motioned between the two of them. "Princess, this is Ger, one of the men who worked alongside me with the rebellion. Ger, I need the forge."

Ger laughed. "You need the forge? You've been missing for weeks, Benje. I had to step in to keep up the forge as a meeting place for the rebellion."

Kailyn's heart sank. Right. The rebellion. A silver gleam flashed through her memory as she remembered her father's death. What had happened in Oleanders since then?

"Never mind that now," Benje said. "Please, Ger. It's important."

Danger! Canis sent Kailyn an image of a dozen guards swiftly approaching. They were galloping down the road toward the library.

"Um, Benje?" she whispered. "There's guards incoming."

Benje paused, listening. The sound of hoofbeats grew louder. His hand went to his sword right as Ger took out a giant ax, the head nearly as big as Canis.

"You're not going anywhere, traitor," Ger growled.

"Run!" Benje hissed, falling into a battle stance as Ger swung his ax.

Kailyn glanced around, wondering where she was going to go when a glimmer caught her eye. She blinked, wondering if she'd imagined it. But no, there on the white wall of the library was a door, right where there should have been one when she'd first come all those weeks ago.

Aru! Canis howled as the sounds of guards got closer. *Danger!*

"Come on, Canis!" Kailyn cried and took off running to the door, reaching it just as the guards entered the courtyard.

"Halt!" the guards said.

The clashing of blades still echoed behind Kailyn, but she didn't turn around. She touched the knob of the door and it silently opened.

Murmuring broke out among the guards, but one of them told the rest to quiet.

"Do not enter the library," he called. "Princess Kailyn, you are under arrest! You are to be brought before Lord Shielen this instant!"

Ignoring them, Kailyn stepped foot into the library and the door slid shut behind her.

Chapter Thirty-Two

Kailyn

The interior of the library was pristine white. Everything hummed with energy, the whole place feeling almost . . . sacred. There were shelves upon shelves of books, scrolls, tablets. Kailyn spied a golden spiral staircase that curled up to a second floor filled with even more knowledge. She gazed at everything in wonder. This . . . this was a temple to learning.

In the center of the library was a great white statue of the Goddess. Kailyn felt herself drawn to the statue, as if by some unknown power. The statue had six arms, and a great white wolf rested next to the carving. Her dress was covered with stars and constellations, and her face was more heavenly than any Kailyn had ever seen. It was ethereal. Sublime. Divine.

She sank down to her knees by the statue, overwhelm washing over her.

Aru? Canis pressed his head against Kailyn's leg, and she reached down to scratch his ears.

"I don't know what to do, Canis," she whispered. "There are guards out there, wanting to arrest me. Benje's fighting Ger, who is much bigger than he is. Everyone looks so scared. And it's absolutely freezing." She sighed, pulling her fur cape closer around her. "Oleanders isn't home anymore."

Tears pricked her eyes. Canis's rough tongue licked her face before she threw her arms around the pup, sobbing. She'd thought by coming back to Oleanders she'd at least find a safe place.

The dragon had been right. Oleanders was no longer her home. Everything had changed.

Now, Lord Shielen ruled everything, and there was still a rebellion happening.

But what could she do? It's not like she could go back to Ligerthia to help Abrina. Her sister hated her. She'd tried to kill her twice and had broken the very sword they needed to defeat the frost giants.

Kailyn was tired. All she wanted was rest. Maybe it would be better for the world to end. Maybe that was the real meaning of the prophecy.

"*Kailyn . . .*"

Kailyn blinked, sitting up. She looked at Canis, who yipped. "Was that you?"

Aru?

No, the pup had never called her by name before. So where was the voice coming from?

"*Kailyn . . .*"

The voice was gentle, resonate, and harmonious. Like the depiction of the Goddess.

Kailyn's eyes went wide, and she knelt in front of the figure, bowing her head in prayer.

"Goddess, I hear you," she whispered.

A sudden *whoosh* filled the library as a golden light illuminated the space, resting on the statue. Kailyn squeezed her eyes shut at the brightness, but it quickly faded. When she opened her eyes again, a woman stood where the statue had been, though this woman only had two arms. Her dress was the deep blue of the midnight sky, with diamond-stars shimmering on it. Her long white hair flowed over her shoulders like clouds. And she glowed with an ephemeral light.

"Rise, my child," the Goddess said.

Kailyn stood up, blinking in amazement. The Goddess had appeared to her? But . . . the Goddess never appeared to anyone. Why? Why did she deserve to have the Goddess speak to her? She was a failure. She'd failed as a princess, she'd failed as a sister, she'd failed as a quester. She'd failed at everything.

"You have come a long way," the Goddess said gently. "Your burdens have been great."

Kailyn nodded mutely while Canis licked her hand. She gently rubbed his head.

"The wolf cub." The Goddess smiled. "How do you like him?"

Canis yipped happily, his tail thumping Kailyn. She smiled. "He's wonderful."

The Goddess nodded. "I thought you would need a companion. And your Florrynian blood gives you access to this great blessing."

Kailyn's smile fell. "But I'm not Florrynian."

The Goddess's eyes filled with starry tears. "I know you doubt the prophecy. You doubt your heritage, and you doubt your place. But do you not remember the dragon, dear one?"

The dragon's voice filled Kailyn's mind, like he was right there, speaking to her. "*Your mother is Queen Jullee of Florryn . . . you are the children of the prophecy . . . Only you can defeat the frost giants raging in the north of Almarryn and save your kingdoms . . .*"

Kailyn's shoulders slumped. "But I'm not Florrynian. Abrina has made that abundantly clear."

"Abrina of Florryn has much anger in her heart. She will need

301

to relinquish it if she is to use the dragonblade. But that is not your role. Your role is to accept your heritage—both parts of it." The Goddess smiled gently. "The dragon is right. You are both Florrynian and Oleanderian. That gives you the unique power to end both the war among your own people and appease the frost giants."

"But how?" Kailyn cried. Canis harrumphed beside her. "I can't wield a sword, the people rebelled because of my father, and I don't have the skills to lead them."

"You do," the Goddess said. "They may be hidden to you, but to me, you shine like a star in the heavens."

Kailyn sighed. It was all too much. She couldn't do what the Goddess asked of her. How was she supposed to end her people's conflict and appease the frost giants? She couldn't even appease her own sister.

She felt a gentle touch on her shoulder and looked up to see the Goddess. A wave of strength filled Kailyn and she saw herself talking to her people, having them lay down their weapons, and talk reasonably among themselves. She saw a government led by the people, with her as queen, listening to their counsel.

And she saw herself kneeling, holding the dragonblade before a frost giant, Abrina at her side doing the same.

Her eyes widened.

"Yes, my child. Do you see?" The Goddess's voice was gentle, but firm. "You have a destiny that is not yet fulfilled."

Kailyn wiped away the tears in her eyes. "But what if I don't want to do this?"

"I will not force you. I cannot force anyone to choose their destiny." The Goddess's smile turned sad. "But you are a child of prophecy. Princess Abrina is your sister. Do not doubt that. You both have such brave hearts. I believe in you."

The Goddess stood up and started to shimmer, fading into light before disappearing, leaving Kailyn and Canis alone in the library.

Kailyn sank to her knees, thinking over what the Goddess had said. The very Goddess of the Heavens believed in her, confirming that Kailyn had a role to play. She left the choice in Kailyn's hands.

Aru? Canis nuzzled his nose against Kailyn's hand. She stroked his muzzle, thinking. She was trapped in the library, Benje was outside fighting. Her sister was in Ligerthia, about to face the frost giants on her own.

Her sister. Kailyn felt tears fill her eyes again. Abrina was her sister. She was Florrynian. About as Florrynian as they came. But when she'd come over to help Kailyn with the sword, and when she'd eyed her appraisingly those few times, Kailyn had seen it. She'd seen Abrina's determination. She'd seen her core strength. And she'd seen her desire there—Abrina had wanted it to be true. She wanted to be Kailyn's sister, even if only temporarily.

Even if Abrina would never accept her, Kailyn still had to help.

But how? She'd been a nuisance and a hindrance to Abrina—the princess herself had said so.

And with her own people . . . she had been isolated from them for years. How could she do this?

You shine like a star in the heavens.

She remembered how she'd felt holding the dragonblade, and how the powerful sword had acted of its own accord. Benje had said that the sword could only be used by one with a pure heart.

She blinked. A pure heart. One who saw the goodness in others. Who believed in them like the Goddess believed in her.

That was it! "Come on, Canis," she said, turning to face the door out of the library. She knew what she needed to do.

Chapter Thirty-Three

Abrina

"Princess, what are we going to do?" Byron's voice was hard, but it pulled Abrina out from her dark thoughts. She hadn't moved from her post by the statue in hours. She couldn't. The sword was broken, Captain Wilen was dead, the world was going to freeze, and it was all her fault.

"I'm-I'm not sure," she said hollowly, feeling numb. "The Oleanderians are gone." She'd woken up early that morning after yet another terrifying nightmare only to see that both the other princess and her guardsman were gone. She'd thought she'd be relieved by their departure. But instead she felt empty. Not even angry. Just empty. They'd taken the only working sword. The other one was in pieces. They were going to die here, frozen into blocks of ice. Just like Captain Wilen.

"We noticed," Byron said grimly. "Did you scare the girl off in the middle of the night?"

"I—" Abrina didn't know what to say. She hadn't. But even if she'd been awake, would she have done anything to stop them? She didn't think so. She was done with this cursed quest. She just wanted to go home.

"Well then." Byron pursed his lips. "I ask you again, Princess. What are we going to do?"

Abrina didn't know.

"We can explore the statues?" she suggested half-heartedly. "Maybe there's something here that could help us?"

"Oh, like a magical sword?" Byron scoffed. "We seem to be short of those."

"Leave her alone, Byron," Zachry said quietly. The man had been very somber since he'd heard Captain Wilen had died. "She's grieving."

She closed her eyes, wincing. He was right—she was grieving. But Byron's jab hurt too. She'd tried this morning to reopen the door to the vault where the other weaponry was, where her grandfather's blade was hidden. But it had been sealed, like the door wasn't even there anymore. They had no weapons. Nothing to defeat the frost giants. And it was all her fault. Just like everything.

"It doesn't matter," she said, sighing. "I have doomed this mission. Without the dragonblades, we do not have a hope of defeating the frost giants." She glanced toward their fire, which was slowly dying. They'd used most of their supply they'd brought from Tigahel. She pushed herself off from the wall, her joints protesting from being in a stiff position all night.

"I'm going to go find more firewood," she said. "Do you two want to prepare the cajuna for departure?"

"Not that it would do us much good," Byron said sourly. "If we don't stop the frost giants here, then they're going to cover the entire world in wretched ice."

She knew he was right, but they had no options anymore. "It's all we can do, Byron."

He glared at her. "This is all your fault, Abrina. If you hadn't driven Princess Kailyn away with your hatred, we'd at least have one working sword, and maybe we'd have a prayer of getting the other sword repaired."

"Yes, well . . ." She cast her eyes around the courtyard, hoping something would materialize that would answer their problems. But nothing did. "There's nothing else we can do, Byron."

She picked up a torch from the fire, turned from the knights, and set off toward the cave entrance. She needed to be alone. She needed to be useful.

Abrina rested her hand on her sword strapped to her side, finding comfort in the familiarity of the blade. She hadn't touched the pieces of the broken dragonblade since she'd discarded it the day before. It wouldn't do her any good to have them with her anyways. She couldn't wield a broken weapon.

Not like she was worthy to access the power of the blade. Just like with her grandfather's sword, she'd failed.

I'm to blame, she thought, her stomach churning. She didn't care where she was going in the long tunnel. Maybe she'd find her own frost giant and die in one last fight.

It didn't matter anymore. Whether she died here or in Florryn, she was going to die fighting the frost giants. There was nothing they could do against them.

The torch reflected off the stone murals the other girl had admired back when they'd first arrived. The shine was somewhat comforting, but it couldn't distract her from her whirling thoughts.

If she had only been able to hold her tongue, and actually commit to working with the girl. If she hadn't been so blinded by centuries of war and hate. She could see the resemblance in the girl to her mother. She had her mother's courage too. The way she had taken the lead, getting Abrina out of the fight with the frost giant earlier. It reminded her of her mother, who would do anything for her people.

Abrina sighed in the semi-darkness of the cave. "Why did it have to be Oleanders?"

Had the princess been from any other kingdom, Abrina knew she'd be more than willing—honestly, even eager—to embrace her as her sister. She'd always wanted one. She'd felt deprived her whole life because of her twin's supposed death. And it wasn't the girl's fault she'd been separated and put in Oleanders. It wasn't her fault the queen of Ligerthia had ruined both of their lives.

Abrina clenched her fist at the thought of the queen. It made her sick. If the queen hadn't tried to bring the prophecy to fruition, the girl never would have been taken, and Abrina would have grown up knowing her sister. She would have had a relationship with her, played with her, perhaps even trained with her. Maybe they both would have found the wolf cub together.

She'd be quite formidable if she knew how to wield a blade, she thought. The thought startled her. The princess had proven to be a formidable opponent. First with the dragon, then with the frost giants. She'd stuck with the quest for so long despite the hatred from Abrina and her knights. She was strong. Grudgingly, Abrina admitted she could see a little of herself in the girl.

If only she'd been willing to set aside her pride earlier.

The dragon's words echoed in her mind. *Set aside your pride, Princess, or you will fail. You will fail us all.* He'd been right. She hadn't been able to set aside her pride, and now, the Oleanderian princess was flying to Goddess-knew-where, and they had only one broken sword, and no chance of completing their quest. And all because of Abrina.

Abrina walked for a while, lost in her thoughts until she became aware of a presence in her mind. It sounded like whisperings. She listened closely, but she couldn't make out the words. But there was something about those whisperings…she wanted to understand them.

She stopped walking, gazing at the murals on the walls. The relief sculptures were exquisite. There were creatures she'd never seen before etched on the walls, living together in harmony. There were depictions of the Ligerthian Knights' Forging tools instead of weapons.

There was also a panel that depicted a grove of trees. There were hundreds of them, all without leaves, but still standing strong and true. The whispering seemed to come from there.

Tentatively, Abrina reached out a hand and touched the stone carving. A rumbling split the air and the panel sank into the ground, revealing another tunnel.

She swallowed and held her torch higher as she took a step forward. The whisperings were louder now, though she still couldn't make out any words. They felt like they were . . . calling her.

She quickened her pace, following the twists and turns of the tunnel until it opened into a wide expanse—she thought she saw the slate gray sky above her, scudded over with puffy white clouds, like a blanket being pulled over the rough timbers of a bed. But that was impossible. They were underground.

Her gaze lowered and she gasped. Her situation had just gotten even more impossible.

Stretching out as far as she could see were thousands of skeletal trees.

These trees didn't have any leaves, just like the carving she'd seen on the panel. Their pale arms extended high toward the heavens and their bark was as white as the driven snow. But there wasn't any snow in the grove. Instead, the ground was polished a blue-gray that reflected the silver sky above. It looked like a giant mirror with trees growing out of it.

The whisperings were louder in this strange, empty forest and Abrina could, at last, make out the words.

"All will be frozen and left to die."

"Dragon's fire is rare, but it will save them. If they choose."

"The world grows old and weary. Perhaps it is time for the world to die."

"Darkness looms ever closer, and it is threatening to swallow all of Alaria."

"Massive columns of snow swirl through the sky, blanketing every-thing in winter. Is this the end?"

"Save Florryn. Save Oleanders. Save Cyron. Save Ligerthia. Save Alaria. Save them. Please."

"Goddess above, can you hear our pleas?"

"Hello?" Abrina called out quietly. "Is anyone there?"

With a rush, the whisperings quieted themselves. A unified voice answered.

"Salutations, young princess."

"Who are you?" she asked. She couldn't see anyone. There weren't even any statues to talk to like at the library or the court-yard. It was simply the sky, the frozen ground, and the trees as far as she could see.

"We are the beings of the Trees of Tears. Some call us tree spirits, but we are much more than that. We are guardians of wisdom and

knowledge. *Some find our grove to share their story. Some find us to forget themselves. And some find us to find themselves. Why have you come?"*

"I'm looking for firewood," she said, deciding to stick with the immediate need. That had been the reason she'd entered the tunnel before, but it wasn't what had brought her here.

"If you are seeking firewood, you shall not find any in this grove. There is firewood to be had in these caverns, but it is not here. This is not a grove you can cut down and burn. We have been here for centuries. Goddess alone knows how long we shall continue to stand guard, collecting the tears of Alaria."

"You said that you offer answers," Abrina said. She did need answers. She needed to know if there was a way to end the frost giants and free Almarryn from their terrible ice without the dragonblades. She needed to know if she could mend this awful rift she'd caused. "I have come with questions."

"Yes, little princess. You have many questions in your heart." The spirits seemed thoughtful as they considered her. *"You also carry much guilt and sorrow. We have collected your tears. We know who you are, Princess Abrina of Florryn."*

Abrina bowed her head. The trees were right. She did carry much guilt and sorrow. Sorrow for the deaths she had seen. Guilt for what she had done to Kailyn. She swallowed. *Kailyn.* Her sister. Who she'd sent away.

"Is there anything I can do to repair the damage? Can I save the quest?"

"'All will be frozen and left to die' is a line from the prophecy that speaks about what will happen if you and your sister fail to unite. The sword is only part of the fracture you have caused, little princess. But it can be repaired."

Her heart started thumping louder. Dare she hope? Could the sword be repaired?

"As for the quest, you cannot complete it alone."

Her heart stopped. Kailyn. She was gone, and she wouldn't be coming back. Abrina knew that. She'd known that the moment she'd woken up and seen that the other princess was gone.

A single solitary tear streamed down her cheek and landed on the frozen blue-gray ground.

All at once, she saw images in the mirror-like surface under the trees.

She saw the fat king of Oleanders get a knife to the stomach, right in front of Kailyn.

Abrina gasped, feeling more tears form in her eyes. To have seen one's own father get murdered like that . . . she hadn't been there the day her father had been killed. But he'd died in battle. Not . . . not like that.

She saw Benje take Kailyn through underground tunnels, not unlike the ones they'd found in Ligerthia. She saw Kailyn find the orphaned wolf cub, and Kailyn and the wolf struggle against that horrible man Mirnabad. She saw Kailyn when she had arrived on the island, struggling up the beach from a shipwreck.

Another tear slid down Abrina's cheek. She hadn't known Kailyn had been shipwrecked.

Then she sucked in a breath as she saw herself pull her sword on Kailyn. She saw Kailyn reeling in horror at the queen's declarations. She saw their company fly on cajuna to the dragon. Then toward Ligerthia. She saw them traveling the frozen wastelands, Kailyn shivering despite her many furs, but trying to hold the sword despite clearly not knowing how. She saw Kailyn use the sword—which had activated of its own accord after Abrina had helped her—to defeat the frost giants that had killed Captain Wilen.

Then she saw herself argue with Kailyn in the underground courtyard, pulling a sword on her the second time. She saw Kailyn crying as she led her cajuna past the company, out into the frozen wastelands, leaving the quest.

A fresh wave of sorrow swept over Abrina. She had wronged her sister, her sister who'd already experienced so much suffering. She saw that clearly now. She had stopped the quest from progressing.

If she had genuinely tried to make an alliance and treat the Oleanderian princess like her sister, would she have left? Abrina didn't know. And now, she supposed, she never would. Kailyn was gone and she could not call her back again.

"It's my fault," she whispered, hanging her head and letting her tears drip into the ground.

"*Your guilt will not heal the rift you have caused, Princess.*"

"But how can I heal the rift between us?" she asked, still staring at the moving images that replayed the damage she had done to her sister. Kailyn. Her long-lost sister. Restored to her, only for Abrina to cast her aside like she was nothing.

"I cannot call her back again."

"*Perhaps not. But the sword can be mended. You can heal the rift in your company. And you, warrior princess, can face the ice giants.*"

"How can I mend the sword?" she asked, not daring to hope. Even if they could mend the sword, it was only one. The set was incomplete. It wouldn't be enough.

"*You cannot. But it is being mended as we speak.*"

Abrina's eyes widened. "Kailyn!" Her sister must have somehow taken the pieces with her. "How did she know how to mend it?"

"*The apprentice knows. The dragon knew.*"

The sparkling vial of dragon's fire glimmered in Abrina's

memory. She grinned. Of course! The dragon had said it could mend anything.

Then her smile fell. "But they're not here." Even if they did somehow manage to mend the sword, it still wasn't there where they could use it.

"That is not the only blade. Mend the rift in your company and you will find you have what you need."

Abrina mulled that over, trying to puzzle out what the spirits meant. She hadn't been a good leader to her men. She'd led them to what was almost guaranteed certain death—and what had been for their captain—but instead of working with them, she'd fought with them.

She needed to apologize. She could start with that.

"Thank you, spirits," she said, bowing to the white trees. It didn't feel strange to her anymore. There was something special about these trees. Something almost . . . holy to them. They deserved her reverence.

"Your quest is not yet done, little princess. We cannot see how the future will play out, but we know that you have your mother's courage and your father's strength. You can find a way to save your people, but you must trust yourself."

If only she could. She had already done so much damage. It seemed almost impossible that she could repair any of it.

"I have one last question, spirits."

She hesitated. Would they even have an answer?

But she had to know.

"Will Kailyn will make it back?" Her voice warbled.

"We do not know all things, little princess." The trees sounded almost apologetic. Abrina sighed and nodded in acquiesce. She supposed it didn't matter. She had to press forward anyway, whether Kailyn was there or not. If she could do anything to stop the frost giants on her own, she had to try.

"But this we do know," the trees went on. *"She is your sister. You must accept this if you are to be successful with your quest."*

Abrina thought about how Kailyn had been so hesitant with the dragonblade, but how she had used the sword, multiple times, with confidence. And suddenly Abrina realized why. Kailyn had a pure heart. She saw the best in others. And she'd been willing to try to see Abrina as her sister. Abrina hung her head. She'd been so wrong. Kailyn *was* her sister. If she was honest with herself, she had known all along.

"Thank you," she said, again bowing to the trees. "You've given me a peace I didn't think I'd find."

"Goddess bless you, Princess Abrina."

Abrina nodded and turned from the Trees of Tears back to the caverns. With acceptance in her heart, she was ready. Even if she didn't have a solid plan in place yet, at least she knew where to start.

Abrina found firewood in the third cavern she searched, behind a door set in a wall that she'd missed on her first exploration of the main cavern. Her mind was still full of what the trees had said. What was she supposed to do to mend the rift in her company? How could they stand a chance against the frost giants when both swords were gone?

The firewood she'd found was the dry wood of a boat. She had no idea how it had ended up in the cavern, but it was fuel. It would burn. Abrina swung her sword to cut up pieces of the deck. It seemed almost a shame as it looked centuries old, but they needed the fuel if they were going to survive in the caves for the next few days.

The next few days. Abrina scoffed as she hacked more wood. If they had a singular dragonblade, that would give them an edge. But what could they do, take on the frost giants by themselves with or without it?

That's exactly what we're going to do. Sword or no sword. She could atone for her mistakes by trying to repair the damage. She'd do everything she could to make sure her people were safe—that Oleanders was safe as well as Florryn. It wasn't fair for Kailyn's people to be killed by the frost giants any more than it was for hers. And if she died trying, it would only be her rightful due. At least then, she'd have done some good with her life.

With renewed determination, Abrina loaded her arms with broken bits of the boat and headed back to camp.

It took her almost two hours to find her way back to the central cave where her men were. Byron and Zachry were deep in discussion by the embers of the fire, their expressions grim.

Abrina walked up to them to drop off her armload of firewood. Byron was the first to notice her.

"So. You're back."

"Yes." She sucked in a breath. She'd never heard him speak so coldly to her before.

"What do you plan on doing now?" Zachry asked softly. "We can't leave the cavern."

"What?" She frowned. "Why?"

"The frost giants are amassing outside. There are other tunnels, sure, but the only one that leads to the outside is barricaded by an army of frost giants."

"No," Abrina whispered. It couldn't be. Not after what the tree spirits had told her. They had a chance to set this right. And *now* they amass? It wasn't fair.

"We couldn't explore very far. There are at least three dozen

315

giants outside, and more were assembling as we scurried back to find shelter. We won't be able to fly out of here." Byron glanced at the cajuna. "We're trapped. We either fight to the death—"

"Or we stay in here and starve," Abrina finished for him. But the trees . . . they had said they might be able to make it. "But we might have a chance—"

"How?" Byron cut her off, his red brows furrowed. "You'll call back your sister? She's gone. This quest is over. We're going to die."

Zachry grunted. "Actually—"

"Shut it, Zachry. I'm not finished," Byron said, sending Zachry a scowl. "We're here, stranded from home. Our captain is dead, our battalion is gone, and we have no way to save ourselves."

Abrina stared at him, the leaden feeling sneaking back into her heart. He was right. But only partially so—if they worked together, maybe they could team up against the frost giants, like they'd done dozens of times in skirmishes on the front. She had to try. All that mattered was stopping the ice and snow. For all of Almarryn.

"We have to try," Abrina said softly. "The people of Florryn, the people of Almarryn, need us. We have to do what we can."

Zachry grunted again. "Princess?"

Byron scowled, ignoring the other knight. "How can we do anything? We don't have a weapon. We don't have the other princess. This prophecy was a fool's mission. We never should have come here in the first place."

"Princess Abrina?" Zachry interrupted for the third time.

Abrina turned to him. "What is it, Zachry?"

Byron harrumphed. "Spit it out, lad."

"I have the other sword." He held up the sheathed dragon-blade. Abrina's eyes widened. Kailyn must have left it behind.

She felt a rush of gratitude for her sister. Perhaps they could make this work.

"By the Palace of Stars . . ." Byron muttered. He glowered at Zachry. "You couldn't have led with that?"

The younger knight shrugged. "You wouldn't let me." He turned to Abrina. "Princess, this rightfully belongs to you."

He offered her the sword and as Abrina picked it up, a rush of golden light filled the underground courtyard. It was warm, but not unbearably so. It tickled, like the summer breezes that blew across the plains toward Heria. It smelled like golden apples and rich pastries, filled to bursting. And it flooded her mind with images of her sister. Kailyn, running on top of the snow with her wolf. Kailyn, laughing with Benje in the courtyard as they examined the First Queen's diary. Kailyn, crying on a cajuna as she fled the quest.

The dragon's voice penetrated her thoughts. *"Do you accept her as your sister?"*

"I do," Abrina thought, meaning every word. She hoped she'd be able to tell Kailyn that someday. If she ever forgave her.

"Then let this sword be my gift to you. Use it well."

Abrina picked up the gleaming sword, grinning. She tossed its weight back and forth and was pleased that it fit her hand just right. *Alaria's hope and salvation.*

Zachry's mouth hung open as he stared at her. "You—you're glowing, Princess."

Abrina looked down at her hands, which were glowing slightly, the same color as the sword. She could still feel the faint summer breeze, but it faded and her hands returned to their natural tan.

"We've got a sword," she said, grinning brightly at him.

"I'm impressed." Byron folded his arms and arched an

eyebrow. "But how do you suggest we take one magic blade and defeat an army of frost giants?"

Abrina turned to Zachry. "What was it that Kailyn said the sword did? It acted of its own accord, right?"

He nodded. "She defeated all three of the giants on her own—the sword shot a column of fire at them, consuming them."

"Right." She nodded once. "Then we'll use this blade and hold off the frost giants on our own."

Byron laughed, a cruel biting sound. "One sword against an army? They're probably planning on invading Florryn. And then Cyron. Oleanders even. Soon all Almarryn will be encased in ice!"

Abrina stared at her knight and the fury that radiated in his eyes. This too was her fault. This was the rift the trees spoke of. She had to win her knights over. They had to do this together.

"Byron," Zachry said warningly. Byron glowered at him.

"What? You think we'll be the only casualties?"

"Byron, we're going to stop the ice," Abrina said firmly, kneeling in front of her knight, crossing her vambrace over her chestplate. Byron looked taken aback. "I promise you. I won't let the giants destroy Almarryn. We can still stop them."

"With one sword?" He shook his head, though his eyes softened slightly. "Face it, Princess. It's impossible."

Zachry cleared his throat. Abrina looked at him and saw him glancing at her pile of wood. "Was there more firewood?"

"Yes. It's behind an unmarked door, then take the fifth cavern down the third tunnel to your left."

He laughed briefly. "How long did it take you to find it?"

"Long enough. I think we could use the extra fire though. It might be useful against the frost giants."

A scoff echoed behind her. "You can't be—"

"Byron," Abrina said, growing irritable. He was really starting to annoy her. She turned to him. "I will do all I can to make this right. But I need you on board with this." She leveled her steely eyes at him. "We're all that's left. And naysaying will not help."

Byron shrugged. "I'm just trying to be realistic, Princess. It's the three of us. Against an army out there."

Abrina nodded. "I know our odds are not good. But we're warriors. This is what we do. We knew this might be a one-way trip. We're going to defeat the frost giants or die trying."

Byron looked a bit taken aback, but he was still staring fiercely at Abrina. "And you expect your firewood to work?"

"I expect you to obey orders," she said, glaring at him now. "You will do your part to defeat the frost giants or I will leave you to them."

Byron stared at her for a long moment and then nodded, saluting Abrina with his arm across his chest. "As you say, Princess. I only hope you know what you're doing."

He motioned for Zachry to follow him and the two started toward the tunnels at the back of the cave. Abrina watched them go.

"So do I," she said to the empty courtyard.

Chapter Thirty-Four

Kailyn

Kailyn stepped outside the library, filled with confidence even as the sound of fighting echoed around her in the frigid air. She could do this. All she had to do was get the second dragonblade, fly back to Ligerthia, and help Abrina.

But to do that, she had to stop the fighting going on around her. Both immediately and in her country.

Benje had managed to defeat Ger—who was lying unconscious—and had taken several of the guards out. There were at least a half dozen guards on the ground. But Benje was panting, his clothing ripped.

"Princess!" he called out when he saw Kailyn. "Stay in the library! It's dangerous out here!"

Kailyn took a shaky breath. It *was* dangerous out there. Could she really do this?

Canis pressed his nose against her, sending her an image of the Goddess.

Believe, was all he managed to convey, which was the most complex thought he'd sent her yet. But it was enough. She took a deeper breath this time, steeling herself to be more like Abrina, who was fearless. She could do this.

"I will go talk to Lord Shielen," she called, surprising herself with how steady her voice was. "If you leave this man to his forge."

Canis growled beside her. *Fight?*

Not yet, she thought. Though she was glad he was willing. He was her backup plan.

"What?" Benje shook his head and managed to punch the guard in front of him, sending him sprawling to the ground. "Don't do it. They want to arrest you!"

"I have to, Benje. You have to fix the sword."

The biggest of the guards grunted. "We have orders to take you and the apprentice to Lord Shielen."

Canis growled again. *Fight?*

"If you don't let the apprentice stay, I will have my wolf attack you," Kailyn said.

The man shook his head. "I'm not scared of some dog. Come on, men!" He motioned the other guards forward, raising their swords.

"Princess!" Benje called, sounding pained. He moved forward to intercept the guards, but he was slower than his usual pace. He was tired.

Kailyn turned to Canis, her heart hammering. *Now. But don't kill them.*

Canis's growl grew louder, and he seemed to almost double in size and fluff in front of Kailyn's very eyes. She blinked. She had no idea he could do that.

The guards lowered their swords, several of them with their mouths hanging open.

"That's—that's an Alarian wolf," one of them managed to stammer.

The other one backed up as Canis stalked him, then shrieked when the wolf jumped, landing on his chest. He screamed. "Get 'im off! Get 'im off!"

The biggest of the guards snarled. "Fine. Call off your dog."

321

Canis, Kailyn thought. *Stop.*

The pup looked up at her, his bright blue eyes shining. *Food?*

No, they are not food. Come here.

The pup bounded back over, still giant and fluffy.

The biggest man motioned to two of his guards. "You two stay with the apprentice. We'll take the princess and her . . . pet . . . to Lord Shielen."

Kailyn walked forward, her head held high. Canis walked beside her, growling at the guards, who followed them.

She felt Benje's eyes on her as she passed, but she couldn't look at him. Benje would only try to stop her, but she had to convince Lord Shielen to stop this oppression of her nation. She had to convince him to lay down arms. Start over.

The walk back to the castle was a blur. Kailyn didn't see many people about, but she felt eyes watching her. She hoped they were friendly. She hoped her people knew that she was on their side, and she was going to change things in Oleanders for the better.

Lord Shielen was waiting for them in the throne room. Along with a large golden man that Kailyn had last seen in Tigahel.

She stopped in her tracks, surprised. "Prince Henri?"

"Princess Kailyn?" The man blinked his blue eyes slowly. "What are you doing here?"

Kailyn was about to ask him the same thing when Lord Shielen spoke.

"Ah, you've met our diplomat," Lord Shielen's eely voice came from the throne. Kailyn stiffened. The throne. Where her father had sat. And died. Lord Shielen now sprawled upon the lush chair. "Princess Kailyn, can I say it is a joy to welcome you to my new Oleanders?"

"This isn't Oleanders," Kailyn spat. "Oleanders is not your kingdom."

"Is that so?" Lord Shielen stood to his full height and walked down the dais toward Kailyn. The hairs on the back of her neck stood up and Canis growled next to her.

"Princess, Oleanders is not your home anymore. You no longer have any claim to the throne." He smirked at her. "But you will still be a delightful pawn in cementing my alliance with Oronia. King Larnik will be most pleased to have you marry his son Zolan, as was the initial agreement. Oleanders and Oronia will then wage war on the rest of the world, conquering them all and uniting them under one empire."

"You snake!" Kailyn hissed, wishing she was as good at fighting as Abrina. If only she had the dragonblade, she could blast him and be done with this . . . *vyko* . . . forever. Canis hissed and tensed next to Kailyn. She was about to let him attack Lord Shielen, but she didn't like the looks of all those guards behind the throne. Canis couldn't take them all.

Wait. Even though that was the last thing she wanted to do.

"Lord Shielen." Prince Henri's voice was level. "This is not what we agreed."

Lord Shielen eyed the prince. "And I don't much care for an alliance with your nation. Oleanders has only ever had trade agreements with Tigahel, and there are far more, shall we say, *lucrative* contracts with Oronia." His eyes gleamed. "Besides, after we've taken over Oleanders, Tigahel will be easy."

Prince Henri's eyes glinted harshly. "Reneging on a trade agreement with Tigahel will be a costly mistake, Lord Shielen."

Lord Shielen shrugged dismissively. "Once Princess Kailyn is married to Prince Zolan, we'll have the military might to take on any nation, land or sea."

Kailyn gritted her teeth. She had to stop this. She had to depose Lord Shielen and reclaim her kingdom. But how?

At that moment, the doors to the throne room burst open. To Kailyn's shock, warriors flying cajuna burst into the room, along with people on the ground, holding swords, knives, some even pots and pans. The force was far more numerous than the guards stationed in the room, though they quickly jumped into the fray, moving to protect Lord Shielen.

Henri moved to block her, Canis standing on Kailyn's other side as clashes, shouting, and bangs echoed around the room.

"What are you doing here?" Prince Henri cried, twirling his staff to create a protective blue sphere of light around Kailyn. He looked right at her, eyes narrowed. "Weren't you supposed to be in Ligerthia with Abrina?"

Kailyn sighed. She hadn't wanted to have this conversation with him just yet. "I-I left the quest."

Prince Henri raised an eyebrow. "Explain."

So as a battle raged around them, cajuna flying through the throne room, guards slashing their swords, people screaming, Kailyn quickly told Prince Henri what had happened in Ligerthia.

"She drew a sword on you." He sighed, sounding deeply disappointed. "Again."

"But we were on our way back to help." Kailyn winced as someone nearby got an arrow to their leg. "We just had to give Benje time to fix the sword."

"He mentioned that," Prince Henri grunted, pulling out a silver moon-shaped pendant from his white robes. "But he wasn't supposed to come back to Oleanders. We had it handled."

Kailyn stared at him. "What?"

Prince Henri patted the necklace and tucked it back into his robes. "It's a communication stone. Benje and I have been in communication since before you left Tigahel to speak with the dragon. My mother sent me to Florryn to deliver supplies, but

Benje had filled me in on the rebellion here in Oleanders. I knew that if the quest were successful, you'd both need a kingdom to come home to. So I've been planning a coordinated attack with the rebellion. My negotiations with Lord Shielen were a distraction. He was never going to agree."

Kailyn blinked. That was a lot to process.

Then she turned and looked out at her people. They were a mess. They were injured and dying right in front of her.

And Lord Shielen was trying to sneak away.

"Canis, stop him," Kailyn said, pointing toward where Lord Shielen was crawling away from the throne, several guards lying injured or dead on the ground before it.

Canis burst through the blue shield and raced across the room to pin Lord Shielen down with his massive fluff.

Kailyn looked up at Henri and at his mystical blue staff that was still emitting a protective shield around them. "How does it do that?"

"Do what?"

She motioned to the sphere. "That."

"It's a Forged staff. That's one of the basic abilities of all Forged weapons. They can all do that."

"Even the dragonblades?" Kailyn asked.

Henri nodded. "I don't know too much about them, but if they're forged weapons, then yes, they should. Why?"

"Could I borrow that?" She motioned toward the staff.

Henri stared at her. "What?"

Kailyn smiled. "I need it."

With a face filled with curiosity, Henri handed her the shimmering blue staff. It hummed with power in Kailyn's hand— it felt like a tree, but it was as solid as metal. Kailyn banged the staff on the ground, like the queen back in the Great Tree.

As she expected, sparks emitted from the staff as it boomed against the tiled floor. Everyone fell silent around them, turning to stare at her.

She handed the staff back to Henri—whose eyes were wide, but who was grinning—and turned to address her people.

"I know these last few years have not been easy for you," she said, hoping her voice didn't shake. "I know you've suffered under my father and under that man." She pointed to Lord Shielen who was still trapped underneath Canis. "I know you don't know me because my father kept me locked away." She bowed her head, sitting with the sting of that memory for a moment.

She lifted her chin. "But this is not the way to achieve peace." Her voice was stronger now as the words came.

"The people of Oleanders have been brave. And your voices need to be heard. I, Princess Kailyn of Oleanders, will listen. We will fix what has been broken. We will start anew!"

The people murmured around her. One man stepped forward. "Princess Kailyn, pardon me, but you've been locked away your whole life. You don't know anything about us."

Kailyn stepped closer to the man, seeing the gaunt circles under his eyes. His clothes hung on his skeletal frame. A dagger glinted at his side, and he looked like he knew how to use it. He'd been through so much. He deserved a rest.

All her people did. They deserved peace.

There'd been enough fighting to last generations.

"I know you've suffered," she said quietly. "And I know that suffering leaves scars."

The man nodded, bowing his head.

"We need help," he whispered.

"I will help you," Kailyn promised, laying a hand on his arm. "Whatever you need. I'm here." She turned to the assembled group. "I give you my word as princess that I will listen to all of you and hear your concerns. You are the lifeblood of Oleanders. Your voices matter!"

The crowd cheered and Canis howled.

Then Canis's howl ended with a whimper.

Pain.

Fear spurred Kailyn's feet across the floor, her people parting in front of her. Lord Shielen shoved Canis's body to the ground, a dagger glinting with blood gripped in his hand, but Kailyn ignored it as she fell to her knees to embrace her fluffy wolf cub.

"Canis! Canis, where are you hurt?"

Pain.

Then she saw it. The blood. It covered vast portions of his fur, matting it together.

"No, no!" She pulled up her skirts and tried to stem the blood, but it just kept coming.

"Canis!"

"He's an Alarian wolf, Princess," Lord Shielen hissed. "Do you know what that means? He's a Florrynian curse. *Oleanderian bane.* An enemy to our people."

"Florryn's not our enemy, Lord Shielen!" Kailyn cried, pressing her gown into Canis's wounds. "You are!"

"Me?" He raised a thin eyebrow. "I've been helping this people."

"No, you haven't," Henri said, standing like a big statue come to life next to Lord Shielen. The prince towered over him. Lord Shielen yelped and started to run, but Henri swung his staff, catching Lord Shielen's knee. The man went down, hitting his head, and skidded to a halt.

Kailyn couldn't stop the tears from streaming down her face as she stroked Canis's soft fur.

A-aru? The wolf whined weakly.

"It's alright, Canis, I'm here. I'm here. I won't let anything happen to you."

But what could she do? He was dying. She knew it, just like she knew when she'd found his injured mother.

She looked up at Henri. "Is there anything we can do?"

But he shook his head, looking morose. "Forged staffs can't heal, Princess."

Pain. Canis's voice in her head was softer now. He was dying.

She bent her head, crying over her wolf's fur. Her constant companion. Her guardian. Her fierce protector. He was leaving her.

He whined again softly as she stroked his muzzle. "It's alright, Canis. It's alright."

But it wasn't alright. She was losing him.

Then a glow nearby caught her eye. She looked up to see Benje, carrying the repaired dragonblade, which was glowing a brilliant gold.

"Princess," he whispered, handing her the blade. It was still warm to the touch. "This is for you."

Shocked, Kailyn took the dragonblade. It felt like the most natural thing in the world to hold it. The dragon on the hilt had a ruby eye that glittered at her. She stared at the Old Alarian words on the blade: *Hilka e dyoin de Alaria.*

Alaria's hope and salvation. Benje had told her what the Old Alarian words meant as they'd poured over the book together, trying to figure out how to get the swords to work.

She glanced from the sword to Canis's side, which was still going up and down, but barely. The wolf was fading.

Henri had said that the Forged staffs couldn't heal. But could Forged blades? Surely if they were blessed by the Goddess, they could do anything.

Kailyn bowed her head, holding the sword aloft like an offering, one hand on the hilt, one on the blade.

"Goddess please," she whispered. "Save Canis. Save him. Please."

The sword glowed brighter and brighter in her hands. Kailyn had to close her eyes as the light grew too intense to look at.

She heard happy yips and opened her eyes. Canis sat in front of her, his normal size, but completely unblemished.

Aru? Sad?

"Canis!" She threw her arms around him. "You're safe."

Safe? He sent her an image of Benje and Kailyn laughed. Canis was whole again. Benje had brought her the blade. He'd made it possible for her to heal her pup. She turned around to see Benje staring at them, a small smile on his lips.

"Kailyn." He bowed his head. "Well done."

"I'm glad the pup is safe," Henri said, standing guard over Lord Shielen's prone body, his blue staff at the ready. "But this isn't over yet." He motioned toward the window and Kailyn gasped. Flurries of white snow were descending from the sky with a vengeance.

She locked eyes with Benje. "The frost giants," she whispered.

"What do we do? What do we do?" one of the women in the room screamed. The man next to her was trying to hold her to keep her calm, but the woman's frantic voice rang out again. "Oleanders never gets snow. We're doomed! We're all going to die!"

Murmuring broke out among the assembled people.

"The snow . . . it means the end of days."

"Lord Shielen's killed us all."

"Is this the Goddess punishing us?"

Kailyn glanced at the crowd, trying to quiet her own mounting anxiety. This couldn't be the end. This wasn't the end.

"No!" she exclaimed.

They kept talking.

She glanced at Canis, who started howling, a loud piercing cry that rose over the noise.

Everyone quieted.

"Thank you." She patted Canis on the head, and she could have sworn the pup was smiling at her. Her heart thrummed with gratitude. She was so grateful he was alive. She didn't think she could bear it if he left her.

She looked at Benje, who nodded. "The snow does not mean we're going to die," she said, her voice picking up steam. "Please. I know how to end this storm."

"How?" a man called out. "It's weather, Princess!"

A couple people laughed nervously.

Kailyn bit her lip, wondering what Abrina would do if she were here. She'd probably smash something to get people to listen to her. Her eyes landed on Henri's staff above Lord Shielen's body, and she repressed a shudder as the man twitched. Henri's staff kept him from moving. She didn't think the staff would help her this time. And smashing things wasn't really her style.

Besides, enough violence had been committed here today. She squared her shoulders, trying to channel her inner Abrina. Abrina, the natural leader.

"Let me deal with the storm. All of you, gather your family and friends to the castle. It's a stronghold. It'll keep you warm."

She looked at Henri and Benje. Worry gnawed at her. She couldn't leave without someone in charge. And they were the only ones she trusted.

"I'm leaving you both in charge," she said to them.

"Princess." Henri bowed his head. "I'll look after them." He motioned for some men to come remove Lord Shielen, before he started moving around the room, checking on each group of people, asking to see if everyone in their family was accounted for.

Kailyn nodded, satisfied. Her people were in good hands.

She made to head toward the door, Canis following, but was stopped by Benje standing in front of her, his arms crossed.

She looked at him, pleading. "Let me through, Benje."

Benje shook his head, his mouth set in a firm line. "No. Absolutely not. You're not flying back to Ligerthia alone."

"Benje . . ." Kailyn sighed. Canis pressed his head into her side, and she stroked his fur. "I won't be alone. I'll have Canis with me."

Aru!

"He's a wonderful warrior. But be that as it may, as we just saw, he's not invincible. And Princess Abrina . . ."

Kailyn swallowed, wondering if the other princess would even want her back.

Then she remembered her visit with the Goddess. The Goddess who believed in her. She could do this. She had to do this. This was bigger than Oleanders, bigger than Florryn, bigger than Tigahel. The world needed her.

"Benje, I have to do this. Abrina and I are the only ones who can save Almarryn."

She hefted the sword, which she hadn't let go of since she'd used it to heal Canis, though its glow was much softer now.

"Besides, the sword is fixed. We'll have both of them."

He worked his jaw. "But you'll be alone . . ."

"No, she won't," Henri said, coming over to them, leading a man who was holding the reins to a purple cajuna. "Jork here and his company will fly with her."

Benje raised an eyebrow. "The Tigahelen advance? But they were just here to aid the rebellion."

"Do you see a rebellion anymore?" Henri asked.

Kailyn looked behind, seeing how the people—both guards and rebels—were helping one another. They'd cleared the wounded from the room, and had started to bring in families, wrapping one another in blankets. Several of the guards had started distributing food. One of the Tigahelen warriors was giving some children rides on the cajuna around the room.

"There's no rebellion anymore. They're all Oleanderians," Kailyn said, smiling.

"We've got this, Princess," Henri said. He nodded once solemnly. "Fly above the clouds—you'll stay out of the storm. Fly hard. Fly swift. Fly true." His eyes softened. "Help Abrina. She needs you."

His eyes shone with a tenderness that made Kailyn smile. She'd seen how Henri and Abrina had interacted together back at Tigahel. She hoped that the two of them would have more time together when all this was done.

"I will," she assured him.

He crossed his chest with his arm. "May the Goddess bless you."

Kailyn nodded her thanks and headed out to the courtyard, Canis right next to her, and Benje not far behind.

Snow was starting to fall in earnest now. It was piling up around barrels, the fountain, and the stables. Kailyn shivered. It had never been this cold in Oleanders. Ever.

The man, Jork, gathered his men and their cajuna, preparing them for takeoff.

Benje took her hand, his calluses as familiar as her favorite book.

"I don't like this," he said. "You could die." His voice dropped to a near whisper and his brown eyes searched Kailyn's face like he was trying to hold onto her for dear life.

"I need to, Benje," Kailyn whispered. She could lose herself in his eyes. She hefted the sword with her other hand. "We are Alaria's hope and salvation. I believe this is the work of the Goddess. I need you to believe it too."

Benje stared at her for a long moment, then nodded. "Alright." He kissed her cheek. Kailyn blinked, feeling a rush of heat fill her insides. "But you better come back."

She smiled sadly. "I'll try."

Chapter Thirty-Five

Abrina

"Ready?" Abrina asked Zachry and Byron. They'd been pre-paring all night, collecting wood and pitch from the tunnels. They'd amassed a large collection of firewood. Zachry had whit-tled as much as he could into arrows. Abrina's plan was to have her knights stand near the entrance and shoot fire at the frost giants while she went out to attack them.

It wasn't a great plan, but she didn't have any other ideas. It's not like she could talk to the frost giants and tell them "Please stop attacking!" She missed Sir Tyir—he would have been able to come up with an even better plan.

But this was what they had.

Her men looked grim, but they both nodded. All three of them had been taking turns standing guard all night, watching the frost giants amass. They couldn't count them, due to the wall of white outside the cave, but the wall had only gotten thicker and thicker since it started. They'd be walking into a frozen cloud.

Byron lit the pile of wood in front of him, dipped the arrow in the flames, and lined up his shot on Abrina's left, Zachry doing the same on her right. Abrina held her dragonblade in one hand, which was slightly glowing, and her regular sword in the other, which wasn't. The weight of both blades was comfortable. She'd been practicing fighting with them all night. She could do this.

They didn't really have a choice.

Abrina nodded at her two men and they both launched their flaming arrows into the cloud of fog. Nothing happened.

"Again," Abrina commanded.

They launched a second volley. Then a third. Then a fourth. Nothing happened.

Abrina squinted at the wall of white, hoping to make sense of it. But she couldn't see anything. Had their flames even penetrated the wall?

She glanced at the dragonblade. *Alaria's hope and salvation.* That's what Henri had told her it said. The dragon, the trees, even her own sister believed they could do this. Kailyn had been able to wield massive amounts of light with her blade that simply engulfed the frost giants. Surely Abrina could do the same, couldn't she?

She brought the glowing blade up to her lips. "Please work," she whispered.

Suddenly, the blade lit up with fire, the scorching heat nearly searing Abrina's eyebrows. But her hand gripping the sword remained cool and untouched.

Abrina smiled grimly. That was more like it.

"How'd you do that?" Zachry asked.

"I don't know," Abrina said. "But I think it'll work against them."

"You don't have to go alone," Byron grumbled. He still sounded put out, but she knew he was loyal to Florryn. He would fight to the last.

"I need you two to keep shooting flames from here, alright? I think this blade," she hoisted the dragonblade, "might change the tide in our favor."

Byron nodded. "Good luck, Princess."

"Goddess be with you," Zachry added.

Abrina nodded, sent a quick prayer up to the Goddess herself, and barreled into the white wall of snow.

Her progress was slow. She couldn't see anything. Walking through the storm felt like walking through a river of mud—which Abrina had tried once when the River Hane had overflowed a few years back, before the civil war.

Her sword burned the fog away around her the further she went. Suddenly, she could see great lumps of boulders. She gasped. These were the frost giants! There had to be a good dozen of them, if not more. All standing there. Watching. Waiting.

Abrina charged the boulder-like legs, which stomped, sending waves of snow toward her. Booms shook the snowy landscape, growls echoed around Abrina. She was alone, knee-deep in enemies.

She'd never felt more alive.

As she sliced and ducked and dodged appendages, the flames of the dragonblade seemed to have a life of their own. As she swung to slice off a leg, the flames jumped up, twirling like some fiery specter, consuming the beast. They spread from monster to monster, devouring them.

Within moments, a half-dozen of them had been destroyed.

She grinned, flipping the dragonblade over in her hand.

"This is almost too easy," she said. She eyed the rest of the horde. "Anyone else want a taste?"

Suddenly, the loudest, deepest roar that Abrina had ever heard shook the ground. A huge creature burst from the ground, sending waves of ice and snow down toward Abrina in an avalanche.

Abrina blanched. "Oh no." She took off running, slipping in her boots on the icy ground, but managed to get in line of sight of the cave, where both Byron and Zachry were waving frantically at her, no longer shooting arrows.

"Princess!" Byron called out. "Come back!"

Abrina stared at the frost giant that was three times taller than any she'd ever seen. She watched as the beast called down a column of snow, sending it blasting her way. She held up both her dragonblade and her regular sword and the fire absorbed the snow, but it sent her staggering backward. By the Goddess, that blast was strong.

"Princess!" Zachry yelled.

Abrina gritted her teeth. She could do this. She had to do this.

Something slammed into her from the side, sending her skidding across the snow.

"Abrina!" one of her knights screeched.

She got to her feet dizzily. The world of white and blue was spinning.

The flames of her sword reared higher, and she shook her head to clear it. She could do this.

"Fire!" she called to her men.

Flaming arrows surged out of the cave, hitting the monster. But they were barely making an impact. These things were much bigger than the adolescents they'd fought at the front.

Abrina wrapped her hands around her swords. She had to take down its legs. The fire would do its job.

But she had to admit, things weren't looking very good.

Even if she took this one down, there were still more of them. They'd just keep coming.

No matter. She was a princess of Florryn. She'd go down fighting.

Screaming, Abrina raised both blades and ran at the frost giant.

Chapter Thirty - Six

Kailyn

I'm coming, Abrina! Kailyn knew they didn't have much time. The snow was getting thicker around her.

But if anyone could hold off the frost giants, she knew the fierce princess of Florryn could. She glanced back at the army following her. Jork and his crew were ready and eager for war. She only hoped that they would be enough. If they all got frozen by the frost giants, they were done for.

Snow. Canis sent her images of the snowy Ligerthian landscape. She nodded. They had to do this. They had to get there. For the hundredth time, she prayed to the Goddess for the cajuna to fly faster.

They had flown above the clouds, like Henri had suggested. But it was frigid. Kailyn only hoped that it would be enough, and that they would arrive in time.

She couldn't see anything from the clouds below her, but Canis's head perked up.

"What is it?" she asked him.

Family, he said. *Fire. Danger.*

Kailyn panicked. If he could smell them, they were close. Possibly even right below them. But with the current cloud cover, it was impossible to see anything.

"Drop down! Drop down!" She yelled at the company following behind her, nudging her cajuna to fly lower into the freezing, icy clouds. She heard Jork bellow out the order to descend. The white expanse of cloud didn't seem to disappear as they flew lower, but Kailyn didn't need to see to know that they had emerged into a battle. She could hear it. And it was bedlam.

She heard loud grunts through the fog as white jagged shapes moved violently toward the incoming cajuna. Kailyn unsheathed her dragonblade, which started glowing a bright golden color and pointed it at the nearest shadow-shape by her.

The sword shot a bolt of fiery energy of its own accord. It flew straight at the monstrous face that bellowed at her, emerging from the dense white fog that swirled around them. She barely had a moment to register the horrifying mouth of razor-sharp icicles before her sword's blast hit the giant. He screamed, a terrible screeching cry that ripped the frigid air into shreds before tumbling out of sight.

"Where are they?" she asked Canis, who was on alert. His ears swiveled at every sound, and he broadcasted images of the ferocious monsters toward her mind, which wasn't keeping her very calm, but she knew he was frightened too.

Family! he said again. Kailyn turned and saw another fiery glow, which was presumably the other sword, charging something big on the ground. She directed her cajuna toward it, but the cajuna crashed in the snow.

Kailyn yelped as she flew into the air and landed in a snowbank. Canis scurried on the snow toward her, licking her face.

"Canis, I'm fine, I'm fine!" she mumbled.

A hand suddenly appeared before her. It was Sir Zachry, who helped her up from the snow.

"Princess Kailyn!" he exclaimed. "You came back."

A shriek sounded behind him and he turned and launched an arrow at a hulking giant. Kailyn lifted her sword and sent a light blast at it, which send the beast staggering away.

"I had to. Where's Abrina?"

Zachry's face was grim. "She took on the biggest one by herself. She went that way." He pointed toward an orange blip, which was drawing nearer and nearer a large blue mountain— bigger than any of the other frost giants Kailyn had seen.

"Abrina!" Kailyn shrieked and ran toward her sister, Canis yipping behind her.

A leg loomed out of the fog and Kailyn would have run into it had Canis not howled at her. *ICE!*

She turned just in time. The leg moved and the creature lumbered toward the cajuna who were dive-bombing the giants from the air. She heard whistling sounds as the cajuna were hit and forced toward the ground, and even bigger thuds as a few of the giants were felled. Screams sounded as the giants dissolved and then reformed. But it was hard to see anything in the swirling vortex of snow. Where was Abrina?

She pointed her dragonblade at the swirling snow. *Help me see my sister!*

The sword started glowing like a miniature sun. Heat radiated off it in waves, nearly choking her, but she waved it in the air, hoping to absorb more fog.

The fog seeped into the sword, and she could suddenly see. But it wasn't good. Abrina was ducking under massive legs, her sword aflame. The giant had a huge long blue icicle sword that he was using to parry Abrina's dragonblade.

Abrina was managing to cut the icicle with her fiery sword, but the giant blade was just too big.

Then Kailyn saw it. The giant was raising its fist—and Abrina wasn't turning! Kailyn didn't even think. She knew she wasn't going to let her sister die. She called a cajuna to her and mounted it, pure adrenaline spurring her on.

Run! she told Canis as she flew as fast as she could toward the frost giant. She could see Canis in her mind, scampering across the snow below her.

Time seemed to move in slow motion as she saw the creature lower its icy fist, clearly aiming to squash Abrina. Kailyn wouldn't let him crush her.

She swung her sword with both fists and somehow lobbed off the hand of the giant, who bellowed in rage. It swatted her from the air with its other hand. She tumbled in circles before landing in a snowdrift again. Canis howled nearby as the giant roared. An enormous blue sword appeared in her vision as the giant turned to her, ready to finish her off. She closed her eyes. This was the end.

A fierce "*NOOOO!*" shattered the air and Kailyn saw a fiery ball of light shoot right past her, hitting the massive giant. He disappeared into a gigantic cloud of snow that swirled into a vortex, heading directly for her. She embraced the wall of cold, her only regret that she had failed her sister.

A wolf howled in the distance. "*ARUUUUUUUUUU!*"

Then the world slowly darkened until she couldn't see or feel or hear anything at all.

Chapter Thirty - Seven

Abrina

"*Noooo!*" Abrina shouted as she watched the giant about to slay Kailyn with his massive blue sword. Her own dragonblade launched a fireball at him, which turned into a flaming mass so big it consumed the giant, turning it into a swirling storm of flakes.

She rushed at the vortex, trying to get to her sister, only to be buried in a mountain of snow.

Abrina spun in the snow, spluttering, trying to claw her way to the surface, but only managing to find a buried human hand. Her breath caught. *Kailyn.*

With the dragonblade in her other hand, Abrina dug out some of the snow around them until she could see Kailyn's prone form.

How deep were they? She couldn't hear anything, not even the thud of the giants' footsteps, or their roars. She'd seen cajuna swoop in right before Kailyn had fallen in front of the giant. What was going on up there? Had Henri come? How? She thought he was in Florryn.

But how else had more cajuna—with warriors—arrived?

Abrina wanted to cry. She didn't know anything. All she knew was that they were buried in ice and snow.

Her dragonblade was no longer on fire, but it was glowing slightly, and she made small dents into the snow as she tried to shovel her way out, but she just kept releasing more flakes that fell on Kailyn's prone body. So she held the sword like a torch and it melted away some of the snow around them, creating a little cave of ice.

"We'll get out of this, Kailyn," she said, her heart pounding. She hoped they would. She wanted to beg Kailyn's forgiveness for chasing her away from the quest. She wanted to thank her for coming back.

Abrina blinked suddenly as hot salty tears pricked her eyes. She wanted to thank her for saving her life. It was absurd, it was brave, but it was absurdly brave, the way she had swooped in like that, lobbing off the giant's hand with the somehow repaired dragonblade. Abrina had been so distracted by the giant's sword that she hadn't seen the hand in the swirling snow.

"Why did you have to be so brave?" she whispered. Kailyn really was a lot like their mother. If Abrina was honest with herself, Kailyn was more like her mother than she was.

She'd gone on the quest for selfish reasons—to prove she could save the world. And now, here she was, buried under Goddess-only-knew how much snow, with her unconscious sister who had sacrificed herself for Abrina—the selfish, judgmental sister who'd pushed Kailyn away, who'd hated her from the moment she had laid eyes on her, who had drawn a sword on her simply because she shared her mother's face.

"What have I done?" Abrina moaned, burying her head in her hands. It was hopeless. The vortex that monstrous giant had created had buried them in so much snow, she knew it was likely she and Kailyn both would die here.

Their only chance was to pray to the Goddess and hope that someone noticed they were missing.

Sometime later, Abrina heard a wolf cry. And it sounded close. "Canis?" she cried out. "Canis! We're down here!"

She felt something press on her mind with great urgency. She jumped, her arm brushing against Kailyn's cold one.

"Canis?" she called out again.

Warmth was the word that flooded her mind. She saw a bunch of wolves curled up, their tails tucked in as they slept together.

"I'm not sure how that's going to help," she muttered. "Go get help, Canis!"

Family?

Abrina had no idea what that meant, but hopefully it meant help. "Yes, family. Go get family!"

A wolf howl echoed above the snow and then the presence in her mind vanished. She looked down at her sister. *Her* family.

Kailyn was out cold, and Abrina could see small patches of ice spread across the girl's cheeks. Abrina swallowed. How reckless it had been for Kailyn to take that attack. But she'd saved her. And now she had to save her so they could end this. Together.

She focused on the sword. "Um . . . warm her up?" she asked the blade.

Nothing happened. It just stayed the same soft golden glow.

Abrina sighed. "Please, magical sword?" Her voice caught. "I need to save my sister."

The sword's glow intensified until it suddenly grew so bright that Abrina had to close her eyes.

"A-Abrina?"

Abrina's eyes flew open. Kailyn was blinking at her. "Wh-what happened?"

"We got buried in a vortex of snow," Abrina said. "Are you alright?"

Kailyn nodded and sat up. Abrina stared at her. They were finally face-to-face, after everything. And they were both alive.

Tears pricked Abrina's eyes.

"Kailyn . . ." her voice croaked. "I'm so, so sorry. You are my sister. I see it now. You're so like Mother, so determined. And you're kind like Father. And . . ." A tear streaked down her cheek. "You're so brave. Not . . . not like me."

Kailyn groaned as she shifted in their small snow cave. "Me? Brave? But I left you, Abrina. I left the quest. I abandoned you. You're the fierce one. You're the brave one. I can't fight like you can."

"But you didn't try to destroy the quest." Abrina hung her head. "Not like I did. You weren't tempted by power. Not like I was. I broke the dragonblade."

She blinked fiercely, the tears streaming down her face.

"Abrina," Kailyn said, and to Abrina's surprise, she found herself embraced in Kailyn's arms. "We all make mistakes," Kailyn murmured. "Our people have abused each other for centuries. But we can set that right."

A warmth spread from Abrina's fingers all the way to her toes. She was right. It didn't matter that they were under several feet of snow. It didn't matter that they might die here. All that mattered was that they were together. Whole again. Family. Like the wolf had said.

"Abrina," Kailyn whispered. "Look."

The two blades—which looked identical, Abrina couldn't even tell which one had been broken—were both glowing brightly now, brighter than Abrina had ever seen them glow before. The one in Abrina's hands hummed with power.

"I think . . . they should be brought together," Kailyn whispered.

Abrina nodded. Without speaking, they both brought their swords together and, as the tips touched, a boom like thunder echoed around them as a great blinding beam of light burst forth, surrounding them.

When it cleared, Abrina saw they were in the middle of the battle, cajuna flying everywhere around large snow-covered lumps, warriors screaming. Flaming arrows glowed in the snow. Instinctively, Abrina stood back-to-back with Kailyn, shielding her from an icy dagger that plunged toward her.

To her surprise, Kailyn turned and thrust her sword up. A great beam of fire burst upward, and the giant stumbled back.

Abrina smiled. Her sister had the heart of a warrior. A true Florrynian.

But Abrina didn't know how long they could last. They fell into a rhythm, running, stabbing, ducking, slicing. She didn't know how long they kept at it, how many giants they avoided.

She didn't know how many warriors were turned to ice.

But they kept fighting, kept going, pressing forward together.

"Abrina," Kailyn said, wheezing after they'd dispatched another frost giant. "We-we can't keep doing this."

"No," Abrina agreed. "But they're not going to stop."

Kailyn nodded, then stuck out her hand. "To the end then?"

Abrina felt a rush of emotion for her warrior sister and embraced her fiercely. "To the end."

They charged another white lump of snow, and this time, Abrina knew. They wouldn't make it. They were weary, battle-worn, and exhausted. There was no way they could keep going.

An icy breath encased her non-flaming, making it grow heavy and cold. She winced at the sting and discarded it, watching as her precious blade turned blue with ice. She gulped. She was next.

"*ARUUUUUUUU!*" A loud piercing howl rose above the noises

of the fighting. The frost giant paused. Abrina whirled around in the swirling snow and gaped. Kailyn laughed.

"It's Canis!" she cried. "And he's not alone!"

Large shapes came out of the snow.

Abrina took advantage of the distraction and wriggled away from the frost giant who'd frozen her sword, who growled and tried to grab her. Kailyn blasted the creature with light from her dragonblade and together, they both started running across the snow.

More howls sounded around them as huge Alarian wolves joined the fight. They were bigger than any wolf Abrina had ever seen, and their pelts were a glorious glowing white. They were all bigger than Canis, though the pup had also grown nearly twice his normal size, and they were growling at the frost giants, who had paused fighting the few remaining men on cajuna.

A booming voice echoed from somewhere close by. "*You dare intrude in our war party, wolfkind?*"

Abrina staggered. The frost giants could . . . talk?

"*CEASE!*" howled one of the wolves. Abrina had no idea which one it was. She just stared at them. There were at least fifty of the majestic creatures.

The sounds of fighting stalled around them as warriors and frost giants alike turned to stare at the newcomers.

"*This does not concern you!*" cried the booming voice of the giants. A wolf howled and the great large shapes grew ever closer.

Abrina shuddered. This wasn't going to be enough. They were going to be frozen—right here, right now.

To her surprise, Kailyn stood, calling out to Canis. The wolf cub bounded over to her.

"Great giants of the north," Kailyn said, her voice booming out across the frozen plain. Abrina stared at her. What was she doing?

"*ARUUUUUUUU!*" Canis howled.

Kailyn smiled, patting Canis's head. "And great wolves. We must end this conflict! We must stop the ice and snow."

Abrina scoffed. She was going to *talk* to the giants? They were beasts, who attacked and destroyed everything in their path. They weren't intelligent.

"*Back off, little human!*" hissed the booming voice. "*The wretched queen of Ligerthia must suffer for her mistakes!*"

Abrina scowled. All this because of the accursed queen? Her blood boiled. If she ever saw that foul woman again, she *would* pay.

"I agree she must be held accountable," Kailyn said, still patting Canis's head. Her voice was far calmer than Abrina's would have been. "But this is not the way, O Great Ones."

"*Such foolishness, girl. The war has only begun. We cannot cease until the whole world is frozen and left to die.*" The giant lifted his ice dagger, leering over Kailyn.

"No!" Abrina lunged forward as the giant dagger met her dragonblade with a brilliant bang and a flash of light. The dagger broke in icy halves which were consumed by the fire of her blade. She smirked. *Good blade.*

The giant hissed.

"*These cursed swords!*"

Abrina's smirk turned into a full-on grin. Those "cursed" swords were the only way they had even a chance of winning.

But Kailyn kept talking.

"The world has not wronged you!" Kailyn said. "It is the queen that your ire is against, not all of Almarryn. Please, I beg you."

Kailyn shot Abrina a look and Abrina's heart twisted. "I know what it's like to make a great mistake. A grave error of judgment."

Kailyn hung her head, staring at her blade before looking up again. "The rest of the world shouldn't suffer because of one woman's mistakes."

"*She caused so much pain,*" the giant's voice boomed. "*So many of us gone.*"

"And that is a tragedy," Abrina found herself saying, standing next to Kailyn. "So many of my people are gone as well. But no new suffering will bring them back. How many of your people will die in this fight to freeze all Almarryn?"

Several of the other giants murmured in assent.

"*We wish to be left alone,*" the giant with the booming voice finally said. "*And never disturbed again. Not even the mountains that surround our homeland.*"

"We can do that," Abrina said breezily. Kailyn shot her a look. "What? I never want to come back to this Goddess-forsaken place."

The giant hissed again. "*The Goddess placed us here to protect this land. To protect its secrets. To protect the art of Forging. But the queen abused us! And the art. She must pay!*"

Kailyn took a deep breath and slipped her hand into Abrina's. Surprised, Abrina squeezed her hand back.

"She will face the consequences of her actions," Kailyn said, her voice firm. "But this is not the way."

"*LISTEN TO HER,*" cried the great howl of the wolf. "*CEASE THIS MONSTROUS FIGHT.*"

The giant hissed. "*We have no quarrel with you, wolves!*"

"You will if you keep this up," Kailyn said. "Your snowy battle will not only damage all of Almarryn, but it will kill every other living thing that can't survive your harsh storms. Including the wolves."

The wolves howled behind her, echoing the sentiment.

Abrina raised an eyebrow, impressed. She hadn't thought of that.

"*What do you propose, little human?*" hissed the giant, his voice sounding . . . slightly warmer. Maybe a single degree warmer. But it was a start.

"Cease fighting. Pull all your forces back to Ligerthia and its surrounding mountains. We won't bother you if you don't bother us."

Abrina felt her squeeze her hand again and she grinned. Kailyn was fearless. Absolutely fearless.

After what felt like an eon, the giant sighed.

"*We agree to your terms. On one condition.*"

Abrina's heart leapt. They were nearly there!

"*We want the blades.*"

Abrina felt like she'd been stabbed in the heart. They couldn't possibly mean . . . *no*. Not the dragonblades! Not after everything they'd been through to get them! Not their power, their magic, no!

Kailyn looked at Abrina and nodded once, fiercely. "For peace."

Abrina felt the fight drain out of her. They had to. They had no choice. Just like she'd had to let go of her grandfather's blade, she now needed to relinquish this one. For peace.

Kailyn knelt on the snow and offered up her glowing blade.

Abrina knelt next to her, offering up her sword as well. It felt like she was giving up a part of her soul.

But when Kailyn beamed at her as the giant scooped up the swords, Abrina realized that she wasn't losing a part of her soul. She was gaining one.

Chapter Thirty-Eight

Kailyn

Kailyn was absolutely exhausted and felt frozen through after the battle. She ached in places she didn't know she could ache. But when Abrina smiled at her, Kailyn felt warmer than a summer's day. They were sisters at last.

They were back in the cavern where they'd started their Ligerthian adventure, a day after the battle. They'd all collapsed for a much-needed rest the night before.

But there was need to mourn. Of the fifty cajuna and warriors who had come with them, only a dozen remained. Jork himself had been caught in a frost giant's blast.

To Kailyn's great surprise, both Sir Zachry and Sir Byron had survived.

"Princess Kailyn!" Sir Byron stared at her, his red hair dusted in ice. "I-I didn't think you'd come back. I—" He hung his head. "I'm ashamed. You've demonstrated that you are truly Florrynian."

"And Oleanderian," Kailyn said, remembering what the dragon and the Goddess had told her. "I am both."

Sir Byron looked ready to protest, but at that moment, Canis bounded across the cave to her, nuzzling her side. She reached down and patted his head.

Food?

"He's so majestic," Sir Zachry said. "Is it true there was a whole pack of them out there earlier? We heard howling."

"There was indeed," Abrina said, coming over to them. "We're about ready to head back to Tigahel. Byron, Zachry, check the cajuna for me."

"And maybe get some food for Canis?" Kailyn called out.

The men saluted them and walked off to examine the cajuna, Canis bounding after them, sending Kailyn thoughts of food.

She shook her head. That pup was always hungry.

Then her heart thumped as she realized what Abrina had said. "Tigahel? You're going back there?"

"Of course." Abrina furrowed her brow. "Isn't that where you got the warriors?"

Kailyn shook her head. "No. They were in Oleanders. Henri and Benje are both there."

"Henri's in Oleanders?" Abrina's mouth dropped open. "*Why* is he there? He was supposed to be in Florryn! Helping *my* people."

"He sort of came to . . . assist with a diplomatic issue in Oleanders," Kailyn said, a little sheepishly. She'd forgotten to tell Abrina she'd seen Henri.

"But that's . . ." Abrina spluttered. Her face settled into its natural scowl. "Fine. Since we're no longer enemies, I suppose I shouldn't begrudge that fact."

Kailyn lifted an eyebrow. "You? Let go of a grudge?"

Abrina's scowl deepened. "I can try, can't I?"

Kailyn laughed. Abrina's mouth quirked into a half-smile before she started laughing, which made Kailyn laugh even harder.

When their laughter calmed down, Kailyn took Abrina's hand. The Florrynian princess stared at her. "What are you doing?"

Kailyn squeezed her hand. "Giving you a hand."

Abrina laughed again and gently pulled her hand away. "Stop that."

Kailyn smiled. Then her smile fell. She was going home to Oleanders. Abrina was going back to Tigahel. They were parting ways. After everything they'd done to save their kingdoms, and their family. "Abrina . . . I . . . I'm sorry."

Abrina quirked an eyebrow. "You're sorry? Why are you sorry? I'm the one who nearly killed you—twice. Had Benje not been there . . ." Abrina shook her head. "I'm the one who let centuries of hate blind me to our current situation. And to the fact that you're my sister. It doesn't matter that you were raised in Oleanders. You are truly Florrynian."

Kailyn smiled sadly. "But I'm Oleanderian too, Abrina. I'm both. And I think I need to be both. Oleanders needs a queen. My people . . ." She shook her head. "They've been through a lot."

"Mine too," Abrina admitted. "There is much to be done to rebuild."

"Yes. There is. But I'm sorry that I'm Oleanderian."

Abrina chuckled. "You can't help it. Any more than I can help detesting those accursed purple fruits Tigahel serves."

"The yilnel fruit?" Kailyn grinned. "They're delicious."

Abrina groaned. "Not you too! They're disgusting."

Kailyn laughed. Then she hugged Abrina, who froze in her embrace for a moment before hugging her back.

"Thank you," Abrina whispered, squeezing Kailyn tighter. "You saved my life, you know."

"And you saved mine," Kailyn whispered. She'd probably still be unconscious if Abrina hadn't used the healing from the dragonblade.

"You're my sister, what was I supposed to do?"

Kailyn smiled, her heart feeling full.

They parted ways after that, Abrina to Tigahel, Kailyn to Oleanders. Abrina told her before they parted to make sure Henri came home to Tigahel. Her eyes glinted with a passion that Kailyn knew was very characteristic of her sister. And she knew how Henri cared about Abrina too.

"If there's a wedding, please promise you'll invite me," Kailyn had said right before they took off.

"You'll be the first," Abrina had promised.

As the cajuna soared across the glittering sea, Kailyn's heart felt more whole than it had been in years. She'd gained a sister and was now heading home to see Benje.

Safe? Canis said in her thoughts. *Home?*

Kailyn smiled. "Yes, Canis. Benje is home."

She missed him terribly. They had barely been separated since she'd first met him. And she found she didn't really want to be away from him.

The way he'd fixed the sword for them . . . and had handed it to her right when she'd needed it.

Canis had been right to call him safe. Benje was.

Benje was waiting for them in the courtyard when Kailyn and Canis finally arrived back in Oleanders. She was tired and weary, but seeing Benje made her feel like she could run on snow for hours.

Snow? Canis asked.

"No. Benje." Kailyn grinned as Canis's ears perked up. He leapt to the ground from the cajuna and ran straight to Benje, who bent down to scratch his ears.

"Benje!" She smiled.

He bowed. "Kailyn."

Safe! Canis yipped and Benje went back to rubbing the wolf cub's ears.

"No need to be so formal," she chided, still feeling giddy at seeing him. Then she noticed he was dressed in white robes with a green sash around his waist, a sword strapped to his side. She blinked. He looked a lot like Henri.

"Benje?" she asked. "What are you wearing?"

"The Ligerthian Knight's robes," came Henri's voice. He had walked out of the castle when Kailyn wasn't looking.

"Henri!" She smiled, then put on her best Abrina face. "Princess Abrina demands you go home to Tigahel."

Henri laughed, a delightfully musical sound. "She put you up to that?"

Kailyn nodded, feeling heat creep into her cheeks.

"Not a bad impression. And I will. I miss my *fyrrel*. But there's something we need to do first. We were waiting for you."

Kailyn frowned, but neither Henri nor Benje said anything more as they led her to the throne room. It was filled with people, but they all looked much happier than the last time Kailyn had seen them.

"Princess Kailyn!" Two familiar faces ran up to her. "You're back!"

"Ilia? Nea?" Kailyn embraced her maids. "Oh, it's so good to see you!" Though her heart echoed a pang at the loss of Myira. Some things had irrevocably changed.

Canis yipped behind her and the maids turned.

"Breath of the Goddess, he's adorable!" Nea squealed. "Can I pet him?"

How about it, Canis? Kailyn asked.

Pets! He sent her an image of the girls rubbing his ears.

Kailyn laughed. "Go ahead."

"Princess Kailyn, if you please," Henri said gently. "There will be time for belly rubs later. We wanted you to be a part of the ceremony before I left."

Kailyn blinked in confusion. "Ceremony?"

Benje bowed again. "My knighting ceremony."

Kailyn's heart leapt within her. "Oh, Benje!"

She was about to hug him, but he held up an arm. "After?" Kailyn nodded and followed Henri to the front of the room.

Henri looked so official in his white robes, the blue sash, and his sapphire staff. He banged the staff on the ground of the raised dais, and everyone turned to face him.

"Welcome, one and all. It is a true pleasure to announce that today, we celebrate not only the return of Princess Kailyn." He paused as the crowd cheered. Kailyn smiled as she waved at her people. "But also to announce the first knighting of a Ligerthian Knight outside Ligerthia or Tigahel in over fifty years. Benje Thornsid. Come forward."

Benje walked, his back straight, his features stoic, and knelt in front of Henri. Kailyn bit her lip. He looked so handsome.

"Benje Thornsid. For years you have desired only one thing. To become a Ligerthian Knight. Is this true?"

Benje lifted his head. "Yes."

"Even though you were sworn to serve my mother, Queen Leilana of Ligerthia and of Tigahel, who abused her power to turn the Ligerthian Knights into her own personal spies, you left her order. You put your principles above your commands. You went above and beyond the call of duty to protect Princess Kailyn, and to reclaim Oleanders, deposing Lord Shielen."

The crowd hissed at the name. Kailyn smiled, unable to help herself. Everyone hated Lord Shielen.

"You also reforged the dragonblade on your own with dragon's fire," Henri said. "All of these are noble in and of themselves. But it is your character, your courage, your compassion, that has shown us all what it means to be a Ligerthian Knight."

Kailyn felt tears spring to her eyes at Henri's words. She'd thought those very things as Benje had truly shown her what a Ligerthian Knight could be.

"So it is a great honor and a privilege to bestow upon you, Benje Thornsid, by the power I hold as Prince of the Tigahelen Archipelago, Lord of the Seventeen Isles, Heir to Ligerthia, and General of the Order of Ligerthian Knights, I now dub thee Sir Benje Thornsid, Knight of the Goddess!" Henri tapped Benje's shoulders with his staff and sparks flew from the end.

The crowd cheered as Benje stood up, unsheathing his sword, and crying out, in Old Alarian, *Gyond de dol, fyeria sheld onno, de Ligerthia e Oleandearn fortal!*"

The crowd cheered even louder. Though Kailyn had no idea what the words meant, she stood, applauding with all her heart. Benje was a knight! Oh, it was everything he had ever dreamed of. She was so happy for him.

But her heart fell. Did that mean Benje was going back with Henri to Tigahel? She knew Henri was going back—Abrina would be waiting for him.

But what about her and Benje? She couldn't imagine a life without him there, protecting her, teaching her, helping her grow.

She needed Benje in her life.

And she was going to tell him.

She tried making her way up through the crowd to reach Benje, Canis yipping at her side. But the wolf kept getting distracted by different pets. Kailyn bit her lip. Benje was a knight now. He had a higher responsibility than to her.

She suddenly found herself getting yanked on the hand, tugged unceremoniously through the crowd until she was right before Benje. Henri nodded once, dusting his hands. "I'm done here. Good luck, Benje. Princess. Send word if you ever need anything."

Benje inclined his head to the prince. "To you as well, Henri."

Henri grinned. "Goddess bless the both of you." And then he turned to the crowd. "Alright everyone, there's a feast waiting for you in the great hall. Let's go."

Canis yipped. *Food?* Then he glanced at Kailyn and Benje, who were standing on the dais together. *Aru?*

"It's alright, Canis," Kailyn said. "I'll be fine."

Safe! Canis gave Kailyn a wolf nod and then bounded out with the crowd toward the food.

Kailyn sighed, watching as the crowd trickled away until it was just her and Benje.

"Congratulations," she said, trying to convey as much enthusiasm into the word as possible. "Where is your first assignment?"

Benje stared at her. "My first assignment?"

"As Ligerthian Knight. Aren't you sworn to serve the Ligerthian royalty?"

Benje shook his head. "No. Henri's doing away with all that."

"But the queen . . ." Kailyn blinked. "Isn't she still in power?"

"She won't be the moment Henri gets back," Benje muttered. "I'd have gone to take her out myself, but Henri told me not to."

She blinked at him. "So Henri's going to be ruler of Tigahel?"

"And Abrina." Benje raised his eyebrows. "How is your sister?"

"Oh, Benje . . . she and I . . ." She looked up at him and saw a little smile playing on his lips. "Don't change the subject here. You never answered my question. Where's your first assignment?"

"Here." Benje's hand fiddled with the handle on his sword.

"Oh, so you're staying in Oleanders?"

"If their princess will have me." He locked eyes with her, and Kailyn saw a question there.

Taking inspiration from her bold sister, Kailyn pulled Benje toward her and kissed him. It was a brilliant kiss, a glimmer of hope that burst inside her like the glow of the dragonblade. It was more wondrous than anything she could have imagined.

"She will," she said when she'd pulled away from him.

Benje merely grinned and pulled her back into his arms, kissing her again. She kissed him back, her heart soaring. This was where she belonged.

Chapter Thirty-Nine

Abrina

Abrina wasn't sure what she was expecting when she got back to Tigahel. It certainly wasn't to find Queen Leilana sitting at the breakfast table sipping tea like nothing had happened.

"You," Abrina said, storming into the room, her hands curled into fists. "You are responsible for this. For all of this."

The queen eyed her over her cup of tea. "Princess Abrina. I'm glad to see you survived. Please, tell me about the quest."

"No." Abrina slammed her fist on the table. "You are in no position to demand anything."

The queen's eyes glinted coldly, and she reached for her scepter. Before she could, Abrina unsheathed her sword and knocked the staff far away from the queen. She pointed her blade at the queen's throat.

"You threaten me, Abrina?" The queen stared at her. "After everything I've done to orchestrate your destiny?" She was unmoving. Unblinking. Like she was made of ice.

"My destiny," Abrina spat, "was never yours to orchestrate." She pointed her sword harder. "Everything was because of you! You caused all this suffering. Every last bit of it. It's entirely your fault."

The queen stared at her, her face stony. "I did what I had to to contain the threat."

Abrina growled. "All the frost giants ever wanted was to

be left alone. But you ruined their lives like you did mine. No longer. You won't get any more chances. You're leaving."

The queen's eyebrows slid up a tiny hair. "You can't demand anything of me. You have no authority here."

"Not yet, but I do, Mother," came a voice that made Abrina's heart skip a beat. Her sword dropped for a split second as she glanced to see Henri near the front of the room.

But in that instant, the queen lunged for her staff.

"No." Henri twirled his own blue staff and knocked the queen's away. She stood there, some of her black hair coming undone from her perfect coiffure.

She snarled. "What are you going to do, Henri? This is my island. Our home, our sanctuary! I raised you here."

"Yes, Mother, you raised me here," Henri said, his voice cold. "But this is no longer your home. You are not welcome here. Not anymore."

"Leave," Abrina added, pointing her sword at the queen again. "Do so now, while we're feeling generous. Or I'll run you through."

The queen gasped and looked right at Henri. "Henri! You wouldn't let this . . . this Florrynian *ikla* kill your mother?"

"Watch your mouth, Mother," Henri said. "She's my bride-to-be."

Abrina felt her lips tug up in a smile. She liked the sound of that.

But they had more important matters at hand. She turned her full-on glower at the queen. "This is your last chance. Leave. Of your own choice. Or we will kill you."

The queen looked back and forth between the two of them, before turning tail and fleeing the room, leaving her scepter behind.

Henri turned to Sir Zachry and Sir Byron, who were both

standing by the door. Abrina hadn't noticed them—she'd been so focused on the queen. "Go after her to make sure she really does leave the island."

The men blinked. "Um . . ." Byron looked hesitant. "I'm sorry, Your Highness, but we only obey Princess Abrina."

Abrina grinned. "It's alright, I agree with the order. Go after her."

They turned to leave. "Oh, and one more thing," Abrina said. Her knights turned to face her. "You obey both me *and* my husband-to-be."

Her knights saluted her and ran out of the room, following the path of the queen.

Abrina waited a half-second until the door was closed and threw herself in Henri's arms. She kissed him with all the longing of her heart and was delighted when he matched her passion with his own. He was her match, her equal. And she never wanted him to be an ocean or a continent away from her ever again.

When she finally pulled back to breathe, she saw his blue eyes twinkling at her. "I missed you too, *fyrrel.*"

"Where have you been?" she demanded. "Kailyn said you were in Oleanders!"

"Kailyn?" He raised an eyebrow. "I think that's the first time I've heard you use her name."

Abrina felt her cheeks heat up. She had a lot to fill Henri in on. "She's my sister, isn't she?"

Henri chuckled. "She is indeed. You should have seen her in Oleanders. A true Florrynian and Oleanderian if I've ever seen one." He kissed her nose. "Tell me everything. And I'll tell you about my adventures in Florryn and Oleanders."

"Florryn?" Her heart hammered. "How is Florryn?"

"Better now. That man Sir Tyir is a good organizer. You should make him Lord of the Keep."

She nodded. That was a smart choice. "I'll have to talk to my mother."

"I don't think you'll have long to wait on that. She's excited to come to the wedding."

She blinked. "W-wedding?"

He arched a brow. "Didn't you just call me your husband-to-be?"

"Well, yes, but we hadn't determined a date. There was this whole . . . incident with the frost giants. And a certain girl from Oleanders."

Henri laughed. "I look forward to hearing all about it. Speaking of those dragonblades though, they would be elegant at our wedding. Maybe you could ask Kailyn to bring hers?"

Abrina shook her head. "I don't have it anymore. Neither does Kailyn. We gave them to the frost giants." A pang echoed in her soul at those words. She would miss that blade until the end of her days, she knew. There was nothing like it in all the world.

Henri's face grew sad. "I can see you have much to tell me."

Abrina nodded. "As do you."

"Indeed. But first, a very important question for you."

She stared at him. "Go on."

"How do you feel about yilnel fruit at the wedding? You know they're my favorite."

She scowled, spinning away from him and picked up the star-shaped fruit on the dining table. "You want some now? I bet I can throw in your mouth!"

Henri waggled his eyebrows. "Try."

Abrina threw the fruit and Henri deflected it with his staff back at Abrina. She ducked and the fruit went sailing overhead. She quirked an eyebrow. "I thought you didn't believe in fighting?"

"Well, I might be convinced every now and then, my *fyrrel*. Depends on who I'm fighting."

She placed a hand on her hip. "You sure you want to take me on?"

"Well, I assume we'll be evenly matched."

She rolled her eyes. "You wish, prince boy."

"Oh, is that a challenge?"

Abrina shook her head. "You don't want to challenge me."

"Maybe I do." He smirked. "Afraid you'll lose?"

"That is it!" She made her hands into fists and slipped into her warrior stance, ready to pummel him. But on first impact, he caught her fist, swinging her around into a kiss that left her feeling all melty, like being in the sun on a warm spring day.

"No fair," she murmured against his lips. "You cheated."

"Ah, but was it really cheating? I have you right where I want you." He kissed her again and Abrina closed her eyes, enjoying every moment of it. Perhaps marriage wasn't so bad after all.

Epilogue

Three Months Later

Abrina looked at herself in the mirror. She looked like a bride, dazzling in a brilliant blue embroidered tunic. She refused to wear a dress—even if it was her wedding day. She still had a sword strapped to her side—the maids who had tried to insist that she shouldn't have a sword at her wedding had faced her wrath and had consented to let her do as she wished. She was glad to have a blade at her side, even if the blade was new. It didn't feel like her old sword she'd lost in that final battle, nor like the dragonblade she'd given up. But it felt most like her, and that was what she wanted.

She did allow the maids to put flowers in her hair though. Just this once.

Her heart fluttered anxiously. Today was the day. The day of her wedding. And she was getting married in Florryn. She'd convinced Henri that Florryn was a better place for the wedding—as much as she was growing to appreciate the trees and the cajuna of Tigahel, she missed home.

Funny. She had left Florryn to get married, but she'd ended up coming back home to marry her prince. She supposed it was fitting. Everything was coming full circle.

Kailyn also looked resplendent, in a white gown tied with a deep blue sash. She held a bouquet of flowers and was grinning.

"You look beautiful," she told Abrina.

Abrina felt heat rush onto her cheeks. It was a new sensation. Having a sister was still taking some getting used to. They'd exchanged letters and talked frequently on the communication stones Henri and Benje wore. She was getting to know her. But she was glad beyond words that Kailyn had come all the way to Florryn to be at her wedding in person.

"Thank you, Kailyn," she said, meaning every word. "So do you."

"Are you ready for this?" Kailyn asked, tugging at her sleeve anxiously.

"Am I ready?" Abrina paused. The past three months had been a blur. She had told Henri that she wanted a Florrynian wedding, and when he suggested that they get married back in Florryn, she had taken him up on that idea. There would be enough time later to sort out the ruling of Tigahel. Right now, she was about to marry the love of her life. And she still didn't know how to feel about it.

Part of her wished to battle frost giants today. Then she'd at least have a reason for all these nerves. But no, she was just walking down an aisle, binding her hands with Henri's, and being pronounced husband and wife in front of the entire kingdom of Florryn, with assembled guests from Tigahel, Cyron, and Oleanders.

And her sister. Abrina was still amazed that Kailyn had found the time to be there in Florryn. Despite the burdens she now labored under trying to repair Oleanders, she had prioritized her sister's wedding. Granted, she had just arrived last night by cajuna (on loan from Tigahel) but she had come. With Benje.

And their mother, the great Queen Jullee, had burst into tears when she saw her long-lost daughter.

And now their family was expanding. But Abrina knew in her heart that this time, she'd be going on an adventure that she wanted. And she would take whatever came. As long as she had Kailyn and Henri by her side.

Woof! Canis yipped. The wolf brushed against Abrina's leg. She laughed, rubbing his head affectionately. And Canis too.

"Canis!" Kailyn cried. "You'll get hair on her tunic."

"He can get hair on my tunic anytime," Abrina said, grinning. She owed the wolf much.

Kailyn rolled her eyes. "You're supposed to be getting married. You definitely don't want to be covered in wolf hair for the wedding. It's like a curse—it never really goes away."

Woof!

"You know it is, Canis. Your fur gets everywhere."

Abrina chuckled and turned to face Kailyn. "You know, all those days ago when I first met you, I was terrified that someone was cursing me. I knew you were family the moment I saw you, but I didn't want to accept it. How was it possible that someone could share my mother's face, someone I'd never met?"

Kailyn shook her head. "That moment was terrifying. I thought you were going to kill me."

Abrina shrugged. "No. I wanted answers." She clasped her hands with Kailyn and looked her sister in the eyes. "And now I have them. I've gotten a sister."

Kailyn smiled, tears in the corner of her eyes. "As did I."

Woof! Canis started tugging on Abrina's tunic, whining.

Kailyn laughed. "He says it's time."

Abrina smiled. "Let's go then. Let's face this together."

And at the chapel, when she joined hands with Henri, and

the cleric wrapped the deep blue and silver ribbons around them while her sister, Benje, Canis, her knights, and her mother looked on, she knew. As long as her family fought beside her, they'd make it through anything. No matter what.

Acknowledgments

This book would not exist if a certain twelve-year-old writer (yours truly) hadn't had the courage to share a very different version of this book with a certain Zachary Spence back in middle school. So thank you, Zach, for encouraging me for all those years. This one is in large part for you.

This book would also not exist without the dozens of people who have shaped me as a writer and fed the flames to keep me going.

First, to my three writing groups: to WGWACA (Avery Morgan, Gabriela Welling, Elizabeth Brown, Megan Hamilton, and Connor Smith) for being the very first writing group to give me feedback and for seeing the very rough draft of TPQ. You guys are awesome!

To the ladies of the Writers Guild (Lauren Johansen, Elisabeth Hyde, and Abby Fielding) for encouraging me and providing lots of laughs.

And to Make Believers (Julia Wagner, Carrie Snider, Cindy Anderson, Amy Trent, Georgia Fritz, Cheree Myatt, and Ashley Stock) for helping me fine-tune my writing and push myself to be an even better writer.

Thank you to all three groups for your feedback, your encouragement, and your support. It means more than I can say.

Another thank you to Megan Hamilton for showing me what this book could look like, and to Avery Morgan for the amazing map. You both made the book so much better.

To my friends and coworkers at Eschler Editing, particularly Angela Eschler, Lindsay Flanagan, Shanda Cottam, Sandi Larsen, Sabine Berlin, and AJ Jepperson for helping me become a better editor and a better writer. Thank you for believing in me.

To the student BYU editing team (Lauren Johansen, Shelby Johnson, and Mason Scholes) for their fantastic work to help me get this book out there. This book vastly improved because of your edits! You guys rock!

To my weekly writing buddies: Natalie Brianne, Michelle Hutchins, and Miri Elliott. I wouldn't have been able to finish my revisions without our online writing sessions!

Another huge thank you to Natalie Brianne for helping me with the layout and finalizing the ebook production of this book. An additional thank you to Lauren Johansen for helping me proofread the final copy.

Also a shout-out to everyone who was an ARC reader for this book. Thank you all so much for your help!

To my newsletter supporters, including Jeremy and Kathryn Madsen, Sunday Corder, Abigail Wincentsen, Zachary Spence, Keilah Kemp, Stephen Lancaster, Thomas Brown, Brooklyn Lorenc, the entire Jackson clan, and everyone else who has ever told me that they're excited to read my words.

Abigail Wincentsen gets another acknowledgment for her fantastic art that brought my characters to life and the fabulous cover! I'm still in awe with how everything turned out. I can't thank you enough—working with you on this project was a dream come true!

To all the wonderful writing friends I've made at conferences over the years. From Arizona to Kansas, your support and kindness have cheered me on throughout some really dark times and has brought me to where I am now. I love you all.

Last of all, to my family, including my remarkable husband who put up with hours upon hours of listening to me ramble about wolves, magic swords, and princesses (who even bought me a sword to celebrate the finishing of this book!). To my mother who inspired me to pick up my own pen as a child. To my siblings for their endless inspiration. To my extended family for their love and support.

And to my father most of all, whose belief in me gave me wings to fly.

About the Author

K.H. Weyerman loves penguins, piano music, princesses, and pajama parties and spends each day trying to juggle those interests around her jobs as a freelance editor, as project manager for Eschler Editing, and working on her books. She graduated with a degree in editing and publishing because she couldn't get enough stories in her life. When she's not writing, editing, or reading, she can be found practicing yoga, teaching piano lessons, designing penguin stickers, or playing dress up with both lightsabers and tiaras. She and her husband live in Olathe, Kansas. You can find her online at khweyerman.com.

www.ingramcontent.com/pod-product-compliance
Lightning Source LLC
Chambersburg PA
CBHW021954130726
47903CB00014B/1359